Becoming Mr. Bingley

BECOMING MR.

BINGLEY

A Novel

SAMANTHA WHITMAN

Printed in the United States of America

First Printing 2018

ISBN-13: 978-1722911379

ISBN-10: 1722911379

Published by CreateSpace

For Stacey

Who convinced me a sequel was not only possible, but absolutely necessary.

"Perhaps it is our imperfections that make us so perfect for one another."

Jane Austen

Prologue

*I*t was the perfect day for a wedding. Elizabeth grimaced as her stomach let out an audible growl, her eyes still screwed tightly shut to the blinding rays of early morning sun. She pushed back the covers, set her bare feet on the veined hardwood floor, and stumbled over to the window. From where she stood, the splendor of Derbyshire was spread out before her like a blanket of downy green grass and tufted trees. The birds trilling a cheerful melody in the hedges below had obviously gotten the memo. She grinned and stretched her arms over her head.

As she turned away from the window her forehead, bottle-green eyes, and sleep tussled auburn hair were just visible in the mirror above the fireplace. She smoothed the flyaway hairs from her face and raked her fingers through her messy braid, shaking the long curls loose over her shoulders. Her eyes drifted to the blue wing chair in the corner, where an ivory Empire waist gown lay draped over the back. She held it up in front of her and admired the delicate lace on the wide collar and the creamy sash at the waist. Her stomach rumbled again. She now deeply regretted not stashing scones in her clutch at tea the previous evening; it would be seemingly forever until the wedding breakfast following the ceremony.

When she was finally dressed and ready, she took one last look in the standing mirror, running through a mental checklist to make sure everything was in order. Hair—high bun with curls—*check. Oh wait, I forgot*

1

the comb with the little pearls. Ok, check. Earrings—*check.* Elbow-length gloves—*oh, crap. Where are my gloves? Oh. Right here in my hand...check.* Inconceivably uncomfortable corset—*oomph! Check.* She readjusted her cleavage, then grabbed her shawl and clutch from the desk and left the room, mindfully picking up her skirt on the way down the stairs. The last thing she needed was to trip and break her neck, or even worse, tear a hole in her dress. When she stepped through the narrow front doors and out into the dazzling sunshine she stopped short and shielded her eyes, gasping as she took in the dreamlike vision before her.

A beautiful white carriage and two majestic matching horses stood waiting for her in the center of the stone pathway. When he noticed her standing by the door, the coachman smiled and inclined his head in Elizabeth's direction as the spotted Hackneys shook their silky manes and sidled impatiently. It was then the door of the carriage opened and a tall, top-hatted man in a black tailcoat stepped out and onto the road. He lifted his head to look at her and grinned, momentarily fixated in unmistakable admiration as his icy-blue eyes surveyed every inch of her appearance.

She studied him carefully as he began to walk toward her, from the dark blond hair peeking out from under his hat down to his white cravat and black riding boots, and back up to his face again. His lips curved upward into a playfully crooked smile, and as she gazed fixedly at his glorious dimples she was suddenly hit by a wave of sensation she couldn't seem to put her finger on—was it a rush of premonition? A surge of déjà vu?

A veritable drowning in his tsunami of sexiness?

She shook the feeling as she watched him bow dramatically, revealing a sportive grin as he straightened back up and lifted his gaze to meet hers. "My lady," he crooned, holding out a white-gloved hand.

2

Yep, there was no doubt whatsoever in her mind—this day was going to be absolutely perfect.

Chapter One

The Previous Day

 lizabeth watched the lush English countryside streak past the passenger side window in a riot of vivid autumn color.

"I still can't believe Bryan is getting married at Pemberley," she mumbled softly, more to herself than anyone else. "How in the world did I miss that when I received the invitation?"

"You do realize it's not actually called Pemberley, right darling?" Charlie gave her a sideways smirk from the driver's side. "It's called Chatsworth House."

"I know that," Elizabeth replied disparagingly, then wrinkled her nose. "But, come on, is there anyone who doesn't just call it Pemberley?" Her eyes briskly skimmed the invitation in her hand. Sure enough, the address was listed as Chatsworth House. *Hmm... Must be a mistake or something.*

"People who aren't obsessed with *Pride and Prejudice*, perhaps?"

"I am *not* obsessed with *Pride and Prejudice*." Elizabeth met his eyes and dropped her sheepish gaze to her lap. "Not as much as I used to be, anyway."

"Well, you might not be obsessed with *Pride and Prejudice*, but it sure sounds like your mate Bryan is."

"I don't know if I would say he is *obsessed…*"

"Oh, no? Could you please explain to me why I'll be dressed as Mr. Peanut, then, love?" Charlie asked with another smirk, gesturing to the top hat on the back seat.

Elizabeth wrinkled her nose. "Because the wedding is at Pemberley, and the bridal party are all wearing Regency era formal wear," she muttered resignedly.

"And remind me just once more—how exactly did I merit the *extraordinary* honor of becoming an usher?" Charlie raised one eyebrow playfully in her direction.

Elizabeth pressed her lips together in a thin line and inhaled slowly. "Because after the accident we rekindled our friendship, and he asked me to be in the wedding. I think asking you was sort of a gesture of goodwill." She smiled sweetly and patted his shoulder. "He wants to be your friend too, you know."

Charlie smirked yet a third time, flashing his magnificent dimples in her direction. "So, the cherries jubilee flambé incident that singed off his mate's eyebrows one week before the wedding had absolutely nothing to do with it?"

Elizabeth chewed on her lower lip. "Well, that may have had a tiny bit to do with it." She leaned over and kissed his cheek. "Thank you for agreeing to it. I know all of this is probably making you a little uncomfortable."

"Oh, come on now, Elle—which bit should make me uncomfortable? Participating in the wedding of a bloke I met only once before, who also happens to be my girlfriend's ex? Or spending the weekend in skintight trousers and a top hat?"

Elizabeth's eyes unfocused slightly at the mental image of his butt in skintight breeches. She forced a pout. "You know, if anyone should be uncomfortable this weekend, it should be me."

"Oh? And why might that be?"

She sighed theatrically. "Well, because we are attending a wedding where the majority of the guests will most likely be single gay men—and you look like that—" she waved her hand in a circular motion in front of his face and chest "—*and* you will be wearing skin tight trousers and a top hat."

Charlie bit his bottom lip and ran his fingers through his hair, his eyebrows knitted together in contemplation. He stared ahead at the road in silence. Elizabeth smiled complacently at his reaction and crossed her boots on the dashboard. Reveling in her victory, she folded her hands on her stomach and gazed out the window once more.

They turned onto a dirt road. After several minutes the thick line of trees cleared to reveal an immense stretch of emerald checkerboard-cut grass. In the distance stood a manor so impressive Charlie brought the car to a momentary halt. Elizabeth dropped her feet to the floor and leaned forward in her seat as they gasped in unison.

"*Pemberley*," Elizabeth breathed. She smiled dreamily as a flood of fanciful memories washed over her, then glanced embarrassingly at Charlie as though he could read her thoughts. His own eyes were wide with appreciation, his lips slightly parted in awe.

"Right. They should definitely rename it," he whispered, giving her a repentant smile.

They watched their destination grow steadily closer as Charlie began to drive again slowly. Seeing in person the designated residence (or one of them) of her favorite literary hero caused her to reminisce on the last time she had been there. It was not in reality, of course (there had not been enough time after moving to England to visit her dream home before the nightmarish car accident that left her in a coma for six weeks)—it was in her own mind. The moment her head hit the windscreen, she closed her eyes to the real world and reopened them to find herself in early 1800s England, as the heroine of her favorite novel, *Pride and Prejudice*.

While her friends and family spent days and nights at the hospital anxiously waiting for her to regain consciousness, Elizabeth was fumbling through a story that in no way resembled the original. No matter how hard she tried to steer the course of events back to the way they were supposed to be, her mind interpreted the feelings and actions of the characters in completely unpredictable ways. Most surprising, however, were her own feelings and actions. Instead of falling for Mr. Darcy (the hero of the novel and the fictional embodiment of manly perfection she had sought after her entire adult life), she found herself falling head over heels in love with his polar opposite, Mr. Bingley. The very moment she allowed herself to embrace a new life with him in her subconscious, she was brought back to the crushing reality of a world where he didn't even exist, and was thoroughly heartbroken. And because anyone she confided in would most likely think she was borderline psychotic for being in love with an imaginary man, she was utterly alone in her despair. She resigned herself to a seemingly irremediable future without him, and attempted to concentrate on anything else to help her forget the time she spent with him.

That is, until she received a letter from the other person involved in the accident and met him at a pub, only to discover he was the very man she had fallen in love with while in her subconscious—quite literally the man of her dreams. He confessed to paying her numerous visits at the hospital during her stay, hoping for the chance to apologize for an accident that had been entirely her fault. Though he obviously had no memory of the time they spent together in her mind, his concern for her well-being fostered an affection he had been unable to disregard. The night they officially met at the pub they felt an immediate connection and mutual attraction for one another, and had been together ever since.

Now that her attachment to England was deep-rooted in love for her sister Jane, the two aunts she had come to adore, and her flourishing new romance with Charlie, she brought him back home with her to Pennsylvania to say goodbye to her life there and then move across the pond permanently. In between packing all her belongings, she introduced him to her parents and her ex-boyfriend Bryan. Her mother (who had been baffled as to how her daughter could become romantically involved with someone whose car she crashed into), gave her hearty approval the instant she saw him face to face. When he complimented her taste in tea and assured her that her chicken tikka masala was the best he ever had, she promptly began planning their wedding.

Her reunion with Bryan was emotional, to say the least. The last time she had seen him while conscious he confessed he was in love with someone else, after they had been in a relationship for an entire year. He admitted that though he loved her dearly, he had never actually been *in* love with her. He waited as long as possible to admit his feelings, because he didn't want to lose the best friend he ever had.

Initially she was angry and hurt, and managed to convince herself she was a victim of unrequited love. But when she found out what it was to be truly in love with someone, she realized she felt exactly the same way about Bryan, and always had. She later discovered he had put his life on hold after her accident, remaining for weeks in England and risking losing his job to be at the hospital when she regained consciousness. It was then she knew exactly how much his friendship meant to her. He was so overjoyed to see her recovered, and truly happy for her that she was with Charlie. Before she returned to England he asked Elizabeth to be his best "man" at his upcoming wedding (a position he purposely left open with the hope Elizabeth might eventually forgive him), and she happily accepted.

Three weeks later, Elizabeth found a modest flat in London. Her sister Jane moved in to help pay the rent, as there was no way she could afford it on her own working remotely as an editor for *Flavor* magazine. Charlie found her a part-time job at the stables where he worked as an instructor, and she loved that she could simultaneously spend time with him and go riding three times a week. Her doctor, who continued to be impressed by the speed of her recovery considering the extent of the injuries she had sustained in the accident, had finally given her official clearance to ride again. It would have been a truly momentous occasion, had she not been secretly riding for the past two months against medical advice.

Summer ended the way it did every year—much too quickly—and early September brought Bryan's wedding. She was very much looking forward to spending an entire weekend with Charlie in the breathtaking scenery of Derbyshire. Autumn had come early to Britain, and the leaves were already changing into a spectacular pallet of crisp, vibrant colors. As Elizabeth rolled her window down to see more clearly the effect the setting sun had on the dazzling display of reds and oranges, the warm breeze that tickled her cheeks smelled earthy and sweet.

"Will we have time to change before tea, you think?" she asked Charlie. "How far is the Cavendish Hotel?"

"Only a few miles further," he replied. "Do you suppose it will be a late evening tonight? I sort of wish I hadn't agreed to join the stag do."

Elizabeth hid a grin with the back of her hand, as she always did when Charlie said something thoroughly British. "Oh come on, it will be fun!" she insisted. "It won't be late—this *is* Bryan we are talking about, after all. He will probably make you all watch the *Pride and Prejudice* miniseries and drink mojitos. I would come with you, but I was up all last night writing my speech and I am completely whooped." She smirked. "*Knackered*, I mean."

"You won't be lonesome for me?" Charlie inquired, a smoldering look in his practically glowing blue eyes.

Elizabeth raised an eyebrow. For a split second she considered telling him no one would miss him. Then she remembered how eager she was for Bryan and Charlie to become friends, and sighed deeply. He *was* a groomsman after all (or usher as it was called in Britain), even if only by default. "Oh, I'll probably dream about you all night." She gave him a provocative smile. "*God*, I hope in those skintight trousers."

Charlie licked his bottom lip, then chewed on it thoughtfully. "Well, we should definitely at least stop to…*change*…before tea." He made a valiant effort to appear as though he had no ulterior motive, though the corners of his mouth were twitching. "I need to iron those trousers before tomorrow, anyway." He broke into an irresistible smile.

Elizabeth felt the familiar swooping sensation somewhere in her stomach she got whenever she saw those dimples. She was convinced that each time they made an appearance, somewhere out there in the cosmos an angel received its wings. "Yes, definitely. We *cannot* have creases obscuring that view, that's for *darn* sure."

That night Elizabeth sat on the edge of the bed in her pink polka-dotted flannel pajamas. She leaned her head against the polished mahogany post and gazed through the window at the night sky. The stars not veiled by wisps of gossamer clouds were glittering over the moonlit expanse of grass below. She watched as the breeze that whistled past the frosted panes made waves across the sea of dark green. Somewhere in the distance crickets were playing their eerie moonlight serenade.

As she drew her eyes away from the window and looked around the dimly lit room, she couldn't quite shake an overwhelming feeling of loneliness. She now wished she hadn't convinced Charlie to stay overnight with the rest of the men in the hotel next door. If he knew she were still awake he would come back to be with her, but she assured him she was headed to bed hours ago. She knew he wouldn't want to wake her up if he thought she was asleep.

It was silly to miss him. She knew exactly where he was at the moment—losing spectacularly at poker in the hotel pub. He was notorious for his inability to bluff due to the endearing way he stuck the tip of his tongue through his teeth whenever he had a good hand. But as her gaze wandered from the fireplace with its electric insert to the not-quite-authentic oil lamp (the electric cord of which was just invisible in the low light), she couldn't help but feel a slight panicky sensation begin to bubble up from somewhere deep inside her chest. There was something about being in that room, with its period décor and candlelight, that brought her right back to her coma-induced delusion, and the last time she had seen Mr. Bingley before she woke up and he disappeared.

She couldn't be more thankful that she met Charlie, Mr. Bingley's real world counterpart. Charlie was absolutely amazing; he was everything she could ever want in a boyfriend. But if she was entirely honest with herself, there were times where she found herself missing the man she knew before they even met. On top of that, she couldn't help but have anxiety over the possibility she might somehow lose Charlie the way she had lost Mr. Bingley.

Which is absolutely crazy—right?

It couldn't be entirely crazy. She and Mr. Bingley had fallen in love and even gotten engaged in her unconscious fantasy that felt so real she sometimes thought maybe it had been. Perhaps any moment now Charlie would confess he remembered everything, and they could start planning their own wedding. She had to remind herself more than once that none of her memories of him as Mr. Bingley were real. *Mr. Bingley* wasn't real—he never was—*Charlie* was real, and they had only been dating for two months.

Elizabeth slid beneath the thick down comforter, leaning over to blow out the candle on the table beside the bed. She laid her head on the cool pillowcase, wincing as a rogue feather threatened to impale her temple. Before she closed her eyes she began listing the things she knew to be true in her head; a mental exercise her neurologist suggested she try whenever things became fuzzy.

1. Mr. Bingley is not real. It was all just a dream.
2. Charlie is real, and he is *incredible.* He is not going to disappear.
3. There is no need to rush into anything. We can take things slow and just see what happens.
4. There are two days left of the weekend to have fun together at Pemberley—Chatsworth House—whatever.
5. Oh, screw it—*Pemberley!*

The next morning, when Elizabeth opened her eyes and focused lazily on the paisley drapes hanging from the bed, she felt a flutter of alarm before she looked down and saw her pink flannel pajamas. With a short laugh at her own foolishness she climbed out of bed. Once she was completely ready, she sat on the bed and waited for Charlie to arrive. As the minutes ticked by she began to wonder where he could be, until a loud knocking sound made her jump to her feet. She threw open the door with a wide grin. Her smile immediately slipped away and she raised her eyebrows in surprise as she found herself face to face with a large bouquet of wildflowers with legs.

The face that peeked around from behind the bouquet was not Charlie's—but a short, bespectacled man with lenses that made his eyes appear cartoonish. He smiled nervously. "Miss Baker?"

"Yes?"

"Right. These are for you, from a Mr….just one mo'…" He pulled an envelope from his suit jacket and held it an inch from his nose. "A Mr. Bon—Bin—"

"Bennet?"

The man frowned. "No." He gave up and held it out to her. "Can you read that, dearie?"

Elizabeth narrowed her eyes. She took the envelope from his outstretched hand with sudden apprehension. When she read the familiar scrawl, she snorted. "Bond," she muttered, rolling her eyes and grinning. "Mr. *Bond*." She looked up at the utterly bewildered man. "Thank you, I'll take them." He handed her the vase. She heard him give a muffled reply and struggled to push aside an enormous sunflower. "What's that?"

"You know James Bond?" the man breathed, with an expression of absolute incredulity.

Elizabeth considered him carefully. "Yes," she deadpanned. "I'm not Miss Baker. I'm actually Miss Moneypenny." His mouth gaped open slightly and she felt the corners of her lips curl upward like the Grinch. "But please don't tell anyone, because —" She raised her eyebrows and looked from side to side down the hallway as he leaned forward eagerly. "I would *hate* to have to kill you."

The porter snapped his jaw shut and backed away slowly. "Have a lovely day!" Elizabeth called as she watched him hurry away without looking back. Chuckling to herself, Elizabeth opened the envelope and read the note inside.

Good morning, my darling. I hope you slept well. Please come downstairs when you are ready—I have a surprise for you.

Charlie

Standing before the full-length mirror for one last look, she stuck a comb in her hair and admired the way the floaty material of her gown swayed with the slightest movement of her hips. Then she threw her phone into her clutch, grabbed her shawl from the desk, and left the room.

When she saw the carriage waiting for her, complete with two majestic horses and a coachman sat high up on a red velvet bench seat, her heart gave a lurch. She blinked and shielded her eyes from the sun—really, everything about this wedding so far was making her feel the need to pinch herself. As the door opened and Charlie stepped out in his top hat, black tailcoat, and riding boots, her heart might as well have stopped altogether. She gaped at him, jaw dropped open, temporarily struck dumb by the uncanny resemblance he bore to—

"My lady." He extended a gloved hand and smiled at her. As she reached her own gloved hand out to take his she felt weak in the knees. "Shall we?"

"Absolutely," Elizabeth breathed. She followed him to the open door of the carriage, too consumed with wistful memories to make her mental list.

Chapter Two

*A*s the carriage made its way down the rocky dirt road to Chatsworth House, Elizabeth watched the scenery crawl past the window with growing anticipation. Every bump in the road caused her to lose her balance and pitch sideways on the seat, but she was determined not to let her head hit the window, as she could not afford another head injury. After the third consecutive soft thud against the glass she rubbed her forehead and skootched closer to Charlie, taking advantage of the opportunity to check him out one more time.

"So…Mr. Bond, eh?" she quipped, raising an amused eyebrow. "I didn't think he wore a cravat."

Charlie shrugged his shoulders and gave her a boyish smile. "When I got everything on, I looked in the mirror and thought—this is a proper suit, really—I look smart! Besides the obvious differences it definitely has a Bond vibe, don't you think?" He pulled the brim of his top hat down rakishly over one eye. "Who else do I remind you of in this getup?"

Elizabeth bit her lip. "Definitely Bond." She unwrinkled her brow. "And will you be trading in your usual cup of Earl Grey for a vodka martini this morning, Double-Oh-Seven? I don't believe Mr. Bond considers tea a real man's drink, does he?"

Charlie placed his arm around her, his hand firmly gripping her corseted waist. He leaned in and whispered softly, "That is the difference between us, my darling. Real men drink tea." He lifted her chin gently with the crook of his finger and kissed her slowly and thoroughly, taking his time. When he finally drew his head back to look into her eyes, he smiled at her dazed expression. "I missed you."

Elizabeth swallowed hard. *You have no idea how much I missed you.* Over his shoulder her eye caught Chatsworth House in the distance. She shook herself free from her reverie and smiled. "Look," she pointed. "We're here."

The carriage came to a stop in front of the building. Charlie helped her out onto the path, and Elizabeth felt a thrill of excitement rush through her as she lifted her gaze to the peak of the breathtaking exterior. They followed a cluster of guests through the enormous doors and entered a room called the Painted Hall, where the ceremony would take place. Elizabeth's jaw dropped shamelessly as she gaped at the ceiling, which was at least three stories high and decorated from one end to the other with a panorama of heavenly beings surrounded by billowy white clouds. Soft morning sunlight filtered in through the windows that lined the balcony on one side, shrouding the elaborate mural on the other side with an ethereal glow. One end of the black-and-white checkered floor boasted a grand staircase, its richly carpeted steps leading to the tantalizing unknown beyond its summit. The entire room appeared gilded; everything, from the banisters and walls to the pillars that held creamy marble busts with eerily vacant expressions, seemed to be covered in gold.

As her eyes hungrily surveyed the length of the room, Elizabeth heard someone call her name from behind and froze in recognition; she would know that smooth voice anywhere. Wheeling around she saw Bryan saunter toward her with a radiant smile on his handsome face. With his black tailcoat, ivory vest, cravat, and top hat he looked almost exactly the same as the first time she laid eyes on him, at the Halloween party he attended dressed as none other than Mr. Darcy himself. Seeing him walk toward her now it was not Mr. Darcy, and not even Bryan she thought of as she grinned back at him. It was someone else entirely—someone she had nearly forgotten until this very moment.

"George!" she cried, and threw her arms around him. The instant she heard herself say the name aloud she realized her mistake. She stepped back quickly, eyes wide with shock at her own foolishness.

What is the matter with me? Elizabeth, get a grip!

Bryan laughed. "Are we calling each other by our middle names now, Lizzie?" He flashed his dazzlingly white teeth. "Or should I say, *Poppy*?"

Elizabeth barely even heard him as her cheeks grew red-hot. She had completely forgotten Bryan's middle name was George! Frowning subconsciously in the direction of an enormous fascinator adorned with peacock feathers, her brain struggled to absorb the uncanny circumstance that her ex-boyfriend bore the same name as his counterpart from her dream; a tidbit of information that had somehow eluded her previously.

In her coma-induced adaptation of *Pride and Prejudice,* Bryan played the role of the villainous George Wickham. However, unlike the

Wickham of the original novel, Bryan's version could hardly be deemed malicious. When she allowed him the chance to tell his side of the story, she learned his bad reputation was unjustly handed to him by Mr. Darcy's evil reprobate of a sister, who had used his already broken heart vindictively to her advantage. It was then she realized just how unfairly she had treated Bryan when they broke up, by making prejudiced assumptions of his character without once considering his own feelings. The bond she formed with Mr. Wickham in her subconscious laid the foundation for her newly reaffirmed friendship with Bryan in reality—with the exception being that he of course had no memory of any of it.

Elizabeth was still looking perplexed when Bryan placed a hand on her shoulder. "I'll be right back," he assured her, and turned in the direction of a gathering of cougar-esque older women eagerly waving him over and devouring him with their eyes as he strolled toward them. Suddenly she felt arms around her waist and heard a voice croon in her ear.

"*Poppy*?" She turned her head to see Charlie grinning over her shoulder as though he had just won the lottery.

She wrinkled her nose. "It was my grandmother's name."

"I *love* it," Charlie insisted, still beaming. "I'm going to call you Poppy from now on."

"Don't even think about it." She swiveled in his arms. "And what is your middle name, Mr. Bond? Danger?"

"Mine is quite dull, actually," Charlie replied. "It's Henry, after Prince Harry."

Elizabeth smiled, picturing her beloved father's face. "Henry is an amazing name." She stood on tiptoe to kiss him on the tip of his nose.

The ceremony was short and sweet—not a bad thing, considering how awkward Elizabeth felt to be standing in front of all of Bryan's family and friends who thought, as she once had, that he would end up marrying *her*. Not that she was regretting participating, of course; she would do absolutely anything for Bryan. But it was nearly impossible to avoid the pitying looks from his mother, who repeatedly wiped genuine tears from her eyes with her handkerchief, and his grandmother, whose fiendish glare seemed to imply it was somehow Elizabeth's fault her precious grandson was marrying another man.

Forcing herself to focus on the minister's words, her eyes wandered to the man standing at the end of the line of ushers on the opposite side— whose blue eyes were currently focused on hers, and hers alone. The intensity of his gaze made her feel like everyone in the room was suddenly dissolving into nonexistence. Her heart picked up the pace as she returned his reassuring smile.

A sudden explosion of applause broke the spell. Elizabeth startled, then produced a ready smile as Bryan and James walked down the center aisle past the small gathering of guests, who continued to clap and wolf-whistle as they passed by. Elizabeth took Charlie's arm and squeezed it. They waited their turn, then followed the wedding party out the front doors into the sunshine.

"You know, I was thinking…" Charlie began, discreetly playing with Elizabeth's fingers as they stood side by side for pictures in the garden.

"About how much the minister reminded you of the one from *The Princess Bride*? Me too! I was so disappointed he didn't start with '*mawage is what bwings us togevah too-day.*'" Elizabeth grinned, then turned to smile obediently at the photographer.

Charlie knit his eyebrows in contemplation. "Now that you mention it…I *knew* he reminded me of someone." He glanced at her sideways and raised one eyebrow in perfect unison with the side of his mouth, then looked straight ahead and beamed for the camera. "Believe it or not, I was actually thinking about something related to *Pride and Prejudice.*"

"Really?" Elizabeth smiled as they began walking to the next photo-op; a staircase-style fountain with jets that sent water arching up into the air and flowing continuously down to the bottom. "Is it because you have finally admitted to yourself we are at Pemberley?" She found his hand and wove her fingers through his.

"Must be," he answered with another smirk. He stopped walking and gave her a solemn look. "I was thinking…if you were to marry me…"

Elizabeth's heart performed a cartwheel in her chest as she slowly turned to face him. Her mouth suddenly felt like it was full of saltine crackers. She swallowed hard, waiting impatiently for him to continue.

"Your second name would be Bennet." His face was quite serious now. "You would be Elizabeth *Bennet.*"

Returning his attentive gaze, Elizabeth gave her best impression of someone that exact thought had not occurred to approximately ten seconds after they first met. "Huh," she squeaked, trying hard to keep her eyes from bulging. "So it would." Her heart was still pounding much too loudly in her ears for wittier banter.

He brought her hand to his lips and kissed it without breaking eye contact. Then he curved one corner of his mouth upward in a maddeningly roguish way and covered her hand with his across his bicep as they walked back to the main building, never uttering another word on the matter.

The wedding party made their way into the great dining room, where the rest of the guests were already drinking champagne and eating hors d'oeuvres. Before she had a chance to gawk properly at the splendor of the room, Elizabeth made a beeline for the closest server and relieved his tray of as many puff pastries as could fit in one hand. She spun around just in time to lift the last flute of champagne from another server hurrying past. With a mouthful of vanilla cream she noticed Charlie's expression and penitently offered him a pastry.

"Sorry," she muttered. "I was *starving*."

The dining table was so huge it held the entire wedding party with ease. From where she sat between Charlie and Bryan's sister Grace, Elizabeth longingly watched the servers carry in tray after tray of delicious looking breakfast food. Moments later, she sighed happily as she dunked her scone into her coffee, feeling the hunger sharks start to dissipate in her stomach. Glancing at Charlie, she saw he was experiencing a similar degree of satisfaction; his eyes were closed as he smiled into his cup of tea.

When breakfast came to an end, everyone made their way out into the Painted Hall once more. Finally Elizabeth would discover what awaited beyond that amazing staircase, as Bryan announced they had plenty of time before the reception to explore the house and grounds. They would reconvene at twilight for a candlelit tour of the Sculpture Gallery; a room Elizabeth had been dying to visit since 2005, when she watched *Pride and Prejudice* for the first time.

As the setting sun kissed the horizon, its dying rays warmed Elizabeth to the very tips of her fingers and toes. A cozy, contented sensation inspired her to yawn drowsily and lean her head against Charlie's shoulder as they casually strolled back to the house. The day had been one of the happiest of her life thus far, and there was still so much more to come. As they entered the candlelit Sculpture Gallery, the flicker of the dancing flames cast shadows onto the milky statues, breathing life into their ghostly forms. Elizabeth traveled slowly from one figure to the next, immersing herself in the otherworldly beauty before her.

She felt a lurch in her middle when she located the familiar face she had admittedly been searching for, high up on a pedestal. Grinning from ear to ear, she grabbed Charlie's hand and pulled him over. "Oh my God, oh my God—look who it is!" she whispered excitedly.

Charlie frowned and put a finger to his lips. "I know this…"

Elizabeth gave him an affronted look. "It's Mr. Darcy!" She tilted her head in disbelief at his less than enthusiastic expression. "Matthew Macfadyen? From the movie? Seriously—I thought you said you loved *Pride and Prejudice*. I'm beginning to think you said that just so I would make out with you the night we met." Noting his look of confusion, she added, "Snog?"

Charlie flashed her a devastating smile. Even with half of his face obscured by darkness, Elizabeth couldn't help but think, *Aaannnddd, boom. Another angel gets its wings.*

"Well, it worked, didn't it?" He wrapped his arms around her from behind, then brushed his lips against the nape of her neck. "I'm only joking, of course—I do love *Pride and Prejudice.* I'm just surprised they left him in here after the film."

Elizabeth smiled. "Well, after all, what would Pemberley be without Mr. Darcy?"

"Too right, love," Charlie mumbled distractedly, his lips now finding their way to her earlobe. "Shall we head out to the marquee now?"

Elizabeth closed her eyes and sighed deeply. "Do we have to?" She opened them again slowly and glanced around the room. "We are the only ones left, you know." She waggled her eyebrows suggestively and gave him a roguish smirk.

Charlie laughed softly. "We do. For two reasons." He gently turned her shoulders so she was facing him. "You are due to give a toast in approximately five minutes. Trust me—that is not nearly enough time for what I have in mind."

Elizabeth's eyebrows rose so high they were in danger of exiting her forehead completely. She gave him a look of mock disapproval.

"And even if there *were* enough time…" His eyes left hers and traveled around the dimly lit gallery. "This is officially the dodgiest room I have ever seen in my entire life. The whole statues in the dark thing is really not my cup of tea, love. I feel like we're in the weeping angel episode of *Doctor Who.*"

Elizabeth wrinkled her nose. "I won't blink, I promise."

Charlie licked his lower lip and grinned. "Elle…" he admonished her.

"Oh-kay," she muttered, shrugging her shoulders in defeat.

Charlie placed his hand on the side of her face and slowly ran his thumb across her extended bottom lip. "On the other hand, you know how much I love it when you pout like this," he whispered, staring longingly at her mouth.

Elizabeth's stomach turned over. She stared at him blankly, her heart pounding in her ears. Did he actually just say that, or had she only imagined it? Why was it that all of a sudden the lines between reality and fantasy were blurring? Was it because of where they were? How they were dressed? She began mentally listing facts until he brought his head down to meet hers, and kissed her in such a devil-may-care manner that she completely forgot her train of thought as she melted into his arms.

Ten minutes later, Elizabeth looked around nervously at the silhouetted faces gathered beneath the glowing strands of fairy lights in the marquee on the front lawn. Although it was not traditional for a woman to give a wedding toast in England, it was also not traditional for a woman to be the best man, and so there she was. Swallowing hard, she brought the microphone to her lips and glanced over at Bryan, whose confident smile did nothing for the enormous lump in her throat. She managed to smile weakly back at him and took a deep breath.

"When Bryan asked me to be his best 'man,' I have to confess I was a little hesitant to say yes at first," she began. "Not because I didn't want to accept—I was honored, actually—I just hate the way I look in a cravat and breeches." She waited for the polite laughter to die out. "We've been through a lot, Bryan and I," she continued, "and when I think of how far we've come, I'm reminded of a quote I stumbled across when googling best man speeches." More laughter.

"It said, 'but your best friend is still your best friend. Even from half a world away. Distance can't sever that connection. Best friends are the kind of people who can survive anything. And when best friends see each other again, after being separated by half a world and more miles than you think you can bear, you pick right up where you left off. After all, that's what best friends do.'" She felt her eyes well up as she turned to face Bryan, who was wiping away a tear with the back of his hand. "I am so happy to be your best friend, Bryan." She quickly brushed away the tears that had spilled over onto her cheeks. "And I am so very happy for you for finding not only a best friend in James, but a soul mate as well. The two of you are perfect together." She paused, remembering the last words Mr. Wickham had spoken to her in her dream. She could see him now as she stared into Bryan's sea-green eyes. "I wish the two of you all of the happiness this world can offer. You deserve it more than anyone I know." She tore her eyes away from his and smiled at her audience, lifting her glass in the air. "To the happy couple!" she cried. Through the raucous applause Elizabeth took her seat next to Charlie, who pulled her close and kissed her forehead.

"That was brilliant," he said softly. "Although you seemed to fade there for a moment. Are you all right, love?"

"I am now." Elizabeth gave him a smile of relief. The music began playing and she watched as couples made their way to the dance floor.

Charlie stood and held out his hand. "Shall we dance, darling?"

Elizabeth grinned. He led her onto the floor and she rested her head against his chest and closed her eyes as Jason Mraz's smooth voice resounded through the marquee with his love song "I Won't Give Up." As the second verse began Charlie sang along in perfect harmony, and she looked up at him with an amused smile. *Of course he can sing—is there*

26

anything he can't do? He smiled back and continued singing to her until the song came to an interlude. Then he whispered softly, "Elle…you must know that I am completely in love with you."

Elizabeth somehow managed to stay cool on the outside as she smiled serenely up at him. On the inside, however, she was running up a hillside in springtime, spontaneously bursting into song whilst surrounded by various forest dwelling wildlife. "You are?"

His confident smile lit up his entire face. *Boom—wings.* "It probably sounds mad, but I feel as though I have loved you forever, even before the night we met." He stopped swaying and took both of her hands in his. "And there's something I have been wanting to ask you."

Elizabeth's heart began drumming over the rhythm of the music as she waited on tenterhooks for him to continue. *What is he going to ask?* He smiled again and opened his mouth, but before he could say anything a hand appeared on his shoulder and a voice called out, "Mind if I cut in?"

Chapter Three

ryan beamed at Charlie and Elizabeth. "Could I borrow the best man for a dance?" he asked hopefully.

Charlie blinked, thoroughly nonplussed. Then he gave him a polite smile. "Of course." Elizabeth watched dispiritedly as he left the dance floor. When she turned back to face Bryan, she tried not to look as disappointed as she felt.

"Thank you for the beautiful speech, Lizzie," he said as he took her hand in his. "It was perfect."

Elizabeth smiled, placing her other hand on his shoulder. "I meant every word, Bryan," she assured him. "I really am so thrilled for you and James."

Bryan glanced over at the table where James was chatting with Charlie. "I can't tell you how happy I am for you too, Lizzie." He winked. "Charlie seems amazing."

Elizabeth followed his gaze. "He is." Charlie caught her looking at him and smiled radiantly back at her, causing her heart to flip-flop in her chest. "I'm in love with him, Bryan." She turned to look at him and they both grinned. When the music came to an end he pulled her close in a tight hug.

"I love you so much, Lizzie." He kissed her cheek gently. "Thank you for being the *best* 'best' man a guy could ask for. If you ever need anything, don't you dare hesitate to call—you know I would do anything for you."

Elizabeth felt her eyes sting with tears. "I love you too, Bryan. I'm going to miss you so much when you head back home to Philly."

They walked back to the table hand in hand. She noticed Bryan give James a meaningful look, and he stood and smiled bashfully at Elizabeth. "May I have the next dance?"

She looked at Charlie wistfully before turning on a convincing smile. "I sure am popular tonight!" she joked. Glancing over her shoulder as she made her third trip to the dance floor, she observed that Bryan had taken the empty seat next to Charlie and engaged him in conversation.

As they swayed stiffly in time with the music, Elizabeth compelled herself to focus her attention on James. They had never been alone together since meeting briefly for the first time in Philadelphia, and she now felt self-conscious as she met his equally timid gaze. Finally having an opportunity to study his features at point-blank range, she could fully understand Bryan's attraction to him. In fact, he was so ridiculously good-looking it would have to be physically impossible *not* to be attracted to him. He was about the same height as herself in heels, allowing her the best vantage point to admire the flecks of green in his steely-blue eyes, which were surrounded by naturally thick lashes. He had perfectly arched eyebrows, a perfectly straight nose, and perfectly shaped pink lips, which Elizabeth noticed were glistening as though he were wearing lip gloss.

He probably is, she thought with an inward eye roll.

Everything about him was just so perfect it made Elizabeth feel plain and inept beside him. Accidently stepping on his foot certainly did nothing for her rapidly withering ego. As their superficial attempts at conversation fizzled into awkward silence ("Did you know that today is Colin Firth's birthday?"), her eyes wandered back to the table where Bryan and Charlie were deep in conversation, easy smiles on both of their faces. Elizabeth wondered what they could be talking about. Could it have anything to do with what Charlie was about to ask her on the dance floor? She simply had to know.

"I'm so sorry, James," she said, taking a step back and removing her hand from his. "I just remembered, I completely forgot to set the basket of sparklers by the door." She smiled apologetically, leaving him standing alone as she walked briskly from the dance floor.

Once safely out of sight, she crept, ninja-style, along the inside wall of the tent until she came within earshot of Bryan and Charlie. She stealthily slipped into an empty chair at the adjacent table with her back to theirs and listened hard for their voices. After a few moments she felt an overwhelming sensation that she was being watched. She slowly turned her head to her left.

A young man no older than twenty—who she initially thought was channeling Lloyd Christmas with his bowl-cut mousy-brown hair and bright orange bowtie, but then realized was probably too young to have even heard of *Dumb and Dumber*—was gaping at her as though he could not believe the gods were smiling on him in such a fortuitous manner.

"Hiya," he said with a smile, exposing a chipped front tooth. *Oh my God—a chipped tooth!* "I'm Walter." He straightened his bowtie. "Welcome to the singles table. Are you single?" He continued to smile at her without blinking.

Elizabeth stared at him in amazement. Seriously, where in the world was Jeff Daniels? A quick glance around the empty table told her Walter was sans wingman. Perhaps he was at the bar "putting out the vibe." She suddenly heard Bryan's disembodied voice and leaned her head back to hear more clearly.

"So I guess you're the new Mr. Darcy, huh?"

"Beg your pardon?" she heard Charlie ask.

"Didn't Lizzie tell you? She is *obsessed* with Mr. Darcy! I thought it was adorable when I met her. We were at the same Halloween party. I went as Darcy because I loved how I looked in the costume (he flicked the brim of his top hat with a smirk)—but Lizzie seemed to *really* be into it. At first I thought maybe she just liked the book. But when she described her previous relationships, it became pretty obvious Mr. Darcy is the prototype for the men she dates."

Elizabeth's jaw dropped indignantly. What in the world was Bryan doing? He was making her sound like a total nut case! She struggled to hear Charlie's response, but the voice to her left overpowered his.

"Do you like magic?" Walter asked. He pulled a wilted rose from his jacket sleeve, uttering an effeminate shriek of pain as a thorn pierced his finger.

Elizabeth gave him an exasperated look. She heard Bryan's voice once more and stuck her nose in the air like a dog on point.

"Well, the men she dated before were almost always dark, brooding, and successful—you know, like Darcy. Though I'm pretty sure none of them could wear the *hell* out of a cravat." He laughed.

Walter skootched his chair closer to Elizabeth, who was now chewing anxiously on her lower lip. "Want to feed each other cake?" he asked hopefully.

Elizabeth distractedly grabbed her fork and speared an oversized vanilla frosted chunk from the plate before her. "Sure." She shoved it into Walter's mouth without even looking at him. He gagged as crumbs fell to his lap, unable to speak.

"No kidding," Charlie was saying. "I wasn't aware she had a 'type.' I'm no Mr. Darcy, that's for sure."

"Well, it's entirely possible Lizzie has changed since the accident," Bryan said as he pushed back his chair. "If *I* crashed into someone that looked like *you*, I would have left Mr. Darcy behind in that ditch along with my car." They both got to their feet and turned in her direction.

Elizabeth gasped. She jerked her head toward Walter so they wouldn't see her face, noticing with a start he was turning a delicate shade of eggplant. She reached over to pound him on the back repeatedly until a mouthful of congealed cake sprayed across the table. He gave her a grateful smile, tears streaming down his florid cheeks. Looking up, she saw Bryan and Charlie walking away, still talking, and cursed under her breath. She stood quickly and walked in the opposite direction, calling over her shoulder, "Bye, Walter."

"Call me!" he squeaked.

Elizabeth slipped through a flap in the marquee and prowled along the outside wall, keeping a careful eye on Bryan and Charlie through the plastic windows. When she arrived at another entrance she pushed through it and strolled nonchalantly up to where they stood with James, near the buffet-style hors d'oeuvres.

"There you are." Charlie smiled.

"Are you all right, Lizzie?" Bryan asked. "You look a little pale." He held out a glass. "Champagne?"

Elizabeth's eyes followed the bubbles as they rose to the top of the glass and then exploded like miniature fireworks. She slapped her forehead with her palm. "The sparklers!" Heaving a large sigh, she looked apologetically at Charlie. "I'll be right back."

As she hurried off to find the basket that held the sheathed sparklers, her head began to whirl with new and terrifying thoughts. *Great. Does Charlie now think I'm only seriously interested in men that remind me of Mr. Darcy? Or that I'm completely crazy for having spent the majority of my life obsessed with a fictional character? What would he think of me if I confessed I gave up Mr. Darcy for yet another imaginary man? He would think I am insane, that's for sure. He would probably regret having told me he loves me. And what if he thinks I don't love him because he's not my type? I didn't even get a chance to tell him the truth before Bryan interrupted us! And why, oh why, would Bryan even think that would be an appropriate topic of conversation with my new boyfriend? "Prototype for the men she dates"— sheesh! I mean, come on! That was* never *even true…was it?*

She set the basket down by the exit of the tent and paused, picturing the men she had dated in the past. True, they had all been tall, dark and handsome, like Mr. Darcy. They all had successful careers centered on the amount of money they made. They had all been rather brooding, conceited, and slightly agoraphobic. And though at one time she believed each one of them to be Mr. Right, they had all been completely *wrong* for her.

What an idiot I was before I met Charlie.

His face swam across her mind and she smiled absentmindedly. Charlie was the antithesis of Mr. Darcy in every way possible, right down to his blond hair and heart-stopping dimpled smile. Yet he was exactly what she wanted, and more importantly, what she *needed*. And he was in love with her! She froze, suddenly remembering their interrupted conversation on the dance floor. *Wait! He was about to ask me something!* Her breath caught in her chest.

What if he was about to ask me to marry him?

The idea that Charlie might have been about to propose right there on the dance floor was so thrilling she completely forgot her insecurities. She began to fight her way through the throng of guests pushing past her to get their sparklers. When she located his face in the crowd she haphazardly threw her arms around his neck and kissed him. He staggered backward in surprise, then wrapped his arms around her and shielded her from the sea of bodies as they parted around their stationary forms.

She waited until the tent was empty before smiling up at him. "By the way…I love you, too," she breathed. As she looked into his blue eyes she felt no need to make a list of facts—there was no doubt in her mind whatsoever as to who it was she was speaking to. "I am so completely in love with you too, Charlie."

Later, as they made their way down the hallway of their hotel, they noticed a gift basket sitting in front of the door to their room. Nestled inside was a bottle of Grey Goose vodka and two leaded crystal martini glasses. Charlie bent down to pick up the envelope tucked in the middle. After opening it carefully, he read aloud from the card inside.

Dear Mr. Bond,

Please accept this offering of my sincerest gratitude for your service to her Majesty's kingdom. It is a prodigious honor to serve yourself and Miss Moneypenny. Please do not hesitate to ring my personal mobile should you need anything at all. Please rest assured sir, your identity is safe with me. I solemnly swear not to inform anyone of your whereabouts.

Your humble servant,

Maurice Trenneman - hotel concierge

Charlie looked up at Elizabeth, who was pressing her lips together to keep from smiling and staring hard at the ceiling. She dropped her gaze to his bewildered face and gave him an innocent smile. "It seems like you have an extremely loyal fan base here in Derbyshire, Mr. Bond."

"So it does." Charlie raised a playful eyebrow. "And are you Miss Moneypenny?" He gestured to the note.

"I would have thought that was obvious," Elizabeth muttered distractedly as she fumbled through her clutch for the room card. "She's *way* cooler than any Bond girl."

"Sexier, too," Charlie added with a slight smirk.

"She's also the only woman on the planet he doesn't objectify." Elizabeth dropped the card and struggled in her corset to retrieve it. "Although he teases her relentlessly with his smooth advances. It's almost as if he's waiting for her to make a move—only she never seems to find the nerve, the poor thing."

"You make it sound like a game of Chess," Charlie laughed. "Would her move be a pin against the king, then?" He winked devilishly.

Elizabeth smiled. "Very clever. But seriously, why does he treat her differently from all of the others?"

Charlie bent down and picked up the card. In one fluid movement he opened the door and held it in place with his foot, then turned around, and, placing his hand on the small of her back, pulled Elizabeth firmly up against his body. "I would have thought that was obvious, darling." He reached down and swept her up into his arms. "He's in love with her."

He carried her into the dimly lit room where, thank goodness, there were no statues. Setting her down gently, he walked over to the fireplace and turned on the gas insert. As she removed the pins in her hair with a sigh of relief, she watched the flames that rose from the neatly stacked faux birch logs illuminate the dimly lit room with a soft incandescent glow. Charlie turned and walked back to where she stood smiling at him, half of her face fiery and lucent, the other eclipsed by his shadow. She placed her hands on his shoulders as he located her waist and pulled her toward him. He took her face in his hands and kissed her with deliberately measured intensity as he brushed a loose tendril away from her forehead and raked his fingers softly through her hair, past her ears to the back of her head. Then he swept the tangle of long auburn curls from her shoulder in order to press his lips softly against the side of her neck.

He turned her in his arms and painstakingly undid the seemingly endless buttons trailing down the back of her gown to her waist. She obediently held her arms above her head as he carefully lifted it off and laid it across the back of the chair. Her pulse quickened as he proceeded to loosen the snakelike strings of her corset, and she let out a sigh of release as he skillfully pulled it apart without removing the stays. Each time his proficient fingers made contact with her bare skin shivers went up and down her spine, until she was covered in goose bumps despite the heat radiating from the fire. He wordlessly allowed the corset to fall to the ground and rubbed his thumbs tenderly across the indentations left by the boning against her rib cage. When his hands found the smooth pink scar that ran down her side he dropped to his knees and kissed it along its entirety. She drew in a long, shuddering breath and then let it out again slowly. Finally, he stood to face her. With a self-satisfied smile he held out her pink polka-dotted pajamas. "You should try and get some rest, love. It's been quite a long day."

She smiled back at him.

My move, Mr. Bond.

Chapter Four

"Speaking of terrifying statues…" Charlie mumbled, with an expression of revulsion that mirrored Elizabeth's. It was the following morning, and they were standing by the edge of the lake at Lyme Park. For their last day before returning to London, Bryan suggested they explore the "real Pemberley," or in other words, the one from the 1995 miniseries. Seeing as she had no objection whatsoever to viewing yet another magnificent home with its awe-inspiring gardens and landscape, Elizabeth was more than willing to join the rest of the bridal party on their excursion. When they arrived, however, there was one not-so-little feature that drew their attention away from the splendor almost the instant they set foot on the property.

In the center of the lake stood Mr. Darcy himself, submerged up to his waist in murky water. He was over ten feet tall, made of what looked suspiciously like papier-mâché, and wore a constipated expression on his unrecognizable face that suggested he was grievously unhappy to be stuck there (which, Elizabeth had to admit, was actually pretty darn accurate for a Darcy representation). The infamous see-through wet shirt was just see-through enough that one need not wonder just how cold the water probably was on that brisk autumn morning.

Elizabeth glanced over at Charlie, completely at a loss for words. Lucky for the two of them, their repulsion went entirely unnoticed by the rest of their party, who were all too busy at the moment being genuinely impressed by the giant Firth-strosity.

As the rest of the group continued without them on their "Pemberley walk" (a guided tour of the filming locations from the miniseries), Charlie turned to Elizabeth. "So, please, tell me…as an esteemed member of the female persuasion…what *is* it about that scene that would compel some poor sap to build a shrine that will now haunt my dreams for all eternity?"

Elizabeth giggled. "Aw, come on, now…" she began, gesturing toward the statue. "You don't think that's hot?" She thought for a moment. "I think it's more that it was completely out of character that makes it such a turn on for most women. You know, because Mr. Darcy is so prim and proper that seeing him strip down and get soaking wet in that paper-thin white shirt that clings to his…" She trailed off, feeling her cheeks blaze from a memory of her coma-induced fantasy that had nothing at all to do with Mr. Darcy.

Mercifully, her phone vibrated in her back pocket at that exact moment. She turned her back on Charlie so he couldn't see her flushed face and checked her messages. She had a new text from Jane.

I can't wait till you get back! I have some news that I am DYING to tell you, so hurry up and come home!! (Excited-face emoji.)

Oh, and I want to hear all about your weekend. Every. Single. Detail. (Winky-face emoji. Kissy-face emoji.)

What are you doing now? Getting into mischief, I hope? (Devil-face emoji.)

Elizabeth was about to text back *of course not* (angel-face emoji), when she glanced up in time to see Charlie walking into the water, his pant legs rolled up to his calves. She stuffed her phone back in her pocket, noticing his navy Chucks scattered forlornly on the grass.

"What are you doing?!" she exclaimed.

He flashed her a crooked grin. "Something completely unexpected."

Elizabeth fought a laugh. "I really don't think you are supposed to go in the water."

"He did," Charlie replied matter-of-factly, pointing at the statue and shrugging his shoulders. "Besides, I need to give you a mental image to replace the one of Colin Firth, don't I?" With that, he turned and dove headfirst into the water.

Elizabeth waited impatiently for him to resurface, torn between amusement and fear of an employee spotting them breaking the rules. When he finally emerged, he stood in the waist deep water and shook his head side to side, droplets of water flying in all directions. He ran his fingers through his hair and gasped from the cold. Then he looked over his shoulder at the statue and attempted to mimic its pose, trying and failing to brood sufficiently.

"Very nice," she laughed. "Now come out before you catch pneumonia. Or worse, we get kicked out."

"There's hardly anyone here!" he called, looking around. He was right. The only other people in sight were a group of college-age girls in the far distance on one side and an elderly couple on the other. "Come on in, the water's, well, the water is absolutely freezing, to be completely honest."

"So come out!" she cried again, walking toward the edge of the water.

"Have I accomplished my goal, then? Will you forever think of my wet shirt instead of Colin Firth's?"

Elizabeth smirked. "Well, you see, *his* is actually see-through."

Charlie looked down at his red and blue plaid button-down shirt. "Bugger! You know, you're absolutely right." He began to unbutton it carefully from top to bottom, exposing his bare chest.

"What. Are. You. *Doing*?" Elizabeth asked, her eyes bulging. "Are you *crazy*?! What if someone sees you?"

"Darling, no one is going to see—" He was interrupted by a catcall from the college girls, who were now staring shamelessly in their direction. Charlie laughed and waved at them before removing his shirt altogether. He balled it up and threw it to Elizabeth, but it fell short and landed at the water's edge.

"All right, pretty boy," Elizabeth chided him, "you can come out now." She glanced over at the girls, who had their phones out and were taking pictures. "I think it's safe to say that I, and at least six other women, will never think of that scene ever again. Or anything else, for that matter." Sheepishly, she took her own phone out and snapped a quick picture. *For, um—you know—posterity's sake*. "Here's your shirt."

She walked to the edge and bent down to pick up the shirt, but just as she reached for it her foot slipped on the wet grass and she pitched forward. Her phone flew out of her hand and landed safely on the ground, but unfortunately she was not as lucky. She fell face-first into the water, her sole reflection on the way in being that at least she got a picture of Charlie's washboard abs first. The implosion of her nerve endings on impact with the freezing water shut out all other mental synapses as she repeatedly slipped on the muddy lake floor and flailed around like a fish in a bucket. When she finally managed to right herself she noticed Charlie standing over her wearing a gratified smirk.

"So nice of you to join me," he said wryly, helping her stand. He gave her a once over with his eyes. "Now I understand completely the appeal of the wet shirt. You look simply *ravishing*, darling."

Elizabeth glanced down at her ivory fisherman sweater and skinny jeans camouflaged in lake sludge and grimaced. She wiped her hand across her stomach and then patted his cheek lovingly, leaving a muddy handprint behind. "Glad I could help with that," she replied with a smug smile.

He grinned and moved in closer, as if to kiss her. Just before his lips met hers he wrapped her in a bear hug and threw his weight backward. They both fell into the water, Elizabeth's shriek of surprise stifled by her unexpected baptism. When she resurfaced she uttered a cry of indignation and struggled awkwardly through the water after him. As soon as she caught up she watched him pull a soaked handkerchief from the back pocket of his jeans and wave it back and forth in the air.

"What is that?" she shrieked.

"A white flag?" He wrinkled his nose.

"I think you might just be the only thirty-year-old on the planet that uses an actual cloth handkerchief," she goaded him.

"Well, you never know, do you, when a damsel in distress might come along." He pulled her toward him and gently wiped a smudge from her cheek with the handkerchief. "And when the love of your life is a tad, err, *accident-prone*, they certainly do come in handy." He gave her a breathtaking smile as he continued to clean the specks of mud from her face.

(*Sigh—wings.*) When he reached her mouth, his eyes darkened slightly and his smile faded. He took her face in his hands and leaned in to kiss her once more, this time with intent. Elizabeth closed her eyes and allowed the world to melt away just for a moment. Then she gave him a saccharine smile, and placing both hands on the top of his head, dunked him unceremoniously beneath the surface. They continued to horse around until they heard a high-pitched "Ahem!" followed by an extremely irate voice calling out, "Just what, pray tell, do you think you are doing?"

Freezing in place like scolded children, they turned slowly and saw a very old, very short man wearing a brown tweed three-piece suit and polished wingtips. He was standing at the water's edge with his hands folded neatly over his rotund belly, staring at them angrily and making *tsk, tsk* noises. His snow-white mutton chops, handlebar mustache, and knitted bushy white eyebrows reminded Elizabeth of Owl from *Winnie the Pooh*.

"Terribly sorry, sir," Charlie began in an unbelievably cool, calm, and collected voice. "This lovely damsel fell into the pond, so, naturally, I had to dive in and rescue her. She can't swim, you see." He offered up his most charming smile. Elizabeth shot him an affronted look (the water they were currently standing in came up to her thighs), then gasped as he suddenly swept her up into his arms. "You're welcome, darling," he finished patronizingly. He carried her out of the water and set her down on the grass.

"I see." The man cleared his throat. "The young lady fell and was unable to swim in the shallow water…and yet you found the time to remove both your shirt and shoes before rescuing her?" He glared dubiously at Charlie's bare chest as he handed him his damp shirt.

Elizabeth and Charlie exchanged looks. Elizabeth bit down hard on her lip to keep from laughing as she picked up her phone and Charlie's navy trainers. "Yes, well, we will be on our way now, if you don't mind, old chap." Charlie struggled into his shirt and pulled on his Chucks. He patted the man on the shoulder. "Smashing pond you've got here, by the way. The statue of Colin Firth enhances the ambiance splendidly."

The man's livid expression promptly transformed to one of pure delight. "I had a hand in the making of it myself, actually." He gazed upon it lovingly. "Don't you think the resemblance is uncanny?"

Charlie grinned. "An excellent likeness. Absolutely swoon-worthy. Well done, mate." He glanced at Elizabeth.

"Dream-like. Hauntingly unforgettable," she contributed, casting a knowing smile back in Charlie's direction.

The man bid them a good day. He shook each of their hands warmly before continuing on with his hands clasped behind his back, whistling a cheerful tune as he went.

As they walked back toward the house, Elizabeth returned to the unsent text to Jane on her phone. She deleted "of course not!" and typed out "you know me…" (Gangster with sunglasses emoji).

What did you do? Jane texted back almost immediately. *Something against the rules, I hope. Did you kiss the bust of Mr. Darcy? I hope you had red lipstick on – send pics!!*

We are at Lyme Park today… I went for a swim in the lake with the Colin Firth statue. (Shocked-face emoji. Devil-face emoji.)

Elizabeth opened the camera to send Jane the picture of Charlie shirtless in the water, noticing as she did that the last picture taken was surprisingly not of him. She opened it. It was a blurry, but perfectly distinguishable image of herself tumbling into the water, her head submerged and her legs in the air. The button must have somehow been pushed when the phone hit the grass. She hit delete before Charlie could see it, and suddenly another text from Jane came in.

You fell in, didn't you? (Belly laughing-face emoji.)

She sighed and put her phone back in her pocket.

That afternoon, no longer smelling of algae thanks to a hot shower, Elizabeth and Charlie were in the car on their way back to London. As excited as she was to hear Jane's mysterious news, Elizabeth couldn't help but feel slightly crestfallen. She and Bryan shared a tearful farewell before they left, and she had no idea the next time she would see him after his return to the States. She was staring out the window despondently when Charlie suddenly spoke up.

"Do you know, my mother has been asking about you?" He glanced at her sideways briefly before looking back at the road.

Elizabeth's eyes widened. She turned away from the window. "She has?"

"Yes, she keeps asking me when she will get to meet you. She and my dad are both eager to have us over to theirs for dinner. I promised I would ask how you felt about it, but assured them I wasn't about to put any pressure on you if you weren't ready to be subjected to an evening of relentless torment. You see, my mum is quite lovely, but my dad and brother are...*characters*." He curled his lip.

"You have a brother?" Elizabeth asked, surprised.

"Tom," Charlie began. "He's a few years older than myself." He smirked. "He said he would drop everything to be there when we are, he is so keen to meet you. Probably thinks he can charm you away from me, which is precisely the reason I have been putting it off, to be honest."

Elizabeth smiled. "I'm not worried." She leaned over and kissed his cheek. "And you shouldn't be either. You're kind of charming yourself, you know."

"So should I tell them yes? Would Friday after next work, you think?"

"Absolutely," Elizabeth said. "I can't wait." She pursed her lips. "And honestly, if *you* can survive meeting my mother, *I* can survive anything your family can dish out. You don't know how terrified I was that five minutes in her presence would be enough to make you swim back to London."

"I really don't know why you would say that," Charlie admonished. "I thought she was absolutely lovely."

Elizabeth rolled her eyes. "Yes, I'm sure you did—meeting you was probably the highlight of her entire year. I could have left the dinner table and swam back to London myself and she would have never even noticed I was gone."

"Ahhh, but you don't swim, remember?" He winked.

Elizabeth sniffed complacently. "I most certainly do swim. Did you forget earlier today at the lake?"

"Oh, is that what you were doing? Funny—it looked an awful lot like drowning to me." Charlie licked his lower lip and grinned.

"I don't mean when I fell in!"

Charlie patted her knee. "It's all right, darling—I know it couldn't be helped." He gave her an earnest look and she smiled gratefully. "You were so turned on by my completely unexpected, stripped-down, soaking wet, Firth-worthy lake scene that as a result you were completely deprived of basic motor skills." He watched her smile falter. "Is that what happened?"

Elizabeth sighed. "Yes, that is exactly what happened," she replied sarcastically. She turned to look out the window to conceal her disloyally crimson cheeks, which were suggesting that, as a matter of fact, it *was* exactly what happened. ⚫

When Charlie dropped her off at her flat she found it surprisingly empty. She left her suitcase by the door and kicked off her moccasins, grabbing the stack of mail from the desk. As she sifted through it she made her way into the tiny kitchen and grabbed a bottle of wine from the fridge, noticing as she pulled it out the Post-it note attached.

Do NOT drink! I'm picking up something special on my way home— we need to celebrate!

—Jane

Now Elizabeth was definitely intrigued. Resisting the urge to change into pajama pants in case Jane's boyfriend Will was with her, she plopped onto the couch and closed her eyes. At that moment the door opened and Jane strolled into the room, a Marks and Spencer carrier bag in each hand.

"Grab some glasses!" she cried excitedly, setting the bags down.

"Does this celebration require pants?" Elizabeth asked cautiously, looking toward the door.

"No, go change," Jane answered. "I'll pour."

On the way to her room, Elizabeth thought to herself how comforting it was to be home. She pulled on her favorite pair of plaid flannel pajama pants and sat down on her unmade bed. Beside her on the nightstand lay her well-worn copy of *Pride and Prejudice*. She smiled, thinking there was no reason to worry about confusing reality with her Regency era dream in London. Her messy room, the noisy traffic outside the window, and most importantly, the ability to breathe freely due to lack of corset were all constant reminders she was right where she belonged. She patted the cover of her book fondly and left the room, eager to hear Jane's news.

Sitting next to her on the sofa, she took the proffered flute from her sister. "So what's the big news?" she asked impatiently. "I hope it's as good as this champagne…mmm…"

Jane took a deep breath. "I'm getting married, Lizzie!" She beamed at her sister's thunderstruck expression. "I'm marrying Mr. Darcy!"

Elizabeth set down her champagne before looking straight into Jane's eyes. "I'm sorry…but what did you just say?"

Chapter Five

*J*ane laughed. "Well, my Mr. Darcy, anyway." She squeezed Elizabeth's shoulder. "Don't worry, not the fictional one from your dreams."

Elizabeth forced a laugh. "Right." She paused. "Wait, so Will proposed? That's amazing! You must be so excited!" She threw her arms around her sister. "Tell me everything!"

"It was completely unexpected," Jane admitted excitedly. Elizabeth smiled, thinking of Charlie's 'completely unexpected' antics at the lake. "He came over and we made dinner together. For dessert he brought out a slice of the cheesecake he bought—you know, from that little bakery you love? Anyway, when I cut into it the ring was inside. Can you believe it? Then he got down on one knee and asked me to marry him!"

Elizabeth smiled. "It was in the dessert?"

"I know, it's cheesy," Jane muttered, coloring. "But we are both kind of cheesy anyway, so it was perfect." She beamed helplessly.

"So, what did he say exactly? How did he ask?"

Jane took a sip from her flute. "He kept it short and sweet. I was too overwhelmed to remember his exact words, but he basically told me how much he admires and loves me."

"I am so thrilled for you, Jane!" Elizabeth hugged her again. "Will is amazing. You guys are going to be so happy together! And now I will have a big brother I can tease forever!" She grinned. "Total win-win!"

Jane laughed. "So…obviously I want you to be my maid of honor. You don't have major plans around a year from now, right?"

"Hmmm…" Elizabeth looked up at the ceiling. "I was going to become a monk and move to Thailand, sooo…" She gave her sister a sarcastic grin. "Of course I will be your maid of honor! It will be so much fun planning the wedding together! So who else is in the bridal party?"

"Well, definitely Will's sister, Millicent," Jane began.

"Will has a sister? I didn't know that!"

Jane pressed her lips together. "Yes, she's six years younger than him. She lives with their parents," she trailed off, staring blankly into the middle distance.

"Anyone else?" Elizabeth prompted her, eyebrows raised.

"Will's friends from the hospital, Andie and Kassy. They met him when he started working there five years ago. He introduced me when you were in the hospital. They are both really great." She smiled. "I've actually gotten pretty close with them both—especially Andie. I think you are going to really like them!"

"That's great! So what about the guys?" Elizabeth asked.

"Will's best man is also a friend from the hospital, Dr. Patel. You know—the Dr. I set you up with the night you met Charlie?" She gave Elizabeth a wry smirk.

Elizabeth flushed. "Oh, right."

"It will be fine, don't worry. He told me there are no hard feelings about it." Jane waved her hand dismissively. "And the other three are two of his mates from uni and his cousin."

"I can bring Charlie as my plus-one, right?" Elizabeth asked.

"Of course you can!" Jane cried. She gave her sister a meaningful look. "Things must be going pretty well if you are including him in your plans a year from now."

Elizabeth blushed. "Well, he did tell me he was in love with me this weekend." She gasped. "And he wanted to ask me something important, but Bryan interrupted him before he could!"

Jane smiled back encouragingly. "You know, two things happened right before Will proposed—we went on a mini-break, and then I met his parents. And you've already gotten the mini-break under your belt…"

Elizabeth chewed on her lower lip. "We're having dinner with his mom and dad next Friday."

"You've found your Mr. Darcy at last!" Jane cried.

"Charlie could not be more different than Mr. Darcy, Jane." Elizabeth sighed contentedly. "And I couldn't love him more for it."

Jane laughed. "See, I told you Mr. Darcy wasn't your type. Charlie's definitely more of a Bingley."

"You were right as always, oh wise one," Elizabeth mumbled. She pulled her legs up in front of her, hugged her knees to her chest, and nursed her champagne distractedly.

"So you said you have plans next Friday, right?" Jane asked. "Are you free next Saturday evening?"

"I think so, why?"

"Because I want to have a dinner party here for the bridal party so everyone can meet. You should invite Charlie! I was thinking it would be fun if we all dressed up for the occasion too. Like a fancy dinner party in a vintage film or something!" Jane gushed.

"That sounds perfect! I will definitely ask him." Elizabeth reached for her phone. "I'm starving. Shouldn't we order a pizza or something?"

"Only you would think about pizza when we are discussing the loves of our lives," Jane said, rolling her eyes.

Elizabeth looked scandalized. "You should know by now, Jane—pizza *is* the love of my life." She put the phone up to her ear. "I only met Charlie a few months ago—but I have been intimately acquainted with pizza since birth." She smiled as Jane rolled her eyes. "Since I was a fetus, actually, seeing as mom craved it during her pregnancy—oh, hey there, Basil, it's Lizzie—" She held up her pointer finger and turned to face the other direction.

Jane made a face at her sister and hurled a throw pillow at the back of her head.

Before she was emotionally prepared, a week went by and Elizabeth found herself in the congested London Underground. She was on her way to Charlie's parents' flat, wearing her favorite floral print blouse, skinny jeans, and riding boots. Though he had a car and was more than willing to drive,

Elizabeth had insisted upon taking the tube, seeing as his parents lived between them and traffic would be at a standstill on a Friday evening in London.

She distracted herself from her surroundings by imagining what Charlie's parents and brother would be like, until she felt an elbow nudge her in the rib cage.

"Sorry," she muttered, and unraveled the ball of yarn she was holding for a woman knitting a pair of what looked suspiciously like underpants beside her. On her other side, a construction worker who smelled like tacos let out an enormous belch. Elizabeth winced, thinking to herself how compelling an argument it was that the smell of tacos (which usually made her mouth water) in reverse was enough to make a person rethink their entire stance on Mexican food.

When she got off at her stop she waited for the crowd to disperse and looked around for Charlie, who was meeting her there. Finally, she found him leaning casually against a wall, legs crossed, holding a bouquet of flowers. She smiled and made her way over to him.

"You didn't have to bring me flowers," she teased him with a coy smile.

"These are for my mum, actually," Charlie admitted. "Roses are her favorite."

Elizabeth blushed. "Oh! Right—I'm sorry!"

Charlie grinned shamelessly. He pulled another bouquet out from behind his back. "I believe these are *your* favorite?"

Elizabeth took the bouquet and kissed him. "Thank you." She smiled down at their friendly-faced blossoms. "I just love daisies."

"They remind me of you," Charlie added, taking her free hand firmly in his.

In the cab Elizabeth turned toward Charlie. "Oh! I can't believe I completely forgot to ask—can you come over tomorrow evening for dinner?"

"Sure," Charlie replied. "Any special occasion?"

"Remember when I called to tell you Jane got engaged? I was supposed to ask you to come to dinner tomorrow evening for everyone in the wedding to meet. I'm so sorry, I don't know what is wrong with my brain lately! I seem to forget everything."

"Well, you did shake it up a bit not too long ago. Maybe you should go a little easy on yourself there, love." Charlie gave her a squeeze. "Of course I'll come. Should I bring anything?"

"No, but—oh! Jane said something about dressing up fancy. She wants it to be like a film or something…"

Charlie frowned. "You mean fancy-dress?"

"Exactly," Elizabeth answered. "A fancy-dress dinner party. At least I think that's what she said."

"You know fancy-dress means costumes in Britain, right? Are you quite sure that's what Jane meant?" Charlie gave her a quizzical look.

"It does?" Elizabeth tried to remember her conversation with Jane. "Hmm… Well, nice of her to clarify! I was just going to wear a black dress and heels—now I have to try to find a costume in time for tomorrow evening? Why in the world would Jane want us to wear costumes anyway? As an icebreaker? Is it like a British thing, to make meeting people feel less awkward? Should I have worn a costume tonight?"

Charlie pulled her close and kissed her forehead. "God, I love you," he whispered with a grin. Then he pointed out his window. "Oh look, we're here."

Elizabeth's jaw nearly hit the floor of the cab. They had arrived at an enormous house with a brick exterior and a myriad of lofty windows, each one of them emitting a warm glow of light that illuminated the perfectly trimmed hedges beneath. "I thought you said your parents lived in a flat," she breathed softly.

"Did I?" Charlie furrowed his brow. "Hmm…I don't remember saying that. Perhaps I have something wrong with my brain as well." He smiled roguishly and helped her out onto the sidewalk.

Elizabeth could feel her heart begin beating wildly in her chest as they walked to the door. It was more than obvious that Charlie's parents were extremely wealthy, seeing as they lived in a verifiable mansion on the outskirts of London. Suddenly she felt extremely underdressed as she looked down at the faded denim on her knees and the stirrup scuffs on her boots.

Charlie rang the doorbell (Mozart's "Canon in D") and as they waited Elizabeth grew increasingly anxious. Suddenly the door was opened by an uncanny Jude Law lookalike, whose glowing blue eyes quickly traveled from Charlie's to Elizabeth's, then back to Charlie's. He broke into a shockingly familiar crooked grin.

"Baby brother!" he cried, shaking Charlie's hand and pulling him in for a bear hug. "How long has it been?"

"Too long, Bro," Charlie gushed. "So good to see you!"

They broke apart and turned in unison to face Elizabeth, their ecstatic smiles nearly identical. "And won't you please introduce me to this absolute stunner you brought with you?"

Charlie gave Elizabeth a knowing smirk. "This is my girlfriend, Elizabeth." He bit his lip. "Elle, this is my brother, Tom."

Elizabeth watched helplessly as Tom took her outstretched hand and kissed it. He smiled flirtatiously up at her with eyes every bit as blue as his brother's. "It is an honor to finally meet you, Elizabeth. You are just as lovely as Charlie described—and much too good for the likes of him, I have absolutely no doubt." He winked at her, flashed another devastating grin, and then stood at considerably full height. "Shall we go inside and find Mum and Dad?" He held the door and gestured for them to enter, then followed them into the foyer, which resembled the entrance to an art gallery. *Or possibly the White House.* The walls were lined with portraits of men and women with varying degrees of indifference in their expressions.

Elizabeth swallowed hard. Trying not to be terrified, she focused her attention on Tom, who they were now following down the cavernous hallway. He was a couple of inches taller than Charlie, with a slender but athletic frame. His hair was a sun-kissed light brown and just long enough to be wavy on top and curled around his ears. He wore a form-fitting blue denim dress shirt with the sleeves rolled up that perfectly matched his eyes, tucked tightly into belted burgundy chinos. On his feet he wore chocolate-brown suede boots. When he grinned at her over his shoulder, massive dimples appeared on each of his cheeks in the exact location of his brother's. As she smiled back bashfully, Elizabeth thought fleetingly that she couldn't wait to meet their mother, if only to congratulate her on a job well done with her offspring.

Upon entering the living room, however, her courage failed her miserably as her eyes traveled from one end to the other. The room was remarkably spacious, with blush velvet sofas, innumerable ivory throw pillows, modern teakwood accent furniture, and a gargantuan crystal chandelier hanging from the cathedral ceiling. In one of the velvet club chairs sat an attractive older man with impeccably styled salt-and-pepper hair, wearing a navy sweater and khakis and balancing a book on one knee. At one end of the sofa, a graceful-looking woman with soft blonde hair pulled up into a flawless French twist sipped daintily from a china teacup. They both looked up as the three of them walked into the room. Elizabeth felt her stomach turn over. Smiling broadly, they both stood and walked quickly across the room to meet them.

Charlie's mother was tall and slender, with striking olive-green eyes. She had an oval-shaped face, a long, straight nose, and thin lips that appeared fuller with their deep scarlet shade. She wore white from head to perfectly manicured toes, accented with pearl earrings and several strands of soft white pearls around her neck. She would have been a highly intimidating presence, were it not for her ready smile that made it clear from whom her sons had inherited their endearing dimples.

"Thomas, why didn't you tell us who was at the door?" she scolded. "I assumed it was only a solicitor when you didn't call for me!" She wrapped her arms around Charlie. "Oh, my Charles! How good it is to hold you in my arms again—our European tour lasted for ages! How long has it been since I saw you last? Three months? More?"

"Far too long, Mum," Charlie answered with a grin, releasing her. He handed her the bouquet of roses. "These are for you."

"Thank you, my darling boy," she replied, and took them in her hands. "Would you believe Thomas brought the exact same bouquet? How well you both know me!" She turned to face Elizabeth. "And this must be the lovely Miss Elizabeth!" She reached out and took her hand. "I have *so* been looking forward to meeting you, my dear. Welcome to our home." She smiled warmly.

Elizabeth beamed. "I am so happy to be here, Mrs. Bennet. Your home is absolutely stunning."

"Please, call me Constance," she insisted. "And thank you." She looked around the room. "We've had to do quite a bit of work to it, but I think it's finally beginning to look a bit less outdated. I'm sure everything looks completely different from the last time Charles graced us with his presence." She cast her son a wry smile.

"Now, now, Constance—go easy on the boy," his father admonished her as he shook his son's hand. "We've only been back a few weeks, after all, and he's been occupied with someone far more captivating than his old Mum and Dad the past few months. Edmund Bennet—it's a pleasure, my dear." He offered his hand to Elizabeth, who tried not to gawk as she shook it. Charlie's dad was like an older version of him, right down to his height, frame, and icy-blue eyes. Between the four of them, Elizabeth had never witnessed a more evident genetic jackpot in her entire life. "And an

American! From which of the former colonies do you hail, Miss Elizabeth?" he inquired.

"You can call me Lizzie," she replied with a grin. "Although Charlie calls me Elle." She turned to smile at him, and he gave her hand a reassuring squeeze. "I'm from Pennsylvania."

"Ah, I see! Such a ruddy shame though, to be known for the unmitigated squander of perfectly fine British tea," Edmund replied with a loud sniff, though his lined blue eyes were twinkling.

Elizabeth looked questioningly at Charlie, who sighed. "He means the Boston Tea Party," he muttered as he rolled his eyes. "Boston is in Massachusetts, Dad."

"Too right it is! Speaking of tea, I am desperate for a cup. Shall we head to the dining room and get dinner over with?" Edmund gestured for the rest of them to follow, winking playfully at Elizabeth when their eyes met.

When dinner was finished, Charlie offered to help his mother in the kitchen with tea and dessert preparations, insisting Elizabeth remain behind and relax. His father left momentarily to locate his book on the Boston Tea Party, eager to prove that it did, in fact, take place in Pennsylvania. Elizabeth watched him go, thinking to herself that things were going much better than she had anticipated. She looked across the table at Tom and grinned when she saw him mouth a silent apology.

"I should probably be prepared to prove him wrong," he said with a sigh, and pulled out a pair of black-framed glasses. As he put them on he only furthered his striking resemblance to Elizabeth's celebrity crush, and she subconsciously gave him a pained look as she stared. "I know." He smirked, pushing them up against the bridge of his nose with one finger. "You're wondering how I could possibly still be single, aren't you?"

Elizabeth produced a high, tinkling laugh. "Actually, yes, I am." She wrinkled her nose, embarrassed.

"I really don't see myself ever getting married," he admitted. "I'd be doing the women of the world a favor. I'm far too afraid of commitment to settle down with anyone. Besides, I've got a lot of love to give, and it would be unfair to put boundaries on it, don't you think? I'd much rather just be a confirmed bachelor for the rest of my life." He laughed at the look on Elizabeth's face. "Don't worry, it's not a Bennet gene. Charlie is keen on the institution of marriage, I assure you. He is such a sap when it comes to love, which is probably the reason he very nearly gave up bachelorhood before he had even fully begun. I wish I could say it's a shame it didn't work out, but I always thought he could do better anyway." He winked at her. "And as usual, I was right."

Elizabeth blinked. "What do you mean?" she whispered. Her heart began to beat faster.

Tom shifted uncomfortably in his seat. "Didn't Charlie tell you?" His debonair smile faded.

"Tell me what?" Elizabeth pressed him.

Tom hesitated, his features conflicted. "He was engaged for six months before he met you."

He was engaged for six months before he met you.

The words echoed in her head as she searched for the proper reply. She opened her mouth but was interrupted by Charlie reentering the room, carrying a tea service on a tray. He stopped short at the look on her face and frowned. "Tom, what did you say to her?" he asked, then smiled broadly at Elizabeth. "I should have warned you. You can't believe a word he says about me."

Chapter Six

*E*lizabeth lay in bed for a long time the next morning, going over the events of the previous evening in her mind. She kept hearing Tom's words over and over again, and though she tried to shut them out, they kept coming back.

He was engaged for six months before he met you.

Who was he engaged to? Why didn't it work out? And why didn't he tell her about it? They had spent countless hours talking about their pasts since that first night at the pub. Not once had he ever mentioned he had almost gotten married!

It must have been extremely painful for him not to want to talk about it. But what happened? To be engaged and then not end up getting married! It must have been something awful. Oh, dear God—what if his fiancée died, and it's too painful for him to talk about it? Maybe I should just ask Tom? She sat up in bed. *Although Charlie did say I can't believe anything Tom says about him. Would he make the whole thing up just to tease me? I really don't think he would do that. If it is true, and Charlie wants to talk about it, he will. I just need to let it go. Besides, whatever happened is in the past, and will stay in the past. No reason to let it interfere with the future—right?*

Feeling determined, she threw back the covers and went to the kitchen to make some coffee. Jane was sitting slumped at the counter on a barstool in her pajamas, her blonde hair crushed against the side of her head on one side and protruding in waves and peaks on the other. She sipped from her "I'm silently correcting your grammar" mug and drowsily patted the stool beside her. "Imbibe yourself with caffeine so you can tell me about last night."

Elizabeth poured herself a cup, contemplating whether or not to confide in her sister what Tom had told her. Climbing onto the stool, she decided against it. If there was any chance at all it could come back around to Charlie it would have to remain a secret. "It was fine," she began softly. "His parents are really great. I don't know why I was so worried about meeting them."

"And his brother?" Jane asked, eyebrows raised. "Is he as cute as Charlie?"

Elizabeth grinned. "Remember the movie *The Holiday*?"

Jane sighed dramatically. "How could I forget it?"

"Well, let's just say I'm still contemplating asking him for his autograph, he looked so much like Jude Law."

"Nice. So when do I get to meet him?"

Elizabeth shook her head in mock disapproval. "You are an engaged woman now, remember?"

"Yes," Jane breathed happily, spreading out her fingers to admire her engagement ring. "Yes, I am, aren't I?" She set down her mug. "And I have an engagement dinner party to prepare for!"

"Do you need help with anything?" Elizabeth asked.

"Will and I are going shopping for groceries and then coming back here to make dinner," Jane answered. "But if you wouldn't mind picking up wine and grabbing some desserts." She smiled and batted her eyelashes at her sister, then rummaged through her purse and handed her a wad of cash.

"What is a maid of honor for, if not to be sent on random errands for the bride?" Elizabeth replied playfully. "I'll go get ready. What time do I need to be back for dinner?"

"I told everyone to try to get here by six, so try to be back at least by five thirty," Jane called over her shoulder as she walked into the bathroom. "And don't forget to tell Charlie!"

"I won't," Elizabeth promised. "He has to work till four today, but it takes him like five minutes to get ready. He'll probably be early, unless he is coming as something that requires makeup." She walked into her room, just missing the look on Jane's face as she stuck her head back through the doorway of the bathroom in confusion.

It took Elizabeth most of the afternoon to fight the weekend crowds and purchase enough wine for eleven people, then struggle to carry the bags to the bakery, where she added a cheesecake and two pies to her load. She had just deposited everything on the floor of the living room when she remembered she still needed to find a costume. Smacking herself on the forehead, she ran back out the door.

It was a quarter to six when she was finally on her way back to the flat, already wearing her costume. After trying it on in the shop she realized she would have no time to change before the guests arrived. Checking the time on her phone, she winced. Most of them were probably already there at this point. Suddenly, her phone rang in her hand, and she was relieved to see Charlie's face pop up instead of her sister's.

"I'm coming, I promise. I'm so sorry, Charlie!" she blurted. "You should see the looks I am getting right now. Jane is never going to hear the end of this, I swear! Costume dinner party…sheesh." She made a face at a group of teenage boys gaping and pointing in her direction. "All right, keep moving! Nothing to see here!"

"Elle," Charlie whispered insistently. "I don't know what you've got on right now, but I'm thinking you are probably going to want to change before you get here."

"What? Why? I'm already here!" She hurried up the stairs, threw open the door, and froze in place as she found herself face to face with a roomful of people with drinks in hand, and most unfortunately for her, looking glamorous in suits and formal dresses. Comparatively, her film-quality Wonder Woman costume (complete with thigh-high boots, gauntlets, and lasso) was just a smidgen out of place.

Her eyes quickly found Charlie, who was still holding the phone up to his ear, eyes wide with surprise and mouth dropped open as he looked her up and down. Very slowly, he lowered his arm and placed his phone in his pocket. Elizabeth wrinkled her nose and squeezed her eyes shut. It was now painfully clear she had somehow misunderstood Jane's words.

Well, at least I didn't go with the giant chicken suit.

Hands on hips, she gave a short laugh. "Well, this is embarrassing," she addressed the room at large. She paused, trying to think of something witty to say as everyone was still staring at her as though she were naked, which (as she tugged at the miniscule skirt attached to her bodice), she thought she might as well be. "You're probably wondering (*Wonder-ing—nice, Lizzie!*) why I am dressed like this…" She pulled the shield from her back and held it before her for coverage.

I should have gone with the giant chicken suit.

She took a few small steps into the room. "I'm meeting Captain America for drinks later," she quipped, placing her hands on her hips.

Jane walked quickly over to her. "Lizzie, why in the name of all that is holy are you wearing a Wonder Woman costume?" she asked calmly.

"I thought you said fancy-dress, and Charlie told me it meant costumes in Britain! This was the only decent one they had left in my size!" she whispered back frantically. "I'm so sorry. I will go change right now!"

"Probably a good idea," Jane replied, then snorted. "Seriously though, something like this could only happen to you. You, and Bridget Jones. It's too bad they didn't have a Playboy Bunny outfit."

"That's hilarious," Elizabeth muttered. She made her way over to where Charlie was leaning against the back of the sofa wearing a highly amused smirk. He was also looking incredibly dapper in a precision-cut black suit complete with a crisp black bow tie and shiny dress shoes. His blond hair was freshly cut with a hard part and slicked down to one side, and his face was smoothly shaved. She gave him a quick kiss, then took a step back to fully appreciate every inch of him before frowning slightly. "Wait, why are you not wearing a costume?" she asked, her eyes narrowed in suspicion.

"I am, actually—I'm a secret service agent," Charlie replied earnestly, straightening his bow tie and smiling. "The name is Bennet." He raised one eyebrow in a thoroughly convincing smolder. "Charles Bennet."

66

Elizabeth smiled back despite herself. "You mean to tell me you rented a suit just so you could come as a secret agent?"

"I probably would have if I were given more than twenty-four hours' notice," he answered wryly. "And if I were absolutely certain you knew what you were talking about." He laughed at the indignant look on Elizabeth's face. "I borrowed this from Tom. Lucky for me it was a bit short on him. Look—I have cuff links and everything!" He held up his wrists excitedly. "I figured a suit was the safest choice. Obviously I ended up a tad overdressed. But then again, since you arrived no one has bothered to give me a second look." He grinned.

"Yes, well…I'm on my way to change now, so I guess the joke's on you." Smiling provocatively, she gently pulled him toward her by the lapels. "I wouldn't let *you* change even if you lived here." She gave him a quick kiss on the lips. "*Mr*. Bennet."

He grinned. "Whilst we're on that subject, there's a question I have been dying to ask."

Elizabeth's smug smile faded. "What is it?"

Charlie leaned in closer. He paused for dramatic effect, making her heart thud in her ears. "This Wonder Woman costume…was it for hire only, or would it be possible to buy it?" He bit his lip and grinned.

Elizabeth considered him for a moment. "I'll make you a deal, Mr. Bennet. You ask Tom to keep the suit, and I will make Wonder Woman a permanent part of my wardrobe." She laughed at the excited look on his face, then strutted to the door of her bedroom and closed the door behind her.

Moments later she rejoined the party, feeling more or less poised in her trusty little black dress and heels (*why didn't I just wear this and be*

Holly Golightly from Breakfast at Tiffany's*?*). Noticing Charlie and Will deep in conversation, she made a beeline to the kitchen for a well-deserved drink. She waited for the man in front of her to finish pouring his glass of wine and felt a small lurch in her stomach when he turned around. It was Dr. Patel, Will's friend. He also happened to be the date Jane set her up with the same night she received a letter from Charlie asking her to meet him at the pub. Although she had agreed to see Dr. Patel again before the end of their date, fate obviously had other plans. Admittedly, she hadn't given him much thought after beginning her relationship with Charlie, but seeing him now for the first time since that night reminded her how inconsiderate and rude she must have come across.

"Dr. Patel!" she exclaimed.

"Ah, Miss. Baker. So we meet again," he replied stonily. His handsome face appeared almost angry, his eyes narrowed.

Elizabeth blinked. "Uh…"

He laughed. "It's a joke! You know, like if I were a villain or something. Sorry, I'm a comic book nerd, I guess." He flashed a dazzling smile. "Absolutely *loved* the Wonder Woman costume, by the way."

"Oh! Thanks." Elizabeth gave a nervous laugh. "It's good to see you again, Dr. Patel."

"Please, call me Char. Great to see you too, Lizzie." He gestured to the counter. "Can I get you a drink?"

She glanced over his shoulder at Jane, who was opening the front door. Two women entered the room and threw their arms around her sister, then gleefully began examining her engagement ring. The one nearest was tall, with glossy black hair pulled neatly in a high bun. Her fuchsia mini dress was complemented by matching lipstick and earrings. The woman beside her was petite, though her stiletto heels made her appear a few inches taller. She had strawberry-blonde curls and a shimmering champagne-hued one-shoulder dress that stopped mid-thigh. Both girls wore expressions of sheer delight on their beautiful faces that made Elizabeth suddenly feel extremely uneasy. "Umm…sure, I'll have…whatever's closest," she muttered distractedly. While she waited for him to pour, she watched Jane call for Will to join her. She thanked Dr. Patel for the drink, then shrank behind the counter and continued to stare across the room in disbelief.

Blinking rapidly, she fought the urge to list facts in her head as her heart pounded a steady rhythm in her ears. It wasn't possible; and yet standing a mere twenty feet away from her were the modern day manifestations of Georgiana Darcy and Caroline Bingley—taking selfies with their mobiles, no less. The fictional characters from *Pride and Prejudice* had cameoed in her coma-induced dream as the sisters of Mr. Darcy and Mr. Bingley, respectively. Though relatively harmless in the original novel, in her mind's version of the story they had both been nothing short of pure, unadulterated evil. In fact, the last time she was face to face with Georgiana, she had impulsively broken her nose with a well-timed right hook.

She snapped out of her reminiscence at the sound of her own name. Looking up, she saw Jane waving her over. She walked toward them slowly, half expecting the two women to begin hurling insults the moment they recognized who she was.

"Lizzie, I want you to meet Will's friends, Andie Frost and Kassy Stark." Jane gave her an excited smile. "They work at the hospital."

"Hey, I'm Elizabeth, Jane's sister," she replied, holding out her hand tentatively as if it might get bitten off.

"Yes, I know exactly who you are!" Andie cried, taking her hand and shaking it firmly. The radiant smile she flashed caught Elizabeth completely off-guard, and she felt her shoulders become rigid.

"You do?" she replied, rather anxiously.

"Of course!" She gestured to the woman beside her. "Kass and I were assigned to you once or twice when you were in hospital! But—oh! You wouldn't remember that, would you, seeing as you were all but unconscious at the time." She gave a light, pleasant little laugh. "I can't believe how quickly you recovered once you woke up. It's like the accident never even happened! You look amazing!"

Elizabeth bit her lip and gave her a small smile. "Thank you," she said softly, trying not to make it sound like a question.

"I'm sorry," Andie replied with another laugh. "I am probably being a bit forward, aren't I? It's just that I feel as if I know you already—all Jane ever talks about is her brilliant little sister!" She looked at Jane, who feigned embarrassment, then conceded with a nod and a smile. "From everything I've heard about you, I just know we are going to become great friends, Elizabeth." She smiled sweetly, displaying perfectly straight white teeth.

Elizabeth found herself at a complete loss for words. She watched helplessly as Jane and Will left to check on the food, leaving her alone with Andie and Kassy. She turned back around to face them, her smile beginning to feel plastered.

"It's going to be great fun all being in the wedding together, isn't it?" Kassy chimed in, nudging Elizabeth with her elbow. "So many fit men to flirt with! Isn't Dr. Patel absolutely swoon-worthy?"

"Umm…" Elizabeth began.

"Speaking of fit men," Andie added under her breath. "Is that Charlie Bennet by the window?"

"It is!" Kassy cried. "What is he doing here?"

Elizabeth followed their gaze. Charlie was standing by the window, looking down at his phone. He glanced up, and, noticing the three of them staring at him, colored. "He's my boyfriend, actually." She beckoned to him and he casually tucked his phone into his pocket and began to walk slowly across the room.

"Charlie Bennet is your boyfriend?" Kassy asked, her eyes wide with astonishment. "That's...unbelievable. Isn't it, Andie?" She gave her friend a knowing smile.

"Why? Do you know him?" Elizabeth asked warily.

Before they could answer, Charlie joined Elizabeth's side and put his arm around her waist. He gave Andie and Kassy a polite smile. "Hello, Kass. Andie."

"Good to see you again, Charlie. It's been a while," Andie replied cautiously, returning his smile. "You look—" her eyes twinkled as they traveled from his hair to his shoes "—really well."

"How do you know each other?" Elizabeth interjected.

Charlie and Andie exchanged measured looks. Andie turned to Elizabeth, her smile unwavering. "Oh, his brother and Will went to Eton together. We were introduced at a dinner party." She looked back at Charlie. "And now you are dating Will's future sister-in-law, and we are all together at a dinner party! Such an unbelievable coincidence, don't you think?" She produced another airy laugh.

"Unbelievable is the most fitting word for it, yes," Charlie replied slowly. His lips curved forcibly upward.

"So…how did the two of you meet?" Kassy asked Elizabeth eagerly.

Elizabeth smiled at Charlie, who squeezed her waist. "We just sort of…bumped into each other."

"Yes!" Kassy exclaimed. "That's right! Don't you remember?" She grabbed Andie's arm. "Jane said her sister was dating the bloke whose car she crashed into!" She gaped at Andie. "And I never told you this—but I thought I saw him in the neuro unit carrying flowers a few months ago! At the time I wasn't sure it was him, but now it makes complete sense. He was visiting her!"

Andie raised her eyebrows. "Wow. Now *that's* unbelievable. A real fairy-tale ending." She smiled warmly at Elizabeth. "Those are hard to come by these days. You really are a lucky girl."

"I'm the lucky one," Charlie cut in, and kissed Elizabeth's forehead.

At that moment Jane called Elizabeth's name. She and Charlie excused themselves and walked over to where Jane and Will were standing by the table of appetizers.

"Lizzie, I want to introduce you to Will's sister, Millicent—or Millie for short." Jane gestured to the person standing with her back facing them.

Millie turned around. She was of medium height and heavyset, with a round face and childlike features that made her appear much younger than she probably was. Her eyes were large and pale blue—made paler by the masses of white-blonde hair pulled tightly into a side ponytail and cascading over one shoulder. She had a short, upturned nose, and her mouth was small and heart shaped. The most striking thing about her appearance, however, was her clothing ensemble. The blouse she wore had the Hogwarts crest proudly centered across the front. Her skirt was covered with the individual crests of the four separate houses of J.K. Rowling's novels—Gryffindor, Ravenclaw, Hufflepuff, and Slytherin. She wore a black hooded cape around her shoulders, and black Doc Martin combat boots with knee-high maroon and gold striped socks. Dangling from her ears were large white owls. She held out her hand to Elizabeth, transferring the wooden wand in it to her other hand, and gave her a reserved smile. "Nice to meet you."

Elizabeth smiled back conspiratorially. "Yes, you too! I can't tell you how glad I am to see that someone else thought Jane wanted us all to wear costumes!"

Millie stared at her blankly. "We were supposed to wear costumes?"

Chapter Seven

When dinner was ready they made their way to the living room, where Jane had set up a folding table and chairs. She had done such an amazing job decorating it reminded Elizabeth of the dining room at *Downton Abbey* instead of the cramped living room of their tiny flat. The table was covered with an embroidered ivory cloth. The delicate china was borrowed from their aunt Bridget, and each place setting was marked by a cloth napkin carefully folded with a handwritten name card. Elizabeth quickly found hers between Charlie's and one that read, 'Winston.' Sensing someone standing beside her, she looked up to see yet another shockingly familiar face.

"Hiya, Miss Baker!"

She found herself staring straight into the amber eyes of none other than the orderly from the hospital who helped her out to the car when she was discharged, and who, coincidentally, called himself "Sanders" due to his infatuation with Kentucky Fried Chicken. He had also made an appearance as Colonel Fitzwilliam, the friend and cousin of Mr. Darcy, while she was in her coma. Both incarnations were equally presumptuous, and even teetering on the edge of creepy.

Elizabeth stood speechless, attempting to make sense of why he would possibly be standing there in her flat. She used the dead air to survey the changes he made in his appearance since the last time she had seen him.

He had grown his reddish-gold hair out to just about chin-level, and his facial hair was now somewhere between stubble and a beard. He admittedly looked quite debonair in his fitted navy suit and tie, and the warm smile he gave her was almost impossible not to reciprocate.

"Hi there, um…Winston?" Elizabeth asked, holding up the place card.

"Yeah, that's me," he admitted sheepishly. "But you can call me—"

"Sanders?" interrupted Elizabeth, one eyebrow raised.

"You remembered!" he cried happily. "Lovely to see you again, Miss Baker."

"Lizzie," she replied, shaking his outstretched hand. "Are you a friend of Will's too?"

"I'm also his cousin, if you can believe it," Sanders said as he took his seat. "Our moms are sisters."

Elizabeth tried to keep a straight face. "No kidding," she muttered. "Who would have guessed?"

"Can you believe Will and your sister are getting married after meeting when you were in hospital?" he asked earnestly. "You could definitely take credit for bringing them together, you know." He gave her a thoughtful smile.

"I know! It's kind of crazy, isn't it?" Elizabeth smiled and shook her head. "Makes you wonder if everything happens for a reason."

"I know exactly what you mean…like perhaps there is a greater purpose to life." He sighed softly and looked down at his wineglass. "Are you religious at all?" he inquired delicately, glancing back up at her.

Taken back, Elizabeth couldn't help but think that maybe she had misjudged him. Sure, he had come across as sort of sleazy when they first met. But maybe that was because she was comparing the real him to her brain's fabricated interpretation of him, and that really wasn't fair. Now that she was actually having a conversation with him, he seemed sweet, genuine, and even a little bit—

"Because you are definitely the answer to all of my prayers." He gave her a wink and a devilish grin.

There it is.

Elizabeth felt her nostrils flare and wrinkled her nose. She drank deeply from her glass until he lost interest in her and struck up a conversation with Kassy, who was seated on his other side.

After dinner Elizabeth ended up sitting beside Millie on the sofa, waiting for Dr. Patel to finish his turn at charades. Kassy and Andie jumped up to hug him when they guessed his film title correctly (*Legally Blonde*), and as Elizabeth's gaze drifted toward Millie their eyes met briefly. She giggled under her breath when Millie mimed puking into her water glass.

"So Millie," she began, "What do you do for a living?"

"I'm a professional cosplayer," Millie answered evenly.

Elizabeth frowned. "I'm sorry…but what exactly is that?"

Millie heaved a sigh. "It's someone who specializes in fandom costume design, and travels to various multi-genre entertainment and comic

76

conventions to display them and win contests." She smoothed the wrinkles in her skirt.

"Oh. I see." Elizabeth tried and failed to hold her tongue. "Doesn't it cost you quite a bit of money to be successful in your career?"

Millie waved her hand dismissively. "Not at all. I still live with my parents, and they are extremely supportive. They foot the bill for every trip I make, and all of my costumes as well." She ran her finger lovingly along the edge of her wand. "They even find conventions I didn't know existed and encourage me to attend, even if it means I'm hardly ever home." She looked up and smiled. "They want me to follow my dreams."

"Oh." Elizabeth bit her lip determinedly. "It's great you have such supportive parents!"

"My boyfriend is really supportive as well."

"You have a boyfriend?"

Millie nodded and reached into her purse. "He couldn't make it tonight due to his busy schedule, but I have a picture of him right here." She handed Elizabeth what appeared to be a well-worn magazine clipping. The young man in the photograph had chestnut hair, glasses, and a lightning bolt-shaped scar on his forehead.

"Umm…Millie?" she began, eyeing the face carefully. "Isn't this Harry Potter?"

"Yes."

"You're dating Harry Potter?" Elizabeth felt her lips twitch.

Millie rolled her eyes. "Of course I'm not dating Harry Potter. You do know Harry Potter is a fictional character, right?" She gave her a patronizing sniff.

"I do—do you?"

Millie sighed deeply. "I'm dating Daniel Radcliffe."

Elizabeth stared at her. "Isn't he the actor who plays Harry Potter?"

"Yes."

Her face was void of even the smallest hint of a smile, so Elizabeth had to assume she was serious. "Wow," she responded slowly. "That's great." Her lips curved upward into a playful smirk. "I'm dating James Bond, myself." She gestured to Charlie, who was in the kitchen adding an olive to his martini.

Millie gave her a pitying look. "You do know James Bond isn't real either, don't you?" she asked, placing a hand on Elizabeth's shoulder. "I think you might have a problem distinguishing between reality and fantasy." She tucked her magazine clipping back into her purse and readjusted her cape carefully.

"Thank you, Millie." Elizabeth gave her a sincere smile. "I'll work on that."

When the evening was over, Elizabeth stood at the door with Jane to bid their guests farewell. She was looking down at the piece of paper on which Andie had written her phone number, imploring Elizabeth to call her to get together later that week, when Charlie put his arms around her waist and asked if she wanted to go for a walk. They made their way down the front steps of the building and onto the sidewalk. The night air had an end of September chill as it gusted between them and Elizabeth shivered involuntarily in her strapless dress. Charlie removed his jacket and placed it around her shoulders. She hugged it tightly beneath her chin and breathed in the scent of his skin still lingering on the collar. "So," he began. "You know how I keep telling you I have something I want to ask?"

Elizabeth gave him a sarcastic smile. "Are you going to ask me what the whip is for?" She furrowed her brow. "Because I have no idea. I'm a little afraid to find out, to be honest."

"You mean the Lasso of Truth?" Charlie laughed at the blank look on her face. "No, not that. I was actually wondering if you would fancy moving in with me."

Elizabeth stopped walking and looked up at him. "Really?"

"Yes, really." He took her hands in his. "I am completely mad about you, Elizabeth Baker. I want yours to be the first face I see in the morning." He gave her a boyish grin. "Every morning."

They came to a bench and Elizabeth sank down onto it. Charlie sat next to her and waited patiently for her answer. Deliberately avoiding his gaze, she bit her lip and looked down at her hands in an effort to disguise her disappointment. She admittedly hoped he had been about to ask her to marry him. Considering what she now knew about his past, there was a good chance it might not happen. It was the worst possible moment for Tom's words to reverberate inside her head.

He was engaged for six months before he met you.

What if he had been hurt so badly that he had no intention of ever marrying? Elizabeth knew she would never be able to content herself with merely living with the man she spent most of her waking moments daydreaming of walking down an aisle with in a white gown. The happy ever after she always imagined included starting a family with the man of her dreams— and getting married was definitely a key factor in that scenario. She knew without a doubt she wanted to spend the rest of her life with him. In fact, she would have probably said yes if he had asked her to marry him the first night they met—but what if he didn't want the same thing?

Looking up at his hopeful face, she pushed her thoughts to the back of her mind. "I would love to move in with you." She sighed as his eyes lit up. "It's just (*I want it to be as an engaged couple*) I, I couldn't do that to Jane. She would, um, never be able to afford the rent on her own."

Could that excuse be any lamer?

"She's getting married, though," Charlie began, "won't she be moving out soon anyway?"

"The wedding isn't until next year." Elizabeth looked down at her shoes. "She didn't say anything to me about moving before then."

"Well, if she does," he said softly, taking her chin in his hand and gently lifting it so she had to look him in the eye. "Will you at least consider moving in with me?" His eyes were round with expectation. "We could get a kitten," he added enticingly.

Elizabeth smiled. He obviously remembered her telling him the story of how she had given away her beloved cat because of an ex-boyfriend, whose "allergies" landed him in prison for making crystal meth out of Sudafed. "What would we name him?"

Charlie grinned. "What was the name of the cat you gave away again?"

Elizabeth smiled sheepishly. "Mr. Darcy." She laughed. "It actually suited him perfectly. He was extremely stand-offish and hated most people except for me."

"Then we will find one that loves everyone and name it Bingley," he decided. "What do you think?"

"Sounds perfect," Elizabeth replied, and kissed him. She made up her mind to try and forget about what Tom had said. After all, Jane wouldn't be moving out for almost a year, and a lot could still happen before then. Maybe he was planning on proposing, and by the time they moved in together they would be engaged. There was no sense in giving it another thought, at least not at that exact moment, when his fingers were in her hair and his lips were just so...

Sigh.

One week later, Elizabeth was about to press send on an article she had just finished editing for *Flavor* magazine when her phone began vibrating on the coffee table. She picked it up and saw that she had a new text from Andie. She had been casually texting back and forth with her since the night of the dinner party, and today she was asking if Elizabeth wanted to meet her for a pint at the bar near the hospital when she finished her shift. She quickly replied *sure!* and set her phone down, thinking how weird it was to be starting a friendship with someone she had deeply hated in her subconscious only months earlier.

She knew it had only been a dream, but it felt so real at the time that even now she found herself struggling to disassociate the real people from their fake counterparts. As she walked into the pub and saw Andie waving her over with a bright smile on her face, Elizabeth thought happily it would probably not be very difficult much longer. Andie's personality was the exact opposite of her mind's version of Georgiana Darcy. She was kind, sweet, and extremely eager to be friends with Elizabeth, who in turn found her enthusiasm easy to requite. It was actually kind of nice, she thought, to have a new friend—one she could confide in. Jane had become so absorbed in the details of her wedding (*and rightly so*), that she had little to no free time to be a sounding board for her sister's endless stream of random thoughts. Perhaps Andie would be the perfect person to talk to about her insecurities when it came to Charlie, especially since she apparently knew him at one point.

Maybe she can tell me what happened with his engagement!

Elizabeth gave her order to the waitress and turned to Andie, who was still wearing her hospital uniform. Not surprisingly, her hair and makeup were flawless, even after an eight hour shift. "Thanks for asking me to come out! I needed a break from my screen."

"I have been wanting to get together since we met!" Andie replied. "I just feel like we have so much in common!"

"We do!" Elizabeth agreed eagerly. "I'm actually jealous of Jane, that she has known you so much longer than I have."

Andie laughed. "Well, I probably would never have met either of you if you hadn't crashed your car and ended up in my unit."

Elizabeth rolled her eyes. "Oh, I'm pretty sure you would have. One thing you will learn about me is that I am hopelessly clumsy." She smiled. "I am constantly getting hurt."

"Well then, I hope for your sake we only see each other outside of the hospital," Andie quipped. "And not only to talk about wedding plans, as much as I dearly love the bride."

Elizabeth took a deep breath. "Actually, I do have something I wanted to ask you about that has nothing to do with the wedding." She bit her lip. "It's something I heard about...someone."

"Oh, really?" Andie leaned in. "Something juicy, I hope!"

"It's about Charlie."

"Oh." Andie sat back slowly in her chair and waited for her to continue.

"You said you met him a long time ago, right? Did you know him well?"

Andie gave her a calculated look. "I suppose you could say that," she confessed. "We dated for a little while, actually."

Elizabeth frowned. "The two of you dated? Was it for a long time?" She nervously wiped the beads of condensation from her glass.

Andie considered her for a moment, running her finger methodically around the rim of her own glass. After what seemed an eternity, she finally spoke. "No, it wasn't. It only lasted a few months."

Elizabeth swallowed again. "Do you mind me asking why it didn't work out?"

Andie paused again. She seemed to be choosing her words carefully. "To be honest, I'm the one who ended things with him." She sighed. "He's a great person, and I liked him a lot, but he had some issues that made me realize it wasn't going to work out."

Elizabeth felt her breath catch in her chest. "Issues?"

"Yeah. Commitment issues, I suppose you could say. It just didn't feel like the relationship was going anywhere, and I wanted more from it than he did." She flicked her eyes sideways in the direction of a group of young men passing by. "It probably had something to do with what happened to him."

Elizabeth's heart began to pound. "What happened to him?"

Andie's eyes met Elizabeth's and she blinked. "Didn't he tell you he was engaged?"

"No, but I heard about it from…someone else," Elizabeth stammered. "I don't know any of the details though."

Andie's eyes flashed with apprehension, then her face became set. "It was before I met him. He was apparently engaged for like half a year or something like that…but she cheated on him."

Elizabeth was aghast. "What—why?!" She looked up at Andie with a horrified expression. "How?!"

Andie sighed. "I really don't think I should be the one to tell you. You should probably just ask him about it."

"No, please!" Elizabeth placed her hand on top of Andie's on the table. "I don't want to make him talk about it if it is too painful. But I have to know what happened. I just have to."

"All right—but don't tell him that I told you," Andie implored resignedly. "I guess she wanted someone with a more successful career. You don't make that much money when you work as a riding instructor, you know."

"But he's doing what he loves," Elizabeth argued. "Isn't that more important than money?"

"For some people," Andie answered thoughtfully. "I know I would love being a nurse more with a pay rise." She gave Elizabeth a rueful smile. "They say money can't buy happiness, but it certainly makes life more fun, wouldn't you say?" She took a long sip of her beer. "Anyway, she left him for the other bloke, and it broke his heart. I don't think he ever even found out who it was. He was never quite the same after that." She paused. "At least according to his brother, anyway, who told me the whole story. He was even cuter than Charlie—I wonder if he's still single?"

Elizabeth ignored her and shook her head furiously. "So she cheated on him with someone who made more money? That is just...*despicable.*"

Andie appeared lost in thought. "Yes, it is," she mumbled softly. Then she smiled. "Especially considering that money can't buy dimples like theirs."

Elizabeth gave her a small smile. "So, you broke up with him because you thought he didn't...want..." she trailed off, tracing the edge of her soggy napkin.

"To get married?" Andie finished for her. "Yes, I got the distinct impression he never intended on settling down, ever." She sighed again. "I mean, I wasn't ready to settle down myself when I was with him, but I wanted it to be a possibility, you know, one day. Otherwise, what is the point of dating? Why not just stay single?" She saw the alarm on Elizabeth's face. "Oh—but that was a long time ago! Years ago!" She squeezed Elizabeth's hand. "It was still fresh for him when we met. I'm sure he's had plenty of time to get over it by now. You are so cute together, really." She smiled sweetly. "And besides, the way the two of you met? It's like a real-life fairy-tale! Of course he will marry you! It's fate!"

Elizabeth smiled back weakly and swallowed hard against the lump that had formed in her throat. After saying goodbye to Andie she slowly made her way back to the flat, the whole way home allowing everything she had heard spin round and round in her head like the spin cycle of a washing machine. She felt her phone vibrate and pulled it out of her purse. Charlie was calling her, his carefree face smiling up at her from her screen. She pressed decline and stuffed it back in. She really didn't want to talk to him at the moment—not when she was experiencing a thousand different feelings with regard to him.

She felt terrible for what he had gone through years before, but she also couldn't help but feel that he should have told her about it by now. The fact that he kept it from her only seemed to further substantiate his apparent disinclination toward marriage—if they were truly meant to spend the rest of their lives together, wouldn't they tell each other everything? Perhaps not the trivial, insignificant details, like which brand of toothpaste they preferred—but surely the staggeringly monumental, life-altering events—like breaking off an engagement because their fiancée cheated on them?

Maybe not if they were worried that telling the other person might cause that other person to look at them differently. Maybe not if it could change how the other person felt about them.

Elizabeth sat down on the front steps outside her flat and felt all the air leave her lungs in one long stream. How dare she feel any sort of resentment toward Charlie for neglecting to tell her about a past relationship, when she still hadn't confessed to having a relationship with someone while in her coma, out of fear he would think she was completely crazy. At least his ex-fiancée was a real person. What would he think if he knew hers was a figment of her imagination, but was so real to her at the time that even after she woke up she still had feelings for him?

Chapter Eight

*S*eptember ended with unseasonably warm weather. Elizabeth made every effort to get in as many hours at the stables as possible before the cold came to stay. It was on a sunny afternoon in the first week of October, as she was sweeping out a stall, that she heard a frantic cry for help coming from somewhere outside the barn.

She ran out into the blinding sunshine just in time to see a horse with a young rider streak past at a full gallop. The little girl had lost control and let go of the reins in order to hold onto the pommel for dear life, and the horse was speeding across the field with no intention of stopping or slowing down. Elizabeth looked around wildly, but with all the noise and activity from the various classes in session around her, no one from the multitude of teachers or students but herself seemed aware of the severity of the situation.

Without hesitation, she ran to the nearest horse and heaved herself up onto it, swinging her leg up and over the saddle and into the other stirrup in one fluid motion. With a forceful flick of the reigns she kicked her heels sharply into the horse's side and it sprang forward into an immediate gallop. She chased after the other horse, closing the gap within minutes. Soon the two horses were neck and neck as they continued to gallop through the field at an alarming pace. The terrified girl was now hunched forward and Elizabeth could see her arms beginning to lose their grip on the saddle. She knew she had to act quickly. She urged her horse even closer, then held onto her reins and pommel tightly with one hand and leaned to reach for the slack reins of the other horse. After a few tries she managed to grab onto them, and pulled back firmly on both sets to slow the horses together.

When they had safely come to a complete stop, Elizabeth reached out to take the visibly shaken little girl's hand. "Are you all right?" she exclaimed. "What happened?"

"I don't know," the girl cried between sobs. "I think something spooked her, I don't know." She burst into tears, her shoulders trembling.

"It's all right now, I promise," Elizabeth soothed. "Everything is going to be fine." She pulled both sets of reins to the left to turn the horses around, and they slowly made their way back toward the stables. Elizabeth spoke reassuringly to the girl as they rode, telling her the story of how she had fallen from a horse when she was young and how she had only recently regained the courage to ride again (leaving out, of course, the small detail that her moment of triumph had occurred within her own mind). By the time they got back the little girl was smiling once again.

She leapt down from her horse and handed her off to a stable hand, then helped the girl down from her saddle, giving her a big hug before sending her off to rejoin her distraught but relieved teacher and classmates. As she watched her animatedly describe her rescue to the class, Elizabeth absentmindedly stroked the horse's side and reminisced on the part of the story she had purposefully omitted.

She moved to the front of the horse, whispering soothing nothings, and reached up to gently rub its nose. Without warning, it jerked its head away from her hand and reared unexpectedly. Before she could even attempt to move out of the way Elizabeth felt the horse's metal shoe hit the side of her head. A searing pain tore its way through her forehead and then suddenly everything faded to black.

The darkness slowly dissolved into fuzzy patches of gold, and then the gold faded away into blue sky speckled with fluffy white clouds. Elizabeth could feel the soft grass beneath her, and she could hear birds chirping somewhere in the distance. She blinked, trying to recall what had made her fall to the ground. Her head felt thick and foggy. She decided to try to sit up, but before her brain could send out the signal to her extremities a familiar face appeared above her and she frowned in confusion.

The eyes that were staring straight into hers in alarm were as blue as the sky beyond them. The blond hair that framed his face, traveling down his jawline and ending in perfectly angled sideburns seemed longer than usual and attractively disheveled. His well-defined lips with their prominent cupid's bow were slightly parted in fear. As her eyes traveled from his face down to his clothing, Elizabeth wondered why he was not wearing the flannel shirt she had seen him in earlier that day. "What happened, Charlie?" she managed to mumble.

A look of bewilderment crossed his features. He took her hands in his and helped her to sit. "You fell from the tree and I caught you. I believe you may have lost consciousness." He gently brushed a blade of grass away from her forehead. "Are you quite all right, Miss…is it Miss Bennet?"

Elizabeth felt the earth begin to spin. The sound of his voice faded along with everything else, until the darkness returned and he was gone.

Chapter Nine

lizabeth opened her eyes. The sky was still blue above her, the grass was still soft beneath her—and the face that looked down at her still bore the same panicked expression. Her breath caught in her chest.

What just happened?

She struggled to sit up, but his hands were strong as they held her shoulders firmly against the ground. "Don't try to get up—we don't know if anything is broken," he insisted. "What in the world happened, Elle?"

The sound of his nickname for her caught her attention, and she immediately ceased in her efforts to push against him. She lay still and observed him more carefully. Yes, it was definitely Charlie—he was clean-shaven and his hair was short with a hard part on one side. He was also wearing his red flannel shirt, and she could smell his Polo cologne. "I have no idea," she replied hazily. "But I think I can get up."

As he helped her sit slowly she felt the earth begin to spin again. She squeezed her eyes shut, the dull twinge of pain on the right side of her head growing more intense with each passing second. Something warm and wet trickled past her temple and she touched it gingerly, noticing as she pulled her hand away that her fingers were slick with bright red blood. Her stomach turned over. "I'm going to be sick," she muttered thickly.

Charlie grabbed the bucket beside him and as she retched into it he gently rubbed her back. "I'm going to ring for an ambulance," he declared. "You need the hospital."

Elizabeth pulled her head back abruptly. "No, I'm fine!" she cried. She looked around at the crowd of people who had gathered around her. "Really. I feel all right now, I promise. I don't need to go to the hospital." A surge of fear raced across her chest. She couldn't go to the hospital with another head injury. She had just gotten her life back, her head was finally starting to feel clear. Going back there would only remind her of everything (and everyone) she had finally begun to forget. With the exception, of course, of a few minutes ago, when it seemed like for a second she had seen—

"Elle, you need stitches," Charlie insisted. "If you don't want an ambulance then I will drive you. Do you think you can stand?"

Elizabeth sighed in resignation. "Yes." She stood, holding Charlie's arm for support. "I don't suppose you'll let me just slap a Band-Aid on it and go home, will you?" The dizziness returned and she closed her eyes till it passed.

"No," Charlie answered, scooping her up into his arms and carrying her. "You're going now."

Twenty stitches and a slew of tests later, Elizabeth was resting somewhat comfortably in her bedroom back at the flat. Her head still throbbed, but at least she didn't have to be admitted to the hospital, which was the last thing she wanted. Instead of having to wait for what could be hours for the results of the lab work and CT scan in the emergency department, they agreed to release her so she could receive a phone call from home and come back in if necessary.

Readjusting her ice pack, she glanced over at Charlie, who was asleep beside her. She watched his eyelashes flutter, and the steady rise and fall of his chest as he breathed. He always slept with one hand resting directly over his heart, as though he were saying the Pledge of Allegiance. She smiled peacefully as she admired every little detail of his physique, from the perfectly formed little dip at the base of his neck to his crossed bare feet, then back up to his sucked-in bottom lip. His top lip kept curving upward slightly, as if any second he was going to smile back at her.

He insisted on staying after bringing her home, as Jane was spending the weekend with Aunt Bridget and Aunt Tessa in Bath. Elizabeth repeatedly assured her panicked sister that she was fine and there was no need to come home early, especially since Charlie was there with her. The chaotic events of the day must have finally caught up with him though; once he was satisfied she was sufficiently comfortable he promptly passed out in the middle of the movie they were watching together.

Elizabeth felt her eyelids become heavy as she listened to the score of beautiful piano music in the background. One of her favorite scenes of *Pride and Prejudice* filled the television screen—an aerial shot of Keira Knightley standing on the cliffs at Stanage Edge with the sunlight dancing across her eyelids and the wind echoing in her ears. She closed her own eyes and allowed the music to distract her from the dull ache radiating behind them. When she opened them again she gasped out loud.

The music was still playing, but she was no longer lying in bed. In fact, she was no longer in her bedroom at her flat, or even in present-day London for that matter; she was standing in a ballroom filled with people wearing Empire waist gowns and tailcoats with top hats. As she breathlessly examined her own glove-covered arms and pale green dress, she quickly came to the conclusion she must be dreaming. Realizing that the last time she had a dream this realistic it had been the result of a head injury, she felt panic immediately begin to set in.

This is just a dream, right? People don't slip into a coma hours after hitting their head—do they? Why didn't I wait for my test results? For crying out loud! This is exactly why they tell you not to fall asleep when you have a concussion!

Before she could think any further on the instructions the doctor had given her she felt someone grab her arm, and looked up in time to see two very familiar faces. They were both grinning from ear to ear, and clearly feverish with excitement.

"You will not believe who we just saw arrive!" Lydia Bennet cried.

"Mr. Bingley and his party!" Kitty Bennet echoed. They both broke into raucous giggles as Lydia pulled Kitty by the hand into the next room.

Elizabeth felt her heart perform a cartwheel in her chest. She slowly turned to look at the doors, exactly where she knew he would be standing. Their eyes met at exactly the same instant, and a jolt of electricity went through her as his face lit up in recognition and he smiled.

Oh, my God.

Her heart was beating frantically, so loudly in her ears it could be heard over the noise of the room as he walked toward her. When he came to stop in front of her she suddenly felt faint.

Was he always this cute?

"What a perfect evening for dancing, is it not?" he exclaimed. He began making the introductions of his party, and Elizabeth managed to tear her eyes away from his long enough to notice with a start Mr. Darcy and Caroline standing by his side, both of them looking at her with mutual expressions of disinterest. "And this is Miss Elizabeth Bennet, and Miss Charlotte Lucas."

Her head jerked to the right. Sure enough, her childhood friend Emma was standing beside her, smiling knowingly and giving her a wink. She still could not seem to find her voice, and instead of speaking she found herself staring awkwardly at each person in the group until a booming voice announced that the dancing was about to begin. She gulped as Mr. Bingley offered his arm to her and gave her a boyish grin. "I do believe I have the honor of the first dance?"

Her heart plummeted into her stomach. She hesitated, unsure of what to do as she gazed helplessly into his brilliantly blue eyes. He extended his gloved hand, and just as she reached out to take it he said softly but clearly, "Elle."

She frowned. *Wait a minute…did he just call me—*

"Elle," he said again, more urgently this time.

Elizabeth blinked. The music suddenly disappeared, along with the room full of people. She was still staring into those brilliantly blue eyes, but instead of Mr. Bingley they belonged to a concerned looking Charlie, whose extended hand was holding her cell phone. "Elle, it's the hospital. They have the results of your CT scan." He helped her sit up and as she looked around, disoriented, she realized she was back in her own bed.

She took the phone from him and put it up to her ear. "This is Elizabeth Ben—Baker," she mumbled." As she listened to the doctor's voice she studied Charlie's face carefully. She felt her mouth drop open in astonishment, and watched as fear flickered across his features. "Thank you," she managed to whisper. "Yes, I will. Goodbye."

She set her phone down on the bed and looked back up at Charlie, who immediately sat down next to her and took her hand in his. "What is it?" he asked apprehensively. "What did he say?"

Elizabeth managed a small smile. "He said the results of the CT scan were normal, that it was just a concussion. He actually said my scan was so clean it was boring, considering how bad it looked after the accident." She pulled at a loose thread on her comforter. "He did say I couldn't participate in any strenuous activities, like riding, for a while. And that I might have some side effects, like headaches or memory loss—but that they would most likely resolve on their own."

Charlie's face lit up in a broad smile. "That's great, Elle!" He kissed her gently. "Did he prescribe you painkillers or anything? Should I go to the chemist and pick them up?"

Elizabeth swallowed. "No, he couldn't prescribe me anything stronger than Paracetamol for the pain."

Charlie frowned. "Why not? You had twenty stitches!"

"He couldn't...because, well..." Elizabeth hesitated, accidentally pulling the thread all the way out and creating a hole in her comforter. She looked up at him in a mixture of trepidation and excitement. "You aren't allowed to take narcotics when you're pregnant."

Charlie stared at her, expressionless. "You're pregnant?" he whispered.

"Apparently," she replied, biting her lip. "I had no idea, I promise." She gave him an apologetic look.

Slowly, his mouth curved upward until he was grinning. "That is the most brilliant news, Elle!" he cried.

She smiled. "Really?"

"Yes!" He swooped in and kissed her. "I mean, it's a little sooner than I expected—but still—I couldn't be more delighted!"

She was so taken back by his enthusiasm she was momentarily at a loss for words. "You wanted us to have a baby?" she asked quietly. "You've thought about things like that?" She had spent so much time lately thinking about his opposition to marriage it seemed unnatural for him to have given any thought to ever wanting children.

He took her other hand and kissed it, then held them both in his and gave them a squeeze. "Bringing a child into the world with the woman I love?" He laughed. "Of course I have thought about it! Nothing would make me happier."

Elizabeth grinned back. Then her head gave a sharp twinge of pain and she winced.

"You should rest," Charlie insisted. He fluffed her pillows and helped her lie back down. "I'm going to ring Jane and tell her you're going to be perfectly fine." He smiled. "I will leave out the rest—I'm sure you would rather tell her the good news yourself." He bent down and kissed her one last time, nuzzling his nose against hers. "God, I love you, Elle."

"I love you, too." She smiled, then felt it falter. "Are you sure you're happy about everything? Even if it isn't the best timing?" She looked down at her hands in her lap.

He gently lifted her chin with one crooked finger so she met his gaze. "I really don't believe I could ever be more content than I am at this very moment." He kissed the end of her nose. "Now get some sleep so we can argue about names. I've got a few in mind already that I just know you will fancy."

She smirked. "I'll just bet you do. Is James one of them?"

He pulled the blanket up and tucked her in, the way her mother used to do when she was a little girl. "It wasn't—but now that you mention it, James would be a top-notch name for a boy, wouldn't it?" He flashed his dimples at her, winked roguishly, and left the room. When she opened her eyes again hours later, she realized it had been a dreamless sleep, and sighed thankfully.

It was just a dream. A fluke. That's all it was.

Two weeks later, on a Friday afternoon, Elizabeth was on her way to a bridal shop with Jane, Andie, Kassy, and Millie to help Jane find a wedding gown. They watched as Jane tried on several dresses, all of which made her look like Kate Middleton on her wedding day. As Jane left to change, the four girls immediately delved into a full-blown discussion on the royal wedding, followed by a series of speculations on the upcoming nuptials of the second prince.

"Prince Harry was supposed to marry me," Kassy whined. "I've been planning it for ages."

"So have I." Andie winked at Elizabeth. "He is such a dish! I have always had a thing for a bad boy. I can't resist them—never could, for that matter."

"Prince Harry isn't a bad boy, is he?" Elizabeth asked, nibbling on a cracker in a futile effort to overcome a particularly brutal bout of morning sickness.

"Oh, yes he is." Kassy sighed appreciatively. "He's always getting into trouble for not following the rules of princely propriety, if you know what I mean." She smirked at the blank look on Elizabeth's face. "Can't keep his clothes on, that one."

"Seriously?" Elizabeth wondered if Charlie's mom, who seemed so prim and proper, knew that her son's namesake apparently had a scandalous reputation.

"Oh, come on now, Kass—it's been ages since he's been starkers on camera," Andie teased. "He's cleaned up his act now he's getting hitched. And therefore lost his appeal completely." She winked again at Elizabeth. "Good boys are just so boring."

"I know of another Harry who likes to break the rules," Millie chimed in. Everyone turned to look at her, waiting for her to continue. When she hesitated, Elizabeth spoke up.

"Harry…Potter?"

"Yep," Millie answered. She glanced around silently at the others, apparently finished with her contribution to the conversation.

"Should we go try on some dresses, then?" Andie asked, nodding encouragingly and standing.

A few minutes later Elizabeth was trying on a bridesmaid dress, struggling to work the zipper on the side. She called for someone to come help her and was a little surprised to see Andie enter the fitting room instead of Jane.

"Jane was helping Millie, so I thought I'd help you do up your zipper," she said to Elizabeth. "Turn around."

Elizabeth obeyed. "So…you like bad boys, huh?" she asked with a smirk.

"I was mostly joking," Andie replied. "Although I have been known to go for a bad boy once or twice." She laughed. "Haven't you?"

Elizabeth considered it. "Well, does it count if you thought they were good boys, until you found out they were bad? Because if it does, I've been with an embarrassing number of bad boys." She wrinkled her nose.

"But you aren't now." Andie smiled genuinely. "Charlie's as good as they come, trust me. He doesn't have a bad bone in his entire body."

"So you don't think I will find out the hard way he has irritable bowel syndrome when he destroys my bathroom, or that he is running a meth lab in his mom's basement? Or that he simultaneously has a wife, fiancée, and girlfriend—the girlfriend being me?"

"No!" Andie burst out laughing. "Those are all ridiculous situations that could never happen to anyone."

Elizabeth pressed her lips together. "Actually, they have all happened to me."

"Oh." Andie focused her attention on the clasp at the top of the zipper, then turned Elizabeth around to face her. "Well, I don't think you need to worry about them happening with Charlie. Have you asked him about his engagement yet?"

"No," Elizabeth began. She smiled, thinking of their little secret. "But things are going really well, so…"

"Oh, really?" Andie asked excitedly. "Has he proposed?"

Elizabeth's smiled faded. "Well, no…"

"Oh." Andie gave her a commiserative smile. "Well, I'm sure he will."

Elizabeth chewed on her lip. "Thanks."

"By the way, that zipper was a little tight." Andie produced an airy laugh. "Are you sure you're a size six?"

"I've been a six for years!" Elizabeth replied indignantly. Her eyes widened as she realized how pointless trying on any size dress was going to be in a very short amount of time. From the sound of it, starting that very moment. She hadn't yet found the right moment to tell Jane her news, but if she didn't tell her soon her thickening stomach would spill the beans for her.

"Maybe in Philadelphia, love, but here in Britain you would be an eight," Andie said with another laugh. "If you told the salesclerk you were a six then she probably gave you what would be a four in the States. I'll go get you a different dress." She left the fitting room.

Elizabeth heaved a sigh of relief. It was nice to know she hadn't already begun to put on weight, but she still needed to tell Jane at some point. She thought that evening when they were alone at the flat would be her best chance, but when they left the bridal shop Jane told her she was meeting Will at a pub and asked if she and Charlie wanted to come with them. As the smell of alcohol now made her nauseous and she couldn't drink even if she wanted to, spending the evening at a pub did not sound like much fun. Charlie was working late to help get the barns ready for the coming winter, so Elizabeth told Jane she had a headache and would probably just head home and go to bed early.

Cozying up in her bedroom with her favorite blanket and a mug of chamomile tea to soothe her stomach, she pressed play on the movie she had chosen, *Jane Eyre,* with swoon-worthy Michael Fassbender as the male lead. She could feel the unfinished article on her laptop chiding her from the end of the bed and closed the lid with her toes. Only half appreciative of Mr. Rochester's form as he galloped across the moors on his gorgeous black stallion, she realized work was not what was bothering her at the moment. It was her conversation with Andie back at the bridal shop. More specifically, it was how she had asked, in a way that seemed as if she already knew the answer, if Charlie had proposed yet. Why did she keep asking her, anyway? After all, she hardly even knew Elizabeth. It wasn't as though they were as close as sisters. Elizabeth hadn't even spoken about it to her actual sister, with the exception of a few days after Bryan's wedding. Although that could simply be because, with everything happening lately, it had been difficult to find time to talk to Jane about anything other than flower arrangements and bands. Maybe she was being too harsh. Maybe Andie really was just trying to get closer by talking about the one thing they had in common aside from the wedding. From the way it sounded she still thought the world of Charlie, even though they had ended their relationship years ago. She cringed, realizing the reason Andie broke up with him was because she thought he never wanted to get married. But that was a long time ago, and so much had happened since then.

Turning her attention back to the movie, she felt a shiver go down her spine as Jane began to suspect Mr. Rochester was keeping a secret from her, and wrapped the blanket more tightly around her shoulders. She decided to try to be more open with Andie, especially since she was making such an effort to become good friends. She was probably only asking about her relationship with Charlie because she just wanted them both to be happy. Besides, maybe he and Andie were never meant to be, and that was why he didn't want to marry her. Elizabeth knew right from the start she and Charlie were meant to spend the rest of their lives together; there was no one else who even compared to him, and never would be.

She smiled as the characters on screen shared their first passionate kiss under a tree. Like Mr. Rochester for Jane, Charlie was the only man Elizabeth could ever love.

Chapter Ten

lizabeth sprang up from her bed, terrified, as a flash of lightning lit up the room followed by a hair-raising crack of thunder. As she waited for her eyes to adjust to the darkness, she wondered how long she had been asleep. She couldn't remember finishing the movie, so it had to have been several hours for it to be as dark as it currently was in her bedroom. Turning toward the window, she was surprised to see it was raining, and hard. Then she realized the window in her bedroom was at least a third the size of the one she was currently looking at.

A sinking feeling, like a rock, settled hard in the pit of her stomach as she gazed down at the bed. There were no gold chevron stripes on the hand-embroidered bedding. She pushed the blankets back and saw that, instead of her flannel bunny pajamas, she was wearing a billowy white nightgown with cap sleeves. Turning her head to the left, she saw Jane sleeping peacefully beside her and felt her breath catch in her chest. She fought the urge to wake her up. Instead, she swung her legs to the side of the bed and set her feet on the cold wood floor, lifted the burning candle beside her by its silver handled base and slowly opened the door, checking over her shoulder to see that Jane was still asleep.

As soon as she stepped through the doorway she was overcome by an inexplicable pull toward the staircase. When she reached the bottom she looked down the hallway and saw a sliver of light stretched across it, right where she knew it would be. Thinking she should turn back, but knowing her resistance was futile, she walked slowly toward the slightly ajar door from which it originated. Swallowing hard, she peeked through the crack into the room.

A large fire was the only source of light. Her eyes skipped past the dimly-lit details of the room and landed on the person she knew would be sitting in one of the armchairs before the fire, reading a book by candlelight. She knew she should go back, that she should simply wait somewhere until she woke up. The only problem was that she just couldn't seem to make her feet move. As she pushed it open slowly to enter the room, the door emitted a prolonged creaking noise, and she gasped.

I forgot it did that!

Horrified, her eyes darted over to the armchair where she saw he was now staring directly back at her with a shocked expression on his face. She took a quick step backward into the hallway, dropping her candle as she stumbled over her own feet.

Crap, crap, crap! Crap on a stick!

In utter incredulity at her own ineptitude, she scrambled to recover the candle before it lit the hallway on fire. Before she could reach it, Mr. Bingley swooped in and picked it up, extinguishing the flame between his finger and thumb. "Miss Elizabeth! Do you need something? Should I call for Mrs. Hughes?" he exclaimed.

Her voice, when she located it, came out as a croak. "No, I'm fine!" She stared helplessly into his eyes, then dropped her gaze to his lips, which were so close to hers as they knelt on the floor she could have kissed them easily if she wanted to. She was suddenly aware of just how much she wanted to and stood up quickly, cheeks blazing. "I, uh, was just looking for a book to read." Realizing how stupid she must sound, she fought the urge to smack her forehead.

"That is precisely what I was doing! This weather makes me mad, truly," he admitted as he stood and gestured to the inside of the room. "Please, come in. I am afraid my library is not nearly as impressive as Darcy's, but you are more than welcome to anything I have."

She smiled as she walked past him into the room. Without even looking she grabbed a book from the shelf, knowing full well it would be *The Mysteries of Udolpho*. Glancing down as she opened it, she smiled when she saw she was right.

"Found a good one?" Mr. Bingley asked. She held it out for him and he smiled. "One of my favorites! Have you read *The Italian*?"

"No, I haven't," she lied shamelessly. Her eyes flicked to the ground, then back up at him. "What is it about?"

He gestured for her to sit in one of the armchairs and cleared his throat before taking a seat in the other and delving into an enthusiastic description of the book's plot. Though Elizabeth appeared to be listening, in actuality she heard absolutely nothing he was saying. She was far too busy studying his every feature, from his disheveled blond hair curling endearingly around his ears to the devastating dimples dancing on both cheeks as he spoke. His muscular chest with its smattering of wiry blond hair peeking through the lacings of his billowy white shirt, and, finally, down to where his knee-length breeches were drawing her attention to his perfectly formed calves and bare feet.

How can he look so much like Charlie, and still not be Charlie? And why on earth am I dreaming about him again? Is it wrong that all I want to do right at this moment is grab him and tear that shirt right off of him? If it's only a dream, does that still make it wrong?

Looking up, she noticed with a start that he was no longer talking. Instead he was gazing at her expectantly, as if he had asked her a question. Her eyes widened in embarrassment.

Uh-oh.

He laughed. "I am obviously boring you half to death."

"Oh, no!" she cried, sitting up straight in her chair. "I'm sorry, I guess I'm just…tired or something."

"Would you allow me to escort you back to your room so you might get some rest?" he inquired. "You could take the book with you if you would like."

"No!" she cried again, a little too forcefully, and blushed. "I mean, would it be all right if I stay here just a little while longer?"

"Of course you may." He gave her a crooked grin. "Would you rather read than listen to me speak?"

She set her book down without removing her eyes from his. "I would much rather listen to you speak," she insisted with a small smile.

"On which subject would you have me declaim? Another captivating novel summary, perhaps?" He laughed, clearly delighted by her eagerness to remain with him.

She sighed deeply. A sharp twinge of longing shot through her chest. She wanted nothing more than to reach out and touch him. Would he feel as real as he looked? Or would her hand go right through him, like a ghost? "Anything," she breathed, staring intently into his eyes.

His smile faded. She could see something like yearning cross his features and his expression suddenly became pained. He bit his bottom lip and ran his fingers through his hair, his eyebrows knitted together as he stared back at her.

It was early morning by the time Elizabeth climbed back into bed beside Jane, weary from staying up all night talking with Mr. Bingley. She smiled at her sister's fluttering eyelashes, then laid back on her down pillow and closed her own eyes.

"Lizzie."

Elizabeth opened her eyes slowly. Everything was so fuzzy she had to blink a few times before Jane materialized over her. "Lizzie," she heard her sister call again.

Now fully in focus, Jane's own eyes had bronze eyeshadow and mascara on them, and her lips were peony pink. Elizabeth frowned as she studied her face lazily. Then her eyes bulged when she remembered the dream and she sat bolt upright in her own bed. "Jane!" she cried.

"Woah! It's all right, Lizzie," Jane soothed. "I was just checking to see if you wanted to get coffee with me before we start packing."

"Packing?" Elizabeth rubbed the sleep from her eyes along with the memory of the sunlight on Mr. Bingley's hair as he slept.

"Yes. We have to get it done because tonight is bonfire night, and I am dying to see the fireworks from the top of the Eye." Jane set down a stack of empty boxes and turned to leave the room. "Hurry and get dressed and we'll go get coffee. We'll get some of those pastries you love. I'll pay."

Elizabeth climbed out of bed and walked zombie-like toward the boxes by the door. Written on the side of each in permanent marker were the words *Elizabeth Room*. Utterly bewildered, she wandered into the living room where she found more boxes. Packing materials covered the counters in the kitchen. She stood perfectly still and gazed around at the mess until Jane reappeared. "Jane, what is all this?" she asked, holding out her hands and turning from side to side.

"I know, it's such a mess. I'm sorry," Jane confessed. "This is why I had to wake you up. You would have slept till the afternoon, and I need your packing expertise."

Elizabeth stared blankly at her. "Are you moving out?"

Jane gave her an impatient look. "Very funny, Lizzie." She began rummaging through her purse. "I know my sunglasses are in here somewhere."

As Elizabeth watched her in silence, she began to rack her brain. Did her sister tell her she was moving out? She could not for the life of her remember Jane ever mentioning it. Surely a conversation that monumental she would recall with ease? "Jane, I can't remember you telling me that you were going to move out."

Jane looked up at her. "Lizzie, we had a long talk about it a few days ago. You really don't remember?"

Elizabeth sank onto the sofa. "No. I can't remember it at all." She felt her eyes well up with tears. "Why are you moving out so soon?"

Jane stopped searching for her sunglasses and walked over to sit beside her sister. She put her arm around her shoulder and pulled her close. "When we talked we both agreed it made sense, Lizzie." She gave her a small smile. "I'm getting married. I have to move out sometime."

Elizabeth blinked at her, hurt. "But how am I supposed to live here without you? I will miss you way too much. Not to mention there is no way I will be able to afford the rent on my own!"

Jane tilted her head to one side and frowned. "But Lizzie," she began, "you're moving out, too."

"I am?" Now Elizabeth was thoroughly confused. Maybe she could forget her sister telling her she was moving out of their flat, but there was no possible chance she could forget she was moving out herself. Was there?

Jane smiled again. "Yes, silly. You're moving in with Charlie." She gave her sister a squeeze. "We both decided it was the best thing for both of you, especially considering there will be three of you soon."

Elizabeth gasped. "You know about the baby?" she whispered.

"Of course I do! You told me when we talked about moving out!" Jane grinned. "And I know I have already mentioned this like a thousand times, but I am just so excited to be an auntie!"

Elizabeth smiled briefly. "So, you are moving in with Will, and I am moving in with Charlie. What about our lease? I don't have enough money to pay the fee to break it."

"We talked about that too," Jane continued, still smiling. "Millie is moving in. Will's parents think it's high time she got her own place and learn the responsibilities that go along with being an adult." She raised an eyebrow. "Although, they will still be paying the rent and pretty much everything else, so I don't know how much learning will get accomplished—but at least she won't be living with them anymore."

Elizabeth gave an uneasy laugh. "So when is all of this happening?"

"Well, that's the thing," Jane replied as she stood. "We really only have today. Will's parents were so excited at the prospect of Millie moving out, I might have told them she could move in here tomorrow. So that leaves the rest of the morning and most of the afternoon to pack everything up and take it by carloads to Will and Charlie's flats. I told both of them to meet us at the bakery in twenty minutes and then we will all come back here and work. So hurry up and get ready!" She began unloading the contents of her purse by handfuls onto the table. "Where the bloody hell are my sunglasses?" Elizabeth walked over, pointing casually to the top of her sister's head. Jane reached up and took her sunglasses out of her hair with a sheepish grin. "Thanks."

"Jane."

"Yeah?" Jane began putting everything back in her purse. Elizabeth thought she saw a can of Mace go inside and looked questioningly at her sister. Jane shrugged. "London is rough," she muttered defensively. "I'm going to get you one, too."

"Great." Elizabeth heaved a sigh. "Why don't I remember our conversation, Jane? You'd think I would remember us talking about moving out of our flat."

Jane paused as she considered her carefully. "It could have something to do with you hitting your head again," she offered. "Didn't the doctor say lapses in memory could be a side effect of your concussion?"

"Yes, he did. But do you think there is any chance I could slip back into the coma?" Elizabeth felt the tears that had begun to well up again spill onto her cheeks. "I, I can't, I don't want…"

Jane came around the table and wrapped her arms around her sister. "Lizzie, it was just a concussion. You don't need to worry about comas, or anything else for that matter. You are going to be perfectly fine." She held her at arm's length and looked her in the eye. "Besides—you're expecting! Isn't pregnancy brain a thing? You probably just had a surge of hormones or something. Or maybe you're just going crazy like I am. I can't even remember putting my sunglasses on my head."

Elizabeth smiled through her tears. "And you don't mind that I'm going to be *very* pregnant at the wedding?"

"Not a bit," Jane assured her with a smile. "I just can't even wait to hold her in my arms! Although, I am slightly jealous you beat me to it." She gave her sister a provocative grin. "Anything else you want to confess to beating me to? An elopement, perhaps?"

Elizabeth forced an unconvincing laugh. "No, not yet. He hasn't asked me anything except to move in with him. At least not anything that I can remember." She changed the subject before Jane could see her frustration. "Wait a minute—did you just call the baby a she?"

Jane grinned again. "Yep. It's a girl. Trust me, I know these things."

Elizabeth laughed, wiping her eyes. "Aren't we supposed to be meeting the guys soon?"

"Yes!" Jane put her sunglasses on. "Go get some clothes on! That is, if you have any that still fit you." She lifted her shades and gave Elizabeth a devilish smirk.

Elizabeth dropped her jaw. "Hey! I'm only ten weeks, you know!"

"I know." Jane sighed dramatically. "I'm just jealous you get to eat whatever you want. I have a dress to fit into, so no more pastries for me."

Elizabeth raised her eyebrows.

"Ok, fine. No more pastries after today." Jane grabbed her phone. "Let's go."

The sun had just begun to set as Charlie carried the last box into the living room of his flat and set it down with a groan. Elizabeth looked around at the stack of boxes. "I thought I had more to my name than this," she muttered sadly.

Charlie laughed. "I think you might have more than me," he said as he kissed her forehead. "That's all right. We will get a lot more, and it won't be yours or mine—but *ours*."

"Sounds good to me." Elizabeth pulled his chin down gently toward her and kissed his lips. "Now tell me, what exactly is going on tonight?"

"It's November fifth," Charlie answered. "Bonfire night."

Elizabeth wrinkled her nose and shrugged.

"Guy Fawkes night?" Charlie rolled his eyes. "It's supposed to be a night to commemorate his failed attempt to blow up the House of Lords in 1605. But now it's mostly just a big, noisy do with loads of fried food and burning effigies." He smiled at the disgruntled look on Elizabeth's face. "There are some smashing fireworks all over London, though."

"Yeah, Jane mentioned she and Will were going to try to get a ride on the Eye while they were going off. She asked if we wanted to come with them. But I don't know if I feel up to battling crowds just now."

Charlie grinned mischievously. "I've got a better idea," he declared, taking her hand. "Come with me."

Intrigued, Elizabeth followed him through the door and onto the lift. They got off on the top floor and walked to the end of the hall until they came to a metal door labeled, *Roof.* She looked questioningly at Charlie, who grinned again and pulled open the door. They climbed a set of rickety stairs, then opened another door to find themselves staring at a twilit sky sparkling with stars. Elizabeth shivered, regretting not grabbing her jacket until Charlie reached down and picked up one of the two thick blankets folded neatly by the door. He wrapped it tightly around her shoulders and led her to the edge of the building, where two folding chairs sat facing the dying sun as it slowly sank beneath the London skyline.

"My lady," he crooned as he held the back of the chair for her, and she beamed as she sat down. Sitting beside her, he reached between them and picked up a bottle and two long-stemmed wineglasses. "Would you care for a drink, love?" he inquired with a self-satisfied smirk.

"Wow, you really thought of everything, didn't you?" she asked, impressed. "But you know I can't drink alcohol."

"Oh, but I *do* know," he agreed smoothly, and rotated the bottle so she could read the label. "Sparkling grape juice?"

She grinned. "Yes, please." She stared out over the city for a moment in awed silence, then looked back at him. "Are we allowed to be up here?"

"Not exactly," he admitted with a roguish smirk. "You're not supposed to swim in the lake at Lyme Park either, but rules never seem to stop me from doing something mad like that." He handed her a glass, then held her free hand in his. "Some moments are worth breaking the rules for, my darling."

He leaned over to kiss her. Just as her lips met his a firework went off in the distance, causing her to jump and slosh grape juice on her face. They both burst out laughing. He pulled his trusty handkerchief with his initials embroidered on it from his pocket and gently wiped her cheeks, then placed his hands on either side of her face and picked up where he left off, as the sky lit up in an explosion of color.

Chapter Eleven

*S*omething cold and wet splashed the side of Elizabeth's face. Instinctively, she brushed it away with her hand, only to discover it was also saturated with droplets. She suddenly became aware she was treading lake water, and nearly cried out before she realized she was wearing a corset and chemise.

Uh-oh. I must be dreaming again. But then that would mean…

She looked around and sure enough, Mr. Bingley was swimming toward her. She let out a shriek of surprise and he laughed at her reaction. Once he caught up she panicked, and impulsively pushed his head under the water. He took such a long time to emerge that she began to worry, and sunk beneath the surface to look for him. The water was freezing, and so murky she could barely see her own hands in front of her. She pushed off from the grimy floor of the lake and rocketed to the top. When she opened her eyes, his face was inches from hers. She shrieked once more.

Together they burst into peals of laughter that quickly tapered off as they struggled to catch their breath. Elizabeth saw his eyes suddenly darken with desire and felt her heart skip a beat. Her body became rigid as he slowly brought his face nearer to hers. He was so close now she could see a thin white scar above one eyebrow, and her own terrified reflection in his desperate blue eyes. She could count every bead of water clinging to his perfect pink lips and eyelashes, and just make out his pulse beating a quick rhythm in the little dip where his collarbones converged.

He placed one hand on her back to draw her closer, and in that brief moment of contact she lost what little restraint she had left. She threw her arms around his neck and kissed him in an uncontrollable compulsion of pent up longing, running her impatient fingers through his wet hair and down the front of his muscular chest. He took hold of her hips and picked her up in his arms. With her legs wrapped tightly around his waist and her mouth still firmly against his, he blindly carried her out of the water and laid her gently down on the grass. He let out a soft groan of anticipation as she pulled him by his biceps roughly down on top of her and sucked in his lower lip.

The forceful breeze that whipped past her ears whispered warning signals to her brain. She froze suddenly, then pushed him away.

What am I doing?!

"I can't do this," she muttered breathlessly. She turned to look at him. "I'm so sorry."

"I am the one who should apologize." He stood and began gathering his scattered clothing from the ground. "I acted reprehensibly."

She smiled despite herself as she pulled her dress over her saturated chemise, corset, and knickers. "I wasn't exactly a shining specimen of integrity myself."

"Yes, but still." He pulled on his boots and took her hands in his. "I was dishonorable, in a manner I never wished to allow as a gentleman toward a lady." He hesitated, his blue eyes twinkling. "Words cannot express how much I honor and respect you, Miss Elizabeth. However, I pray you will give me leave to try."

Uh-oh.

Alarm bells began going off in Elizabeth's brain. This was the part she had royally screwed up last time. He was about to propose, and this time there was no ridiculous misunderstanding preventing her from saying yes.

He studied her hands in his for a moment, then brought them to his lips and kissed them gently. He acknowledged her wistful expression and smiled back with confidence. "Miss, Elizabeth, you must know that I am completely and irrevocably in love with you."

She stared at him, unable to speak. She knew she should stop him. She should tell him the truth—he was just a figment of her imagination, and she was in love with someone else who was real. But as she watched him drop to one knee and smile hopefully back up at her, a part of her willed him to continue. After all, if Charlie really did struggle with the idea of marriage, she might never get another proposal. Certainly not one as beautiful as the one she already knew Mr. Bingley was about to give.

"From the first moment I saw you I have loved you, heart and soul. Every word that has passed between us since then has only strengthened my admiration of your character. With each new day I find myself further captivated by your beauty. Indeed, I cannot concentrate on anything for thinking of your breathtaking smile. There is nothing at Netherfield that does not remind me of you. I see your loveliness in every flower in the garden, every book that lines the walls of the library, every drop of rain that falls over the fields. Your presence is felt everywhere and in everything, and I cannot imagine living there any longer without you as my wife. Please tell me that I have a chance. Allow me to endeavor to make you happy every minute of every day, for the rest of your life. For you are all I could ever need to make me happy for the rest of mine."

Elizabeth, replete with a thousand contradicting emotions, was unable to answer directly. Instead, a succession of rapid-fire musings bombarded her already conflicted mind. She stared down at their hands.

I have to say no, right? I have to tell him the truth. And yet I really don't think I can hurt him like I did last time. This is only a dream, after all. When I wake up it will be as if it never even happened. If I say yes I won't break Mr. Bingley's heart, and I won't be hurting Charlie, because none of this is real anyway. In fact, maybe this is happening for a reason. Maybe I am being given another chance to make up for the way I responded last time. Maybe this is my brain's way of healing itself, and I have to just let it play out till the end before I can finally put it all behind me. I'd really only be saying yes in order to move on with my life, not because I am still in love with Mr. Bingley. I mean, that would be ridiculous, considering I now have Charlie.

Right?

She looked up at him. He was gazing at her expectantly, with an intensity in his eyes that made her heart turn over in her chest. She immediately forgot her train of thought, along with her ability to reason. "Yes," she blurted out, before she could stop herself.

His eyes widened. "You will be my wife?" The smile he gave her could have easily replaced the sun.

She grinned back. "Yes."

He stood quickly and wrapped his arms around her. Then he lifted her off the ground and spun her around once before setting her back down again. "I am the most fortunate man in the entire world this day!" he exclaimed. "Truly, I do not believe my happiness could ever be as complete as it is this very moment."

I think I could be totally fine even if Charlie never proposes to me after a dream this, well, dreamy.

Elizabeth opened her eyes. For a few seconds she was unsure of where she was. Then she realized as she looked around the room that she was lying in the king-sized bed at Charlie's flat. Her outstretched arm was flung across his empty pillow. In alarm, she jerked her head to see the covers pushed back and an indent where his head should have been. The sunlight streaming in through the window was causing something on her hand to glitter with refracted light, and as she looked at it more carefully her jaw dropped open. On her finger was the most beautiful diamond ring she had ever seen, and she had absolutely no memory of how it got there.

Chapter Twelve

*P*ulling herself upright, she brought her hand closer to examine the ring. It was absolutely stunning, with a vintage charm that had Charlie's name written all over it. In desperation she began to retrace the events of the previous evening. He must have asked her to marry him at some point while they were on the roof. The last thing she could recall clearly was the start of the fireworks. When did he propose? And why couldn't she remember it to save her life?

She heard a sudden noise to her right and turned to see Charlie enter the room. Clearly a morning person, he was already dressed in an incredibly attractive navy cowl-neck sweater with brown suede patches on the elbows, dark-wash jeans, and a smile that promptly replaced caffeine as the first thing she needed to start her day. To complete this fantasy brought to life, he was also carrying a tray laden with various breakfast items.

"Good morning, my love," he greeted her as he set the tray down and sat down. "Sleep well?" He handed her a mug of coffee just the way she liked it, then began pouring milk into his own cup of tea.

Elizabeth gave him a brief nod and smile, all the while unavailingly trying to remember his proposal. It was as though her mind had been wiped clean. All she could seem to remember at the moment was the dream she now felt guilty about having (*What in the world was that all about—am I having a surge of pregnancy hormones, or what?*), especially since she could recall every single second of it with absolute clarity. She tried not to allow the panic bubbling up inside of her to show as she leaned forward and gave him a quick kiss. "Yes."

Why am I forgetting things? Is it because I hit my head again? And why are they not insignificant things, like paying my phone bill or putting on deodorant? First I completely space on talking with Jane about moving out of our flat. Now I can't remember the one thing I have longed for since the night I met Charlie—the one thing I thought might never happen! And now it has, and I should be ecstatic, except that I can't even remember it happening! What if he asks me about it and I can't give him an answer? Or worse, what if it keeps happening and I don't remember other major events, like our wedding? Oh, no—what if I forget the birth of our child? How can I be responsible for another human being if I can't even be responsible for myself?

"You all right, love?" Charlie's voice broke her from her thoughts and she looked up at him. "You look worried about something."

She glanced down at the ring glistening on her finger.

"Regretting it?" Charlie asked tentatively.

Elizabeth jerked her head up in time to see his look of misgiving. She felt her eyes fill with tears. "No, of course not! It's just..." She paused.

"Elle, what is it?" Charlie put his arm around her.

Her face crumpled in unison with the scone she dunked into her coffee. She shook her head. She couldn't tell him the truth. How would he feel if he found out she had no memory of his proposal? "I don't think I can eat anything right now, and you went to all the trouble to make breakfast."

Charlie's furrowed brow unraveled and he bit his lip to hide a smile. "Well, I don't think buying scones and putting them on a plate really counts as making breakfast." He kissed the end of her nose and brushed the tears from her cheeks with his thumbs. "Do you think you feel well enough to go out? I believe I have a promise to fulfill." He grinned.

Elizabeth smiled weakly back. She took a few sips of her coffee and admired the ring winking at her from the handle of her mug.

Maybe it's not important that I can't remember how *it happened. The most important thing is that it* did *happen. We're engaged!*

•

Charlie did not tell Elizabeth the purpose of their outing, but when they arrived at a building with a large sign that read *Humane Society*, she had a pretty good hunch. Sure enough, the employee at the front desk seemed to be expecting them. She led them to a very loud room filled with cats of all shapes and sizes. In one corner a litter of kittens clawed their way to the front of the cage in order to be seen (and heard) more prominently. Elizabeth was immediately drawn to a small black and white kitten with pale blue eyes. His markings made him appear as though he were wearing a tiny, kitten-sized black suit. She grinned at Charlie. "I think it has to be the one that looks like a mini secret service agent, don't you?"

"Absolutely, I do." He turned to the employee. "We'll take Mr. Bond over here."

On the way back to Charlie's flat, Elizabeth ran her fingers along the kitten's downy fur as it lay sleeping in her lap. Her ring kept catching the sunlight with the slightest movement, and she couldn't help but stare at it admiringly. "Charlie, this is the most beautiful ring I have ever seen in my life," she breathed.

"I'm so glad you like it," he replied with a delighted smile. "It belonged to my great-grandmother."

"Really?"

"I thought about getting you a new one, but this one definitely seemed more *you*." He gave her a meaningful look. "I know how much you love stepping into history."

"I love it." She blinked, her eyes stinging with fresh tears. It was embarrassing, really, how easily she cried these days. "I can't wait to show Jane. She is going to lose her mind when she hears we're engaged!"

Charlie smirked. "You already told her, remember? You rang her immediately afterward."

Elizabeth wrinkled her nose. *That does sound like something I would do.* "Right." She pressed her lips together. "I guess I forgot about...that part."

"Did you also forget we are going to Will and Jane's for dinner tonight to celebrate?"

Elizabeth blew air out through her lips. "No." She gave him a smirk, then caught him looking at her and grimaced. "Yes."

Charlie laughed. "Wow, those pregnancy hormones must be intense for you to forget an entire conversation with your sister!" He glanced at Elizabeth, who was chewing anxiously on her lower lip. "Or was it that I produced such a romantic masterpiece of elocution it made you forget the entire evening?" He waggled his eyebrows and grinned.

"Yep, that was definitely it," she replied with a silent sob.

That evening, when they arrived at Will's flat and knocked on the door, Elizabeth was taken back to see Tom's staggeringly handsome face when it opened. "Tom?" She returned his contagious smile. "What are you doing here?"

Tom gave his brother a combination handshake/hug, then faced Elizabeth. He leaned in to kiss her cheek. "Do you really think I would miss an opportunity to congratulate my little brother and his future bride?" He pulled her in for a tight hug. "And I hear there is more than one cause for celebration?" he inquired, lowering his voice and raising a provocative eyebrow.

Elizabeth gave Charlie a look of disbelief. "You told your brother?"

"You told your sister," he retorted, with an unabashed smile.

She smiled and shook her head, then followed Tom inside where she was immediately accosted by her sister.

"Let me see the ring!" Jane cried. "It's *gorgeous*."

Elizabeth beamed. She looked past her to see a group of people gathered in the kitchen. Andie, Kassy, and Dr. Patel were deep in conversation, drinks in hand. They all laughed at something Tom said as he rejoined their group.

A small sense of disappointment came over Elizabeth as she watched them flirt shamelessly with one other. She had hoped it would just be Will and Jane celebrating, though Tom was definitely a welcome addition. For some reason she couldn't quite put her finger on, sharing the moment with the rest of them seemed to cheapen it. She hid the feeling, however, as Andie caught her eye and smiled, then walked briskly over to her.

"Congratulations," she cooed, giving Elizabeth a quick hug. She held her hand out for Charlie to shake. "I am *so* happy for you both."

"Thanks, Andie."

"Were you absolutely stunned?" she whispered in Elizabeth's ear. "I know I was when Jane told me."

Elizabeth gave her a small smile. "It was definitely a wonderful surprise." *You don't need to know how much of a surprise it actually was.*

Andie studied her face carefully for a moment, then looked away as the doorbell rang. Tom answered it, then walked back into the room carrying a stack of pizza boxes. Jane laughed at the excited look on Elizabeth's face. "I didn't think you would want a fancy dinner. Pizza and beer—(she wrinkled her nose) or, in your case, root beer—seemed much more you."

Elizabeth placed a hand over her heart and sniffed dramatically. "You know me so well." She leaned in closer. "You haven't told the others about the baby, right?"

"Of course not!" Jane whispered vehemently. "I mean, I told Will, but he won't spill the beans, I promise."

Once they were all comfortably seated in various spots all over the living room with disposable plates of pizza on their laps, Will raised his beer. "I would like to make a toast." He cleared his throat. "To Lizzie and Charlie," he said. "Officially the most efficient couple I have ever met. Talk about getting things done!" He grinned. "Congratulations to the both of you. Not only on your engagement, but also on your growing family!" Jane elbowed him sharply in the ribs and he let out a grunt. "What? Was I not supposed to mention that part?"

Elizabeth bit her lip and looked around at Dr. Patel, Kassy, and Andie, who were all wearing similar expressions of astonishment. Andie shook her head. "Wait—what?"

Will mouthed a silent apology and Elizabeth shrugged her shoulders dismissively in reply. "We weren't going to announce anything until I went for my first sonogram—but I'm pregnant." She gave the room at large a nervous smile.

Jane wiggled gleefully in her chair and cast excited looks in her sister's direction. Tom, Will, and Charlie were all beaming. Elizabeth smiled and glanced at the others, whose expressions had not changed. They all still looked as though they couldn't believe what they had just heard. Finally Andie met her gaze and turned on a megawatt smile. "Wow!" she cried. "That is just so *great!*" Kassy and Dr. Patel nodded in agreement.

Once she fielded the seemingly endless questions (When are you due? How are you going to fit into your bridesmaid dress? Have you felt ill at all? Is that why you look peaky?), Elizabeth made her way into the kitchen for a napkin. She turned to see Andie walking up to her.

"Why didn't you tell me you were pregnant?" Andie admonished, her expression wounded. "I would have kept it a secret, you know."

"Oh! Um, well..." Elizabeth glanced down at her feet. "We didn't even tell our parents yet."

Andie's eyes widened. "So did he propose the day you found out?"

"No, it was just last night. We've known about the baby for about a month now." She gave her a sheepish smile.

"Just last night? Oh…" Andie toyed with her bracelets and avoided Elizabeth's gaze, her eyebrows raised.

"What is it?" Elizabeth asked, her smile faltering.

Andie looked up slowly. She saw the look on Elizabeth's face and unwrinkled her brow. "Oh! Nothing!"

"Are you sure?"

Andie hesitated, then took Elizabeth's hand and squeezed it. "I was just thinking how great it is that something finally forced him to overcome his fear of marriage, that's all. You really are a lucky girl, Lizzie. And I really am so happy for you." Her face lit up in one of her signature smiles.

"Thank you," Elizabeth replied slowly. She watched Andie turn away from her and walk to where Kassy and Tom were sitting together. Her eyes found Charlie, who was listening to Jane speak with a carefree smile. When he glanced up and saw Elizabeth looking at him, his features became sober with concern. He excused himself and walked toward her.

"All right, Elle?" He swept her hair from her shoulder and took her face in his hands. "What is it?"

Elizabeth melted at his touch. "Nothing, I'm fine." She smiled.

His face relaxed. "Ready to go home?"

"Yes." She stifled a yawn. "I'm exhausted."

"We probably should get going anyway," he added. "I'm a little nervous to see what that kitten has done to the flat whilst we've been gone, to be honest."

On the way home, Elizabeth couldn't stop thinking about what Andie had said. She was fairly certain she was just reading into things as usual. Her hormones were making her even more sensitive than normal, but it sounded like she was implying the only reason Charlie proposed to her was because she was pregnant.

An entire week passed by without any major occurrences of disremembering (unless of course still having forgotten to tell the seamstress she was expecting counted), as well as a complete lack of dreams, which made Elizabeth feel as though her life was finally getting back on track. That is, until one evening, after eating turkey curry that was more curry than turkey, her stomach began churning with painful cramps and she was unable to sleep. She got out of bed and took every bottle of medicine out of the cabinet in search of something safe to take during pregnancy. Paracetamol with sleep aid being the winner, she swallowed two pills with a large sip of water and got back into bed. It began to work its magic in no time at all, and she felt her body relax until she finally fell asleep.

As she drowsily opened her eyes, Elizabeth found herself staring into the flames of a strangely familiar fireplace. She frowned, squeezed her eyes shut once more and then opened them again slowly. The fireplace was still there, along with an enormous mural inside a gilded frame. The elaborate sitting room at Netherfield was dimly lit with candles, but glancing down at her lap she could very clearly see that she was wearing a pale blue gown. She looked to her right and saw Mr. Darcy and Jane sitting in armchairs by the window, deep in conversation. As her eyes slowly scanned to the left she noticed with a start Georgiana and Caroline sat primly on the blue sofa directly across from hers. They both smiled at her in unison. She curved her lips tentatively upward in reply, then continued to look to the left, where she was even more surprised to see two men who looked suspiciously like Tom and Dr. Patel standing with Mr. Bingley by the back wall.

It was more than obvious she was dreaming again, but unlike the others, it was definitely not a scene she remembered from her coma. It was safe to say she had absolutely no clue as to what would happen next.

This must be what would have happened if I had said yes to Mr. Bingley's proposal in the first place.

Her eyes widened as Mr. Bingley suddenly smiled in her direction, causing both Tom and Dr. Patel to turn and look at her.

I wonder what part these two will get to play.

Before she could speculate further she felt someone sit down beside her and turned her head to see Georgiana gazing at her. The *Mona Lisa* smile on her face struck terror in her heart. Was she about to return the favor from their last encounter and punch her in the face?

"Miss Elizabeth," she began, her tone surprisingly benevolent. "I am so pleased to make your acquaintance at long last. My brother has appraised me of your congenial character, and I have been longing to know you myself for quite some time now."

Elizabeth stared at her, nonplussed. Then she realized that her altercation with Georgiana occurred much later in the story, when she went to Pemberley to tell Mr. Darcy that Jane loved him. Still, it was hard to believe she was pleased to make her acquaintance, especially since it was highly likely that Caroline hadn't given her "character" a glowing reference. She and Caroline never did get along, probably due to Caroline's belief that Elizabeth was pursuing Mr. Darcy (which wasn't inaccurate). She wondered what Caroline thought now that she was engaged to Mr. Bingley, her own brother. She looked over at her apprehensively, and saw her gazing at him as he laughed with the other two men. Then she turned back to face Georgiana.

"Yes, um, it's nice to meet you too, Georgiana," she replied cautiously.

"You must be very much looking forward to becoming the mistress of such a beautiful home," Georgiana continued. "Caroline tells me you have accepted Mr. Bingley's hand in marriage! How wonderful! I can assure you that you could do no better. He is one of the finest gentlemen I have ever known, and he is such an excellent friend to my own dear brother."

Elizabeth scrutinized her smiling face. She seemed so genuine, and yet there was something artificial in her eyes. "Yes, he is." Looking over at her sister and Mr. Darcy, she saw him actually smile while he listened to Jane speak. "And your brother is one of the finest gentlemen *I* have ever known."

Georgiana shrugged. "He is tolerable, I suppose." She stood and smoothed her skirt. "Excuse me, Miss Elizabeth. I have a pressing question to ask Mr. Pattle in regard to the East India Trading Company's foreign policy."

Elizabeth watched her saunter toward "Mr. Pattle," who acknowledged her with a devastatingly handsome smile. *Yes, I'm sure foreign policy is the only thing on your mind, Georgiana. You might not be evil this time around, but you are still an incurable flirt.*

She looked away to see Caroline's eyes on her and swallowed hard. If she remembered correctly (and remembering things was not her strong suit at the moment), the last interaction she had with Caroline before Mr. Bingley's proposal was at the Netherfield ball, where she threw daggers at Elizabeth with her eyes while she danced with Mr. Darcy. And the occasion before that, Elizabeth had accidently voiced aloud that she would run through a field of horse crap if it meant she could get away from her faster.

Therefore as Caroline rose and walked from one sofa to the other, primly taking Georgiana's vacated seat beside her, Elizabeth could feel her heart begin to beat faster. She forced herself to look Caroline in the eye and was astonished to see that she was smiling back.

"Miss Elizabeth," she sighed. "I would like to make amends for my less than amiable behavior toward you in the past. Now that we are destined to be sisters, my greatest wish is to become more intimately acquainted. My acrimony toward you was entirely unfounded, as I am now fully aware. I must make a confession—I foolishly believed us to be adversaries for Mr. Darcy's affection."

Elizabeth widened her eyes. "Wow, Caroline," she began. "That's, um…great." She looked over at Jane. "But, I think Mr. Darcy…I mean, he might just be…" she trailed off, looking uncomfortable.

Caroline smiled. "My affection for Mr. Darcy was also unfounded, as I have very recently come to acknowledge. He is a remarkable gentleman, and a most advantageous match, however…" Her eyes flicked sideways in the direction of Mr. Bingley and Tom. "My own brother has demonstrated for me the merits of marrying for love, instead of advantage." She looked back at Elizabeth and smiled sheepishly, her cheeks bright pink. "There is truly something in his manner of thinking, to be sure."

Elizabeth was so astounded she couldn't even speak. Georgiana was no longer out for blood when it came to her and Mr. Bingley's relationship, and Caroline was no longer an unmitigated snob who planned on making Mr. Darcy her own personal sugar daddy? This was officially the strangest dream she had had so far, and yet as she returned Mr. Bingley's heart-stopping smile, she couldn't help but feel elated. Clearly, she had made the right choice by saying yes when he proposed. It really did seem like everything was working out nicely, and perhaps closure with all of the characters would mean no more confusing dreams from that point on, and she could focus solely on Charlie.

Mr. Bingley and Tom approached the sofa. "Miss Elizabeth," Mr. Bingley began with a playful smile. "One of my contemporaries from my days at Eton, Mr. Thomas Baker, has just brought to my attention the heinous crime I have committed against him by not introducing the two of you before this evening." He gestured to Tom. "I assured him I would make amends at once. Miss Elizabeth Bennet, may I introduce you to Mr. Thomas Baker, one of my oldest and dearest friends."

Elizabeth watched as they flashed synchronized crooked smiles in her direction, their matching dimples making her heart flutter. She held out her hand to Mr. Baker (*of course his name is Baker—why not?*). He bowed low before her. She watched helplessly as he took her outstretched hand and kissed it gently, then smiled flirtatiously up at her with eyes every bit as blue as his brother's. *Make that his oldest and dearest friend's.* "It is a prodigious honor to finally meet you, Miss Elizabeth. You are just as lovely as Charles described—and much too good for the likes of him, I have absolutely no doubt."

He winked at her with a devastating grin, and then stood at considerably full height. Both he and Mr. Bingley then took seats beside herself and Caroline on the sofa. Tom immediately engaged in conversation with Caroline, who flushed scarlet and beamed helplessly up at him. Likewise, Elizabeth felt the familiar swoop in her stomach she received whenever Mr. Bingley was close to her.

"Enjoying yourself, my darling?" he asked, handing her a glass of wine. She looked at it with longing before realizing it was a dream, and she could drink all the wine she wanted.

"Of course," she breathed, fighting the desire to wrap her arms around him and kiss him.

He laughed. "I myself have been thinking this entire evening of how instead of playing host and entertaining guests, I would much rather entertain my desire for the two of us to escape to the stables together." Elizabeth raised her eyebrows. "After your astounding performance at the lake, I have been desperate to take you for another vigorous ride."

Elizabeth snorted into her glass, nearly spitting her mouthful of wine back into it. She grinned at him, eyes glassy with tears, trying not to laugh as he gave her a look of mystified concern. "Yes, that definitely sounds more...*enjoyable*," she replied, and chewed her lip. She couldn't help but think that if he were Charlie, he would have been taking advantage of an irresistible opportunity for euphemism, not merely referring to horseback riding like Mr. Bingley.

He grinned roguishly and stood, then glanced around the room fleetingly at the others. Seeing that they were all either talking or playing cards, he held out his hand and helped her up. He discreetly pulled her close, so that her body was pressed up against his and she could feel the warmth radiating from his skin, and whispered in her ear, "I do not believe we will be missed." Then he brushed his lips softly against the side of her neck. She raised one eyebrow and followed him eagerly out of the room.

Maybe he is more like Charlie than I thought.

Moments later, as they raced across the English countryside, she felt the familiar sensation of reckless abandonment that riding horses gave her and sighed contentedly. The wind in her ears blocked out all thought. It was a feeling of absolute freedom, an escape from everything currently weighing on her mind. Even if it wasn't real, it was perfect. It was—

—an excellent note to end this entire fantasy on. I really think I can face anything the real world could possibly dish out after this.

Chapter Thirteen

The first thought that entered Elizabeth's mind when she regained consciousness was that she had never felt colder in her entire life. Once the shock of the room temperature wore off, a completely new torrent of sensations began to register before she even opened her eyes. Her entire body was simultaneously stiff and relaxed, her aching muscles slack. Her head felt thick and impossibly heavy. A painful throbbing in her right hand demanded her immediate attention. She reached across her torso, and feeling something hard taped to it was instantly seared by a rush of panic in her chest. Her eyes sprang open and she looked around wildly, receiving validation of the sickening fear that had begun to well up inside her.

She was lying in a hospital bed.

Instinctively her hands went to her head. She was relieved to discover it was free of bandages and not missing sections of hair. She pulled back the flimsy coverlet to see that her leg appeared normal, not diminished as though it had recently been casted. A quick examination of the rest of her body not concealed by her gown gave her no answers as to why she would be in the hospital. Could she still be dreaming?

Thinking of her dream caused the sickening fear to increase as she realized she must have forgotten another significant event.

No. No, no, no…

Sitting up straight, trepidation tore through her like wildfire as she saw she was alone in the room. She needed answers to the questions that were reverberating through her mind. Unable to bring herself to pull out her IV so she could leave the room, she stared at the door and mentally willed someone, anyone, to walk through it. Almost on cue, the door swung open and Charlie entered the room, his head hung low and his broad shoulders drooped. He glanced up at her, stopping short when he saw she was awake. The look in his eyes when they met hers covered her with a fresh wave of goose bumps and made the room begin to spin. She fought the imminent syncope with every ounce of willpower in her being and swallowed the lump in her throat as she watched him sit hesitantly at the foot of her bed.

Now that she was seconds away from the answer to her most pressing question, she found herself incapable of asking it. Instead, she listened to her heart pound in her chest and stared into Charlie's red-rimmed, glassy blue eyes. It was more than obvious he was unwilling or possibly unable to speak, and for what felt like an eternity they simply sat and stared down at their laps in deafening silence. Finally, he took her icy hand in his and squeezed it. Without looking up he whispered brokenly, "Elle, I'm so sorry."

The spinning sensation returned with a vengeance. She gripped the edge of the bed with her free hand and felt her eyes fill with irrepressible tears. With the lump in her throat now threatening to choke her, she took a shaky breath and forced herself to speak aloud. "What happened, Charlie?"

He raised his head to look her squarely in the eye. She could almost see pity mixed in with the heartbreaking sorrow in his expression as he tilted his head to one side. "You don't remember?"

A new emotion registered as she lay back down and squeezed her eyes shut—shame. They had obviously both gone through a horrifying ordeal, yet he would have to carry the burden of it with him for the rest of his life alone, because for whatever reason her brain had chosen to erase it from her memory. Although the major details were missing, in her heart she already knew exactly what happened. Though she knew she had to, she didn't want to answer; she didn't want him to hate her for her ineptitude. "No," she whispered.

Tears spilled over onto his cheeks and he hastily wiped them away. He studied her face for a moment before inhaling sharply, then letting it out slowly. "Elle, you woke up screaming in the middle of the night. At first I thought you were having a nightmare..." His voice quavered. He dropped his head and fresh tears fell from his eyes and onto his trembling hands. "I called 999, they sent an ambulance. Everything happened so fast..." He trailed off, letting out a muffled sob.

Her vision was now completely clouded with tears, but she made no effort to clear it. "Did I lose the baby?" she mumbled almost inaudibly.

He nodded.

She covered her face with her hands and sobbed silently, her shoulders racked with grief. He moved closer and gently pulled her toward him. Yielding, she buried her head in his chest as he held her tight. She clung to him like a life preserver in a sea of anguish she might otherwise drown in without him. They both cried till they had no tears left to cry. Then they simply held each other until the door opened and a doctor in a long white lab coat entered the room.

"I am so sorry to intrude," he said quietly. "I was hoping to speak with Miss Baker alone, if I may."

Charlie moved to stand, but Elizabeth squeezed his arm. "Can he please stay?" she asked desperately, her voice shaking. "He's my fiancé."

"Of course." The doctor took a seat in the chair beside the bed. He looked at each of them carefully before speaking. "I want to offer my deepest condolences to both of you. I know you must have a lot of questions. I wish I had more answers to give you, but unfortunately I can really only give you my conjectures based on the lab results we received of your bloodwork, Miss Baker."

Neither of them replied, so he continued. "Your CBC showed that your platelet count is low, which indicates possible kidney dysfunction. I reviewed your medical history and noticed you had one of your kidneys removed as a result of a car accident eight months ago, so I ordered a glomerular filtration rate test, which measures how well your remaining kidney is filtering waste from your blood. It came back much lower than I hoped it would, suggesting your kidney has recently been under substantial duress. I'm going to send you for a sonogram this afternoon to see how it looks and determine the steps we need to take to improve its function, with the hope you won't need a transplant in the future."

Elizabeth stared at him blankly. Most of what he said sounded like a steady humming in her ears, but one thing was perfectly and devastatingly clear—her own dysfunctional body had caused her to miscarry. She glanced at Charlie, who looked as confused as she felt. From her desperate need for answers she found the strength to ask, "Is my kidney the reason I lost the baby?"

The doctor frowned. "It is certainly not definite…but I believe so." He gave them a sympathetic look and continued. "There is no absolute reason why a miscarriage occurs, no matter how optimal the mother's health may be. Ten to twenty-five percent of all pregnancies end in miscarriage, with the majority of them the result of chromosomal abnormalities in the fetus—very few are caused by a physical complication. That being said, I typically advise my nephrectomy patients not to get pregnant for at least two years following their procedure. Pregnancy is stressful on a body with two fully functioning kidneys. Having only one takes an even greater toll, and the strain can sometimes induce spontaneous abortion. In your specific case, Miss Baker, based on your lab work and without having the results of a sonogram, I can only make the assumption your remaining kidney was simply not strong enough to support both you and your baby, and your body reacted defensively."

Elizabeth dropped her gaze to her lap. Her hands were trembling; she could not make them be still. Closing her eyes momentarily, she felt the shaking cease as Charlie took them in his and held them tightly. She wanted to look up at him, but was too afraid of what she would see in his eyes. Then she heard his voice and involuntarily glanced upward.

"Has her kidney been irreparably damaged?" he asked, a note of deep concern in his voice.

"Without further testing I can only tell you what the bloodwork shows, which is that her levels are currently not within the normal range for healthy function. Her blood pressure is also much higher than normal, which also is indicative of kidney disease—although it could also simply be a result of the miscarriage. We will know much more this afternoon, I promise." The doctor stood up from his chair. "I will leave the two of you alone now. Please try to get some rest, Miss Baker."

They watched him exit the room, then looked back at each other. Elizabeth could feel the lump returning as she fought the tears threatening to brim over her eyelashes again. A small seed of anger began growing inside her as she listened to the doctor's words echo through her head.

Your kidney was simply not strong enough to support both you and your baby.

It was not her fault, really—she knew it was not. And yet it was. It *was* all her fault. *Her* stupid brain that didn't work correctly. *Her* stupid body that should have kept her child safe, but instead chose to protect itself. She suddenly felt furious with herself, not only for the miscarriage, but for the inability to remember having it. Not only had she failed her baby, but Charlie as well. How could he even love her now, after everything she had put him through? It was no wonder, really, that he had misgivings about marriage, considering his first fiancée cheated on him and his second was a blundering invalid who lost his baby. He deserved so much better than her. He deserved someone—whole.

The tears that ran down her cheeks as she avoided his face were raw with indignation on his behalf. A sudden noise pierced the heavy silence. They both turned to look to where her purse sat on the chair as her phone began to ring. Charlie reached over to retrieve it, and recognizing the face on the screen, muttered softly, "It's Jane. Do you want to answer it?"

She shook her head adamantly. "Can you please tell her what happened? I can't...I just can't..."

"Of course I can," he said, "I'll be right back." He left the room, closing the door behind him.

Alone in the room, Elizabeth had plenty of opportunity for her emotions to continue to consume her. Jane knew by now, but there were so many people she would have to tell about the miscarriage. How would she ever find the words? When the initial accident occurred she had been treated as if she might break in half at any moment by everyone she knew and loved. How would they treat her now that she knew what it was to be truly broken—not merely in half, but shattered into a thousand splintered pieces? Would Charlie treat her differently? Would he harbor resentment toward her? Would he feel obligated to take care of her? And what if she never recovered? What if her kidney continued to deteriorate until she needed dialysis, or a transplant, or she died? What if her forgetting became worse and worse until she no longer remembered anything or anyone at all? What if one night she slipped into a dream from which she never awakened? She thought fleetingly that perhaps it wouldn't be so bad, then hated herself for her own selfishness.

She felt incredibly foolish for what she had considered to be hardship in her life before now. In fact, the longer she thought about how immature she had been right up until the accident, the more foolish she felt. She heard the door open once more and feigned sleep, feeling grateful when the door closed again and she saw the room was still empty. She didn't want to talk to anyone at the moment, especially if it were another doctor with more bad news. She didn't even want to think any longer—she couldn't stand listening to her own panicked voice in her head. She wanted to escape, to be anyone else for a while. Anyone but her.

"Miss Elizabeth Bennet!"

Elizabeth jerked her head upward to find herself looking into the amiable blue eyes of none other than Lady Catherine de Bourgh. Before she could even react she was swept up into her arms. "How good of you to come see me, at long last! My dear nephew Fitzwilliam and Mrs. Collins have told me so much about you I feel as if we are kin." She held her at arm's length and studied her carefully. "You look a bit peaky, my dear. Are you quite well?"

"She is tired from the journey, dear Aunt," a voice to her right called brightly. She turned to see Georgiana smiling at her, along with her own sister Jane at her side. "The carriage was terribly unsteady. Not one of us slept the entire journey from Netherfield, even for a moment. And Miss Elizabeth, the poor dear, must have hit her head against the window at least a dozen times. She most likely has a terrible headache by this time." She gave Elizabeth a wink.

"I know just the thing to revive your spirits, Miss Elizabeth." Lady Catherine placed her hand through the crook of her arm and held it firmly. "Let us adjourn to the sitting room and have some tea and a game or two of whist." Leaning closer, she whispered in her ear, "And I must hear all about this dashing young gentleman of yours! What a shame he could not join us this evening! When will I have the privilege to meet him?"

Looking around, Elizabeth saw that, sure enough, Mr. Bingley was nowhere in sight. "I, umm..."

"Charles is en route from London as we speak, Lady Catherine," another voice rang out. It was Caroline. She gave Elizabeth a warm smile, then took Lady Catherine's other arm. "He had some legal matters to attend to. However he did not wish to deprive your ladyship of Miss Elizabeth's promised visit any longer, and bid myself and Georgiana accompany her in his stead. He should be arriving on the morrow, before we dine."

"Lovely! My nephews will arrive forenoon, and I have invited Mr. and Mrs. Collins to join us as well. What an impressive party we shall make!" Lady Catherine led them from the entrance hall into the drawing room, where the five of them plus her daughter Anne (who this time around vaguely resembled Millie) spent the evening. Then Elizabeth was shown to a guest room the size of Charlie's entire flat. She climbed into the enormous poster bed and lay awake wondering why she hadn't woken up yet, and how her brain could torture her with yet another dream at her lowest moment. After what seemed hours, she closed her weary eyelids.

"I gave her something to help her sleep, so she might be in and out the rest of the evening."

"Is it all right if I stay the night? I don't want to leave her."

"Certainly. I would hate for the poor dear to be alone, should she wake up. She has been through enough this past year, hasn't she?"

"I'm sorry, ma'am, but do you know her?"

"I was her nurse when she was here the last time, after that ghastly accident. Such a sweet little thing. I can't even imagine what this must be doing to her. And you too, of course, young man. I am just so sorry for the both of you."

"Thank you."

"I'll just go and see if I can scare up an extra pillow and blanket. You let me know if there is anything else I can do for either of you."

"Thank you, I will."

Morning sun filtered through the window and streaked across Elizabeth's hair and face. She blinked several times before she managed to focus on the bed, which, with its tall mahogany posts and blue silk drapes, definitely did not belong in any hospital. Frowning, she sat up and looked around her. The door opened and a woman in a long white apron entered carrying a tea service. She set it down carefully beside the bed and began pouring the liquid from the teapot into a hand-painted cup as Elizabeth observed her in confused silence.

"Is there anything more I can get for you, miss?" she asked as she stood up straight and clasped her hands together behind her back.

Elizabeth's voice was scratchy from disuse. "No, thank you." She watched the maid curtsey and walk out of the room, closing the door behind her. She stared at nothing in particular for several minutes before taking the teacup and slowly sipping the bitter liquid. Part of her wanted to simply stay in bed until she woke up, to avoid the illusion that awaited her on the other side of the bedroom door. On the other hand, reality was going to be difficult to face; at least in her dreams everything was going right. It couldn't hurt to postpone the inevitable for just a little while, could it? And besides, only in her dreams did she have Lady Catherine, whose mere presence was somehow comforting. And she certainly could use some comforting at the moment.

She got dressed and ventured downstairs to find the rest of the women already deep in conversation in the drawing room. Elizabeth managed to smile back at Jane, who looked relieved and gestured for her to sit beside her on the sofa.

"Did you sleep well?" she asked Elizabeth. "Your cheeks are pale."

"I'm fine." She smiled.

"Oh! Miss Elizabeth!" Lady Catherine called. "I was about to escort Miss Darcy and Miss Bingley to the library as they have been looking for something new to read. I would ask yourself and Miss Bennet to join us, but I am sure you are highly anxious to greet Mr. and Mrs. Collins. Perhaps the two of you would prefer to venture to the parsonage for a visit?"

Elizabeth looked warily at Jane, who shrugged unhelpfully. "No book on earth could be more captivating than a visit with Mr. Collins, Lady Catherine," she muttered sarcastically.

Of course. Just when I think things are going right in my dreams, Mr. Collins shows up. Why not?

They set out shortly after breakfast, the fresh air and natural beauty of the gardens lifting Elizabeth's spirits. When they reached the dirt road that led to the parsonage they heard horse hooves in the distance and saw a carriage approaching. It slowed to a stop, and Elizabeth felt a flutter in her stomach at the prospect of Mr. Bingley stepping out onto the road. As the door swung open, however, it was not Mr. Bingley but Mr. Darcy who climbed out, followed by Colonel Fitzwilliam. Jane immediately flushed scarlet and beamed, while Elizabeth tried her best not to show her disappointment and gave them both a polite smile.

"Miss Bennet! Miss Elizabeth!" Mr. Darcy exclaimed. "Good day to you both! Allow me to introduce my cousin, Colonel Fitzwilliam." He turned to face Elizabeth. "How do you find Rosings, Miss Elizabeth? Extraordinary, is it not?" He gave her an uncharacteristically enthusiastic smile, which made her own cheeks blaze with embarrassment.

She never did tell Jane everything that happened the last time she visited Lady Catherine. While in her coma and undergoing a procedure that required anesthesia in the real world, she spent an entire evening acting as though she were drunk. She even ended up kissing Mr. Darcy impulsively when he escorted her to the parsonage at the end of the night. She had no memory of it the next morning, but was given every sordid detail by the one other person who had witnessed the entire debacle and was at that very moment standing uncomfortably close to her—Colonel Fitzwilliam. Apparently she had even used the word extraordinary to describe how good of a kisser Mr. Darcy was. If he had chosen to use it now as a means to torment her and make her blush furiously, he had greatly succeeded.

Her eyes traveled from Mr. Darcy's to Colonel Fitzwilliam's, and she cringed to see the latter waggle his eyebrows provocatively at her. She quickly looked back at Mr. Darcy. "Not as *extraordinary* as the last time we were both here, I can promise you that, Mr. Darcy. At least I sincerely hope not. I have no clue what drugs they have me on at the moment..." She trailed off under her breath as she noticed the looks of bewilderment she was receiving from the men.

Oh, right. Last time never happened, since I changed the course of events this time. Which means I never visited the parsonage. Or Rosings. And it means I never drunkenly kissed Mr. Darcy (He probably thinks I'm drunk this very moment), and never even met Colonel Fitzwilliam, who apparently is still just a huge creep.

Breaking free from her thoughts, she gave Mr. Darcy what she hoped came across as a sober smile. "Would you care to visit the parsonage with us, Mr. Darcy?"

"Truth be told, I was hoping Miss Bennet would accompany me to greet my aunt." He gave Jane a knowing smile. "I was unable to better coincide our arrivals and I believe I have occasion to introduce her myself." He looked back at Elizabeth and winked conspiratorially. "However, I am certain the colonel would be more than willing to escort you to the parsonage, Miss Elizabeth."

She glanced reluctantly at Colonel Fitzwilliam, who was grinning and holding out his arm. She wrinkled her nose, then turned to say goodbye to Jane and Mr. Darcy, who had already climbed into the carriage and shut the door.

"Shall we?" Colonel Fitzwilliam proposed. "Unless you would prefer to walk the gardens instead?"

She considered it, her head cocked to one side. Then she shook her head firmly. "No, Lady Catherine will probably ask how I liked the shelving in the parsonage or something. I suppose we should just get it over with."

When they arrived at the parsonage, Mr. Collins was standing at the end of the pathway. He looked like a kid at Christmas with no idea which present to open first as he spotted them walking toward him. Leaping back and forth from one foot to another and wringing his hands together excitedly, he shouted," Miss Elizabeth! Did you see the carriage pass by? I do believe Mr. Darcy has just arrived at Rosings!"

Elizabeth gave him a sarcastic smile. "It is so good to see you again too, Mr. Collins."

He made an ungainly bow, stumbling forward. "Yes, forgive me, where are my manners?" He turned away from Elizabeth. "How wonderful to see you again, Colonel Fitzwilliam! And how kind of you to visit my humble abode so soon after your arrival! Miss Elizabeth Bennet is more than capable of walking to the parsonage alone. It was unnecessary for you to escort her when you are expected at Rosings! Surely Lady Catherine is awaiting your presence?"

Elizabeth met Colonel Fitzwilliam's gaze and rolled her eyes. He winked back at her. "It is an unmitigated honor to accompany a lady as esteemed by Lady Catherine as Miss Elizabeth," he answered resolutely. "My dear aunt would be ashamed to have me as her nephew if I allowed such a distinguished guest to tour the grounds unescorted."

"Oh! Yes, of course!" Mr. Collins chirped. "I have often taken it upon myself to escort the Miss Bennets on their walks to Meryton, unfortunate as they are not to have daily access to their family's confined single carriage. Lady Catherine often graciously condescends to bestow her kindness upon persons of low social standing. Indeed, the lower the rank of an individual, the greater her compassion is for their well-being."

Elizabeth couldn't help herself, she really couldn't. "You are so right, Mr. Collins. Didn't you mention once you owe everything in your life to Lady Catherine?"

Mr. Collins beamed. "Why yes, Miss Elizabeth, what an excellent memory you possess! Lady Catherine has always been especially attentive to my own welfare. Though I daresay she views her generosity as a heavenly investment, the return of which I flatter myself is sevenfold. She certainly seemed extremely grateful for the conclusion of last weeks' sermon, to be sure."

Elizabeth choked on a repressed laugh as she looked at Colonel Fitzwilliam's incredulous expression. Then she frowned slightly as his face suddenly became concerned and he reached down to take her hand in his. "Elle," he said softly.

"Yes?" she asked, her brow furrowed in confusion.

"Elle," he repeated, more insistently. His amber eyes almost seemed to be lightening to a pale blue. She blinked hard.

I am definitely on something.

Standing over her, with an urgent look in his icy-blue eyes, was Charlie.

Elle?" he whispered. "The doctor wants to speak with you about the results of the sonogram." He looked both exhausted and anxious.

Elizabeth sat up in her hospital bed. The doctor was standing by the door, clutching a clipboard and giving her a harrowing look.

Oh, no.

Chapter Fourteen

*T*he doctor pulled the chair nearer to the bed and sat down. He glanced at Elizabeth briefly before opening the substantial folder of medical records in his hands and clearing his throat. "I received the results of the sonogram, Miss Baker," he began. "There were a few other lab tests that came back as well." He exhaled deeply. "I have both good news and bad news for you."

Elizabeth looked at Charlie, whose eyes were full of apprehension.

"The good news is, your kidney shows no sign of disease as of now. There were no obstructions or infections of any kind, though it does appear to be slightly enlarged, which is an indication of stress. There was, however, significant stenosis, or narrowing, of the renal artery that could lead to problems in the future. I'm going to send you for a renal angiogram today to either confirm or rule it out."

"Is that the bad news?" Charlie asked.

The doctor sighed. "It could be. As the kidneys are the blood filtering units of the body, a narrowing of their vessels and arteries places additional strain on the organs themselves. High blood pressure and physical or emotional stress only increases the risk of disease. There are medications that help treat renal artery stenosis, as well as lifestyle changes you can make such as reducing caffeine and alcohol and maintaining a healthy diet, that will significantly improve the function of your kidney. However, if you were to become pregnant again, either in the near future or even years from now, you would be considered extremely high risk. The physical stress it would put on your body would be incredibly dangerous for both you and your fetus, resulting in possible spontaneous abortion or premature birth, not to mention the risk of losing your remaining kidney."

Elizabeth stared hard at the loose threading on her blanket. Finally, she looked back up at him. "Does that mean I can't have children?" she whispered.

"I certainly wouldn't recommend it," the doctor replied firmly. His stern look transformed into one of compassion. "I'm very sorry, I know that is not what you want to hear at this moment."

Elizabeth returned to staring at the blanket. She felt as though he had just stabbed her in the chest with a scalpel; the pain was so acutely tangible.

"I will check in on you later this evening, Miss Baker," the doctor said as he stood and returned the chair to its corner. "I would like you to remain here for at least another day or two, until your blood pressure lowers and your levels improve. We can discuss medications tomorrow."

Charlie looked at Elizabeth, who was staring unresponsively at her hands. "Thank you," he muttered to the doctor as he left the room and closed the door behind him.

Several minutes passed before Charlie managed to ask in a strangled voice, "Elle?"

She made no effort to reply, as she did not trust herself not to burst into tears, though her eyes felt dry and scratchy, as though they were full of sand. The piercing sensation in her chest was quickly subsiding into a dull ache she knew would become permanent. She tried to swallow, but her throat felt even drier than her eyes.

Charlie pulled her close, wrapping his arm around her shoulders. She could hear the steady rhythm of his heart through the fabric of his sweater. She realized she could no longer hear her own heart drumming in her ears, and wondered if it had stopped beating altogether.

"It's going to be all right, Elle," Charlie whispered soothingly. His voice sounded muffled with her ear pressed against his chest. "We're going to get through this."

Elizabeth pulled her head away and looked up into his eyes. She was instantly reminded of the first time she had seen those eyes gazing intently into her own. Although, she thought suddenly, she had actually seen them for weeks before that night at the pub, except that they belonged to someone else entirely.

For the first time since she woke from her coma she wondered how her unconscious brain could create someone who looked exactly like an actual person. Was it possible she had woken up at some point after the accident? Charlie told her he came to visit her in the hospital multiple times while she was in the coma. Had she seen his face, then slipped back into her subconscious, where he manifested himself as a character from her favorite novel? How she wished she had been awake all those times Charlie visited. She would have fallen in love with him first, avoiding the confusion and guilt she felt now for loving both of them at the same time. How she wished she had never been in the accident to begin with.

If I had never been in the accident, I never would have met either of them. And that would be so much worse.

She knew Jane, if she were there, would tell her everything happened the way it did because it was meant to be; that she was meant to be with

153

Charlie. She wanted to believe it, and yet, if it were true, why did it seem like their relationship continually faced insurmountable obstacles? If it was meant to be, why did it feel like everything was working against them? Like everything was falling apart?

With a fresh stab of pain she realized it had nothing to do with Charlie; he was the most incredible man in existence. Even if he did struggle with the idea of marriage, and even if he had only proposed because he felt it was the right thing to do, his misgivings were not the reason for their problems.

It's all my fault.

She had caused the accident that put her in a coma and left her with only one kidney. *She* had reinjured her brain at the stables, triggering confusing dreams and affecting her memory. *She* had gotten pregnant too soon. *She* lost the baby because of her own ignorance. *She* was the one who would never carry another of her own. And *she* was the one whose physical health was unstable, and would inevitably cause her to become a burden to her loved ones—especially Charlie.

She couldn't do that to him. She loved him too much to be a burden to him. He deserved better than that. He deserved someone whole.

He does deserve someone whole. Someone he can marry without any fear for her health. Someone who can give him beautiful children of his own that look just like him. Someone he can grow old with.

And that someone isn't me.

"No," she whispered, tears streaming down her face. "We won't."

154

Charlie squeezed her hand. "We will. We'll get through this together."

She exhaled shakily and forced herself to look at him. "Charlie, I can't ask that of you."

"Ask what of me?" He frowned in confusion.

"I can't let you stay with me not knowing what will happen. I don't know how long my kidney will continue to work."

Charlie's face was stern. "I am not going anywhere, Elle. We will just take it one day at a time." He unknit his eyebrows. "Besides, the doctor said your kidney showed no sign of disease, and that the stenosis can be treated." He managed a small smile.

Elizabeth sighed. "Even if that is true…" She felt her chin quiver. His face was blurry through her tears and she blinked them away in frustration. "Charlie, I can't have children."

She saw his eyes become glassy with fresh tears, though his expression didn't change. "That's all right." He looked down at their hands. "We will figure it out."

Elizabeth's heart lurched. She pulled her hands away from his and buried her face in them.

Charlie looked up at her. "Elle. We will," he insisted. "There are other ways to have children. We could always adopt."

She shook her head silently.

"Elizabeth, look at me," he said softly, and she lowered her hands. He took them in his and kissed them before continuing in a steady voice,

"The loss of this baby is devastating." He paused and swallowed hard. "And the pain is so fresh right now it feels like it will never subside. But time will help heal the wound, Elle. I promise it will."

Elizabeth stared at him. His words were comforting, but instead of reassuring her, she only felt more decided about what she knew she had to do. No matter what he said about adoption, she knew how much he wanted a child of his own, because of how thrilled he was when he found out she was pregnant. He would be giving up the chance if he chose to stay with her. She couldn't be so selfish as to allow him to make that choice. "No, Charlie," she whispered firmly. "You deserve to have children of your own." She looked down at the engagement ring glistening on her finger and began to carefully remove it with her other hand.

Charlie dropped his gaze to her hands. Then his eyes darted back up to meet hers, full of fear. He made a soft whimpering noise. "Elle, please don't do this."

She held the ring in her hand and, taking one last look, held it out to him. "I can't let you marry me, Charlie. I want you to be happy."

"I *am* happy, Elle!" he cried. "Please, believe me! I have never been happier in my entire life than I've been since the night I met you!" He closed her hand around the ring and held it tightly. "And I am not the least bit afraid of what lies in store for us, because whatever it is I know we will face it together!"

Elizabeth hesitated. It was time to come clean. "But that's just it, Charlie. We won't face everything together."

Charlie frowned. "What do you mean?"

"I should have told you the first time it happened, but I was too afraid of what you would think of me."

"What is it?" He gave her a concerned look.

She sighed. "Ever since the accident at the stables, I have been forgetting things."

"You had a concussion! I'm sure that is perfectly normal, Elle. And between how busy you have been with Jane's wedding plans and work, and everything else that has been going on you were bound to forget to do a few things."

"No," she admitted softly. "It's not things that I forgot to do." She hung her head in shame. "I can't remember entire evenings."

A moment passed in silence as Charlie thought hard. "Has it happened more than once?"

"Yes." She exhaled slowly. "The first time it happened was the night Jane and I decided to move out. I have absolutely no memory of the entire conversation."

Charlie's expression was unreadable. "And the other evenings?"

Elizabeth grimaced. "The night you proposed."

A shadow of regret fleetingly crossed over Charlie's features. "You don't remember me proposing?"

"I remember the roof. I remember the fireworks starting," Elizabeth said quickly. "But the next thing I can remember clearly is waking up with the ring on my finger." She decided against telling him about the dreams; she was already feeling guilty enough at the moment.

Charlie sighed and looked down at the blanket. What felt like forever passed before he said quietly, "Losing the baby was one of the evenings you forgot, isn't it?"

Elizabeth's eyes were burning so intensely she had to squeeze them shut against the pain. "Yes," she breathed. "And I am so completely ashamed you went through it alone, because I can't remember it."

They sat in silence for several minutes, avoiding each other's gaze. Then Elizabeth held her shaking hand with the ring between her fingers out to him once more. "I'm so sorry, Charlie."

He reached past her outstretched fingers to take her face in his hands. "This is just one more thing we will figure out as we go, Elle. The memory lapses are probably just from the concussion. It will get better."

"What if it doesn't, though?" she implored. "What if it gets worse? What if I forget days or weeks, or even years? What if I forget who you are?"

"I would never allow that to happen," he insisted, then leaned forward and kissed her.

She kissed him back slowly, knowing in her heart it would probably be for the last time. She could taste the saltiness of tears on his lips, though who they belonged to, she couldn't tell. When she drew her head back she saw that he was almost smiling. The glimmer of hope in his eyes caused her to break down once more. "We have to say goodbye, Charlie," she muttered between sobs. "I can't live with the guilt of knowing you deserved better for the rest of my life. It would make me miserable. I would end up hating myself for it."

His face became solemn. He slowly lowered his hands from her cheeks and leaned backward. "I would never want you to be unhappy because of me, Elle. If what you really want is for me to go, then I will go." His chin quivered. "Are you sure this is what you want?"

She hesitated. No, it was not what she wanted. What she wanted more than anything else was to reverse time and meet him before the accident—maybe at the restaurant as her blind date. What she wanted was the assurance of a long, healthy life, so she could marry him and they could grow old together, raise their children, and watch them begin lives of their own. What she wanted in that very moment was to throw her arms around him and tell him how much she loved him; that she had never known real love before, and that she never wanted to cause him another second of pain for the rest of his life.

"Yes," she lied. "It is what I want." She took his hand and turned it over so his palm faced up, then opened his fingers and placed the ring inside. Then she gently closed his hand with hers and let it linger for a few seconds before removing it. "I'm sorry," she whispered.

He stared down at his hand in silence. After a moment he stood and slowly walked toward the door. He reached out to turn the handle, then stopped and looked back at her with tears in his eyes. "I need you to know something, Elle. You think I deserve better than you, but you have it completely backward." He paused, his face now resolute. "I could live a hundred lifetimes and still never be worthy of your love."

It took everything inside her for Elizabeth not to speak. Instead, she dropped her gaze to her hands, which were trembling again.

"If you need time and space to work through things, of course I will give it to you," he continued. "And if you still decide you would rather not marry me, I promise I won't press you to change your mind." He turned the handle and pulled the door open. "But I won't give up on us, Elle, because I love you. More than I have ever loved anyone. And nothing—*nothing*—could ever change that."

He turned and left the room. The door clicked shut behind him, and Elizabeth hoped against hope it would open again and he would reenter the room. But it didn't. She was very much alone. Lying back on her pillow, she cried herself to sleep.

Elizabeth blinked.

She was sitting at Lady Catherine's dining table, staring at a plate of something slimy and depressingly gray in color. Realizing they were raw oysters, she bit her lip in distaste and looked up to see Colonel Fitzwilliam smiling at her from across the table. To his immediate left and right were Georgiana and Caroline, with Mr. Darcy and Jane seated beside Georgiana. Lady Catherine sat at the head of the table, with her daughter Anne, Mr. Collins and Charlotte to Elizabeth's left. To her left was an empty chair, which she assumed was for Mr. Bingley. She wondered why he hadn't arrived yet, then realized she was completely unsure of how she would feel once he did. Would she be happy to see him? Would it be too painful so soon after losing Charlie?

She listened for cues from the conversation around her as to what was going on. The topics seemed to shuffle between the weather and the meal, so no information of actual relevance was ascertained. As the meal continued, Elizabeth rapped her foot against the leg of the table and grew more and more anxious about seeing Mr. Bingley. She knew he wasn't Charlie, and yet at that moment she wanted nothing more than to see that familiar face. She took a long sip from her wineglass and fielded questions from Lady Catherine about her visit to the parsonage ("What did you think of the shelving in the closets upstairs? They were my own personal suggestion, after all!").

Several minutes later, as she was listening half-heartedly to the less than thrilling story of Mr. Collins's proposal from Charlotte, she finally heard his name spoken aloud by Lady Catherine. "Miss Bingley, where on earth is your dear brother, Mr. Bingley? Has he been delayed on the road, do you think?"

"Indeed, I hope not, Lady Catherine," Caroline replied sincerely. "He should have arrived by this time. I hope he hasn't met with any difficulties. I know he was most anxious to meet your ladyship."

"I am certain he is merely increasing our anticipation with his tardiness. Let us adjourn to the drawing room for entertainment whilst we await his arrival, shall we?"

Elizabeth followed the others into the drawing room, taking a seat in the furthest chair and attempting to remain inconspicuous. The last time she was in Lady Catherine's drawing room, she had been asked to play the piano for everyone. She then proceeded to delight (or possibly horrify) her audience with a rousing rendition of "Heart and Soul" and "Chopsticks" while under the influence of a large dose of anesthesia in the real world. Despite the fact it hadn't actually happened after she changed the course of events in this second set of dreams, she had absolutely no desire to make a fool of herself. In fact, no amount of anesthesia (or alcohol, for that matter) in the world could entice her to—

"Miss Elizabeth! Do you play the pianoforte?" Lady Catherine called from across the room.

Everyone turned to look at her expectantly. "No!" she barked, then realizing she probably sounded a tad overdramatic, attempted to recover her dignity by smoothing her skirt and adding calmly, "Err, that is, no, Lady Catherine. I cannot play the pianoforte." She smiled confidently.

That was close.

"Oh! Such a pity. Do you sing, then?" Lady Catherine pressed her.

Elizabeth thought for a moment. She *could* sing, sort of, but that sounded even less appealing than playing "Chopsticks." Besides, what in the world could she sing that they would even recognize? She had no clue what songs were popular in Regency England. Before she could open her mouth to reply, Georgiana offered, "Miss Elizabeth sings like a starling, Lady Catherine! Miss Bennet praised her ability the last evening we were all together at Netherfield!" She gave Jane a conspiratorial smirk.

Elizabeth cast a murderous glance at her before giving Jane a look of indignation. Georgiana smiled encouragingly and motioned to the front of the room with a slight twitch of her head.

"Wonderful!" Lady Catherine cried. "Let us hear you sing, Miss Elizabeth!" She gestured with her hand to the open space in front of them.

Elizabeth glanced around the room before drooping her shoulders and standing. She really was in no mood to argue. It was just a dream, after all, one she would most likely forget all about anyway. There was also every possibility she would wake up any second and avoid embarrassing herself entirely. She walked over to the piano and turned around to face the others, who were all waiting eagerly for her performance.

She racked her brain for the oldest song she could think of, but only came up with "Yankee Doodle Dandy," which, considering her audience, would probably not be well received. Just before she decided to go for it regardless, she was reminded of a song her grandmother used to sing to her when she was a little girl, and took a deep breath.

"Lavender blue, dilly dilly, lavender green," she sang softly as she examined her fingernails.

"If I were king, dilly dilly, I'd need a queen…"

She glanced up nervously, but no one seemed on the verge of laughter, so she inhaled and continued.

"Who told me so, dilly dilly,

Who told me so,

I told myself, dilly dilly,

I told my—"

She stopped short, her breath catching in her chest as she looked up and saw Mr. Bingley standing in the doorway. Her heart began to beat frantically. He gave her a devastating smile, that indistinguishable smile of Charlie's she might never see again. She could sense everyone staring at her in bewilderment and tried to continue singing, but was incapacitated by the sight of him. Instead she stood frozen, helplessly fixed to the spot, until he opened his mouth and, most astonishingly, began to sing in a clear, pleasant voice as he walked slowly toward her.

"If your dilly dilly heart feels a dilly dilly way,

And if you answer yes,

In a pretty little church, on a dilly dilly day,

You'll be wed in a dilly dilly dress of…"

He took her gloved hand in his and gazed lovingly into her eyes. She felt somehow relieved and terrified simultaneously as she stared back at him. He nodded encouragingly, and she managed to find her voice as they sang in unison.

"Lavender blue, dilly dilly,

Lavender green,

Then I'll be king, dilly dilly,

And you'll be my queen."

The room erupted in delighted applause, but still Elizabeth could not tear her eyes away from his. He grinned at her, dimples flashing, and raised her gloved hand to kiss it gently.

She tried to return his smile, but it faltered as she realized she couldn't remember the last time Charlie smiled at her that way. Had he already begun to fade from her memory? Her face crumpled. She removed her hand from his and pressed her fingers against her lips. Without hesitation, she walked across the room into the hallway, and then through the gargantuan doors to the twilit stone pathway outside.

Chapter Fifteen

By the time Elizabeth reached the manicured shrubs lining the stone pathway she was no longer crying. She began feverishly pacing back and forth, deliberating what to do. She knew it didn't really matter what she said or did—sooner or later she would simply wake up and it would all be irrelevant. But she also knew that, selfishly, she really didn't *want* to wake up. She wanted to remain in this dream world, where she was perfectly healthy. Where she still had almost everything she needed to be happy.

Everything except Charlie.

It didn't matter that she could wake up any moment. It didn't matter that it wasn't real. What *was* real, at least in that moment, was the fact that a wonderful, amazing man loved her and wanted to marry her—and no matter how much he looked like Charlie or even acted like him, he *wasn't* Charlie. It was time to tell Mr. Bingley the truth (or at least some version of the truth), and say goodbye to him. It was time for her to move on from her dreams and face reality once and for all, even if it meant never seeing either of them again and ending up alone.

She heard footsteps and looked up to see Mr. Bingley walking toward her, his face heavy with concern.

"Lizzie, what is it?" he asked, placing a hand on her arm. "What happened?"

One look into his soulful blue eyes and her willpower unraveled like a loose thread. "I, it's just, we…" She cocked her head to one side and frowned. "Wait a minute, did you just call me Lizzie?"

A servant walked past the nearby carriage and glanced over at them with curiosity. Elizabeth felt Mr. Bingley take her arm and escort her farther down the path. She could just make out his coy smile in the dark. "Well, you see, Miss Elizabeth, now that we are engaged to be married, I am allowed a more intimate form of address." He placed his hand on the small of her back and pulled her closer. "I myself am partial to Lizzie, however, if you prefer Elizabeth…"

She melted at his touch and muttered distractedly, "Lizzie…I prefer Lizzie." Her heart gave a lurch. "Mr. Bingley," she began regretfully.

"If I am allowed to call you Lizzie, then you must call me Charles," he interrupted with a sly grin. "Unless you would prefer Charlie?"

Elizabeth gaped at him. "What?"

He laughed. "The moment we met, when you fell from the tree, you addressed me as 'Charlie.' I have never been called anything but Charles my entire life. Therefore, the instant I heard it spoken aloud from your lips, I somehow knew I was destined to love you." He kissed her hand. "I know it probably makes me sound mad."

Oh, God.

"It doesn't make you sound mad," she replied slowly, a wave of nausea washing over her. She gnawed on her lip. "It's just…"

His smile faded away. "What is it, my love? Are you unhappy?"

Her eyes welled up with uninhibited tears; This was going to hurt. "I am so very sorry—you don't know how sorry I am—but I...I can't marry you."

His body tensed and he scrutinized her face. "May I ask you for the reason?"

She thought for a moment. What reason could she give that would make any sense to him? Because he wasn't a real person? Because it wasn't possible to shut out her problems in the real world and dream forever, even if she wanted to? Because he reminded her too much of someone who *was* real, and it was excruciatingly painful to keep seeing his face in her dreams when it wasn't really him?

I can't tell him that!

"I...I can't tell you," she murmured. Her tears spilled over her eyelashes and onto her cheeks.

"Elizabeth, if you are afraid to accept my hand because of your lack of fortune, you must know that it means nothing to me," he insisted emphatically, taking her hands in his.

Hearing the words he spoke the last time she refused him drove a wedge further into her already splintered heart. "No, it's not that. I promise."

His eyes became glassy with tears. He blinked them away before looking back into hers. "Then...you do not return my love?" he asked quietly.

Elizabeth glanced down at her feet. The last time he asked her that same question, she had lied to him and told him she didn't love him. She remembered the broken look in his eyes, as if she had mortally wounded him with her words. She couldn't lie to him again. Looking back up at him, she whispered softly, "I do love you..."

Relief flooded his features. "Then what is it, my love?" he asked. "Whatever it may be, we will address it together."

She hesitated. "No, we can't. It's not...something that can be fixed. I am so very sorry...I should never have said yes in the first place." She took a deep breath. "I wish things were different—*believe* me—but they just aren't."

"And you can offer no hope that you might ever feel...differently?" he asked, his voice quavering with emotion.

She could not trust herself to speak. She couldn't even look up at him for fear he would see regret in her gaze. Instead she shook her head silently, the tears coming faster as the last flicker of hope died out in his eyes. He exhaled deeply as he gently let go of her hands. "Then I will bid you farewell, my darling, and wish you every happiness." He turned and walked away, leaving her standing alone. When he reached the door he gave her one last haunting look over his shoulder. Then he walked inside and closed it behind him.

"I was just about to leave. I didn't know how long you would be asleep."

Elizabeth opened her eyes. She saw a face begin to materialize and blinked a few times before identifying it as belonging to someone from the twenty-first century. "Andie?"

Andie was seated at the foot of her bed wearing nursing scrubs. She gave Elizabeth a rueful smile. "I just started my shift, but I had to come see you." She sighed. "Jane was here and she told me what happened. Lizzie, I am just *so* sorry." She leaned forward and gave Elizabeth a stiff hug.

Elizabeth's eyes began to sting as she hugged her back. "Thank you."

Andie released her and leaned back to look in her eyes. "Are you all right? Jane said there was a problem with your kidney?"

"I'll be fine," Elizabeth replied weakly. "It will get better eventually, I guess. I don't really know..."

Andie looked around the room. "Where's Charlie? Shouldn't he be here with you?"

The sound of his name caused Elizabeth's stomach to turn over. Her eyes stung worse than ever, but she had no more tears left. "He's not here." For a reason she couldn't put her finger on she really didn't want to talk to Andie about it, but she knew the news would come out sooner or later anyway. "We...we broke up."

Andie's face remained impassive. "You broke up?" she repeated carefully. "Why? Was it because of what happened?"

Elizabeth wished more than anything it was Jane sitting in front of her, not Andie. But then again, apart from her sister, Andie was probably the only person she could talk to at the moment, and she desperately needed to talk to someone. "Yes...it is." She rubbed her burning eyes with her fingers and took a deep breath before looking back at Andie. "The doctor told me I can never have children because of my kidney."

Andie gave her a long, contemplative look, then raised her eyebrows and slouched her shoulders. "Wow," she breathed. "That is…awful." She moved to sit beside Elizabeth and placed an arm around her. "Did Charlie break up with you because you can't have children?"

"No," Elizabeth replied firmly, shaking her head. "I broke up with him."

"You broke up with him?" Andie asked, bemused. "Why?"

Elizabeth glanced briefly at her face, then hung her head shamefully. "Because he should be with someone who can have children," she admitted. "He should be with someone he can have a future with. Someone who can give him everything he deserves."

She half expected Andie to tell her she was crazy. That she had made a huge mistake by breaking up with him. That of course Charlie didn't care about any of that, because he loved her more than anything. That she should admit she lied to him, marry him, and spend the rest of her life with him, regardless of what may or may not happen in the future. It was what Jane would have said if she were there—she had absolutely no doubt.

She was therefore rather taken back when she heard her say, "It's probably for the best." Looking up at her in disbelief, she saw Andie's eyes widen. "Sorry! That is what my mother always says to me when something doesn't work out the way I hoped it would." She gave her an apologetic look. "Usually because of my own stupidity. I have a tendency to bugger things up for myself most of the time."

Elizabeth frowned. "I can relate to that."

"Do you think that is what happened with Charlie?" she asked carefully. "Do you think you made a mistake?"

Elizabeth paused. "I don't know, Andie." She sighed. "But I do know that he wanted this baby *so* much. So I know that even if he would never admit it, he would regret never having one of his own."

She wished Andie would tell her it wasn't true. But when she looked up at her from under her eyelashes, she was disappointed once again. "He did tell me once how much he was looking forward to one day becoming a father."

Elizabeth suddenly felt so heartsick she wanted nothing more than to be left alone. She slowly pulled away from Andie's arms. "Andie, my head hurts. Is there any chance I could have some medicine?"

"Of course!" Andie stood quickly. "I have to get back to work anyway. I'll have your nurse bring you some of the good stuff." She smiled and headed for the door. "Oh, and I think Jane is still around. Want me to send her in?"

"Yes." Elizabeth faked a smile. "Thanks, Andie."

"Of course!" She turned the handle, then looked back over her shoulder. "Everything will work out the way it was meant to in the end, Lizzie, I can promise you *that*," she declared with a knowing smile. "If you need someone to confide in, you know I'm here for you—right?"

"Right." Elizabeth waited for her to walk through the door and close it behind her. Then she wiped the smile from her face and narrowed her eyes.

When Jane came into the room she stood in the doorway and gave her sister a fearful look. When she saw Elizabeth's face collapse, she burst into tears and rushed over to the bedside to throw her arms around her. Elizabeth allowed herself to simply be held in silence for several minutes.

Then she lifted her eyes to meet her sister's. "Jane," she whispered. "What am I going to do now?"

Jane brought her hand up to gently brush the tears from Elizabeth's cheeks. "It's going to be all right," she soothed. "I promise."

"I really don't think it is," Elizabeth replied shakily. She told Jane what had happened with Charlie. Jane's response was exactly how Elizabeth imagined it. After giving Jane her most compelling arguments for why she couldn't be with him, she sighed. "Where am I going to live, Jane? I know Aunt Tessa and Aunt Bridget would let me stay with them, but I don't want them to be constantly worried about me. I don't even want them to know about any of this, really."

"You can stay with me until you figure things out," Jane answered decidedly.

"I'm sure Will wouldn't appreciate someone sleeping on his couch," Elizabeth replied. "And you have so much going on right now with the wedding. You don't need me getting in the way."

"You are *not* in the way," Jane emphasized. "You are my sister." She kissed Elizabeth's forehead. "And besides, it won't be for long. I know everything is going to work out with Charlie. He is your soul mate, Lizzie. You belong together."

Elizabeth looked away and noticed his forgotten sweater draped across the arm of the chair. She felt a fresh ache in her chest. "Do you think Will could move my stuff out of Charlie's flat for me?" she pleaded desperately. "I can't do it, Jane. I just can't see him right now."

Jane gave her a compassionate look. "Lizzie..." she began. "Please, think about this before you do anything you will regret."

172

"I *have* thought about it, Jane. I want him to be happy." She glanced back at the sweater, the ache now becoming unbearable. "His happiness is more important to me than my own."

Jane surveyed her sister's face carefully, then nodded in defeat.

"Thank you, Jane," Elizabeth murmured. "Thank Will for me, too."

"I will." She smiled sadly. "He's meeting the lads after work for a fitting, but I will have him go over to Charlie's after that." She stood, then followed Elizabeth's gaze to the chair and sighed. "Andie told me you are being discharged tomorrow morning. Do you want me to come pick you up? Or do you think you might call Charlie tonight to talk things over?" She gave her sister a hopeful look.

Elizabeth reluctantly pulled her eyes away from the chair and looked at Jane. "I would be so grateful if you came. Are you sure you don't mind?"

Jane's expression was subdued. "No, I don't mind at all." She leaned over to kiss Elizabeth's forehead once more. "Get some rest, Lizzie. I will be here bright and early."

"I love you, Jane."

"I love you too, Lizzie."

Once Jane left the room, Elizabeth slid out from the covers and walked over to the chair. She picked up the sweater and held it up to her face, breathing in Charlie's cologne and letting a muffled whimper escape her lips. Then she got back into bed and hugged it against her chest. For the rest of the day and most of the night, she lay awake staring at the closed door and checking her phone in vain. Whenever she felt her eyelids droop she forced them open again, until she allowed them to close for just a few seconds and those seconds stretched into minutes, and then the minutes stretched into hours.

When morning came Elizabeth opened her eyes and realized, much to her relief, she had mercifully slept without dreaming. She changed into her normal clothes and waited to be discharged. She no longer felt the crushing loneliness and despair that had consumed her the previous night. Instead, an empty, hollow sensation spread through her like a poison, leaving her void of emotion of any kind and causing her to stare out of the window in silence the entire drive to Jane and Will's flat. Although Jane repeatedly stole concerned glances in her sister's direction, she wisely did not attempt to engage Elizabeth in conversation. She allowed her to retreat to the guest bedroom and close the door behind her when they arrived, where she remained for several hours. Jane had been true to her word; boxes filled one corner of the room with Elizabeth's name on each one, thanks to Will. She eyed them despondently, thinking how the sight of all of her earthly belongings stacked in cardboard boxes was like a metaphor for her life—she didn't belong anywhere.

She noticed something white lying on top of one of the boxes. Puzzled, she walked over to see what it was. She held out a trembling hand to pick up a crisp white envelope with her name written on the outside in Charlie's familiar scrawl. Unsure of what to do, she simply stared at it. Should she read it? Probably not—it would only weaken her resolve. She pulled her worn copy of *Pride and Prejudice* out of the open box at her feet and tucked it carefully between the pages, then placed it carefully back in the box and closed the lid.

Over the next few weeks, Elizabeth distracted herself from her slow recuperation (a painful reminder of the magnitude of her loss) and the permanent ache of missing Charlie, by becoming absorbed in her work for *Flavor* magazine. She spent her days and most of her nights on her laptop, editing article after article and asking for more work once she finished them. Her boss was so impressed with her sudden motivation he suggested she try writing some articles of her own; a proposition she gladly accepted. Anything to keep her from the downward spiral of depressing thoughts she was perpetually susceptible of falling victim to. Her preoccupation served more than one purpose; if she worked late into the night she wouldn't have any opportunity to dream. When she did sleep it was undisturbed, probably the result of sheer exhaustion. It was a huge relief—she never wanted to dream again.

When she wasn't working, she was helping Jane with wedding plans. It was convenient for her to be living with the bride, so she could spend hours discussing silverware and cake designs, on her part with only half-hearted enthusiasm. Will's parents, who were eager to showcase their wealth through the impending nuptials of their cherished firstborn, were sparing no expense; the wedding was going to be incredibly lavish.

Will and Jane were gracious hosts, but as the third week drew to a close Elizabeth could tell she was beginning to wear out her welcome, though neither of them would ever admit to it. She needed to find a more permanent place to live and let them get back to their normal routine. Her aunts were out of the question as they still believed her to be living with Charlie, and she could never afford to pay rent on her own. She considered Andie, but she knew she wouldn't be able to handle her pitying looks and patronizing condolences, even if they were well meant.

That left one last option, which Elizabeth voiced aloud to Jane one afternoon, and then immediately regretted.

"That would be perfect!" Jane cried excitedly. "I'm sure Millie would *love* it if you moved in with her!"

"Really?" Elizabeth asked warily. She had half hoped Jane would talk her out of it.

"Yes!" Jane clapped her hands together. "She was just telling Will how lonely she was living by herself!"

"What about Daniel Radcliffe?" Elizabeth bit her lip.

"Who?"

"Her boyfriend," she replied, holding back a smile. "She told me she was dating Daniel Radcliffe."

Jane frowned. "Well, I didn't know she had a boyfriend, but since I have never even met him, my guess is that he isn't around very often."

"I'd say that's a pretty good guess."

Elizabeth broke into a smile for the first time in weeks as she realized her sister had no clue who Daniel Radcliffe was, causing Jane's eyes to widen with delight. "Well, I think it's a great idea. You would be a good example of a mature adult for her, and she is really fun when you get to know her. She might be just what you need right now."

"I was pretty immature myself, until recently." Elizabeth's smile melted away. "And now I'm not a good example of anything, unless it's what not to do."

176

Jane gave her a squeeze. "I'll call Millie and give her the good news." She kissed her sister's cheek. "Thank you, Lizzie. It means a lot to me that you would be willing to move in with my future sister-in-law. I know she is a bit, well, unique—but she *is* family now."

Elizabeth managed a small smile. "True." She sighed. "And it will be nice to be back in our comfortable old flat again. Maybe the familiarity will be healing in some strange way."

Jane pressed her lips together in a thin line. "Umm...well...about that," she began awkwardly.

A week later, Elizabeth stood facing the unmistakable front door with its faded and peeling green paint. Seconds after she knocked Millie pulled it open and gave her an excited smile. "Lizzie!"

Elizabeth leaned down to pick up a box and her purse next to her feet and followed Millie through the door. Once inside, her mouth fell open as she looked around the room and nearly dropped everything in her hands. "Millie, what the actual hell?"

Chapter Sixteen

What once was Elizabeth and Jane's shabby chic living room was now completely unrecognizable. The walls had been painted a deep maroon. The partition between the kitchen and bedroom doors held aged portraits inside vintage-looking frames, while the opposite open wall space was adorned by an enormous and remarkably lifelike stag's head, complete with antlers. The windows were encased with floor to ceiling maroon and gold paisley drapes, and in front of them were two well-worn leather armchairs. A chess board was carved into the table separating them, the shiny rooks and pawns looking as though they had never actually been used. A massive bookshelf held at least one hundred books at one end of the room, guarded by a full-sized suit of armor in the corner. On a display stand behind the champagne-hued sofa antique instruments including a large ornamental hourglass, a brass telescope, and a sepia-toned world globe were lined neatly in a row. Over the small fireplace, its gas insert emitting a cheerful fire, was an ornate gilded mirror. The wooden mantel was lined with lit pillared candles, the melted wax dripping down the sides into solidified puddles at their base.

Elizabeth set her purse down on the mahogany secretary's desk beside the door. When she finished gaping at the authentic feather quill dipped into a bottle of actual ink, she rolled the brass seal with the letter "m" on it between her fingers and attempted to pick her chin up off of the floor. "Millie, this is just…wow…"

"Do you like it?" Millie asked eagerly.

Elizabeth looked around once more. The resemblance to the library at Netherfield would have been uncanny, were it not for a small tapestry bearing the Hogwarts crest beneath the stag and a display of magic wands on a shelf above the desk. She smiled despite herself. "I absolutely love it."

Millie beamed with delight. "I call it the common room."

"Ahhh." Elizabeth nodded appreciatively in recognition of the term. "But which one?"

"Gryffindor, obviously."

Elizabeth managed to keep a straight face. "Obviously." She shrugged out of her coat sleeves. "So where do you keep all the memorabilia you were telling me about?"

"Oh, I keep it all in my bedroom," Millie admitted shamelessly. "I wouldn't want anyone thinking I am a total geek."

"Millie, no one would ever think that of you," Elizabeth muttered solemnly, though her twitching lips betrayed her. She looked away quickly. "The detail in this room is incredible though, really. Where on earth did you manage to find it all?"

"Oh, you know, here and there…" Millie caught Elizabeth's eye and blushed. "My parents."

Elizabeth smiled. "So, do you have any plans tonight, Millie? Will I finally get to meet your boyfriend?"

Millie shook her head. "No, he is in Los Angeles at the moment, at a convention."

"That's too bad." Elizabeth shrugged her shoulders. "Any ideas, then? Hopefully something that doesn't require leaving the flat? I'm not feeling very sociable at the moment."

"Right." Millie gave her a compassionate look. "Will told me what happened. I'm so sorry, Lizzie."

"Thanks, Millie." Elizabeth reached out to spin the globe and vaguely watched it rotate. "I'll be all right."

"I know just the thing to cheer you up," Millie replied confidently.

Elizabeth glanced up, her expression wary. "Oh, yeah?"

Half an hour later she was curled up on the sofa in her pajamas, watching *Harry Potter and the Sorcerer's Stone* fill the television screen. She took the opportunity while Millie headed to the kitchen for snacks to check her phone—still no calls or texts from Charlie. He was obviously extremely angry with her, and how could she blame him? She was the one who told him to leave.

Millie walked back into the room and held out a glass of amber-colored liquid. "Butterbeer?"

Elizabeth eyed the glass distastefully. "What's in it?"

"Oh, it's mostly cream soda and butterscotch syrup—"

"That's OK, Millie…" Elizabeth looked at her phone, which had just notified her of an incoming text. She was disappointed to discover it was only Jane, asking her how things were going.

"—with vanilla vodka and butterscotch schnapps."

Elizabeth jerked her head back toward the glass. She had been expressly forbidden from alcohol consumption by the doctor, and Jane had taken it upon herself to make sure she followed his orders while she lived with her. But Jane wasn't there…and it had been so long…and she was in dire need of liquid reprieve…

Surely one glass won't hurt anything?

She thanked Millie and took a sip. "Holy Hogwarts! That is *fantastic!*" she cried, her upper lip covered in a whipped cream mustache.

"I know, right?" Millie smiled and drank deeply from her own glass. "I made loads of it for our film marathon."

"Oh! I don't know if I can watch more than one movie, Millie," Elizabeth admitted as she took another sip. "I'm really not that into Harry Potter, to be honest."

Three hours (and too many glasses of butterbeer to count) later, Elizabeth was wearing a set of wizard robes with the hood pulled low over her eyes. She pointed a wooden wand at the wall, directly between the stag's antlers, and struggled to focus. "La mimosas!" she blurted, then hiccupped loudly. She frowned at Millie. "It didn't work."

"You pronounced it wrong," Millie slurred, readjusting her own robes to cover her ample bosom. "You have to put the emphasis on the correct syllable. Didn't you pay attention to the film?"

"Of course I did!" Elizabeth looked affronted. "I just need to loosen up my wrist. Maybe one more glass of butterbeer would help…"

"It's all gone," Millie replied sadly, holding up the empty pitcher. "It must have disapparated." She pushed her bushy hair out of her eyes; she and

Elizabeth had taken turns teasing each other's hair to make it look like Hermione's, causing them both to appear as though they had recently been electrocuted.

"Nooooo…" Elizabeth whined. She flopped into one of the armchairs and blew raspberries at the clump of hair that had fallen in front of her mouth, eyes crossed in order to see it better. "Well, what should we do now?" She dazedly scanned the room, pausing at the stag and drawing in her breath sharply. "Millie—look! It worked! He's smiling at me!"

"Behold!"

Millie and Elizabeth stood in the doorway of Millie's bedroom. It was like a mecca for nerds; every fandom in existence seemed to be represented in one form or another. Posters, clothing, action figures, and various miscellany occupied every square inch of the room. Even the bedding was covered in characters and stuffed animals. And standing in one corner, in all of his glory, was Harry Potter himself.

"Oh…my…word," Elizabeth breathed. She took a few tentative steps toward him, her hands clasped over her heart. "It is *such* an honor to meet you, Mr. Potter."

She stood gaping at him until Millie joined her side. "That's not him."

"Oh! Right!" Elizabeth blushed. "I am so sorry! I mean, *Mr. Radcliffe.*"

"No." Millie shook her head forcefully, losing her balance and clutching Elizabeth's arm for support. "No." She extended her arm and pointed. "I mean, that's a cardboard cutout."

Elizabeth squinted hard and swayed forward to examine him more closely. "Oh." She grinned stupidly at Millie. They burst into raucous laughter and collapsed in a heap on the floor.

After they were officially placed in their houses by the authentic reproduction sorting hat (Elizabeth had to admit it was right on the money with Hufflepuff), and taking turns trying on every costume Millie owned and snapping selfies, the two girls lay side by side on Millie's bed, exhausted. Elizabeth gazed across the room at the cardboard Harry and sighed deeply. "Millie, it is just so...so...*cool*," she murmured sluggishly. "That you are dating a celebrity."

Millie propped herself up with her elbow. "So, you believe me, then?" She grinned, then gagged as she pulled a long strand of hair out of her mouth.

"*Totally*." Elizabeth rolled onto her hip to face her. "I *totally* believe you, Millie."

"*Thank* you! I don't think anyone else does. Not even my own family, though I have no clue why not." Millie scratched her head and frowned. "It's probably that they are just jealous, because he is so fit."

"That's got to be it," Elizabeth agreed enthusiastically. "I bet he *is* fit—probably from all the broomstick frying...frying...*flying!* And you know what else? He's kind of got this super-hot, like, *sexy librarian* vibe, too—I can't believe I never noticed it before! If he ever decides to quit being a wizard—I mean an actor—he could *definitely* be a part-time model for, like, toothpaste. Or he could always be a...a...*sexy librarian*."

"*Yes!* I love you for saying that, Lizzie! And I love *you*, too." Millie sat up suddenly. "You know what?" she asked soberly, eyes round with intensity.

Elizabeth tried to push herself up with her hands. Missing the bed on one side, she nearly fell to the floor. "What?"

Millie grinned. "We are going to be best friends."

Elizabeth smiled back in agreement. "We are *definitely* best friends, Millie." She fell back onto the pillow and closed her eyes. "Best friends of ever. I mean, *forever*."

"I am going to take you with me to the next cosplay convention."

"I'm so *there*." Elizabeth opened her eyes wide. "Oh! Another use for my Wonder Woman costume!"

When Elizabeth woke up she was lying in bed, staring up at the canopied ceiling in a small room with pale blue and white striped walls. It took a few seconds, but she soon knew exactly where she was—her bedroom at Longbourn.

Nooooo.

Looking around, she was aware that beside the fact she was dreaming *yet again*, something was wrong.

All of Jane's things are gone.

She quickly got out of bed and tore open the wardrobe. Only her own dresses hung inside; all of Jane's were missing.

Did she marry Mr. Darcy?

Unable to face what awaited her outside the door after the memory of the last dream she decided to climb back into bed, pull the covers over her head, and simply wait to wake up again. Just before she drifted off to sleep, the door burst open and slammed into the wall with a deafening bang. Lydia and Kitty Bennet flew into the room and leapt onto the bed.

"Lizzie!" cried Lydia, her long dark braids flying out from under her cap. "We are walking to Meryton after breakfast! Do come with us! It will be such fun to see the officers!"

Elizabeth pulled the blankets away from her face and frowned. "Officers?"

"Yes, of course!" exclaimed Kitty. "The militia! Soldiers in uniform! Hundreds of them!"

"There is only one gentleman in uniform who catches Lizzie's eye," Lydia said with a smirk. Kitty collapsed in a fit of giggles.

Elizabeth felt more confused than ever. Then suddenly her eyes widened with realization. "George!"

Both girls fell silent. "Are you engaged to Mr. Wickham?" Lydia breathed. "We thought you were merely besotted with him."

"What?"

"He *is* remarkably handsome," added Kitty with a knowing smile.

"I am *not* engaged to George—I mean, Mr. Wickham!" Elizabeth cried exasperatedly. "That is ridiculous! And I am definitely *not* besotted with him!"

"Then why did you dissolve your engagement to Mr. Bingley?" Lydia demanded bluntly.

"Lydia!" Kitty admonished.

"I would like to know the reason!" Lydia shot Elizabeth a scandalized look. "He seemed to be in love with you—although why he would choose you, only heaven knows—and he is even more handsome and infinitely wealthier than Mr. Wickham!"

"I...I can't explain it to you," Elizabeth stammered. She wished she could melt into the floor. "It won't make any sense to you, trust me. But it was *not* because of Mr. Wickham."

"Well, you should know, Lizzie, Miss Darcy has been spreading a malicious falsehood that you ended your engagement with Mr. Bingley because you are in love with Mr. Wickham." Far from appearing concerned for her sister, Lydia's expression was exultant to be the bearer of such sensational gossip. Kitty, however, merely glanced uneasily from one girl to the other with increasing apprehension.

"What? Georgiana?" Elizabeth's mind began to spin. "Why on earth would she do that?"

"Perhaps she thought it the truth?" Kitty offered tentatively. "After all, *we* believed it to be." She cringed at the outraged look on Elizabeth's face. "The night we were introduced to him you spent the entire evening in his company. It seemed as though you were purposefully ignorant of anyone else in the room. The occasions we have been in his presence since have all

186

been remarkably similar, with the two of you smiling, laughing, and talking intimately and unreservedly."

"Yes—because we are *friends*! Friends can laugh and talk. It doesn't mean I'm in *love* with him!" Elizabeth's affronted expression changed as she felt a stab of fear. "Oh, no—did Georgiana tell Mr. Bingley that I am in love with George—*ugh*—Mr. Wickham?"

Lydia and Kitty looked warily at each other, then back at Elizabeth. They didn't answer her, but they didn't need to. She felt a sudden and strong impulse to see her actual sister. "Where is Jane?"

The girls looked at each other again. "Jane is on her bridal tour with Mr. Darcy," Kitty replied slowly. "They have been gone a fortnight."

"Oh. Right." Elizabeth's disappointment was quickly replaced by a sinking weight of dread inside her stomach. "I have to go to Netherfield and talk to Mr. Bingley."

"You could join us on our walk to Meryton and then continue on to Netherfield!" Lydia suggested eagerly.

Though she wanted nothing more than to walk alone so she could think without incessant chatter in her ears, Elizabeth agreed. She dressed quickly and headed downstairs to breakfast, where she found the dream version of her mother already seated at the table beside Mary. A sting of longing to throw her arms around her was interrupted by the realization that her father was noticeably absent. She wondered if he had already had enough socialization for the day and excused himself to his library for some peace and quiet. The thought made her smile, though she wished she could see his handsome face just for a moment; it had been so long since she had seen it in person. She had just taken a seat across from her mother and opened her mouth to ask where he was when Mrs. Bennet abruptly pushed her chair backward and stood. She cast her daughter an apoplectic look and hurried from the room without speaking.

Elizabeth was momentarily baffled by the uncharacteristic behavior; her mother had never before possessed the ability to hold her tongue. Then she realized she was probably irate with her for ending things with Mr. Bingley, a handsome, highly-connected gentleman with a large income. In fact, the loss of such an impressive potential son-in-law most likely had provoked her to wrath of a hitherto unprecedented scale. As a result, she probably had decided never to speak to Elizabeth again, just like in the novel.

She wondered what her actual mother would do if she knew she had ended things with Charlie. At least she never even told her they had gotten engaged. Or for that matter, that she was pregnant and lost the baby. Or even the struggles she was having with her health. She marveled at her own ability to keep it all from her parents. Was it possible she had subconsciously assumed they were preoccupied with Jane's wedding details, and didn't want to bother them? If she was truly honest with herself, she had to admit it was most likely because she was terrified of what her mother's reaction would be to her second daughter's train wreck of a life in comparison to her successful and boast-worthy firstborn.

She sat frozen in her chair as her mind processed this new revelation about her relationship with her mother. Then she was brought back to the room by the eager voices of Lydia and Kitty, urging her to hurry as the sky was becoming overcast. They set off for Meryton shortly after, with Mary trailing along disparagingly in their wake. Once they reached the town they were immediately swallowed by a sea of red coats. As much as she desperately wanted to see Mr. Wickham, who was as close to Bryan as she would get either in her dreams or in reality (as he was currently an ocean away in Philadelphia), Elizabeth knew she needed to find Mr. Bingley as quickly as possible. She said goodbye to her sisters and continued on to Netherfield through the beautiful English countryside.

The sky grew bleak and ominous. Elizabeth looked up at the menacing clouds and startled as a crack of thunder echoed through the fields. Raindrops pelted her uplifted face and immediately escalated to a downpour. The sheer irony of it all was so ridiculous that she began to laugh out loud as she quickly became drenched from head to toe. Suddenly, a lightbulb went off inside her head. The last time she walked to Netherfield and it began to rain, she took shelter under the branches of a tree, and was rescued by Mr. Bingley on horseback! Maybe if she waited for him, he would rescue her a second time!

There was a large tree not far from where she stood. She ran underneath it and leaned against the trunk, listening hard for the sound of approaching horses. For almost an hour she could hear nothing but the raindrops against the leaves of the tree and the steady beating of her own heart. Discouraged, she sank to a squat and ran her fingers through her wet hair.

He's not coming.

The instant she admitted it to herself the rain stopped so abruptly it was as if it had been waiting for her to say it aloud. She walked out slowly from under the tree. Gathering the folds of her saturated skirt, she continued to trudge along until she saw Netherfield in the distance.

The first sight of Mr. Bingley's magnificent house caused her heart to perform a cartwheel in her chest that had absolutely nothing to do with its grandeur. In her panic to discredit Georgiana's rumor she completely forgot that she was going to have to see Mr. Bingley once more in order to do it. The only reason she found the courage to tell him she couldn't marry him in the first place was because she was certain it would be the last time she would ever dream about him. Despite her determination to face reality and move on with her life, her brain obviously had other plans. It was going to be extremely difficult to maintain her resolve once she saw his face and heard his voice again, especially since she was missing Charlie so badly she almost couldn't breathe.

Would she really be able to tell him a second time that she couldn't marry him after she cleared up the misunderstanding about Mr. Wickham? Did she even want to? She really did love him, after all. She could deny it all she wanted, but she knew deep down a part of her always would. And it would certainly be nice if her life weren't a disaster in both reality *and* her dreams.

Plus she really, *really* wanted to kiss him again…

Making up her mind to tell him she made a mistake, she knocked on the door and waited, an anxious smile on her face. She was ushered inside by a bored-looking butler, who escorted her into the drawing room and announced her presence. Expecting Mr. Bingley to be seated in one of the chairs, or possibly Caroline, she was taken back to see Georgiana Darcy herself alone in the room. Upon seeing Elizabeth in the doorway, Georgiana's eyes widened with surprise, and quite possibly a smidgen of something else—was it fear?

"Miss Elizabeth!" Georgiana exclaimed. Her eyes traveled the length of her wet and muddy clothing, making Elizabeth feel vulnerable. "What—whatever are you doing here?"

"I came to speak with Mr. Bingley," she answered determinedly. "What are *you* doing here?"

Georgiana considered her carefully before she spoke. "I am staying with Caroline whilst my brother is away from Pemberley. She had no desire to remain at Netherfield alone."

Elizabeth frowned. "Alone?"

A glint of indignation could be clearly seen in Georgiana's brown eyes. "Yes, alone. Mr. Bingley is not here."

Elizabeth tried to mask her disappointment. "What about Caroline? Is she around?"

"Caroline is indisposed for the time being." Georgiana raised a perfectly arched eyebrow and glared at Elizabeth. "Thanks to you."

"Me?" She tried to think of what she could have done to upset Caroline, but came up empty. "Why because of me?"

"She is greatly concerned for her brother." Georgiana scowled. "For his well-being. I believe you must know why?"

Elizabeth sighed. "Yes, I do. I—I made a mistake, Georgiana. That's why I'm here, I need to talk to him. Do you know when he will be back?"

"No," Georgiana replied flatly. "Not even he possesses the answer to that question. It may be that he never returns to Netherfield."

Elizabeth remembered the last time she hurt him, when she was in the coma. She bit her lip. "Is he in London?" she asked hopefully. Her mind began to think of ways to get there without the use of Mr. Darcy's carriage. She had to find a way to find him before she woke up again.

Georgiana hesitated; she seemed to be actually enjoying herself now. "No." She shot Elizabeth an accusatory glare. "He joined the militia."

Chapter Seventeen

*E*lizabeth's heart plummeted. "What?"

"Once he departed Rosings, Mr. Bingley made the rash decision to join the militia. He appraised my brother of his plans, telling him he felt it his duty as an Englishman to serve his country in its time of need. He then left almost immediately." Georgiana sneered at Elizabeth. "And it is your fault."

For a few seconds, Elizabeth felt overcome with remorse for the part she played in his decision. Then she remembered the reason she had come to Netherfield in the first place. "And you had absolutely nothing to do with it, Georgiana?"

"Excuse me?"

"When exactly did you tell him I was in love with Mr. Wickham?" Elizabeth asked slowly and carefully.

Georgiana's nostrils flared. "That is entirely irrelevant."

"When?" Elizabeth asked again, her voice low and dangerous.

"At Rosings," Georgiana admitted. "When neither of you returned following your appalling vocal performance, from which you fled the room in tears (Elizabeth made a face at her), Miss Bennet left to search for you and discovered Mr. Bingley in the foyer, alone and visibly distressed. I overheard their entire conversation from behind a door. He confessed you told him you would not marry him, though you would not give a reason for it. Miss

Bennet reassured him of your love for him, and asked him to wait whilst she spoke with you. As soon as she departed, I approached him and confessed to hearing what was said. When he asked if I believed you might have a change of heart, I told him you would not. I told him the reason you would not marry him was that you were in love with someone else. When he asked who the gentleman was, I told him it was Mr. Wickham." She met Elizabeth's gaze. "It was extremely satisfying to watch the sorrow in his eyes increase as I embellished my falsehood, telling him you never actually loved him, and that you regretted accepting his proposal the moment he asked."

Elizabeth stared at her in astonishment, tears clouding her vision. "Why would you do something like that?"

Georgiana smirked. "Partially because, as a result of your own foolishness, you unwittingly handed me the perfect opportunity to console Mr. Bingley and turn his affection toward myself. Now that he has purchased Netherfield and is considered part of the landed gentry, he is a most advantageous match, to be sure. And also partially because I despise Mr. Wickham. I hoped perhaps Mr. Bingley and my brother would seek him out, and possibly assault him for the part they believe he played in the entire pantomime. Honestly, it would all be far more amusing than even Shakespeare."

"Wow," Elizabeth muttered, her upper lip curling in disdain. "I can't believe I thought you might actually be a decent human being this time around, Georgiana. I don't know why I doubted my instincts, really, you are just the worst." She could hear her heart pounding relentlessly in her ears. "As was your plan. Mr. Bingley would never assault anyone." Her eyes narrowed. "Although, I myself have absolutely no problem with violence, if the situation calls for it."

Georgiana's eyes grew round and she took a small step backward. "If you dare strike me it will only incense my brother, as well as aid my quest for Mr. Bingley's affection."

"I doubt that very much," Elizabeth retorted, thinking of Mr. Darcy's reaction the last time. "Besides, I'm not sure how you plan to gain Mr. Bingley's affection if he is in the militia."

Georgiana glanced down at the floor. "I admit, I did not anticipate what his response would be toward the vilification of your character." She looked back up at Elizabeth. "It seems I greatly underestimated the depth of his affection for you. Apparently the loss of your love is more devastating to him than the potential loss of his own life in battle." She rolled her eyes.

"He is not going to be in any battle," Elizabeth seethed. "He is probably stationed at Meryton with the regiment there. I'm going to find him and tell him the truth. I'm sure it's not too late for him to change his mind."

"And what exactly is the truth, Miss Elizabeth?" Georgiana asked superciliously. "What was the reason you would not marry him?" Her baleful eyes stared menacingly into Elizabeth's.

Elizabeth hesitated, temporarily at a loss for words. Then she set her jaw firmly and stood at full height. "A much better question is, why am I wasting time standing here talking to you?" She turned to leave, then stopped abruptly and spun around again. She walked briskly up to where Georgiana stood, until their faces were within inches of each other. Georgiana became rigid, her expression uneasy. "You need to leave Netherfield, Georgiana. Now. And don't you dare go back to Pemberley—leave your brother and my sister alone. Go back to the seventh level of hell, where you belong," she threatened through a clenched jaw. "And if you even so much as show your face in my dreams again, I will, I'll—OK, admittedly, there's not a whole lot I can do about it, because I have now officially lost control of my life in both reality and my subconscious, not that I ever really had it in the first place. But seriously, just *don't*."

Bye, Felicia!

She walked out of the room without looking back, feeling a sort of triumph at having put Georgiana in her place without resorting to punching her in the teeth. As soon as she was back in the dismal outdoors, however, a vice gripped her heart. Mr. Bingley had joined the militia because of her. He couldn't be in any real danger, though, if he were stationed at Meryton with the other officers, right? She knew little of English military history, but from what she had read in Jane Austen's novels, the local militia were different from the regular army. They typically stayed on home soil, keeping the peace by suppressing riots and taking over policing duties normally performed by the regulars. By doing this they freed up army soldiers for battle abroad. Surely Mr. Bingley, a gentleman with an inheritance and high connections, would be made captain of the local regiment, and be kept from direct combat.

Right?

Elizabeth headed back toward Meryton, with a fresh urgency in her step that caused her to stumble more than once and splash mud onto her hem. When she reached the town her eyes darted back and forth among the flood of red coats for the familiar blond head and dimpled smile. After several minutes of searching in vain she had an epiphany. She fought her way through the crowd to the tiny pub with the rusty sign hanging from the door that read, *The Swan.* She stepped inside and waited for her eyes to adjust to the darkness. The only light filtering in from the windows that lined one wall was speckled with particles of dust, and Elizabeth sneezed as she walked through it. Everyone at the bar looked over in her direction. When they saw her standing there, forehead glistening with sweat, her hair falling from its bun in loose curls, and her hem six inches deep with mud, they immediately fell silent and stared. Elizabeth watched their eyes on her with acute self-awareness. Before she found her voice, another from the furthest corner of the room called out, "Miss Elizabeth?"

She smiled without even locating him in the shadows; she knew exactly who that smooth voice belonged to. Quickly, she walked over to where it originated, grinning when she saw Mr. Wickham's handsome face. He stood and reached for her hand, then bent over to kiss it. "Miss Elizabeth, what on earth are you doing in a disreputable place such as this? You could have been harmed!"

She ignored his look of concern and threw her arms around him. "George!" Releasing him, she flushed at his astonishment, remembering they did not call one another by their first names at this point in her coma. "I mean, Mr. Wickham." She reached for the back of the nearest chair and dropped roughly into it.

Mr. Wickham gave her a knowing smile and returned to his own seat. "Would you like a drink, Miss Elizabeth?"

"God, yes," she replied eagerly, and watched as he casually gestured to the bartender. A glass of whiskey was set before her. She looked at it uncertainly, then picked it up and threw it back in one long gulp. She set the empty glass back down on the table and waited for the burning to subside, watching Mr. Wickham's eyes widen in what was unmistakable admiration.

"What brings you to Meryton, Miss Elizabeth?" he asked. "I did not expect to see you again for quite some time, considering the whispers I have recently heard." His lips curved upward in a roguish smirk.

Elizabeth cringed. "I am so, so sorry about that," she muttered. "I swear there is no truth to it. I love you like a brother, and that is all."

Mr. Wickham frowned. "And I love you like a sister, Miss Elizabeth." His lips twitched. "But what, pray tell, does that have to do with your engagement to Mr. Bingley?"

"Wait, so you haven't heard a rumor that I broke off my engagement to Mr. Bingley because I am in love with you?"

Mr. Wickham's eyes bulged. "What?" he exclaimed. "You broke off your engagement? Why?"

Elizabeth sighed. She licked her lip and stared into his eyes, considering him. Should she tell him the truth? Would he think she was completely crazy? "I...had to."

Mr. Wickham's expression suddenly became dangerous. "Was it Darcy? Did he persuade Bingley to break off the engagement because of your lack of fortune?"

"No!" Elizabeth cried, shaking her head. "No, it wasn't Mr. Darcy."

"Was it Miss Darcy, then?" His eyes flashed with rage. "Did she threaten you?"

Again Elizabeth paused, considering him. *Well, that is certainly easier than trying to explain that none of this is real.* "Yes." She looked at him from under her eyelashes. "Yes, she did."

Mr. Wickham left his chair and sank to one knee in front of her. He took her hands from her lap and held them firmly in his. "I do not know what she may have done or said to cause you to destroy your own happiness—but you must believe me when I say that you are ten thousand times the woman Georgiana Darcy is, Elizabeth. Do not even dare to compare yourself with her."

Elizabeth smiled despite herself; she could remember all too well him using those exact words once before. "Thank you, George." She sighed. "But even though Georgiana is clearly a minion of Satan, it doesn't change the fact that I don't deserve a second chance with Mr. Bingley—you don't know how badly I hurt him. He probably despises me now."

Mr. Wickham kissed her hand. "You would never intentionally hurt anyone, Elizabeth. Your description of Georgiana is more than accurate—she merely seeks to devour." He gave her a rueful smile. "It is more than obvious that Charles Bingley's heart is solely in your possession, just as it is obvious that you and he belong together. If you love him, find him. Go to him, wherever that may be, and tell him that you love him." His eyes glistened with repressed tears. "It is a truth universally acknowledged, Miss Elizabeth, that no matter how badly they may hurt us…the ones we love could never cause us to despise them."

He stood. Elizabeth felt her own eyes fill with tears, as well as an overwhelming flood of emotion for the incredible man before her. She placed her arms around his waist and laid her head on his chest as he held her tight. Then she took a step back so she could look him in the eyes. "Where can I find him, George?" she asked.

Mr. Wickham was still holding her arms in his hands as he shook his head in confusion. "What do you mean?"

199

Elizabeth frowned. "Have you not seen him yet?"

He released her and tilted his head in confusion. "Seen him?"

"Yes, he should be here somewhere," she admitted uncomfortably. "He joined the militia."

Mr. Wickham's eyes widened. He stared without speaking for a full minute. Then he gave her a determined look. "I have not seen him, love. But I know how we can determine his whereabouts."

He led her out into the sunshine. They shielded their eyes and waited for a carriage to pass before crossing the street. She followed him to a building guarded by officers, their guns crossed over the threshold. Elizabeth glanced nervously at Mr. Wickham, who merely gave them an effortless smile. "Officer Wickham and Miss Elizabeth Bennet to see the captain."

They removed their weapons and allowed them to pass. Once inside, they were met by a buzz of activity which seemed to stem from one centrally located room, where several men in uniform stood around a mahogany table with weathered maps spread across its surface. At the center of the group, and most distinguishable in his oversized three-cornered hat with a large feather and gold tasseled shoulder cuffs on his scarlet jacket, was the captain. He was significantly older than the other men, with white hair pulled back in a ribbon at the base of his neck and many wrinkles on his wizened but handsome face. When he looked up and saw Elizabeth standing in the doorway his tense features relaxed. He waved his hand dismissively at the rest of the men, and they promptly filed past her and out of the room.

"May I help you, miss?" he inquired. His voice was assertive but kind.

Elizabeth looked questioningly at Mr. Wickham. She had no idea if or how she should address a captain in the English militia.

"This is Miss Elizabeth Bennet, Captain Langley," Mr. Wickham began after bowing. "She is seeking a gentleman she believes may have joined the regiment here at Meryton recently."

"What is his surname, Miss Bennet?"

Elizabeth stepped forward, her desire for answers overcoming her fear. "Bingley," she answered. "His name is Charles Bingley."

The captain placed a finger to his lips. "Bingley." His face lit up in recognition. "Ah, yes! Mr. Bingley joined as an officer here in Meryton several weeks past. However, considering his elevated rank I decided to relocate him to the regime of the Duke of Wellington, who was more than willing to accept him as an officer in the British army."

Elizabeth cast an uneasy glance at Mr. Wickham, who met her gaze, then dropped his head and exhaled deeply. She looked back at the captain. "Please, sir," her voice quavered. "Where is the Duke of Wellington's regime?"

"Spain."

A cold rush raced through her core to her extremities. She instinctively locked her knees—realizing too late it was a grave mistake as the room began to fade into darkness. She grabbed Mr. Wickham's hand. "George," she whispered, before collapsing into his arms.

"Lizzie?"

Elizabeth's eyes flew open. She could see nothing in the pitch black surrounding her on all sides. Then she felt the hood that completely covered her face lift away. Her frizzy hair fell like curtains, obscuring her view, so she blew it out of the way and looked up. Jane was standing over her, with one hand on her hip and a severe look in her eyes. She tried to move, but her brain was too fuzzy to send the signal out to her arms and legs. "Jane?" Lifting her head slightly, she squeezed her eyes shut to prevent them from being pushed straight out of her skull. "Ohhhh," she groaned.

"Please, take your time."

She managed to pull her hands up beneath her torso in order to push herself to an upright position. She attempted to swallow, but her mouth was as dry as the Sahara, and twice as hot. The jackhammer on her temple refused to cease its drilling. "Where am I?" she croaked.

A voice beside her suddenly cried out, "Release the kraken!" Startled, she jerked her head to see Millie's foot inches from her face. She was sprawled, spread-eagled and upside down next to her, apparently talking in her sleep as she was already back to snoring heavily. She was also still wearing her black Hogwarts robes, though hers had twisted round to cover her from the front, the hood on backward over her face.

Elizabeth followed Jane to the kitchen, stumbling several times along the way. She pulled herself onto a stool, and, pushing the empty popcorn bowls and bottle of vodka aside, laid her cheek down on the cool tile of the counter. A few seconds later, Jane set a mug of coffee down in front of her and sat on the other stool. Elizabeth could sense, by the fact that she still hadn't spoken aloud since they left the bedroom, her sister was not in the mood for pleasantries. She stole a hesitant look in her direction; yep, that was not a face of someone simply stopping by for a friendly cup of coffee and a chat. She waited a tension-filled moment, then cleared her throat. "How did you get in?"

"I still have a key."

"Jane, I—" Elizabeth began.

"Lizzie, why on earth would you do something like that?"

Angry tears welled up in Jane's eyes. Elizabeth was momentarily stunned into silence. What could she have done to make her so upset? "Something like what, Jane?"

Jane shook her head. "You know damn well the doctor said you shouldn't drink alcohol—why would you deliberately do something you know could make you sick? You were so good about it the entire time you stayed with me! Then you move out, and the very first thing you do is get smashed with my fiancés little sister?!" She sniffed. "You were supposed to be an example for her of what an adult looks like!"

Elizabeth gave her a sheepish smile. "Well, I told you I wasn't a paragon of maturity, didn't I?"

"It's not funny, Lizzie!" Jane shouted. Tears were now streaming freely down her cheeks. Her hands trembled around her mug. "You don't know what I've been through this past year! I had to watch you lie unconscious in a hospital bed for over a month, with half your body covered in plaster! You were clinically dead for two minutes when they performed the surgery to remove your kidney! Your brain started bleeding, and they had to drill a hole in your skull to remove it, so you wouldn't have permanent brain damage! I didn't sleep for weeks, because I was too afraid that if I closed my eyes, you would die and I would never see you again—that I would never again hear your contagious laugh, or see your eyes light up when you get excited about something. You are so worried about your imperfections causing people unhappiness, that you completely overlook the fact that it is *you* who make the people who love you happy, imperfections and all! My unhappiness—and *Charlie's* unhappiness—could only be caused by the misery of a life without you in it!" She paused, too overcome with emotion to continue. After a few minutes, she added in a quiet voice, "I thought I was going to lose you, Lizzie, I really did." She met her sister's gaze. "And now, after everything that has happened, and how deeply it has affected you, I have just felt so incredibly helpless. I don't know how I can make things better for you, but I refuse to sit back and allow you to get sick again because you don't value the joy you bring to the lives of everyone who knows you."

Elizabeth set down her mug and wrapped her arms around her sister. She wiped her saturated cheeks with her palms. "Jane," she whispered. "I am so sorry. I have been so selfish, you're right." She sighed. "I've spent way too much time lately wallowing in self-pity, yet somehow believing I'm being selfless by pushing everyone I love away. I know if the situation were reversed, and you were the one with the uncertain future, I would want nothing more than to be included in it. In fact, there is nothing you could do to keep me from being with you."

Jane kissed Elizabeth's forehead. "Just promise me you won't drink like that again, that's all I'm asking." She leaned back and gave her a small smile. "Not that I don't love hearing that—I really do—but I'm your sister. You couldn't push me away if you tried."

Elizabeth smiled, then made a face. "I'd be afraid to try after today, anyway—you are *terrifying* when you're mad."

Jane held back a grin. "This is true." Her face became serious. "Lizzie, the things you just said..."

"Yeah?"

"Do you think maybe they were meant for someone else?" she asked hopefully.

Elizabeth dropped her gaze to her mug and smiled. Then she looked back up at Jane, a penitent look on her face. "I should call him, shouldn't I?"

Jane's eyes lit up and she grinned. "I think so." She tousled her sister's frizzy hair. "After you charge your mobile. It's dead. I tried to call you like five times this morning. I thought maybe you had just forgotten about meeting me at the florist."

"The florist!" Elizabeth smacked her forehead. "Jane, I am so, so sorry!"

"It's all right," Jane said brightly. "When I couldn't reach you I called Andie. She was more than happy to come."

"Andie?" Elizabeth frowned. "Oh."

"Anyway," she continued, "I have to get going. I am headed to the bakery to pick up the cake samples."

"I'll go!" Elizabeth cried eagerly.

A muffled voice from the bedroom snorted loudly, then called out, "Go! And may the force be with you!"

"Are you sure?" Jane asked. "It would be a huge help, actually, if you're really feeling up to it. I have so many other errands to run."

"I don't mind!" Elizabeth hopped down from her stool. "I'll go now!"

Jane eyed her ensemble warily. Her bunny pajama pants and slippers clashed horrible with her black Hogwarts robes. "You might want to change first," she offered with a wink.

An hour later, Elizabeth was on her way to the bakery. She buttoned her red trench coat against the bitter December air and pulled her white scarf up higher on her neck. As she entered, she paused for a second and allowed the warmth and the sweet smell of baked goods to permeate her lungs. She navigated her way through the crowd of people waiting to be seated at the café, admiring the Christmas decorations along the way, and walked up to the counter. Once she inquired about the cake samples, she waited while the clerk left to retrieve them.

She leaned against the glass display case, purposefully avoiding the wonderland of sugar and carbs within, and smiled as she recalled her earlier conversation with Jane. It was not at all surprising her sister would be the one to make her realize how foolish she had been, and how selfish. She had no right to determine Charlie's happiness for him—only he could decide what made him happy. And if Jane's words were true, it was simply being with her that made him happy, not whether she was a perfect physical specimen. He loved her, and he wanted to spend the rest of his life with her. She had been incredibly obtuse to think for even a minute he could ever have any misgivings about their relationship.

She decided to call Charlie as soon as she finished her errand and ask him to meet her somewhere, so she could apologize to him for trying to protect him by shutting him out of her life.

Maybe we could even meet here, at the bakery.

Her eyes roamed the room, admiring the various pairings of people enjoying a late breakfast. There were several couples laughing and talking; the sight sent a shockwave of longing through Elizabeth's chest. She missed Charlie so badly, she could almost imagine that the man sitting across the room with his back to her was him. He had the same blond hair with the hard part, wore the same sweater with the patches on the elbows that was his favorite, and even held his mug of tea the same way, with his pinky finger outside the handle...

Her heart gave a lurch—it *was* Charlie! She watched as he set down his mug and pulled out a pair of glasses (*Glasses? When did he get glasses?*). He picked up what appeared to be a magazine with one hand and bowed his head as he began to read. Elizabeth's heart gave another lurch as she recognized the face of the person sitting directly across from him, who had reached out to take his free hand lying on the table and was carefully watching him with a provocative gleam in her dark brown eyes.

It was Andie.

Chapter Eighteen

lizabeth watched in horror as Andie's eyes drifted slowly upward and locked onto hers. She saw shock register in her expression before frantically spinning around and mentally imploring one of the employees to give her the bag of cake samples so she could make a run for it. No one seemed to notice her, however, and with her heart palpitating she stole a furtive glance over one shoulder. Much to her dismay, Andie was walking over to her with a poised smile. With a jerk of her head back to their table, she saw Charlie still seated, seemingly unaware of her presence.

"Lizzie?" Andie whispered as she approached. "What are you doing here?" She reached out to give Elizabeth a hug.

Elizabeth stiffened. She took a step back to avoid Andie's embrace. She could feel rage boil up inside her as her brain quickly eliminated the very few possible scenarios where Andie was innocent. She glared at her. It was uncanny, really, the resemblance she bore to Georgiana Darcy; they both had the same back-stabbing look in their eyes. "A better question, Andie…is what are *you* doing here?" Her voice came out low and dangerous. "With Charlie?"

"Lizzie…" Andie sighed. She gave Elizabeth a pitying look. After a moment she admitted shamelessly, "We're on a date."

Elizabeth felt a wave of nausea wash over her. "A date?"

Andie glanced back at Charlie, who still had not looked up from his magazine. "Yes, a date." She looked back at Elizabeth. "When I saw him at Jane's engagement dinner, I fell for him all over again. I realized immediately I made a huge mistake when I ended things with him. You have no idea how much it hurt me to see him with you—to watch the two of you get engaged, then find out you were pregnant—yet still have to act as though I was happy for you." She smirked. "I can't even tell you how excited I was to hear you broke up with him. I did feel a little bit bad that you lost the baby, but it does make things so much easier—him not being stuck with the burden of helping to raise a kid."

Elizabeth's mouth gaped open in disbelief. She tried to speak, but the lump in her throat had returned with vengeance as she listened to Andie's words. She swallowed against it, feeling her eyes begin to sting. "He loves me, Andie. I know he does." She met her gaze with determination. "Just because he agreed to go on one date with you doesn't mean he wants to be with you."

"Oh, you poor darling." Andie placed her hand on Elizabeth's shoulder. "*He's* the one who called *me*."

"What?" The noise of the room faded. Elizabeth clutched the edge of the display case for support; she would not pass out.

"Yes." Andie's eyes were triumphant. "He needed someone to talk to, someone he has history with. You broke his heart, Lizzie, and I'm here to pick up the pieces. He met me first, remember? Years before he met you. If we had stayed together, I have no doubt in my mind we would be married for years by now, because I would have quelled all of his doubts about marriage. I can make him happy. I can give him everything he deserves, unlike you. You said yourself that he deserves someone whole, someone who can give him children. I told you that everything was going to work out the way it was supposed to in the end—and this is what is supposed to happen. He told me he is ready to move on, ready to give us another chance. If you really cared about him, you would let him go." She patted her shoulder patronizingly. "Why don't you try to move on, too? I can set you up with someone, if you'd like. Someone who doesn't care about ever having kids."

At that moment, a voice behind the counter called out, "Elizabeth Baker?" Elizabeth turned to grab the bag from the clerk. She stepped past Andie without another word and headed for the door. She heard Charlie call out, "Elle?" and stopped in her tracks to see him rising from his chair, an astonished look on his face. Panic welled up inside her. She couldn't talk to him after what Andie just said. She pivoted on the spot and collided roughly with someone carrying a tray of pie slices. Cringing, she looked down to see her trench coat covered in whipped cream and assorted fillings. A hush fell over the room as heads swiveled to stare at her.

She glanced up in time to see Charlie walking briskly toward her. "Elle, are you all right?"

As she furiously blinked to clear her vision, she allowed herself one last look into his eyes. Gathering up the remains of her dignity, she muttered, "I have to go," and exited through the door and out onto the street, where she promptly burst into tears.

When she arrived back at the flat it was empty. She made a beeline for the bathroom, where she peeled off her coat and threw it in a heap onto the floor. She plugged the drain of the tub and turned on the tap, watching as steaming water slowly rose higher and higher. Grabbing the bag of lavender Epsom salt in the closet, she carefully sprinkled a small amount into the water, then turned the bag upside down and dumped the entire contents into the tub. The calming scent filled the air. She undressed and stepped into the scalding water, allowing the searing pain to distract her from her even more painful thoughts. Once her skin adjusted to the temperature, she sank down to chin-level in the water and closed her eyes.

The scene at the bakery replayed over and over in her mind. She felt betrayed—not so much by Andie, who she had a sneaking suspicion after their conversation at the hospital would turn out to be evil—but by Charlie. He called Andie to ask her on a date? He told her he was ready to move on? It seemed impossible, considering his last words to her before he left the hospital, and yet she had seen the proof with her own eyes. Taking a deep breath, she held it and submerged beneath the surface. The water blocked out all sound except for the beating of her own heart in her ears. When she ran out of air she grasped the sides and pulled herself up, sloshing water over the side of the tub and onto the floor. She scrambled to save her phone from the encroaching stream, noticing as she picked it up she had six missed calls in the last hour. All from Charlie.

A week passed by uneventfully. Elizabeth stayed indoors as much as possible to avoid the holiday festivities, that in years past she couldn't get enough of, but now felt shallow and meaningless. She couldn't see the point of buying a Christmas tree and decorating it—a favorite pastime since she was a little girl and her father would hold her high on his shoulders so she could place the star at the top. She couldn't muster the energy to shop for presents, and instead ordered them online and had them delivered to her door. She made no plans for Christmas Eve or Christmas Day; though Jane insisted at the very least she join her, Will, and Millie at their aunt's flat for Christmas dinner, along with Will's parents.

Jane had been more than sympathetic when Elizabeth recounted what happened at the bakery, though she neglected to tell her it was Andie who Charlie was with. Having to confess to her sister that her friend and bridesmaid was now dating Charlie was like salt in an open wound, and would cause major problems with the wedding. Jane was already stressed to the max with the planning, the last thing she needed was to deal with a disgruntled wedding party. Elizabeth would just have to avoid Andie at all costs (with the exception of vital events), until the wedding was over. Then she would never have to see her again.

"Well, I'm off."

Elizabeth sat up straight in her armchair, setting her laptop down on the table beside her. "Have fun, Millie."

"You're still coming tomorrow, right?" Millie asked, taking a seat in the chair next to her and pulling her *Dr. Who* beanie low over her blonde head.

"I'm planning on it, as long as I don't have to work." Elizabeth avoided her hopeful gaze.

"It's Christmas Eve, Lizzie!" Millie cried exasperatedly. "For God's sake—take a break from work for one bloody day! It will still be there when you get back!" She wrapped her matching scarf several times around her neck and over half of her face. "Mmm mmmm mmm mmmm mmmm mm mmmmmmm?"

"What?"

Millie pulled the scarf down. "I said, why don't you come with me tonight? We will have fun! I can make some butterbeer," she added enticingly.

Elizabeth smiled, thinking of Jane's inevitable reaction to their drinking together again. "That's all right, Millie. I have to finish this article, anyway." She squeezed Millie's hand fondly. "Drink some butterbeer for me, though."

"I will." Millie grabbed her overnight bag and headed to the door. "See you tomorrow, Lizzie. Happy early Christmas."

Elizabeth smiled. "Happy Christmas, Millie." She watched the door close behind her, then settled back down with her laptop. A few minutes later, she nearly jumped out of her skin as something thudded against the window behind her head. She rose from her chair and frowned at what appeared to be a snowball splattered against the glass.

Looking down at the sidewalk, she saw Millie grinning broadly. "It's snowing!" she shouted excitedly, waving her arms around in a circle at the swiftly falling flakes.

Elizabeth gave her a thumbs-up and watched her climb into a taxi and pull away. She continued to gaze admiringly at the snow, thinking to herself that the enormous flakes resembled cotton balls against the twilit sky. The metaphor reminded her of the night of her car accident, when she had a similar thought right before the slick road caused her to crash into Charlie's car and into a ditch. Shuddering, she pulled the curtains closed.

Ten minutes later, there was a knock at the door. Elizabeth rolled her eyes, wondering what Millie could have possibly forgotten. *Probably to kiss her cardboard cutout goodbye.* She held back a laugh as she pictured Millie making out with it. On her way to the door, she grabbed a blanket from the back of the sofa and wrapped it around her shoulders. "Coming, Millie!" she called, and threw open the door. She gasped.

Charlie stood on the threshold, the lapels of his navy pea coat pulled up around his neck and a dusting of snowflakes in his attractively messy hair. In his arms he held Bingley, their cat. "Elle," he began desperately. "I'm sorry to intrude, but you won't answer your phone, and I had to see you." He held out the cat, and instinctively she reached out and took him from his arms. He immediately began purring furiously and rubbing his nose against Elizabeth's cheek.

Wordlessly, she gestured for him to enter, feeling self-conscious in her pajamas and blanket. He followed her to the sofa, where they both sat uncomfortably on the edge of the cushion. Bingley took turns kneading each of their laps and purring like a motor boat while they stared at each other in silence. Finally, Charlie cleared his throat. "Elle, the day at the bakery—"

"Charlie, it's all right!" Elizabeth cried. She couldn't hear him give an explanation for why he was dating Andie—it would be too much for her to bear. "I know why you were there."

"You do?" Charlie looked embarrassed.

"Yes, Andie told me." Elizabeth dropped her gaze to her lap, where Bingley was curled up in a ball of contentment. She began to stroke him absentmindedly. "She said you called her." Without glancing up, she added, "Did you?"

"I did," Charlie admitted quietly.

They sat in silence again for what seemed to Elizabeth an agonizing length of time. She looked at him just in time to see him open his mouth once more, and, terrified of what he was about to say, blurted out, "So, it's settled, then."

"What's settled?" he asked.

"Both of us moving on." She forced herself to meet his gaze. She thought she saw pain in his eyes, and the irony that he should be the one injured by his own words only furthered her resolve. "We should probably move on."

"Elle, I wasn't—"

"Charlie, please don't!" she begged, her voice shaking. "Please don't make an excuse! I saw what you were doing with my own eyes!" She took a few deep breaths and looked up at him. He was gaping at her as though she had struck him across the face. "I really can't talk about it anymore. I just. It hurts too much." She stood, picking up the cat and offering him to Charlie. "Please, just leave."

Charlie stood slowly, tears glistening in his eyes. "You should keep him," he whispered. "He misses you." He walked over to the door. She followed, watching as he opened it and then hesitated. "I never meant to hurt you, Elle." The tears fell from his eyelashes onto his cheeks. "I'm so sorry if I did." He turned back reluctantly and walked into the hallway.

Elizabeth stood facing the open door, her mind racing. She wanted to be angry with him, but the only emotion she felt as she stared at the empty space he had occupied only seconds before was fear. Fear that she would never see him again. Fear that the last memory he would have of her was of her telling him to leave. She couldn't let her hurtful words be the last thing he heard her say to him. After all, he may have broken her heart—but she had broken his first, so badly she would not be the least bit surprised if he hated her for it.

No matter how badly they may hurt us...the ones we love could never cause us to despise them.

He didn't despise her, therefore he must still love her in some way, even if he had moved on with someone new. And she knew without a doubt she would continue to love him, no matter what he said or did, forever. She had to tell him so. Or, at the very least, she had to let him know she didn't hate him.

She ran out the door of the flat in her bunny slippers, the blanket flying behind her like a cape. When she reached the heavy door to the street she pulled it open and raced down the steps. He had just opened the door to his car when she located him in the diminishing light. "Charlie, wait!" she cried, wishing she hadn't ditched the blanket in the hallway. The snow was coating her hair and eyelashes, and her bare feet were quickly becoming numb inside her slippers. She pulled the sleeves of her thin sweater down over her hands.

He closed the door of his car and walked to meet her as she plodded toward him. "I'm sorry," she said breathlessly, "For what I said."

He noticed her shivering and at once began to remove his coat. He wrapped it around her shoulders and, without thinking, began to rub her arms.

She gave him a small smile. "Thank you."

Charlie's lip curved upward, exposing a dimple. "You're welcome."

Elizabeth allowed herself a moment to simply stare at his features, memorizing them. His brilliantly blue eyes, framed by soft, dark blond lashes and speckled with snowflakes. The kissable little indent above his top lip. The stubble on his jaw. Those devastating dimples that appeared on each pink with cold cheek. He smiled, and the skin surrounding his eyes creased. She traced the lines of his face with her mind, etching them permanently into her memory. The beginnings of wrinkles when he smiled made it almost possible to see what he would look like as a much older man—but with a sting of heartache she realized she would most likely never get the opportunity. The realization was so painful she reacted out of sheer desperation, and stood on tiptoe to kiss him on the lips. They were so warm, and so soft. He kissed her back, just as urgently, as the snow fell gently around them. When they finally parted he nuzzled his nose against hers before drawing his head back to look into her eyes.

She followed the curve of his lip with her fingertip, then held his face in her cold hand. He covered it with his, warming it instantly, and pulled it gently away to plant a kiss on her palm. "Elle, about Andie," he began softly.

She shivered, not from the cold, but from something else entirely. Her name spoken aloud cast a frosty chill over the coziness of the moment, freezing the last heated seconds of passion they would ever have together. She looked sadly up into his eyes, her heart suddenly feeling as icy as they were blue. "Charlie, it's all right." She swallowed the pesky lump in her throat. "I knew when I broke off our engagement I would have to accept the fact that you would eventually find someone else." She didn't want to let him know exactly how much it killed her to see him with someone else; it would be unfair. "It's for the best, really. We both should be with someone who makes us happy, someone who can give us what we deserve. I'll find someone too, I'm sure. Someone who doesn't care about ever having kids. It's true, if you think about it. We were never really meant to be together in the first place. You should have been married for years by now."

He staggered backward as though she had mortally wounded him with her words. "Is that really how you feel?"

No, I really feel like choking out that frigid bitch.

"I have to let you go, Charlie." She sighed. "And you have to do the same." She turned and walked away, leaving him standing alone in the snow.

I hate myself.

Elizabeth went back inside. She found Bingley in the hallway and scooped him up. She walked to the window and watched Charlie climb into his car and pull away from the curb. After sitting in the armchair despondently for over an hour she retreated to her bedroom, where she pulled the covers up to her chin and counted down the minutes to midnight on her alarm clock. Then she kept counting. Each hour came and went, until the sun had fully risen and she still hadn't slept.

It was late morning when Elizabeth heard a knock at the door mid-sip on Millie's Gryffindor mug. She startled, spilling coffee onto her shirt. What if it were Charlie? She hesitated, then realized he had no reason to ever return after the previous evening. She opened the door.

Carol singers stood in the hallway, their old-fashioned costumes causing Elizabeth's heart to skip a beat. Without warning, they commenced with "God Rest Ye Merry Gentlemen" in harmonized vibrato, smiling excessively at the end of each line. Elizabeth watched politely, all the while wishing they would stop and move on to the next door. After five verses they finally paused for breath, but before Elizabeth could even open her mouth to thank them, they launched unabated into "Good King Wenceslas."

Her phone began to vibrate in her hand, and for once she was thrilled to see her mother's number on the screen. She mimed an apology, holding up her ringing phone, and closed the door in the middle of the second verse. Then she answered it, waiting for the cursing in the hallway to cease before saying brightly, "Hi, Mom!"

"Merry Christmas, Lizzie!" Her mother's voice sounded strained.

"Oh, right. Merry Christmas, Mom." She sighed. "How are you and Dad?"

"Oh, we are doing all right."

Elizabeth frowned. Something in her mother's lack of enthusiasm felt like a warning signal. "Are you sure?"

"Well, it's your father…"

"Dad?! Is he OK?" Elizabeth's heart plummeted into her stomach.

"Oh! Yes, he is fine," her mom assured her. Elizabeth heaved a sigh of relief as she continued. "He has just not been himself lately, that's all."

"What do you mean?"

"I don't know." Elizabeth could hear her mother's voice waver. "He seems so tired. And he hasn't shoveled the back deck off once since it started snowing in November. You know how much he loves to shovel the back deck. He normally spends hours out there doing it." She sniffed.

"Yes, I do know," Elizabeth replied softly. "Has he been to a doctor?"

"Oh, you know your father," her mother sighed. "He wouldn't go to a doctor unless he were dying. That's how I know he is still all right."

Elizabeth's eyes stung with tears. "Well, please let me know if anything changes. I miss you both so much."

"I will, darling. We miss you too, especially your father. He keeps telling me he is worried that you are unhappy, which I assure him is nonsense considering you have a wonderful job and an absolutely dream-worthy boyfriend. I am just so proud of both of my daughters for finding such amazing young men to spend their lives with. It is a gift even more meaningful to me than the photo album you sent us, which I cannot wait to fill with pictures of my hopefully not-so-distant-future grandchildren!"

Elizabeth stared numbly at the wall, tears now falling freely onto her stained shirt. When she didn't reply, her mother continued.

"I should probably go, sweetie. I still have to give your sister a ring. I will see you both soon—March will be here before we know it! And I'm sure we will be returning sooner rather than later for another wedding! Merry Christmas, my love! Give Charlie a kiss from me!"

Elizabeth could tell from her excited tone her mother was grinning. She couldn't bear to end the conversation on a disappointing note by confessing the truth. "Merry Christmas, Mom. Give my love to Dad."

She hung up.

When she arrived at her aunts' flat for Christmas dinner, she looked only a little better than she felt. She greeted Jane, Will, and Millie, and politely shook Mr. and Mrs. Davis's hands as she was introduced. They were like reverse images of their children; Mrs. Davis was tall and lean, with Will's dark hair, green eyes, and perfectly arched eyebrows, while Mr. Davis resembled Millie, though his hair had changed from blond to snow white. Though they both had pleasant smiles, Mrs. Davis was similar to Will in her natural reserve and dry sense of humor that bordered on sarcasm. Mr. Davis's personality mirrored his daughter's; they both had an easygoing nature and an ability to put people at ease, not to mention make them laugh.

Elizabeth headed down the hallway to find her aunts. On her way she nearly ran into two young girls staring down at their phones, and gasped as she saw their faces. She had almost forgotten that Aunt Tessa's boyfriend had two daughters, who had manifested during her coma as Lydia and Kitty Bennet! She uttered a stunned apology and watched them pass by without as much as a glance in her direction. The daughter of Aunt Bridget's boyfriend sat at the upright piano in the wide hallway, playing a Christmas carol with a solemn expression. *Mary!* She smiled before continuing on to the kitchen and felt a warmth in her chest as she saw her Aunt Tessa and Aunt Bridget arguing over the thickness of the gravy. Her eyes welled up with tears, but she managed to give both of them a convincing smile as they took turns smothering her with hugs and kisses.

"Darling, you look as though you haven't slept in days!" Aunt Tessa cried as she inspected her niece's bloodshot eyes. "That is exactly the problem with these modern-day work from home jobs—they never allow you to take a break! You'll work yourself to death, Lizzie darling!"

Elizabeth gave her a small smile. "I'm fine, Aunt Tessa, really." She watched her remove an apple pie from the oven and felt a hand on her arm. Turning her head, she saw her Aunt Bridget giving her a look of concern.

"Jane told us about Charlie, Lizzie," she whispered sadly. "I am just so sorry." She pulled Elizabeth in for a hug, her red bob tickling her nose. She held her at arm's length and smiled ruefully. "You will find someone Lizzie, someone much better suited for you, I promise you." Her voice sounded confident, though her eyes betrayed her; it was more than obvious she thought Charlie had been perfectly suited for her.

Elizabeth forced a fake smile in reply, wondering just how much Jane had told their aunts. As Aunt Bridget kissed her cheek and left the room she felt relieved; if she had known about the miscarriage she definitely would have mentioned it.

As she looked around the table at dinner, Elizabeth couldn't help but smile as she watched her aunts laughing and talking with their boyfriends. Though they had each confessed to having longstanding beaus while Elizabeth was in the hospital following her car accident, they decided not to move out of the flat they shared since they were young women. They had gotten so accustomed to one another's presence over the years, it would be far too difficult to separate at this stage of their lives. Both men had their own homes and grown children of their own, but as she observed them she couldn't help but think they looked like one big happy family. Her eyes met Jane's, and they both smiled; their sweet aunts deserved every bit of happiness they had found for themselves, considering what they had both been through with Aunt Tessa's battle with cancer ten years prior.

When dinner was over, Millie brought out the Christmas crackers, and they had a blast exploding them to see what was inside. They wore their paper hats and crowns while eating dessert. Aunt Tessa insisted everyone try the Christmas pudding she had made from scratch, while Aunt Bridget argued her mincemeat pie was not to be missed. No one touched the forlorn fruitcake that sat like a log in the center of the table, but everyone found a two pence in their pudding.

They opened presents around the Christmas tree, taking turns so everyone had a chance to be properly embarrassed by their gifts. Jane nearly fell off her chair in a fit of giggles as Will opened a swimsuit from Millie that was covered with Harry Potter's face. He had his turn to laugh, however, when Jane held up in front of everyone a set of pink furry handcuffs from Elizabeth that she had strategically wrapped in a gift box from Harrods.

It was the most blissful evening Elizabeth had spent in recent memory. When she climbed into her own bed back at the flat well after midnight, she felt completely exhausted, but nearly perfectly content. There was only one thing missing, one person, who would have made her happiness complete.

Chapter Nineteen

*M*orning came. Elizabeth heard birds trilling outside the window. Without opening her eyes she squeezed them shut and pulled the blanket over her head. She knew instantly what the sound of birds trilling meant; her lack of sleep and subsequent exhaustion had caused her to dream once more. She had absolutely no desire to find out what had occurred in her subconscious since she discovered Mr. Bingley had been sent to Spain. Surely everyone must hate her for provoking him to join the militia in the first place. Especially—

"Lizzie!" a voice cried from behind the closed door of her Longbourn bedroom. "A letter from Miss Bingley!"

Especially Caroline.

She cringed as the door burst open and Lydia and Kitty flew into the room, followed by a sullen Mary. They waved an envelope around her face as it emerged from the covers. "The messenger says you are to open it at once!" Lydia implored. "It is urgent!"

Elizabeth pulled the blanket back over her head. "You can open it, Lydia."

She heard the envelope being ripped open, followed by a tense moment of silence. "She bids you come to Netherfield at once!" she heard Kitty cry suddenly.

She pushed the blanket off of her and sat up. "Is that all it says?"

"Yes!" Kitty and Lydia looked at each other. Elizabeth watched them engage in a wordless conversation with their eyes.

"Do you suppose he is returning to Netherfield?" Mary contributed.

Elizabeth's eyes widened. Of course! Why else would Caroline ask her to come to Netherfield? She threw the covers off her feet and leaped from the bed. "I'll go as soon as I'm dressed!" She peeked down the front of her chemise at her naked body and turned to look at the others, who had not budged. "Um...can you guys, you know...leave?"

They filed out of the room, leaving Elizabeth to herself. She had become quite adept at dressing alone in Regency wear, though she had given up entirely on the corset since no one was around to tighten the stays. Once she located her trusty breeches and pulled them on beneath her dress, she threw on her stockings and shoes and quickly braided her hair down one side of her neck as there was no sense in wasting more time doing anything fancy. She splashed water from the basin onto her face and ran out of the room.

Just before she left the house through the front door, she noticed her mother sitting alone in a chair by the window, a half-completed cross-stitch on her lap. She was staring in silence out the window at the trees. Elizabeth felt compelled to approach, despite believing she might be the cause of her apparent despondency. She walked slowly toward her. "Mom?"

Mrs. Bennet looked away from the window at her daughter. "Oh! Lizzie," she gasped. "Are you going somewhere?"

Elizabeth frowned at her; something obviously wasn't right. "Um, yes, actually. I received a letter from Car—Miss Bingley, asking me to come to Netherfield at once." She knew she shouldn't say anything, in case she were wrong, but she couldn't bear the sadness in her mother's eyes. "I think Mr. Bingley might be returning home."

"Oh! How wonderful." Her mother looked out the window once more.

Elizabeth followed her gaze and saw a carriage approaching. "Is someone coming?" she asked.

"What?" her mother asked without looking at her. "Oh, yes. I sent for the physician. Mr. Bennet is not well."

"What's wrong?" Elizabeth felt a sense of foreboding.

Mrs. Bennet rose from her chair. She walked to where Elizabeth stood and took her hands in hers. "I am not certain, Lizzie." Her eyes became glassy. "I am placing my faith in God and the physician to restore your father to health. Lord knows what I would do without him." Her face crumpled and she threw her arms around her daughter's neck.

Elizabeth held her, her own eyes brimming with tears. "He will be all right, I know he will." They both looked to the front door, where the butler had opened it to admit the physician. "Do you want me to stay with you?"

"No." Mrs. Bennet patted her hand. "Your father would not want you to see him in a weakened state. He did not even wish me to send for the physician." She gave Elizabeth a small smile. "Go to Netherfield, Lizzie. I pray to God you are right, and our dear Mr. Bingley will soon be returned to us." She left the sitting room to meet the physician in the foyer, leaving Elizabeth alone to debate whether to stay or go.

With regret she left the house and began the three mile walk to Netherfield. Along the way she thought about the scene she had just left. Her mother must have been terribly concerned for her father to not have allowed one comment about her severed engagement to Mr. Bingley, or the inevitability of Mr. Collins kicking them out of Longbourn escape her lips. She must be terribly worried about him, then. She saw his face in her mind and felt an aching in her chest for him. She remembered her actual mother telling her that her father would not go see a doctor unless he were dying. If the physician was sent to visit Mr. Bennet, could that mean—?

She shook the terrifying thought from her mind as Netherfield came into view and her heart flip-flopped in her chest. What if she were wrong about Mr. Bingley returning home, and instead he was being sent even farther away? What if he was doing such a good job as a soldier that he was promoted to an even higher rank and didn't *want* to return home? What if he *was* returning home, but he never wanted to see her again after the things she had said to him?

She pushed aside her fears and summoned the courage to knock on the gargantuan front door. Just as she raised her hand, it flew open and a top-hatted man walked through with his head lowered. He nearly collided with her, but stopped short and looked up just in time. Elizabeth drew in her breath and stumbled backward as she found herself staring helplessly into his piercing blue eyes.

"Tom!" Elizabeth cried. She blushed furiously as he gave her a bewildered look. "Mr. Baker."

"Miss Bennet?" Something like apprehension registered in his expression before he bowed deeply. "Forgive me, I was just leaving for Pemberley. I must make haste, there is not a moment to lose." He walked past her, then stopped abruptly and turned. He took a few steps forward and gave her an empathetic glance, his eyes glistening with repressed tears. "I believe Caroline is expecting your presence in the drawing room, Miss Elizabeth." He hesitated, then reached out to take her hand, giving it a squeeze. "I, that is to say, you…" he faltered. His shoulders slumped as he quickly kissed her hand, then walked away without another word.

Elizabeth stood frozen on the threshold, her heart beating wildly. She placed an unsteady hand on the doorframe and gasped for breath, yanking the strings that tied her bonnet loose beneath her chin and whipping it off her head roughly. Everything about Mr. Baker's demeanor suggested what she already knew in her heart to be true—Mr. Bingley was not coming back to Netherfield.

The very last thing she wanted to do at that moment was to see Caroline, but she knew she had to hear it spoken aloud, otherwise she would never be able to believe it for herself. With Herculean effort she forced herself to breathe normally once more. She wiped her eyes with her sleeves and swallowed the lump in her throat, then walked through the open door. The foyer was deadly quiet; the hallway deserted. The absence of life made the house feel as though it had been abandoned, and the notion that it could soon be truth made Elizabeth light-headed. She crept along the hallway until she came to the doorway of the drawing room.

At one end of the sofa, very much alone and holding a handkerchief to her eyes, sat Caroline. She looked tiny from where Elizabeth stood in the doorway, and helpless, like a lost child. Compassion coursed through Elizabeth's veins at the sight of her. She walked quickly and without thinking over to the sofa, her fear suddenly outweighed by guilt. If Mr. Bingley wasn't coming back, if he had decided to stay in the military and pursue his career, it was because of her. She never once paused to consider the effect her actions would have on the lives of Mr. Bingley's family and friends when she broke his heart. In fact, she hadn't even thought about the impact it would have on Mr. Bingley himself; she was too busy trying to be self-righteous. The realization made her nauseous as she approached his obviously crestfallen sister.

"Caroline?" she whispered tentatively.

Caroline looked up. Her eyes were red and glassy, as though she had been crying for hours. She sat stiffly beside her, then placed a hand on her shoulder. Instantly, Caroline dropped the handkerchief and threw her arms around Elizabeth's neck. She burst into heart-wrenching sobs, her entire body shaking from the effort. Elizabeth felt her body tense from the unexpected proximity, then relaxed and held her. She struggled from her vantage point to read the name on the letter sitting in Caroline's lap, but before she could she felt Caroline release her and lean back.

"Miss Elizabeth," she managed through sobs. "I am sorry to have sent you so cryptic a letter, but I did not wish to divulge such distressing news in so detached a manner."

The vice on Elizabeth's heart began to turn, tightening its grip. "What is it, Caroline?" she breathed. "What happened?"

Caroline took Elizabeth's trembling hand from her lap and held it tightly. She took a deep breath. "I was paid a visit by Captain Langley yesterday evening. He informed me that my brother Charles—" she choked on his name and tensed "—my brother Charles is missing in action in Vittoria." She slowly met Elizabeth's terrified gaze. "He is presumed dead."

Chapter Twenty

*W*hen she realized it was Mr. Bingley, her eyes grew round in astonishment. His eyes locked onto hers and his mouth curved upward into a devastating smile. She smiled back at him, realizing that he reminded her of the final scene in the movie version of Pride and Prejudice. As her heart beat rapidly in her chest she knew without a shadow of a doubt this was infinitely better than any movie.

He stopped just before he reached her. "How did you know I would be here?" she asked breathlessly.

He smiled and shrugged his shoulders. "This is a sacred place."

She glanced around her at the canopy of feathery leaves that veiled them from the shadow of night and smiled. "Yes, it is."

He gazed longingly at her for a moment. "Miss Elizabeth, I did not get the chance to speak to you at Pemberley, though I desperately desired to."

Elizabeth dropped her gaze to her feet. "Yes, I really am sorry about that." She glanced up at him from under her eyelashes. "What was it that you wanted to speak to me about?"

Mr. Bingley came closer, hesitating before taking her hands in his. "You are so cold!" he exclaimed. He took off his coat and wrapped it around her shoulders.

"Thank you." Elizabeth *pulled the jacket tightly around her and breathed in deeply the scent of his skin still lingering on the collar.*

"Miss Elizabeth," he began determinedly. *"A good friend of mine came to visit me yesterday. He said I should seek you out—that I should attempt just once more to profess how ardently I admire and love you. Those were his exact words. He believed your feelings may have changed since our departure from Netherfield, and he would not leave until I vowed to declare my love for you a second time. Although I confess, I did not require much convincing."*

Elizabeth felt her cheeks grow warmer. "He sounds like quite the guy, this friend of yours."

"The greatest I have ever known." He smiled.

Elizabeth frowned. "But where did he find you? I went to your house in London, but they said you had left. Where did you go?"

"Netherfield," Mr. Bingley replied.

"Netherfield?" Elizabeth asked. *"Why did you go back there?"*

"Well, you see," he began, brushing a loose tendril of hair away from her face. *"There is a girl that lives nearby…and though she has already refused me once, I am afraid I am still mad for her."*

Elizabeth smiled. Then she remembered Caroline telling her he was probably already engaged. "What about Georgiana?" she asked hesitantly.

"Miss Darcy?" He looked at her inquisitively. *"What about her?"*

"You didn't propose to her?" Elizabeth murmured, staring hard at the ground.

Mr. Bingley put his index finger under her chin and gently lifted it. "Now, Miss Elizabeth," he admonished. "Do you truly believe I could ever desire a mere mortal like Georgiana Darcy, when I am already madly in love with a goddess such as yourself?"

"Well, she does have a pretty face," Elizabeth replied with a small shrug. "I mean, she did..." She gave him a sullen look.

Mr. Bingley placed his hand on the side of her face and slowly ran his thumb across her lower lip. "Have I ever told you how much I love it when you pout like this?" he asked, staring covetously at her mouth.

Elizabeth looked up at him. "You do?"

"Oh, yes," he breathed, taking a step closer. "It makes me want to kiss you so badly."

Elizabeth smiled. "Well," she began slowly, "then I suppose you probably should. Quickly. Before it goes away."

He held her face gently with both hands as he kissed her, his lips warm and soft against hers. She felt shockwaves of pleasure course through her entire body as she melted into his arms. Then she pulled her head back abruptly and squinted up at him. "Wait a minute," she said indignantly. "Do I pout a lot?"

He leaned his forehead against hers and smiled with his eyes still closed. "Not nearly enough," he whispered, and pulled her closer.

"Miss Elizabeth?"

Caroline's blue eyes came back into focus. The soothing evening breeze in Elizabeth's ears diminished into jarring silence. She blinked. "Yes?"

"Did you hear me?" Caroline was holding the letter out in front of her. "This is for you."

Elizabeth held out a trembling hand to take the crisp white envelope with her name written on the outside in Mr. Bingley's familiar scrawl. "How did you get this?" she mumbled weakly.

"It has been in my possession," Caroline answered sadly. "Charles entrusted it to me before he left to join the militia. He beseeched me to present it to you should anything happen to him." Her face crumpled.

Elizabeth stared numbly at the envelope. "What did happen to him, Caroline?" she whispered.

Caroline took several lengthy breaths before she could continue. "Captain Langley gave me an account of the battle, though I did not apprehend much of it. His general, the Marquess of Wellington, divided his army into four columns to attack the French, with Charles amid the third in the south. They crossed a river, where the enemy was waiting for them with fifty canons. They lost eighteen-hundred men." She shuddered. "Charles is thought to have been among them."

Elizabeth closed her eyes against the onslaught of vertigo that overcame her. She waited for it to pass, then opened them again. "I am so sorry, Caroline."

"As am I," Caroline replied. She squeezed Elizabeth's hand. "And not merely for the loss of a dear brother, but also of a sister. For I know, that, given time, that is what you would have undoubtedly become."

The tears that had been repressed until that moment flooded Elizabeth's eyes as she felt the depth of Caroline's sentiment. She gave her a rueful smile; Mr. Bingley would have loved to see the two of them share such a sincere and heartfelt moment. After several moments of mutual silence, she muttered softly, "What will you do now, Caroline? Will you go back to London?"

"No. I will remain here, at Netherfield." She looked around the room. "It is all I have left of Charles."

Elizabeth followed her gaze along the cavernous walls. "Alone?"

Caroline managed a small smile. "No." She looked almost apologetically at Elizabeth. "I have accepted an offer of marriage from Mr. Baker."

Elizabeth's eyes widened. "Tom?" she gasped. "I mean, Mr. Thomas Baker? When did this happen?"

"It has been a fortnight." Caroline's cheeks were pink. "Though I feel ashamed to even mention it at such a sorrowful time."

"Don't be ashamed." Elizabeth smiled. "That is so wonderful, Caroline. I am so happy for you both." She leaned over to give her a quick hug. "Charlie—Charles—would have wanted his little sister to be happy and taken care of," she added firmly, holding back her tears. "And I can think of no one he would have wanted more for the job than his oldest and dearest friend. Tom—Mr. Baker—is absolutely amazing."

"Yes, he is." Caroline gave her a sheepish look. "It seems improbable I could ever have thought anyone else to be better suited for myself."

Elizabeth's stomach turned over as she realized she meant Mr. Darcy. "Caroline," she began uneasily. "Mr. Baker said he was on his way to Pemberley."

Caroline's smiled melted away. "Yes, I bid him go and apprise Mr. Darcy…" She trailed off into painful silence.

"Right." Elizabeth swallowed. Of course Mr. Darcy would need to be informed of the fate of *his* dearest friend. She just wished she could have been the one to tell him. Especially since Jane would be terribly heartbroken and worried for her sister once the news reached her.

Terribly heartbroken and worried.

Their father! Elizabeth had been away from Longbourn too long already; she had to get back so she could see for herself how he was. The physician might still be there, and perhaps by that time he knew what was wrong and how to cure him. She stood quickly, the envelope still firmly in her grasp. "I am so sorry, Caroline, but I have to go. My father is very sick."

Caroline joined her, rising smoothly and placing a warm hand on her arm. "Of course! I am sorry to have called you away from him! He will be in my prayers, Miss Elizabeth." She reached down to her sash and removed the handkerchief, then offered it to Elizabeth. "Please, take this," she insisted. "It belonged to Charles. I know he would want you to have it."

Elizabeth held the handkerchief in her hand, rotating it until she located his embroidered initials, C.B. on the edge. It was the same handkerchief, with the very same initials Charlie used to wipe the mud from her cheeks the day at the lake. "Thank you, Caroline," she whispered softly.

"Please, do come and visit me often, Miss Elizabeth," Caroline pleaded. "I would love the pleasure of your company."

"I will," Elizabeth assured her, thinking to herself that it would never be possible, as she was determined to find a way to end these agonizing dreams. Her heart chided her after one look at the hopeful look in Caroline's eyes, and she sighed. "I promise."

Elizabeth's eyes sprung open as a disembodied voice near her head suddenly began shrieking, "All Aboard," and Ozzy Osbourne's maniacal laugh rang sharply in her ears. She looked around wildly for the source, but there was no one else in her bedroom. Rolling over onto her stomach, she spread her arms through the sheets of her bed in an ungainly breaststroke, sweeping an indignant Bingley from his preferred spot beside her pillow. He hissed at her as her hand finally closed around her phone. "Damn it, Millie!" she shouted, realizing she must have changed her ringtone as a prank at some point the previous evening.

She held it before her bleary eyes and focused on the number. It was her boss, calling from Pennsylvania. With an elevated heart rate she answered it. "Hey, Robb!" she trilled nervously.

"Lizzie! I'm so glad I reached you!" Robb exclaimed. "You're not in bed, are you?"

Where else does he think I could possibly be at five in the morning, the day after Christmas?

236

"I am, Robb." She rubbed her eyes. "Shouldn't you be at (she did some quick math) midnight? How can you possibly be working, anyway?" She smiled. "Today is Boxing Day, mate!"

"Uh-oh," he uttered playfully. "It sounds like you have already lost your Philly drawl, girl. How do you order a cheesesteak? Or do they even have them over there, *across the pond*?"

She cringed at his atrocious attempt at a Cockney accent. "They do, but they are terrible," she replied sadly. "And they look at me like I have three heads when I say whiz instead of cheese."

"Tragic," Robb sighed dramatically. "Well, perhaps I can entice you to come back home and have the real deal again."

Elizabeth sat up. "What do you mean?"

"There's a position opening up I think you might be interested in," he began eagerly. "Stu is finally retiring."

"You mean Stuart Martin, editorial director?" Elizabeth felt her heart skip a beat. "*That's* the position you think I might be interested in?" She bit her lip. *That job pays more than triple my current salary.*

"Absolutely." She could tell from the sound of his voice he was smiling. "You'll have earned it, too, with all the extra hours you've been putting in lately, not to mention your years of editing experience. I don't think anyone at the office works harder than you do, let alone from another country." He laughed. "You must be bored to tears over there. You'll probably be glad to come home, won't you?"

"Come home?"

"Yeah, home to Philly." He paused. "If you accept editorial director, you'll have to move back to Pennsylvania."

Elizabeth's frantically beating heart plunged into her stomach. "Oh."

"There are a few other candidates, but you're my first choice, Lizzie," Robb encouraged her. "I would love it if you'd accept. I think you're a perfect fit for the position."

Elizabeth hesitated. If she moved back to Philadelphia, she would hardly ever see Jane or her aunts.

And I would never see Charlie again.

She squeezed her stinging eyes closed as she remembered the last thing she had said to him before leaving him standing alone in the snow.

I have to let you go, Charlie. And you have to do the same.

Letting him go meant not seeing him again, ever. And even if she did, it would be with Andie at his side.

"I want the job, Robb," she replied decisively. "But there is no possible way I could move back to Philly until after my sister's wedding in March."

"I can work with that!" Robb assured her. "We can just start with the mountain of paperwork you need to go through first, anyway! When is the wedding?"

"March third."

"Can we tentatively say you'll start a week after that, then?" Robb asked.

Elizabeth felt the vice tighten. She took a deep breath. "Yes."

"Excellent!" Robb cried. "Then I'll be the first to congratulate you, Miss Editorial Director!"

"Thank you," Elizabeth replied quietly.

"I'll be in touch soon. Have fun at the boxing match today!" Robb exclaimed before hanging up.

Elizabeth set her phone down on the bed. She lay back and stared at the ceiling.

It was the right thing to do. I need a fresh start.

If it was the right thing to do, then why did it feel like her heart was being crushed slowly? The pain was so intense she had trouble breathing. She got out of bed and began pacing around the room. She looked at the clock—it was only six in the morning, far too early to go anywhere. Crawling back into bed in defeat, she gasped as the choking sensation worsened, the tightening in her chest becoming unbearable.

I'm having an anxiety attack, aren't I? That is what this is!

As she struggled for breath, a wave of nausea hit her hard. She jumped up and ran for the bathroom, making it just in time. Too weak to stand, she sank down along the wall in a heap on the cold tile of the bathroom floor. She held her head in her hands as she rocked back and forth, trying to keep it together as hot tears streamed down her bloodless cheeks.

This can't happen again. I have Jane's wedding to get through. I have to move back to the States and start my new job.

I have to see a doctor.

What seemed like hours later, she was finally able to stand. She returned to her room and climbed weakly back into bed. Feeling around for it without looking, she picked up her phone to call the doctor, then remembered it was a bank holiday. She felt the panic rise up again as she realized she would have to wait till the next day to be seen. Exhausted, she forced her eyes closed and eventually drifted off to sleep.

The sky was bright with stars. Elizabeth could just make out Venus shining brighter than the rest as she laid her head against Mr. Bingley's chest and sighed contentedly. He was sitting at the base of the tree with his arms around her waist, his fingers interwoven with hers. Though she wanted more than anything to simply be with him in that moment, there were still some unanswered questions in her mind. She lifted her head upward and asked, "How did you really know I would be here tonight?"

He smiled. "I had a suspicion." He gazed down at her skeptical eyes and laughed. "That is to say, a suspicion, and a confirmation from Miss Bennet after I went to Longbourn first. Not only did she blame herself entirely for the misunderstanding that caused you to refuse me, she also informed me of the most likely place you might have gone to be alone."

"It wasn't her fault. It was all mine. If I hadn't been so blind to what was right in front of my face I would have seen that it was Mr. Darcy Jane was in love with. And I also would have realized that I was in love with you from the first moment I saw you. Well, the first moment I saw you properly, that is. Fainting sort of puts a damper on love at first sight. When I think of how much more time I could have spent with you..." She hung her head and sighed. As she felt his lips graze the nape of her neck her mouth curved into a

sly smile. "So, how long do you think it will take Jane to wake up and notice that I haven't returned?"

He laughed again. "Perhaps she will think we have eloped."

She raised her eyebrows at him. "Not a bad idea, actually." She smiled. "Although, you haven't asked me to marry you yet." He gave her a look of incredulity and she blushed. "I mean, not tonight, anyway."

Grinning, he brought his mouth down to her ear and whispered, "Miss Elizabeth Bennet...will you marry me?"

"All aboard! Ha, ha, ha, ha!"

Elizabeth grabbed her phone. "What?" she shouted into it. She felt overwhelmingly disoriented.

"Whoa, Lizzie!" Jane teased. "Chill! You should be up by now, anyway!"

"What time is it?"

"It's almost noon." Elizabeth could hear laughter in the background as Jane continued. "I wanted to see if you and Millie would like to meet me at the flat for lunch."

Elizabeth hesitated. "Is it just you?"

"No, Andie and Kassy are with me."

"I can't." Elizabeth thought quickly of an excuse. "I already promised Millie I would watch the second Harry Potter film with her."

"Oh, all right," Jane replied disappointedly. "Just don't let her make butterbeer again." More laughter.

Did Jane tell Andie and Kassy about getting drunk with Millie?!

The thought made Elizabeth angry. "Jane, I have to tell you something," she muttered. "Can you go somewhere private?"

"Sure, hang on." She heard scuffling and footsteps. "OK, I'm in the bathroom. What is it? Is everything all right? Are you feeling sick? I told you not to eat that fruitcake last night!"

"No, it's not that." Elizabeth took a deep breath and told her sister about the promotion.

"Wow," Jane breathed when she finished. "That is an amazing opportunity, Lizzie." She paused. "Is it really what you want?"

"I think so." Elizabeth thought fleetingly of Andie in her sister's flat, laughing at anecdotes of her stupidity. She imagined Charlie and Will there as well, and all of them perfectly happy without her. "Yes, it is."

"Then I am happy for you," Jane replied, in a tone that suggested she was definitely not completely happy for her. "I should go, though. I will call you tomorrow, OK?"

"Sure." Elizabeth looked up and noticed Millie hovering in her doorway, her hair matted on one side. "Talk to you tomorrow." She hung up. "Good morn—afternoon, Millie."

"Did I hear you say you wanted to watch the second Harry Potter film?" Millie asked hopefully.

"Absolutely, I do." Elizabeth gave her a sly smile. "But first, can I borrow your phone for a second?"

The next morning Elizabeth called the hospital to make an appointment with her neurologist. When she mentioned that she thought she might be suffering from anxiety, his secretary suggested she see a psychiatrist instead. She found an open time slot with the hospital's chief psychiatrist for that very afternoon. At three o'clock on the dot, Elizabeth found herself sitting in an exam room wearing a flimsy cotton gown she thought a tad unnecessary, considering the problem was in her mind.

The door opened, and the doctor entered the room. Elizabeth immediately crossed her arms and legs and sat up straight on the table as she stared in disbelief at his smooth mocha skin, dazzling smile, and the nametag on his crisp white jacket that read, Dr. Charu Patel.

Chapter Twenty-One

"*L*izzie!" Dr. Patel exclaimed. "Lovely to see you!' He flashed a charming grin. "It's been a while."

Elizabeth felt torn between a desire to flee the room, and a paralyzing fear of her hospital gown opening in the process and exposing her backside.

Why, oh why, did I have to wear the panties Millie gave me for Christmas with 'Mischief Managed' written on them today, of all days?

"Hey, Dr. Patel," she greeted him breezily, her arms still crossed stiffly across her stomach. "I didn't know you were a psychiatrist."

"Yep." He took a seat on the stool and spun to face her. "I try not to mention it outside of work. Otherwise people wouldn't just be themselves when I'm around, for fear I might be diagnosing them." He smirked. "Don't you just hate it when people pretend to be someone they're not?"

Elizabeth jiggled her foot impatiently. "Yeah."

"That's what I like about you, Lizzie." He stared down at her chart in his lap. "You are never fake—unlike so many others out there."

She took the opportunity while he was looking down to consider him carefully. Could he be referring to Andie? He knew her longer than she did, after all. Perhaps he had known all along she was merely pretending to be Elizabeth's friend.

Dr. Patel eyed her gown. "Would you be more comfortable changing back into your regular clothes? The gowns in here are more for physical exams. You know you didn't have to put one on, right?"

Elizabeth gave an inward eye roll at her own idiocy. "Yes, please."

He left the room. When she was dressed she opened the door for him to reenter.

"So, anyway," he continued. "It says here you are having some issues with anxiety?" He glanced up at her. "Can you elaborate for me?"

She cleared her throat. "I think I might have had an attack yesterday."

"Can you describe the symptoms?"

"My chest hurt. I couldn't breathe." She began to pick at her cuticles. "I threw up."

"Hmmm…" He scratched the stubble along his jaw. "Have you experienced symptoms like that before yesterday?"

"Yes."

"About how long, would you say, have they been occurring? Is there a specific event you can trace the beginning of your symptoms back to?"

She hesitated, thinking. Her anxiety really began the day after her miscarriage and breakup with Charlie, but there was no way on earth she was about to confide in Dr. Patel about any of it. "I hit my head again a couple of months ago. I think that's when it started."

Dr. Patel knit his eyebrows and narrowed his eyes as he scrutinized her face. He appeared to be deciding whether or not to bring up the elephant in the room he knew she was trying to avoid discussing. After a few seconds his features relaxed; he had chosen to humor her. "After hitting your head, did you have any headaches? Loss of memory? Dreams?"

Elizabeth was so grateful he had not mentioned Charlie's name that she blurted out, "Yes! I mean, yes to the loss of memory and the dreams."

"Interesting." He bit the end of his pen. "Can you tell me about the dreams? Are they good dreams, or bad?"

"Both." Elizabeth chewed her lower lip.

Dr. Patel tilted his head, one eyebrow raised as he waited for her to continue.

Elizabeth sighed. She took a deep breath. "When I was in the coma after the car accident, I dreamed that I was…someone else. It felt so real, like I was actually living another life. I became so absorbed in the fantasy that when I woke up I had a hard time disengaging from it." She gave him a shameful look.

"Go on," he encouraged her gently.

"I started to move on with my actual life, recovering and getting back to work—"

"—and being set up on blind dates with stodgy doctors," he quipped, then grinned. "Sorry! I just always wondered what would have happened, had we gotten that second date."

Elizabeth flushed. "About that, I really am so sorry, Dr. Patel." She wrinkled her nose. "I never meant to leave you hanging like that."

He waved his hand. "It's all right, things don't always go the way we plan. That's life for you." He shrugged, then smiled ruefully. "I'm the one who's sorry for interrupting, please go on."

Elizabeth paused a moment to think. "I thought everything was getting back to normal, but then at the stables a horse reared and hit me with its shoe, knocking me unconscious for a moment, and…" She looked up to see Dr. Patel waiting patiently for her to finish. "I saw the man I fell in love with again." She cringed, realizing how crazy she must sound.

Dr. Patel frowned. "Charlie?" he asked softly.

Elizabeth made a face. "No, not Charlie. Someone else." She stole a furtive glance at him. "Someone not real. Someone I met while in the fantasy world."

"Right." Dr. Patel made a note on her chart.

"I sound absolutely crazy, don't I?" Elizabeth muttered sadly.

Dr. Patel looked up at her, compassion in his features. "Of course you don't sound mad, Lizzie. What you are experiencing is perfectly normal." He saw the doubt in her eyes and smiled. "I'm not just saying that, I promise."

"Really?" She gave him a hopeful look.

"Of course." He leaned forward. "There is no real way of knowing what exactly goes on inside a person's brain when they are in a coma, at least not in a psychological sense. However, I myself believe that it is entirely possible for what you described to occur. Unlike typical dreams within normal sleep patterns, the dream you experienced whilst in the coma most likely gave you a heightened sense of reality due to the altered level of conscious state you were in at the time. The places and people you encountered would therefore be as real to you as those in the real world, and the relationships you cultivated, as well as the emotions attached to them, would be indistinguishable to those you make in reality."

Elizabeth struggled to process his words. "So then, is it possible for the people from my coma to resemble people from the real world? To look and sound the same as real people?"

"I don't see why not." He folded his hands together. "We often incorporate our friends and family in our dreams."

"Yes, but what about people I never met before the accident?" she pressed him. "Is it possible for me to have met them first in my coma, as someone else entirely?"

Dr. Patel paused. "I'm not sure, but it is possible you may have regained a level of consciousness at some point when those people were in your hospital room, before slipping back into an unconscious state. Perhaps you heard their voice, and even saw their face—thus creating a persona within your mind before you knew them."

Elizabeth sat in silence, flabbergasted. She had just one more question. "Is it possible to love two separate people at the same time—even if one of them isn't real—if I keep having the dreams?" She dropped her chin in embarrassment.

And even if I can never be with either of them ever again?

"What makes you think they are two separate people?"

Elizabeth jerked her head upward. She gaped at him for a moment while he gazed back at her with confidence. Then he checked his watch.

"Bugger!" He gave her an apologetic look. "I have to get to my next session." He held out his hand to help her hop down from the table and shook it. "I would love to continue our conversation, Lizzie. You can always make another appointment with me, anytime you like." He gave her a bashful smile. "Or maybe we could talk over dinner? I could finally get that second date?"

Elizabeth blushed furiously. "Umm, I don't know, Dr. Patel. I don't think I'm quite ready to date right now. It's just too soon."

"Would you at least think about it?"

Elizabeth smiled. "Sure." She hung her thumbs in the back pockets of her jeans and rocked back and forth on the heels of her Uggs. "Thanks for seeing me, by the way. I actually feel a lot better right now."

"No problem at all. I live to hear my patients say that." He gave her such an endearing look her heart fluttered at the sight. "If you have any more symptoms, though, don't hesitate to give me a call, day or night. I'll give you my card." He pulled it out from the chest pocket of his lab coat, pausing to write something on it. "I can always prescribe you something if you need it." He handed her the card. "That's my personal mobile, by the way—just in case you change your mind about dinner. I know an excellent little bistro we could try."

He escorted her out to the hallway. As she turned to wave at him over her shoulder, he flashed one last devastating grin and winked.

It was then she realized she completely forgot to tell him she was moving back to Pennsylvania.

The next morning, Elizabeth was lounging on the sofa with her laptop, editing an article entitled, "Fifty Desserts that Include Kale," and trying not to be heartsick at the waste of perfectly good desserts. There was a knock at the door. She got up slowly to answer it, wondering who it could possibly be at nine in the morning. Her heart gave a feeble lurch as she imagined Charlie standing there, but shook the ridiculous thought and pulled the door open to find Jane standing on the threshold. Her eyes were swollen and red, and full of fresh tears. Elizabeth felt a cold rush extend to the very tips of her fingers; she knew instantly something was very, *very* wrong. "Jane, what is it?" she whispered in trepidation.

"Mom called me, about an hour ago," Jane managed to mutter between breaths. "She said Dad had a heart attack."

Elizabeth's heart began to pound in her ears. She threw her arms around Jane and hugged her. Then she pulled her by the hand into the room and led her to the sofa, where they both sat. "When did this happen?"

"Yesterday." Jane buried her face in her palms.

"Is he all right?" Elizabeth placed a trembling hand on her sister's knee. "Jane!"

Jane lowered her arms and inhaled deeply. "I think so. He is in the hospital, but—oh, Lizzie—what if he dies?"

"He's not going to die, Jane," Elizabeth reassured her. She ignored the searing pain in her chest as the vice began to tighten once again. "He's going to be fine." She couldn't help but think of her dream, and the unknown fate of Mr. Bennet. "He *has* to be fine."

"I want to go be with him, but I can't," Jane sobbed. "My passport expired six months ago. I should have renewed it, but there was just too much going on at the time, and I forgot, I, I didn't know…"

"It's all right, Jane!" Elizabeth soothed. She squeezed her hand. "I can go! I will look for a flight right now!"

"How can you afford a flight to Philly right now, Lizzie?" Jane shook her head sadly. "Do you even have room on your credit card?"

"I have been working so much overtime lately, that even with the nearly constant pizza deliveries, I have more than enough. Trust me." She gave her sister a weak smile. "Or I can tell Robb I'm coming in to fill out paperwork and have it comped as a business trip. Either way, I'm going."

She pulled her computer into her lap. Miraculously, there was a flight from Heathrow to Philadelphia International Airport that left in three hours. If she threw some clothes in a bag and had Jane drive her to the airport, she could make it in time. "I'll be right back, Jane." She hopped up and headed to her bedroom. In the doorway, she called over her shoulder, "Can you get my passport? It's on the bookshelf, inside the second Harry Potter book." She rolled her eyes at the look of confusion from her sister. "Don't ask—Millie told me the safest place for anything valuable is inside 'the chamber of secrets.' Our San Diego Comic-Con tickets for next summer are in there too—again, don't ask."

She ran to her room to pack, leaving Jane alone in the living room to find the book. She realized she left her phone on the sofa when she thought she heard it ring, but it stopped before she could determine whether the voice she heard yelled out "all aboard," or "passport." When she had everything haphazardly thrown into her suitcase, taking a detour to the bathroom for her makeup and blow-dryer, she reentered the living room. "All set!" she called. "Did my phone ring?"

Jane gave her a sheepish look, her eyes still swollen. "Yes."

Elizabeth frowned. "Was it Mom? Is Dad OK?"

"It wasn't Mom." Jane wrinkled her nose. "It was Charlie, actually."

Elizabeth's heart flip-flopped. "It was? Did you talk to him?"

"Don't worry," Jane said quickly, "I told him you were in a hurry; that you were on your way to the airport for Philly." She bit her lip. "I didn't tell him about Dad, though. I guess I probably should have, huh?"

Elizabeth froze in place, her heart thumping in her chest. Why was Charlie calling her? And why was he calling her *now*?

"Lizzie?" Jane's voice brought her back from her panicked thoughts. "We need to go if you're going to make that flight."

"Right!" She grabbed the handle of her suitcase. "Oh!"

"What is it?"

"Someone needs to make sure Bingley eats while I'm gone. Will you tell Millie to feed him? I don't even know if she's aware he exists. He's spent the last few days lounging between the sheets of my bed." She gazed pleadingly at Jane.

"Sure," Jane muttered, her eyes narrowed.

Elizabeth gave a sigh of relief and followed her out the door and into the hallway. "Lizzie?" she heard Jane ask as they got into the lift.

"Yeah?"

"I know it's really none of my business…" Jane gave her an incensed look. "But who the *hell* is this Bingley bloke?"

Chapter Twenty-Two

raffic was at a mid-morning standstill in London. By the time Elizabeth reached the airport and made it through security, she had to race to make it to her gate. Her flight had already begun to board, so she joined the queue and followed the other passengers down the Jetway onto the plane. She took the first empty aisle seat she could find and kicked her carry-on beneath the seat in front of her.

Feeling the eyes of the person next to her watching her every move, she turned and gave her a polite smile. The woman, whose black hair was suspiciously free of grays despite her being well into her sixties, immediately ceased chewing an enormous wad of gum in order to flash a beauty pageant grin; exposing both sets of fuchsia lipstick tarnished teeth. She continued to watch as Elizabeth leaned over to pull out her phone. Once she lost interest, she looked back down at her tablet and began unsuccessfully attempting to tap the screen with the two-inch, hot-pink talons extended from her fingertips. Elizabeth took a quick peek past her to the woman in the window seat, who had both armrests locked in a death-grip with her eyes closed.

Elizabeth returned to her phone. She sent Jane a quick text to let her know she made it safely onto the plane, and promised to call as soon as she landed in Philly. She noticed she had a new voicemail, and was about to check it when she realized it was Charlie's number. Staring at the screen for several minutes, she finally decided to listen to it. Her finger was poised to type in her password when the stewardess interrupted her.

"Pardon me, dear," she began in a sugary voice that did not match her eyes, which were mutinous. "The captain has asked for all electronic devices to be safely stowed for takeoff."

"Oh! I'm sorry," Elizabeth gasped, and tucked her phone carefully into the front pocket of her carry-on.

The stewardess muttered, "*Thank* you," and moved on to her next victim.

Elizabeth glanced at the woman beside her, who winked and pulled her tablet back out from its hiding place under her shirt and returned to the book she was reading, *Twilight*. Or at least she pretended to read; her eyes seemed to spend far more time scanning the cabin. The woman in the window seat unleashed her grip with one hand and began to frantically cross herself as the plane taxied down the runway. Elizabeth glanced out the window to watch the ascent. As the city of London grew smaller and smaller until it was obscured by clouds, she wondered what it would feel like to be leaving it behind for the last time after the wedding in March. She recalled the last time she was on a plane headed to Philly, only six months prior. With a twinge of pain she remembered Charlie asleep on her shoulder as she watched the city she loved grow increasingly smaller until the clouds veiled it in a blanket of white mist. He was joining her on a trip home to pack all of her belongings, then return to London for what she planned on being a permanent relocation. With a sigh, she realized that if nothing else, everything she had faced since then had taught her not to put her faith in plans, as they almost never worked out the way she hoped they would.

Several hours later, it was the woman next to her who was asleep on her shoulder and breathing heavily in her ear. Elizabeth sat stiffly, unable to move. She saw the tablet on her lap still open to the first page of *Twilight*, and though at first wasn't the slightest bit interested in interspecies love triangles, began to read out of an inability to do anything else. When she finished the page, she carefully lifted her hand and swiped the screen to continue reading.

She had just gotten to the part where Bella realized Edward was a vampire, and was gripped with anticipation against her will as to how she would react, when the woman's gum fell out of her gaping mouth and onto Elizabeth's lap. Her eyes bulged as she stared at it in disgust. What was she supposed to do with it? At that moment, the woman produced a snore so loud she woke herself up, and jerked her head upright. She glanced at Elizabeth in horror, and seeing the gum on her lap, immediately scooped it up and popped it back in her mouth. Then she returned to reading on her tablet, staring in confusion at the page as she had absolutely no clue how she had gotten that far into the story.

When the plane finally landed around three in the afternoon, Elizabeth retrieved her suitcase from baggage claim and headed to the car rentals. The old fear began to rear its ugly head the closer she got to the Alamo sign; it would be the first time she had driven since her accident. At least she was in the states, where the steering wheel was on the left where it was supposed to be. As she waited for the woman behind the counter, whose nametag read "Bitsy," to check for availability since she didn't have time to reserve a car before she left, she texted Jane for the hospital information.

"So it looks like we have two options for you, miss," Bitsy began brightly. "A Dodge Charger, or a Smart car."

"Definitely the Charger," Elizabeth replied firmly, thinking she would never be caught dead in a Smart car.

"Let me just have Martin check and see if it is still here. Sometimes our system is slow to refresh."

Half an hour later, Elizabeth was cramped behind the wheel of the Smart car, her suitcase just fitting in the seat beside her. She drove the hour to where her parents lived in Levittown, pulling in to the hospital's parking garage around five thirty. She rushed to the cardiac floor and found the right room. Just before she opened the door she felt fear bubble up inside her at what awaited her inside; she had never seen her father anything less than his spry, jovial self. And she had certainly never seen him lying in a hospital bed hooked up to medical equipment.

The room was silent except for the humming and beeping of the monitors. Her mother was curled up in a chair near the bed, fast asleep and using her balled-up coat as a pillow. Her missing pearls and absence of pristine makeup told Elizabeth much more about her anxiety level than she could have herself had she been awake. Her mother had not left the house without either for as long as she could remember.

She glanced reluctantly at her father, who was lying in the bed and also appeared asleep. His face was ashen, his chin bore a five-o'clock shadow. His cheeks had a hollow appearance, as if he had lost a considerable amount of weight in a short time. Elizabeth approached him slowly, and as she sat carefully at the foot of the bed he opened his eyes. When he saw it was her, he gave her a slow smile. "Lizzie," he sighed happily.

"Dad." She moved closer and tried not to cry as she took his hand in hers. "How are you feeling?"

"Never better, love." He winked. "Though I could use a stiff drink."

She smiled. It was just like her father to make jokes at such a serious time.

"Where's Janie?" he asked, looking around the room.

"She wanted to come, Dad, she practically climbed into my suitcase." Elizabeth watched him smile at the mental image. "Her passport was expired." She looked up. "Actually, she is probably freaking out waiting for me to call and tell her that I have seen with my own eyes you're all right." She gave his monitor a wary glance. "You *are* going to be all right, aren't you? What did the doctors say?"

"I'm going to be just fine." He pressed the button to elevate his bed so he could sit up. "I just need to lower my cholesterol. And find a way to eliminate the stress they tell me I am suffering from." They both looked over at her mother, who smiled in her sleep, then back at each other. "I told them it would be impossible, considering I am completely mad for her." Her dad gave her another wink and a shameless grin.

Elizabeth bit her lip, trying not to smile. "Well, you better do what they say. You have a very important duty to fulfill in a couple of months, you know."

"That I do."

"Jane is going to be the most beautiful bride ever, Dad. Wait till you see her dress, you are going to be blown away. She is so happy with the way everything is coming together for the wedding," Elizabeth gushed.

Her dad's warm smile faltered. "And what about you, my darling girl?" He gave her hand a squeeze. "How are you feeling?"

Elizabeth frowned. "What do you mean?"

He hesitated. "Jane told me about Charlie."

Her eyes grew wide. "Does Mom know?"

"No," he assured her. "She knew you would rather tell your mother on your own time, but she thought one of us should know what you have been going through." His eyes glistened with tears. "Lizzie, I am so sorry about the baby."

Elizabeth's face crumpled as the tears she had been holding back for several hours flowed freely down her cheeks. "When did Jane tell you everything?"

"She called when you were staying with her. Please don't be angry with your sister, Lizzie. She was just so worried, and didn't know how to help you. She said you were told you could never have another baby because of your health, and that you thought Charlie would be sacrificing his happiness to stay with you. She said you stopped eating and sleeping, that you holed yourself up in a room and worked for days on end, without taking a break." His eyes were full of anguish as they gazed straight into hers.

The vice on her heart was suddenly squeezing it so aggressively Elizabeth was certain she was about to have a heart attack of her own. Her mother was not the stress the doctors had been referring to—the stress that had nearly killed her beloved father—it was *her*. Her, and her hot mess of a life. There had to be something positive she could offer him instead, so he would stop worrying about her and risk another attack. "Speaking of work, they offered me a promotion, Dad—editorial director! I'm going to be moving back to Philly after the wedding!" She gave him a small smile. "I'll be able to help keep your cholesterol in check. No more stiff drinks for you, my friend. I can't drink either, because of my kidney, so we'll be a match made in heaven."

"Lizzie…" her dad began sadly. "You can't move back to Philly."

"Why not?"

"Because you belong in London. You belong with Charlie." He gave her a stern look. "He wants to marry you, you know."

"Dad," Elizabeth muttered. She looked down at their hands. "Charlie is with someone else now. And even if he wasn't, I don't think he wants to get married, ever. He, well, something happened to him in his past that ruined the idea of marriage for him." She returned his gaze with great effort. "I think the only reason he was going to marry me was because of the baby."

Her dad shook his head slowly. "Elizabeth Poppy Baker," he scolded. "Please tell me that is not the reason you ended things with him."

Elizabeth felt slightly taken back. "No, it wasn't! I mean—I guess maybe it could have been a contributing factor, on some level—but I had already resigned myself to the idea that he was only marrying me because he felt like it was the right thing to do."

Her dad sighed. "Lizzie, Charlie asked for my permission to marry you the very first day I met him, back in June."

Elizabeth's breath caught in her chest. "What?"

"He apologized for it being so soon after the two of you met. He said, even at that point, he had no doubt whatsoever that you were the woman he wanted to marry and spend the rest of his life with." He paused. "I don't know who this poor girl is you say he is with, but honestly, I'm just sorry for her. She has no idea how mad he is for you."

His words should have comforted her, but somehow hearing them only made Elizabeth feel even more miserable. She had been completely wrong. Charlie never had misgivings about marriage. He didn't want to marry her merely because he felt it was the right thing to do. In fact, if her dad was telling her the truth, (and it had to be, considering he had never once lied to her), Charlie had known he wanted to marry her only weeks after they first met! And she had ruined everything because of her own stupid fears and insecurities. She had driven him away with her own foolish assumptions, not once, but *twice*. She had driven him right into the arms of someone else, and now there was nothing she could do about it, because she was the one who told him they had to let each other go.

"You should get some rest, Dad." Her voice was strangled. "I'm going to call Jane." She stood and bent down to kiss his cheek. "I'll be back in a few minutes."

He gave her a defeated look and patted her hand. She glanced over at her mother, who was still peacefully sleeping in the chair, then left the room. In the hallway, she buried her face in her hands and cried until she saw someone walking in her direction. Then she hastily wiped her cheeks and walked to the waiting room to call Jane.

Elizabeth spent the rest of the evening with her parents. After much convincing (not only of her fearful mother but also herself as she glanced out the hospital window), Elizabeth drove her home in the freshly falling snow so she could get a solid night's sleep and a decent shower, making a solemn vow to pick her up again first thing in the morning. She then returned to the hospital and took her place in the stiff chair in her father's hospital room, where she managed to sneak in a few hours of sleep between replaying her conversation with him in her head.

The following afternoon she drove back to Philly and checked into a hotel. The next morning she was going to *Flavor* magazine to meet with Robb and fill out paperwork, then ask her friend Juliet Evans, a journalist, out to lunch. The day after that, New Year's Eve, she was going to make a surprise visit to Bryan and James's apartment, and hope they would include her in whatever plans they had for the evening, as she had no desire to ring in yet another year by herself.

She got to bed early, exhausted from lack of sleep, and fell asleep almost as soon as her head hit the pillow. When morning came, she was relieved that she still hadn't had any dreams. Perhaps talking to Dr. Patel had helped after all. She smiled as she remembered the way he had grinned and winked at her as she walked away from him.

In the morning, Elizabeth carefully ironed her favorite pencil skirt and blouse. She took extra time curling her hair and applied more makeup than she normally did. She wanted to make sure she appeared worthy of the editorial director position. She entered the building and took the elevator to the fifth floor, labeled Editing/Journalism, and noticed several women clustered around the expansive front desk. They were bent over what appeared to be a men's magazine, and were chittering like squirrels in a tree. As she grew closer, she recognized them as Tina from marketing, and Erica and Heather from finance. Juliet sat watching them with hawk-eyed scrutiny from her perch on the top of the desk, her expression a mixture of irritation and boredom.

"Damn," Heather was saying. "Can he be any cuter? Look at that smolder!"

"Seriously," Erica agreed. "And look at this picture of him—that smile could melt a glacier!"

"He was so gorgeous in the last movie he was in—you know, the one with what's her name, with the huge boobs?" Tina asked with a disdainful look at the others.

"Ugh. Yeah, Whitney Monroe. I hate her for breaking his heart when they dated a few years back." Heather muttered. "It was like he disappeared off the face of the planet for a while. I don't know what made him realize she wasn't worth the depression, but thank God he finally got over her. And at least now we know they're only acting when they make out, right?"

"Aren't they engaged?" Juliet offered, and they all turned to look at her as if just noticing she was there. She replied with a noncommittal shrug. "I heard they were getting married."

"Who are you guys checking out?" Elizabeth asked as she joined them. She craned her neck to look at the article; a photospread of the popular (*And pretty darn gorgeous, if I do say so myself.*) British actor, Graham McKenzie.

"Lizzie! Oh, my God!" Juliet jumped up and ran around the desk to throw her arms around her. "What are you doing here? You look incredible!"

Elizabeth hugged her back, then released her so she could see her face when she told her the news. "I'm coming back to Philly, Jules!" She decided against telling her about the promotion in front of the others. "I move back in March!"

"That's the best news I have heard in months!" Juliet clasped her hands together and bounced up and down in her heels. "It has been a *very* long year without a comrade in the war against idiocy." She flashed the other women a look of repugnance.

Elizabeth grinned. "I have to go see Robb, but do you want to get lunch? I am dying to catch up!"

"Absolutely!" Juliet cried. "It's not too early for champagne, right?"

"Never! I will come get you when I'm done."

After filling out the necessary paperwork and touring her new office with Robb (*It has a window!*), Elizabeth stopped back at the desk to pick up Juliet. They went to one of their favorite restaurants in the city, a Parisian-style bistro called Parc, and sat by the windows that overlooked the snow-covered fairy land that was Rittenhouse Square. As they sipped champagne (*Just one glass, Jane. I swear.*), Elizabeth filled Juliet in on life in London, leaving out the more personal details such as her car accident, coma, and Charlie. She decided there was plenty of time to mention the fact that she almost died when she returned for good. When Juliet asked if she had ever met anyone famous, Elizabeth choked back the urge to tell her that her flat mate was dating Harry Potter. Instead, she shook her head sadly. "No one! Jane even dragged me to see Colin Firth's house, and even though we stood on the sidewalk for what felt like ten hours, he never even peeked through the curtains."

"Still obsessed with him, then?" Juliet swept her long chestnut bangs away from her doe-eyed baby blues and smirked. "You always loved that *Pride and Prejudice* miniseries."

264

Elizabeth shook her head dismissively. "Now, Jules, you know I prefer the movie version." She smiled. "Although I will say the miniseries is definitely growing on me, especially since it reminds me of Bryan now."

Juliet's cherry red lips formed a perfect 'O.' "That's right! How *is* Bryan? He got married, right?"

"Yep." Elizabeth gave her a small smile. "In England, actually. I was in the wedding. I'm going to surprise him tomorrow with a visit." Imagining the look on Bryan's face when he saw her in Philly made her shiver with anticipation. It had been so long since she had last seen him, at least in real life; she could still very clearly see him sitting across from her in a bright red militia jacket with a glass of whiskey in his hand, telling her to find Mr. Bingley and reassure him of her love.

When Elizabeth awoke the next day and rolled over to check the time on the alarm clock beside the bed, she gasped—it was already early afternoon. After a late night of talking, eating their weight in junk food, and watching a cheesy rom-com with Juliet, the room darkening drapes on the window had done far too adequate a job of tricking her brain into thinking it was still night. She pushed the empty cookie trays off the bed with her bare feet as she got up and trudged to the window, piling her hair on top of her head in a messy bun. Then she threw open the curtains and staggered backward as the glaring sun instantly blinded her.

Once she was showered and dressed for the day, she hopped into her Smart car and entered the address of Bryan and James's apartment into her phone's GPS. With increasing excitement she pulled into the building's parking garage and found an empty spot, noticing with a laugh she only took up half of it when she got out. She entered the lobby and gasped; she had forgotten just how stunning it was. When she got into the elevator, she pushed the button for the penthouse suite, and as the doors opened she was so overwhelmed by the entrance hall she almost forgot to get out. It was filled with more pieces of art along its ivory walls than a museum. Even though she had seen it once before when she was last in Philadelphia, it still held the ability to leave her speechless.

She rang the doorbell and waited, her heart beating fast. The seconds ticked by, and still no one came to the door. She rang it once more with a sense of foreboding. She had not even considered the possibility that they might not be at home. The more she thought about it, the more stupid she felt—of course they weren't home—it was four o'clock on New Year's Eve! They were probably at the first of several parties they would be attending that night. Or even more likely, they weren't even in town!

She waited ten more minutes, wondering if she should just give up and call Bryan. She would be incredibly disappointed to let him know where she was standing at that moment, as she had hoped to make it a surprise. As a compromise, she decided to text, *Hey Bryan! Missing you tons! What are your NYE plans?* As she waited for the reply, she wandered the hallway to admire the paintings and sculptures. Finally, her phone vibrated in her hand.

Missing you too, babe! We are in NYC for New Year's – back home in a few days. Love you, kisses! —Bryan

Tears stung her eyes as she took one last look of longing at the front door. In a few days, she would be back home herself—or at least home for another few months. She wouldn't even get to see him before she left for London. And his brief and uncharacteristically concise reply left her feeling lonelier than before; even her best friend had better things to do than have a conversation with her.

She got back in her car. The drive back to her hotel took well over an hour due to the holiday traffic, as everyone in the city was on their way to ring in the New Year with family and friends. She contemplated just continuing on to the hospital to be with her parents, but with the congestion on the roads and the snow that began to fall, it would be a miracle if she made it in time for midnight.

When she got to her room, she kicked off her heels one at a time and changed back into her pajamas. She piled her hair back on top of her head, then grabbed the pint of Ben and Jerry's ice cream she and Juliet hadn't eaten the night before from the refrigerator. Climbing into bed, she buried herself up to her neck in the blankets and turned on the television. She watched in disbelief as the words *Pride and Prejudice* filled the screen, letting a cry of mirth escape her lips at the sheer irony. She made no effort to change it, however, and eventually became absorbed in the witty banter and sexual tension between Colin Firth and Jennifer Ehle.

The room grew darker and darker around her as evening turned to night, until the soft flicker of the television was the only source of light; it cast a ghostly sheen on everything in the room. Her ice cream container now sat in a chocolate puddle on the nightstand. Elizabeth sniffed. She remembered how lonely she had felt last New Year's Eve, when she had watched the very same miniseries by herself after breaking up with Bryan. At the time, she thought she would be alone for the rest of her life. But that was before she met Charlie, and spent what was easily the best six months of her life with him. Now, one year later, she was right back where she started, feeling even more hopeless when it came to her future.

The red numbers of the clock on the table beside her switched to midnight. Elizabeth ruefully wished that somewhere out there Charlie was staring at the numbers on a clock, missing her as much as she missed him.

Happy New Year, Charlie.

Chapter Twenty-Three

lizabeth spent two more days with her parents before she flew back to London. She helped her father get settled comfortably at home after being discharged, and made sure her mother felt confident enough for her to leave them. On her last day, she considered telling her mother everything her father already knew, but when she looked into her weary eyes she couldn't bring herself to give her more to worry about. Instead, she hugged and kissed them both. With promises to pick them up at Heathrow before the wedding, got in her car for the drive back to the airport.

Just before she pulled away, her father knocked on the window. As she lowered it, he placed his elbows on the door and leaned in. "I just wanted you to know, Lizzie," he began. "Your mother and I will support whichever decision you make with regard to staying in London or moving back to Philly." He kissed her forehead. "But please, don't give up on Charlie because you think he would be sacrificing his happiness to be with you." He smiled. "I once knew a young man just like Charlie, who had been wounded so deeply by a previous relationship he thought he could never love anyone again. Until one day, when he was at the pub, the most beautiful creature he had ever laid eyes on walked in and sat down at the other end of the bar. It was as if electricity surged between them. In that instant he knew, without a shadow of doubt, he simply *had* to marry her, so he could spend every moment by her side for the rest of his days. And when life handed them a curve ball, and she told him they had to say goodbye and move on with their lives separately because he would be sacrificing his happiness to stay with her, he risked everything to prove to her that they belonged together. He never once regretted his decision, not even for a second." He paused. "And do you know why he did that, my darling girl?"

Elizabeth wiped the tears from her eyes with her palms and smiled. "Why, Dad?"

"Because the one thing that made him happier than anyone or anything else on this earth, the one thing that he couldn't live without, the one thing he could live a hundred lifetimes and still never be worthy of—was *her*." He cupped her face in his calloused palm. "I love you, my sweet Lizzie ladybug. I will see you in March."

"I love you too, Dad."

She returned her rental car, thankful to finally be rid of it, and checked her luggage. When she received her ticket, she noticed her flight had assigned seats, and that she had somehow managed to score one by the window. Once she boarded the plane and kicked her carry-on beneath the seat in front of her, she set the copy of *Twilight* she had purchased in one of the airport bookstores (*Only, you know, for the principle of finishing what you start.*) on her lap and looked out the window at the tarmac. A few minutes later, she felt someone take the seat next to her and turned to see an extremely attractive man smiling at her. He dropped his gaze to the book on her lap, and she felt her cheeks blaze; why couldn't she have picked up the copy of *Hamlet* that was right next to it on the shelf instead? She looked back up at him, thinking hard; she knew that smile from somewhere, but where was it?

Sliding the book from her lap to underneath one leg, she curved her lips upward in reply. Then she turned to stare straight ahead at the inflight magazine stashed in the pocket in front of her. Beside it, someone had left behind their copy of a popular men's magazine. She reached for it, and as she pulled it upward her eyes bulged at the photo on the cover—she now knew exactly where she had seen that smile. The handsome face staring back at her was identical to the one currently checking his email on his phone beside her, his elbow grazing hers on the hand rest.

Elizabeth bit her lip. She was on an eight-hour flight with none other than Graham McKenzie, A-list movie star and Britain's most eligible bachelor. Or, at least until recently, when he got engaged to his girlfriend who was also an actor. She casually pulled her book back out and folded the cover to the back so he couldn't see it, pretending to read. After a minute, her eyes flitted sideways to check him out. He was wearing an expensive steel-blue suit; the jacket of which was neatly folded over his carry-on. The buttons of his white dress shirt were under a considerable amount of strain from his impressive pectorals, and a smattering of chest hair peeked out from below the open collar. His square jaw was defined with well-trimmed stubble that continued across his upper lip and in a neat vertical line beneath his pouty bottom lip. He had an amazing head of thick, short-cropped caramel-brown curls that begged to be raked through with one's fingers; Elizabeth couldn't take her eyes away from the single curl that fell enticingly over the side of his forehead. As his gray eyes found hers, she realized in horror she had forgotten to pretend to read and was now gaping at him, her book in a forlorn heap on the floor. She immediately turned into a lobster from the neck up and went back to her book.

About halfway through the flight, Elizabeth finished her book, closing it with a contented sigh. She glanced at Graham, who had his head tipped back and his eyes closed. It wasn't her best idea, but she thought it would be worth it to try and get a selfie with him to show Jane when she got to London. She pulled out her phone and held it up, trying to find the best angle. Concentrating hard, she gasped as she saw his eyes open. He looked straight at the phone in her outstretched hand.

"Come on now, love," he grinned as he sat up. "If you wanted a selfie, you should have just asked!" He placed his arm around her shoulder and pulled her against his chest. He flashed a movie star smile at her phone as her mouth fell open in a comical 'O' of surprise. "Smile, darling!" he prompted, and she blindly obeyed as she snapped the picture.

He released her and leaned back into his own seat, still not looking away from her crimson cheeks. Holding out his hand, he said, "I'm Graham McKenzie, by the way—but I'm assuming you already knew that?" He nodded toward her phone with a smirk.

"Elizabeth Baker," she muttered as she shook his hand. "I'm so sorry. I wanted a picture for my sister, but I should have asked first. I do know who you are, but really only because of…" She showed him the magazine. "I mean, I have seen your films—and they are all wonderful—but if I hadn't just seen you in this photospread at work, I would have thought you were just some randomly gorgeous man." Her eyes grew round and she began to chew her lip.

He laughed. "Where do you work, Elizabeth?"

"I work for *Flavor* magazine. I'm about to become editorial director, actually." Her cheeks now felt like the equivalent of molten lava.

"Really? I'm mad about cooking!" He put a finger to his lips. "I may have actually gotten a few recipes from *Flavor* magazine, come to think of it."

They dove into a lengthy conversation about food, books ("I can't say I'm into vampires and werewolves, myself, but I do love a bit of Shakespeare now and then—have you read *Hamlet*?"), and movies. Elizabeth asked him if he had ever met Daniel Radcliffe, to which he replied he had worked with him recently.

"Did he happen to mention if he had a girlfriend, by any chance?" she asked hopefully. If Graham confirmed he didn't, she could take the mickey out of Millie when she got home.

Graham raised his eyebrows. "I'm hurt, Elizabeth," he breathed, one hand held defensively over his heart. "That you would ask if another celebrity has a girlfriend, after spending nearly eight hours with *me*." He smirked. "This has practically been a date, you know." He gestured to their tray tables, which held empty plastic flutes and packets of peanuts. "We did get to know one another over dinner and drinks, after all."

Elizabeth couldn't think of a witty retort, so she simply grinned back at him in silence.

They continued talking until the plane landed at Heathrow. When they collected their bags, exchanged numbers in order to stay in touch, and said their goodbyes, Graham called over his shoulder as he walked away, "Oh! I just remembered!"

"Yes?" Elizabeth asked, whirling around.

"Daniel Radcliffe," he began, pointing his finger in her direction. "I think he does have a girlfriend. He brought her to the premiere last year.

She's blonde, with blue eyes. But not nearly as beautiful as you, Elizabeth—believe me." He gave her a wink and a grin, then turned and walked away with his suitcase behind him.

When she finally set her suitcase down in the doorway of her flat, she heaved a sigh of relief and felt her way through the darkness to her bedroom, where she didn't even bother to change before collapsing onto her bed and falling asleep.

The next morning, she stumbled out to make coffee, sitting in one of the stools at the counter to wait for it to brew. Millie came into the room, her blonde hair braided on top of her head like a Bavarian milkmaid. She plopped down next to Elizabeth and closed her eyes. "I missed you," she mumbled softly.

"Rough week?" Elizabeth asked, amused.

"Yes." Millie sighed. She opened her blue eyes and focused them on Elizabeth's. "You have no idea what I have been through."

"Please, do tell." Elizabeth tried not to smile at the inevitable list of trivial misfortunes Millie was about to rattle off. Until that point, the worst difficulty her flat mate had faced since they met was having to get a part-time job as a tour guide at Madame Tussauds. She had entertained Elizabeth many an evening with her tales of woe at having to explain to tourists numerous times a day that 1) the wax figures were not the actual, live celebrities who gathered daily for photo ops at the meager cost of $39.95 a ticket 2) the wax figures were not, in fact, anatomically correct, and she was not at liberty to "prove it," and 3) she could neither confirm nor deny the presence of bodily fluids on the faces of the wax figures, although she was now officially an expert in lipstick removal.

"Well," Millie began. "First, I woke up to find you went on holiday, which was highly inconvenient considering you forced me to become addicted to caffeine, and I don't know how to use the coffee machine. I tried, but it was doing my bloody head in, so I gave up and went back to bed. I ended up skiving off work and nearly got sacked."

"Never minding the fact that I left because my dad had a *heart attack*; you could have just made a cup of tea, you know." Elizabeth rolled her eyes.

Millie's mouth gaped open. "Your dad had a heart attack?" She stared at the floor. "I'm so sorry, I didn't know! And to think I saw my brother the next day, and he didn't even bloody mention it! No one tells me anything!"

"It's OK, Millie. Really, he's going to be fine." Elizabeth suddenly felt sick to her stomach as she realized she still had not told Millie about moving back to Philadelphia. For some strange reason, she just couldn't seem to bring herself to mention it now as she watched Millie's reaction. "Go on, what else happened while I was gone?"

"Well, now I feel like I shouldn't even say anything else." Millie sipped her coffee with a shameful look in her eyes. She glanced warily at Elizabeth.

Elizabeth smiled. "Come on, it must be something good." She raised her eyebrows expectantly.

Millie returned her smile. "Oh, it is—wait till you hear this." She took another slow sip to increase the anticipation. "I found a stray cat in our flat! I was in the loo one morning—and it's a good thing I was, because I definitely would have shat myself otherwise—when I heard this strange scratching noise and saw it stick its hands underneath the door. Bloody hell—it was like a horror film!"

Elizabeth laughed. "That was Bingley, Millie. He's my cat." She made a face. "And cats have paws, not hands."

Millie froze, her eyes wide. "It was your cat? Since when do you have a cat?"

"He was Charlie's and mine," Elizabeth mumbled. "He brought him over here on Christmas Eve." She sighed. "I should have told you about him, Millie, I'm sorry. I guess I just got caught up in the holiday, and then I went to the doctor after having an anxiety attack (Millie's eyes boggled)—another thing I should have told you about—and then everything with my dad happened, and I guess with all the chaos, I forgot. I told Jane to tell you to feed him, though. Did she?"

"No," Millie whispered, her voice barely audible. "She never said a word."

"That's OK. I'm sure she was too upset at the time to remember. Thank goodness you found him, though." Elizabeth smiled. "I missed him so much, I can't wait to snuggle him again. Where is he now?"

Millie's face still bore the same shocked expression. Several seconds passed before she managed to mutter, "He's not here anymore, Lizzie. I, I didn't know he belonged to anyone, and I didn't think we were technically allowed to have animals here, so I got rid of him."

Chapter Twenty-Four

*T*he loss of her last connection with Charlie sent Elizabeth headlong into a stupor of apathy for the next few weeks. She returned to working round the clock in an effort to block out her own self-destructive thoughts, as well as the irritatingly blissful, carefree lives that everyone around her clearly lived. Not that she dared allow her unhappiness to show on the outside. Whenever she was around Jane or Millie she managed to act as though she were as excited as they were to talk about wedding bands and guest lists, or *Game of Thrones* fan theories for the new season, respectively.

What she really needed was someone to talk to about her true feelings. As she sat on the sofa one morning, drinking her coffee and staring blindly at the stag head on the opposite wall, she twiddled the business card Dr. Patel had given her between her fingers. She remembered how much better she felt the last time she talked to him. They had not, however, talked about Charlie; Elizabeth felt that he was not something she wanted to talk about with another man, even if that man was a psychiatrist. She could talk to him about her dad, though, and possibly her new position at work and her uneasiness with regard to it.

She gazed at the handwritten mobile number he had added to the bottom of the card. She could call him right now, and ask him to meet her for coffee sometime soon. Of course, that could easily be misconstrued as a date, and Elizabeth did not want to give him the wrong idea. Perhaps Charlie was finding it easy to take her own advice when it came to moving on, but she was struggling with the very idea of finding someone new. At some point, though, she was going to have to give another man a chance—and why not Dr. Patel? He was cute, charming, and seemed to genuinely like her. She thought for a moment. If she had never received the flowers and letter from Charlie the night of their blind date, she probably would have said yes to second date. If she never met Charlie at the pub, would she still be dating Dr. Patel now? He was Will's best friend, after all; it would make sense for her to be with someone she inevitably would see a lot of anyway.

Oh, right.

But then again, probably not, since she was moving back to the States soon. The smartest thing for her to do, then, would be to keep working, and not even think about being romantically involved with anyone, at least until she was settled back in Philly. She could do that, right?

I can just be one of those career-minded types that focus all their time and energy on getting ahead in the business world, and, because they have no time for relationships, end up all alone with fifteen cats for children.

A sob escaped her lips and she buried her head in her hands.

Cat.

That evening she met Jane for an early dinner. While they were discussing wedding details, the waiter approached and asked if they would like a drink. Jane ordered a chardonnay, then looked at Elizabeth, who sighed and asked for an iced tea. Jane smiled. "You're going to really hate me at the hen party on Friday, aren't you?" she asked.

Elizabeth's spine went rigid. *The hen party.* In the midst of shutting out the world and absorbing herself in editing for the previous month, she had completely forgotten to plan the British version of a bachelorette party for her sister. "Oh! No, of course not," she sputtered. "I'm so excited! Wait till you see what I've got planned for you." She chewed her lip anxiously, then stopped for fear Jane would know she was lying.

Jane smirked. "I know you forgot about the hen party, Lizzie." She traced the placemat with her finger. "With everything that has been going on lately, I honestly don't expect you to have remembered, anyway." She glanced up at her sister. "I still haven't thanked you for going home to see Dad. I should have gone. I have been feeling so guilty about not being there for him and Mom, and for not being there more for you, too." Her chin wrinkled. "Millie told me about Bingley. I am so, so sorry, Lizzie—it's all my fault. I didn't know she had gotten rid of him until it was too late."

"It's all right, Jane." Elizabeth willed herself not to cry in front of her sister when she clearly felt terrible about what happened. "It's no one's fault. I just wish I knew where he went. I was going to check the shelter, but Millie told me she asked Will if he knew anyone who wanted a cat, and someone apparently was more than willing to take him. Not that it matters at this point, but do you know who it might have been?"

Jane shook her head. "No. I wish I did. Will never even told me about it—I went to spend a few days with Aunt Bridget and Aunt Tessa when you were in Philly, since I had the week off from work and they were so upset about Dad. By the time I got back, Bingley was long gone." She looked down at her lap.

Elizabeth sighed. "Well, it sounds like he found a good home, at least."

"Yeah."

"Anyway," Elizabeth began with a small smile, "I really am excited about the hen party. There's still more than enough time for me to plan something awesome. I can get Millie to help! Although, she would probably want to have us all dress up like Harry Potter characters and LARP or something." She took a large sip of tea and chewed on a piece of ice.

"LARP?" Jane asked warily.

"Live action role playing," Elizabeth explained, then shook her head. "Don't ask."

Jane laughed. Then she made a sheepish face at her sister. "I wouldn't worry about the hen party, Lizzie," she said slowly.

"Why not?"

"Because Andie told me she would love to take over and plan everything, and since you weren't here, and considering how stressed you have been lately, I thought maybe it would be for the best to let her." She wrinkled her nose.

Elizabeth frowned. "Oh." She tried not to look as disappointed as she felt. Andie was now taking over the one event Elizabeth got to plan for her sister before the wedding? It wasn't as if she were having a bridal shower, which was traditional in the U.S., but not Britain. Was there anything else Andie was going to take away from Elizabeth?

"Don't worry, Lizzie," Jane soothed. "It's just a stupid hen party—one single night of meaningless partying. It's not like she's going to take your place as maid of honor or anything."

Elizabeth's nostrils flared. *I'd love to see her try.* "I know." She wondered what in the world her sister saw in Andie, anyway. Couldn't she see for herself just how two-faced she was? *Probably not.* Andie only showed the side of her personality she wanted people to see. In Jane's case it was that of a caring, thoughtful friend; not a manipulative, backstabbing liar who pretended to care about someone until that someone stood between them and what they thought they deserved. She was so convincing in her role that she apparently even had Charlie fooled—and he was usually so good at discerning other people's intentions. Elizabeth wished she could make them both see the truth about Andie, but she knew it was the type of thing they would have to realize for themselves. She just hoped it happened before Andie hurt either of them as badly as herself.

Friday evening finally arrived; the night of the dreaded hen party. Elizabeth and Millie helped each other get ready, then stood side by side in the mirror to admire their work. Millie's hair was pulled up high on her head in a ponytail and curled. She had drawn wings with black eyeliner on her eyelids that were slightly uneven, but were covered so sufficiently with blue sparkly eyeshadow it was impossible to tell. Her dress, an equally shimmery blue sequined number that Elizabeth picked out for her, flattered her ample assets and made her eyes pop. The overall effect was only slightly diminished by the black Doc Martin's she chose to accessorize with on her feet, and those darned white owl earrings she had insisted upon wearing in her ears.

Elizabeth felt surprisingly glamorous in the emerald-green mini dress she had picked out for herself earlier that week. It was extremely daring for her usual taste—the sweetheart neckline accentuated her cleavage, the mid-thigh length, in combination with her ankle strap heels, showed off tons of bare leg, and overall it was so tight that it hugged her curves like a Formula One car—but damn it if she didn't feel daring at the moment. She left her long auburn hair down and curled it so that it fell over her shoulders and down her back in a satisfying manner. Then she gave herself some smoky eyes that made their green shade almost glow, a neutral lipstick, and some dangly silver earrings. Smiling at her reflection, she felt ready to face Andie.

They waited by the window for the others to show up. Right on time, a black Jaguar pulled up to the curb, and they watched in awe as the window rolled down and Andie and Kassy stuck their heads out. The two of them shouted something unintelligible up at them with feverishly excited expressions on their flawlessly made-up faces. Once Millie and Elizabeth had climbed into the back seat of the car and slid across the leather beside Kassy, they noticed Jane in the passenger side, beaming at them.

"Wow," Elizabeth mumbled softly, impressed against her will. "This car is unbelievable, Andie."

"I know, right?" Andie countered. "My dad loaned it to me for tonight. He threatened to disown me if anything happened to it, but it is totally worth the risk. Only the best for my dearest friend, the beautiful bride!"

Elizabeth met Millie's gaze. Millie rolled her eyes, and Elizabeth smiled gratefully. At least someone besides herself was not fooled by Andie's virtuous act.

"You look incredible, Lizzie," Kassy gushed admiringly as she surveyed her ensemble. "You too, Millie."

"Thanks, Kass." Elizabeth smiled. "You do, too. How are things?"

Kassy blushed and dropped her gaze to her lap. "Oh, never better." She hesitated, then glanced back up at Elizabeth. "And you? How is your dad feeling? Jane told us about his heart attack—that must have been so scary!"

Elizabeth felt a sudden warmth toward her for her concern. "He is good, Kass, thank you for asking. He just had a checkup last week. They say he will be in tiptop shape to walk Jane down the aisle in a few weeks."

"That's so great! I know Jane was really worried about his health." Kassy frowned. "And how about you, Lizzie? How is your, um, kidney doing?"

"Really well, actually," Elizabeth answered with confidence. "The doctor told me a couple of weeks ago that it has fully recovered. He said it was functioning like a perfectly healthy, normal kidney now."

"I'm so happy for you!" Kassy reached over and squeezed her hand. She lowered her voice. "I really mean it, Lizzie. You deserve to be happy. I hope everything works out, you know, the way I just know it's supposed to." She gave Elizabeth a meaningful look. "No matter how it seems right now."

Elizabeth was taken back by her ambiguously meaningful choice of words. Again she felt affection for her compassion. "Thank you, Kassy," she whispered. She felt her eyes sting with tears and looked away until it passed.

"Ladies, it's time to accessorize!" Andie, who had been talking nonstop with Jane in the front seat, held a Marks and Spencer bag over one shoulder. "We are going to get so tipsy tonight!"

"Oh, no, we can't," Jane urged her. "It wouldn't be fair to Lizzie, since she can't drink alcohol."

"Oh, I'm sure Lizzie doesn't mind—right Lizzie?" Andie looked at Elizabeth in the rearview mirror and smiled. "It's Jane's one and only hen party, after all! Besides, it works out perfectly that she can't drink, because someone needs to be the designated driver!"

Millie leaned over to whisper in Elizabeth's ear, "I say we get her good and plastered and then ditch her somewhere. Then we can steal the car and see what this bad boy can really do."

When they reached the restaurant, and were adequately distinguishable as a group in their matching feather boas and plastic crowns, they were escorted to a table directly overlooking the Thames. On the way they received several nods of admiration from a table of young men, who continued to smile in their direction once they had taken their seats. Elizabeth found herself in between Millie and Kassy, with Andie and Jane across from her. She hesitantly returned the smile of a particularly attractive dark-haired man from the table in the corner, feeling her cheeks turn pink as she did so.

They ordered drinks, and when they arrived the waiter set down a tall glass of pink liquid with an orange slice before Elizabeth, which she immediately recognized as a tumbler-sized 'Sex on the Beach.' She stared at it in confusion.

"Lizzie!" admonished Jane.

"Jane, do you really think I would ever, in a million years, order a 'Sex on the Beach' for myself?" she asked exasperatedly, then turned to the waiter. "Excuse me, but I didn't order this."

"I know," he replied with a wink. "It's from that lad over there with the tight buns."

Elizabeth's eyes widened in surprise at the waiter. Then she followed his gaze to the same dark-haired man, who raised his own drink and flashed her a devilish grin in reply.

"Ooooo, Lizzie," Andie teased. "You should totally send him something in return."

"I'm not going to flirt with him."

"Why not? You are the only single hen in our party, after all." Andie shot a challenging look at Elizabeth, who glared back at her with flames dancing in her pupils. Andie blinked rapidly in defeat. "Excepting Millie, of course."

"I'm not single, actually. I have a boyfriend who's famous," Millie stated matter-of-factly.

Everyone at the table turned to gawk at her, instantly diffusing the tension. They ordered dinner. While the others were deep in conversation, Elizabeth turned to Millie. "Millie," she began desperately. "I need you to do me a favor, and not drink tonight."

"Oh, my God, why not?" Millie whispered. "Because I seriously think completely off my trolley is the only way I'm going to get through it."

Elizabeth's face became solemn. "Because I can't drive, Millie." She sighed deeply. "I haven't driven a car in Britain since my accident. I can't do it with the steering wheel on the other side."

Millie smiled, placing her hand on Elizabeth's arm. "No worries, bestie, I got you."

Elizabeth gave her a relieved grin. She unthinkingly sipped her 'Sex on the Beach' as she gazed out at the river.

"So where are we headed after this, Andie?" Jane inquired, her eyes lit up with excitement.

"Oh ho ho, wouldn't you like to know?" Andie answered in a sing-song voice. She rubbed her hands together in a conniving sort of way and winked at the others conspiratorially.

"Where are we going?" Elizabeth whispered to Millie.

"I found gift bags for each of us in the back of the Jag," Millie confessed. "Inside was a mini bottle of liquor, a pink cowboy hat, and a rolled wad each of what looked like fifty quid, so…are you thinking what I'm thinking?"

Elizabeth grimaced, closing her eyes. "Yes."

Millie sighed. "Well, I'm not wasting my fifty quid on bail just to try and tip a drunk cow in the middle of winter. Not again, anyway." She rolled her eyes at Elizabeth. "Fool me twice—am I right?"

If Jane were truly Andie's 'dearest friend,' wouldn't Andie already know she would never in her entire life want to go to a strip club? Her stupidity is about to ruin Jane's night!

As Elizabeth watched with her eyes narrowed Andie taking selfies with Jane across the table and ignoring the rest of their group, she was suddenly hit by a lightning bolt of inspiration. "I'll be right back," she told Millie and Kassy.

After dessert, they climbed back into the car. Jane, Andie, and Kassy were all slightly buzzed after two drinks each at the restaurant, so Andie willingly handed the keys over to Elizabeth, who then handed them to Millie. Millie grinned roguishly. "Go time," she muttered under her breath.

Elizabeth pulled out her phone and punched an address into the GPS. "If you guys don't mind," she called airily over her shoulder, "we're just going to take a little detour before we continue on with whatever it is Andie has planned." She exchanged smirks with Millie, who revved the powerful engine and let out an almost indecently enthusiastic groan of appreciation.

Half an hour later, Millie pulled into a car park. Andie glanced out her window. "Where are we?"

"You'll see," said Elizabeth. "It's just a short walk from here."

They clustered together in the freezing night air and walked until they came to Swallow Street. Making their way past a few restaurants, Andie called out, "Lizzie, Jane wants some decent entertainment, not more food. This is supposed to be a night she won't ever forget—remember?"

When they arrived at an ordinary, unlabeled brown door in a towering building at the end of the street, Elizabeth stopped walking and smiled. "Oh, trust me, Andie." She mockingly rubbed her hands together in a conniving sort of way and winked at her conspiratorially. "It will be."

She knocked on the door. It was opened by a muscle-bound man dressed all in black, with a headset on his head and an irritable look on his face. Elizabeth leaned in to mumble something nervously in his ear. He gestured for them to wait a moment, then turned and began to talk into his headset. Finally he turned around again, and, showing them the way with his tree trunk of an arm, allowed them to enter.

"Seriously, Lizzie, what the hell?" Andie asked, grabbing Elizabeth's arm roughly as they made their way down a dark hallway. "This is *not* part of my plan!"

"It's probably for the best." Elizabeth shook her hand off and smiled at the shocked look on her face. "Isn't that what you always say when something doesn't work out the way you hoped it would?" She gave her a would-be apologetic look, then turned and grinned as they entered a series of rooms lavishly decorated in hues of pink, burgundy, and purple. An elevated, mirror-backed bar faced an expansive dance floor in the center of the main room, and surrounding it were countless round tables and pink velvet tufted benches and chairs. Maroon silk curtains hung from the ceiling, which was glittering with thousands of multicolored lights and disco balls. Glamorous partygoers filled every inch of the space; laughing, talking, drinking, and dancing to the thunderous music selected by the DJ in one corner.

"Lizzie," Jane shouted over the noise. "Is this the Cuckoo Club? How in the world did you get us in here?" She was beaming with delight as she swayed back and forth with the beat of the music.

As if in reply, a male voice yelled, "Lizzie!" and they all turned. Sauntering toward them, wearing a sharp gray suit and tie and a devastating smile, was none other than Graham McKenzie, running his fingers through his curls exactly like the cologne advertisement he had most recently appeared in. He strolled up to their group and gave Elizabeth a hug. When he released her, he stepped back in order to look her up and down. "You look absolutely smashing, love! So glad you could come!"

Elizabeth flushed. She turned to introduce the others, who were all, except for Millie, huddled together and staring, drop-jawed, back and forth between her and Graham. "This is my sister Jane, the bride-to-be," she told him.

"Lovely to meet you, Jane," Graham crooned seductively, taking her hand and kissing it. "Even lovelier to meet you before you become a married woman." He gave her a playful wink.

Jane turned beet red and grinned like a Cheshire cat.

Graham turned back to Elizabeth. "I have to dash for just a bit, but I reserved a table for your party. I'll be back soon, I promise." He kissed her cheek and disappeared into the crowd.

The girls made their way through the dancing couples to the tables beyond the dance floor. They found one that bore a place card with Graham's name on it and filed one by one onto the silky smooth velvet bench.

"This is easily the most amazing night of my entire life already," Jane gushed as she gazed happily around the room. She grabbed Elizabeth's hand. "Geez, Lizzie—*Graham McKenzie*? How is it possible that you met him and didn't tell me?" She leaned back and sighed dramatically. "He is *so* unbelievably gorgeous."

"He really is. I think I might pass out!" Kassy cried. "You are so lucky to be close with Graham McKenzie, Lizzie! I had no idea! Who else do you know that's famous?"

Elizabeth grinned. "Well, I'm hoping to be introduced to another celebrity any day now," she answered with a suggestive look at Millie, who nodded smugly in reply and gave her a thumbs-up.

Andie sat in silence, sulking as she listened to their conversation. "I need a drink," she grumbled, and pulled the drink menu closer to inspect it. "Bloody hell! Lizzie, did you even consider how much everything was going to cost here when you chose to ruin our plans? *We* aren't celebrities, you know. I can't even afford a cocktail!"

Millie rotated in her seat so her back was facing Andie, and, reaching into her bosom, exposed several wads of cash along the neckline of her dress for Elizabeth to see. "We can, though, I swiped it from the gift bags." She smirked devilishly.

Before Elizabeth could respond to Millie's misconduct, someone appeared before them and set a bottle down on the table. "Compliments of Mr. McKenzie, in celebration of the bride," he explained. He gave each of them a flute and a napkin. Then, with a dramatic flair, he popped the cork from the bottle and began to pour. When he walked away, Kassy picked up the empty bottle. "Jane," she breathed, giving her arm a shake. "This is bloody *Cristal*!"

Jane and Kassy began to squeal as they grinned at Elizabeth, who raised her glass. "To Jane," she declared boldly. "Who is not only my *dearest friend*, but someone with whom I share a bond even closer, and even more unbreakable—my *sister*. I hope I've helped make this a night to remember. Cheers!" She held her glass out for the others to clink, Andie adding hers reluctantly at the last minute. With a tearful nod of approval from Jane, Elizabeth took a few sips of her champagne, smiling triumphantly to herself over the rim of her glass.

Millie tipped back her glass and drained it in one long sip, then balked at the look on Elizabeth's face. "It's just one glass." She gave her a dismissive wave of her hand. "Don't worry, I'm still plenty good to drive."

When Graham returned to their table, he brought along with him two of his friends; one of whom was a fellow A-list actor, who just happened to have appeared in the latest Bond film, and one well-known musician, who ironically was a member of Jane's favorite band. He asked if they would like to dance, and they filed back out to wholeheartedly join them on the dance floor.

As she paused for a breather at the bar several hours later, Elizabeth noticed Kassy sitting alone at their table and asked Graham to excuse her. She walked over to sit by her side. "You all right?" she asked, struggling to be heard over the music.

"Oh yes, I am having the most amazing time!" Kassy exclaimed, her words only slightly garbled as she sipped her third glass of champagne. She smiled. "I was just feeling a little, um, tired is all." She gestured across the room, where Graham was now dancing to Bruno Mars with an uncommonly bouncy Jane. "I still can't believe you know Graham McKenzie, Lizzie! He seems to really like you, too—oh, my God!" She slapped her cheeks with her palms. "You're not dating him, are you?"

Elizabeth gave a short laugh, her eyes wide. "Ha! No, definitely not," she replied. "He has a girlfriend, you know. She's an actress too, and about a thousand times prettier than me." She wrinkled her nose. "I met him on a plane recently, and we hit it off. We're just friends, I promise."

"Still." Kassy raised a sluggish eyebrow. "Still, I can't say I have any celebrity friends, especially ones that will get me into a swanky club and buy expensive champagne for a bunch of girls they don't even know. Andie's hopping mad, you know." She grinned.

"I'm sure she is," Elizabeth giggled. She quickly located her by the bar, her hand on the knee of the man next to her. Elizabeth looked quickly away from her back to Kassy. "So, what about you, Kass?" she asked eagerly. "Are you dating anyone?"

Kassy bit her lip. Her cheeks turned pink. "Yes."

"Do I know him?"

She hesitated, then looked down at her empty glass. "Yes."

Elizabeth smiled. "Is it Tom?"

Kassy's face remained unchanged except for her eyes, which sparkled briefly before she answered. "How did you know?"

"Oh, just a hunch." Elizabeth grinned, then gave her an earnest look. "The two of you are perfect for each other, Kass. I'm really happy for you both."

Kassy blushed. She gave Elizabeth a relieved smile. "Thank you, Lizzie."

Elizabeth stood. "I'll be right back," she promised. She turned, then felt Kassy's hand on her arm and looked back.

"Lizzie," Kassy began soberly, "There's something you should know about Andie."

Elizabeth frowned. She opened her mouth to speak.

"Speaking of the devil." Millie appeared at Elizabeth's side, half dragging a limp Andie behind her. "I just caught this one snogging some bloke at the bar." She dumped her unceremoniously onto the bench with a satisfied smirk. "I'm not going to lie, it was fun to watch him nearly wet himself when I told him she was married to 'The Mountain' from *Game of Thrones*."

"Where's Jane?" Elizabeth asked nervously as she scanned the room. She gasped as she suddenly saw her approaching, her hands around Graham's neck as he carried her in his arms. "Jane! What happened?"

Jane giggled, then cringed in pain.

"She made a valiant attempt at 'the worm' before someone stepped on her," Graham explained. He gave Elizabeth an apologetic smile.

"We should probably get her home." Elizabeth helped steady her sister as Graham carefully set her down. "Do you think you can walk to the car?"

"Sure!" Jane took a few wobbly steps, then collapsed into a chair and clutched her ankle.

Elizabeth sighed.

"I'll carry her," Graham offered. He swept her back up into his arms as Jane beamed at him helplessly.

"Are you sure?" Elizabeth felt humiliated; this was not how she imagined the end of this night, with a legitimate movie star carrying her injured sister and escorting her inebriated friends to their car. "It's like a quarter of a mile."

"I'll be fine," he grunted. He managed a convincing smile.

Elizabeth rounded up Kassy and Andie, the latter of which threw an arm around her neck as they stumbled outside.

When they arrived at the car; a ten minute walk that turned into an hour with rest stops, Millie opened the back door so Graham could help Jane inside. Once she was seated, Elizabeth watched in horror as she pulled him in by the tie and planted a drunken kiss on his unprepared lips. "My hero!" she mumbled, then released him and fell back against the seat with her eyes closed.

Graham straightened up and glanced at Elizabeth, his face flushed.

What is it, like, a Baker family trait to kiss a man you hardly know while you're intoxicated?

"Time to go," she announced abruptly, and closed the door after Kassy had climbed in beside Jane. With Andie still draped on her shoulder, she faced Graham. "Thank you *so* much for tonight, Graham," she gushed. "It was completely unforgettable. Well," she added, glancing back at the car, "I hope except for that kiss, at least in your case." She wrinkled her nose. "Sorry about that. At least it's too late for paparazzi, right?"

Graham laughed. "It was my pleasure, Lizzie. I was thrilled to get a ring from you! Anytime you want to get together, let me know. If I'm in London we will make it happen." As her hands were currently occupied, he leaned in to gently kiss her cheek.

Elizabeth felt the spot where his lips touched her face burn. "I'm actually moving back to the States soon," she admitted.

"Well, I'm in New York more than I am home," he confessed. "We can meet up and grab some dim sum." He laughed. "Or I could make it for you—I found a brilliant recipe in a magazine I think you might just be familiar with."

She grinned. "Sounds good to me."

Once he left, she hauled Andie over to the other side of the car and struggled to open the door. As she bent her head down to help her inside, Andie's phone fell onto the pavement. Elizabeth picked it up, noticing it had automatically opened to a recent text message. She didn't mean to look—but a picture she had sent to Kassy caught her eye. She clicked on it to make it bigger. Her heart plummeted into her stomach; she suddenly felt on the verge of losing both her dinner and expensive champagne.

Chapter Twenty-Five

$\mathcal{O}$nce Millie and Elizabeth had delivered Jane safely home to Will they dropped off Kassy at her flat, then drove back to theirs.

"How are we going to get Andie home?" Elizabeth asked, gazing at her unconscious form in the back seat.

"*Bollocks*! I completely forgot." Millie frowned. Then she curved her lips upward in a perfect imitation of the Grinch. "I'll take her home."

"How are you going to get back?"

Millie shrugged. "I'll take a taxi."

Elizabeth tilted her head. "I don't know if that's the best plan, Millie."

"Do you really want her spending the night here with us?"

"No." Elizabeth shook her head firmly. "Definitely not."

"OK, then." Millie waited for Elizabeth to get out of the car. "I'll be back." She peeled away from the curb and disappeared around the deserted corner.

Elizabeth went inside and kicked her heels off, sinking onto the sofa to massage her sore feet. She tried to wait up for Millie's return, but eventually succumbed to exhaustion and curled up in the only position her skintight dress would allow. Before she knew it, the room was filled with harsh afternoon light and the music of the busy street below.

She sat up, waiting for a rush of vertigo to pass before scanning the room for Millie. Sure enough, she made it safely home and was now lying flat on her back in the middle of the floor, sound asleep and snoring. Elizabeth chuckled to herself as she tiptoed past her to make coffee. She checked her phone—it was two in the afternoon! She sat on one of the stools and clutched her mug in both hands as she watched Millie snore on the rug. When she finally awoke with a start she sat up and looked dazedly over to where Elizabeth was sitting.

"What year is it?"

"I don't know, I didn't notice when I got out of the TARDIS." Elizabeth rolled her eyes and held up the coffeepot, gesturing for her to join her. Millie stumbled over and took a seat on the other stool. She reached into her mouth and pulled out her retainer, along with a trail of saliva, and set it on the counter as Elizabeth watched in revulsion.

"Ew, Millie, what did you do—go and get your retainer from your bedroom and then come back and pass out on the rug?"

"I carry it in my purse," Millie answered hoarsely. She cleared her throat. "Someone once told me that my teeth are my best feature, so now I take keeping them that way very seriously."

"Right." Elizabeth smiled. "So, how did last night go?"

Millie took a long drag from her mug and mustered the strength to cast her a wicked grin. "I got her home, no problem."

Elizabeth gave her a look. "OK." She raised an eyebrow. "So what's with the evil smile, then?"

"Well, before I brought her home, I took the car for a little joy ride." Millie laughed as Elizabeth shook her head in disapproval. "And I may have taken the turns a tad too fast—" she paused for dramatic effect "—because she totally tossed her cookies all over her dad's leather seat."

Elizabeth knew it was wrong to grin, but she couldn't help it.

"Oh, by the way," Millie added, "I have a gift for you." She walked across the room to get her purse, along with a mysterious black bag. She set the bag on the counter, and Elizabeth reached in to pull out an unopened bottle of Cristal.

"Millie!" she cried. "I don't even want to know how and when you got this, but you know darn well I can't drink it!"

"It's not for you," Millie chided her. "That's *my* gift, graciously and unknowingly provided by our good friend Andie last night with her dirty strip club money." She gave Elizabeth a wink. "This is *your* gift." She pulled her phone from her purse and fiddled with it, then handed it to Elizabeth. On the screen was a picture of Andie kissing the random man at the bar the previous evening. "I snapped this last night," she admitted boldly. "You're welcome."

Elizabeth sighed. "What am I supposed to do with that, Millie?"

"Blackmail her, of course." Millie snorted. "I can't wait to see the look on her face when you do."

"Why would I blackmail her?"

Millie frowned. "To get her to break up with Charlie, obviously. Threaten to show him the picture unless she agrees to never see him again."

"You've been watching too many films, Millie," Elizabeth admonished. "Real life doesn't work that way. Besides, I could never consciously do something that I know would hurt Charlie. He has to realize Andie is a terrible excuse for a human for himself."

"Well, I'm sending it to you anyway," Millie insisted. "You might change your mind." She hopped down from the stool. "I'm going to shower, so I can wash the smell of vomit out of my hair." Grinning, she added, "I'm going to hang on to the mental image of Andie lying in it in the back seat of that Jag, though."

Elizabeth smiled. "Thanks for all your help last night, Millie. It's been a really rough couple of months. It felt good to win one."

"I got you, bestie." Millie shot her a finger gun. She placed a hand on her hip. "We really carpéd the bloody hell out of that diem, didn't we?"

Elizabeth laughed. "We really did."

The following morning Elizabeth found herself alone in the flat. As it was a Sunday, Millie had left to accompany her parents to church and then brunch afterward. She asked if Elizabeth wanted to come with her, and she briefly considered it as Jane and Will would also be there, but in the end she decided to stay home and get some packing done. Time was running out before she would be moving back to Philly, and the next month would be a whirlwind of wedding activities. It would be fairly easy since she really only needed to throw things back in the stack of empty boxes that lined one wall of her bedroom.

She had just begun to work up a sweat in her yoga pants and AC/DC T-shirt, her hair tied back with a red bandanna, when there was a knock at the door. "Just a minute!" Elizabeth called from her bedroom. She finished taping the box on her bed and hustled through the living room to the door. She threw it open, and her heart skipped a beat as she recognized who was standing on the threshold.

Dr. Patel, looking extremely dapper in dark wash jeans and a hunter green sweater with a navy-blue plaid scarf wrapped around his neck, smiled appreciatively as he took in her disheveled appearance. "Hey, Lizzie," he greeted her.

She had no time to reply, as her eyes traveled immediately down to his arms, which were holding a small black and white cat. "*Bingley!*" she cried, and reached out to take him as Dr. Patel held him out to her.

Bingley instantly began purring and nuzzling her neck as she hugged his warm little body against hers. For a second, she had completely forgotten Dr. Patel was still standing in the hallway. "Please, come in!" she exclaimed, and gestured for him to follow her inside.

They sat on the sofa, Elizabeth still stroking Bingley's silky fur as he made himself comfortable on her lap. "How? I mean, where? When?" she stammered, gaping at Dr. Patel's satisfied grin.

He laughed. "A while back, Will asked around at the hospital if anyone wanted a cat Millie found wandering around. I love cats, so I thought why not? But a few days ago he said he talked to Jane, and she told him the cat belonged to you." He reached out to scratch Bingley's ear. "I was going to just give him back to Will, but I couldn't resist an opportunity to play the hero and deliver him myself." Elizabeth beamed at him, tears in her eyes.

"Honestly," he continued, "that look makes having to give him up completely worth it."

"You have no idea how happy I am to have him back, Dr. Patel," she breathed.

"Please, call me Char," he insisted. "And it was nothing. Really."

"Well, it is everything to me." She gave him an earnest look. "Seriously, how can I ever thank you enough?"

He smiled. "Well, you could agree to let me take you out to dinner."

Elizabeth stopped petting Bingley and looked up at him. She considered it. It didn't really make sense for her to start dating anyone with her move now only a little over a month away. More than that, though, she really didn't want to start dating anyone else, ever.

But then again, he did just give her the greatest gift she had received in a very long time. Surely, she could say yes to one date as a thank you?

"OK." She saw his eyes light up and gave him a small smile.

"Really?" He looked as though he couldn't believe his good luck.

"Sure, why not?" She watched Bingley walk across the sofa to Dr. Patel. He made a few consecutive circles and then plopped down on his lap, purring contentedly. Elizabeth grinned. "How about next Friday?"

"Perfect! I'll pick you up, say, seven?"

"Sounds great." She stood. "Can I get you some coffee? I can make a fresh pot."

He got to his feet and waved his hand. "Oh, no, thank you. I wish I could, but I have to go get ready for my shift." She followed him to the door, where he turned and gave her a winsome smile. "I can't wait for Friday." Then he walked through the door and down the hallway.

Elizabeth closed the door. She sank back down on the sofa, lost in thought, as Bingley jumped up on the back and began vigorously nuzzling her head. Now that she actually thought about it, she regretted agreeing to go out with Dr. Patel. It wouldn't be fair of her to give him false hope; and she knew she could never think of him as more than just a friend. Her heart belonged to Charlie, and always would. She would have to come clean on their date and tell him the truth. At least she had an entire week to think of how exactly she was going to let him down without hurting him too badly.

When Friday arrived, Dr. Patel picked her up right on time and took her to his favorite bistro. Since Jane wasn't around, she only felt slightly guilty ordering a drink, and as she sipped it she smiled across the table at Dr. Patel. He seemed to be reveling in her company; his handsome smile was more enthusiastic than a dog in the window of a car. "So," he began, "are you getting excited about the wedding?"

"I'm excited to see Jane and Will get married," she replied insipidly. She shrugged. "I can't say I'm particularly excited for the wedding, though. Or the final dress fitting next week, for that matter."

Dr. Patel looked back at her and grinned. "Not enjoying spending so much time with the bridesmaids? I don't blame you one bit—that's a lot of estrogen to be dealing with."

Elizabeth sighed. "Yeah, I guess you could say that." She glanced down at the table. "Although it's really just one bridesmaid who is the problem."

Dr. Patel paused a moment. "It's Andie, isn't it?"

Elizabeth's head popped back up. "How did you know?" she asked.

He shook his head. "Andie's quite a character. I mean, I'm used to her personality by now, but I'd be the first to agree that she can be a tad overbearing. She has quite a talent for getting what she wants by any means necessary, and taking no prisoners in the process."

"I've noticed." Elizabeth stared determinedly at her wineglass.

Dr. Patel watched her for a moment. Then he said, "If I were you, Lizzie, I would just ignore Andie. Find something to take your mind off of her and Charlie, like, oh I don't know, seeing a film with me next week." He flashed her a charming grin.

She tried to smile back at him, but it quickly turned into a frown. Dr. Patel had basically confirmed for her that Andie and Charlie were getting serious with their relationship. She remembered the picture she had seen by accident on Andie's phone, and her heart gave a lurch as she was hit by a sudden realization. Andie was more than likely going to bring Charlie with her to the wedding as her plus one, and Elizabeth would have to face the agony of seeing them together, as well as suffer the indignity of spending the evening completely alone, without a date. "Would you be my date for the wedding, Dr. Patel?" she blurted out.

His smile melted away and he raised his eyebrows in surprise. "Really?"

"Well, I mean, it would only make sense, wouldn't it?" she added with a smile. "I'm the maid of honor and you're the best man, after all."

He looked at her as though she had just handed him the moon. "It makes perfect sense," he agreed. "I would be honored."

So much for not giving him false hope, Elizabeth, you complete idiot.

She decided to try another tactic. Perhaps she could deter any thoughts of romance on his part by subtly cluing him in to her impending move to Philly. "You know, to be honest, I can't wait for this wedding to be over," she began tactfully.

"I totally get that." He nodded in agreement. "Weddings are great in theory, but end up being more stressful than anything else." He looked away thoughtfully. "When I get married, I think I will just skip all the drama and elope on a tropical beach somewhere."

Elizabeth was distracted from her train of thought. "You want to get married?"

"Of course I do," he answered with a smile. "Doesn't everyone?"

She didn't answer. Instead, she looked back down at her glass. After a moment, she looked up at him from under her eyelashes and asked softly, "Do you want kids?"

"Now that is a question I would have to answer with a definite no," he replied firmly.

Elizabeth was so surprised by his answer she nearly dropped her fork. "Why not?"

He made a face. "I have a sister that has seven kids, all under the age of twelve. I love spending time with them—don't get me wrong—but I am more than ready to go back home at the end of the day and enjoy the peace and quiet. Plus, I think it would be maddening to not be able to come and go as I choose, you know? I want to travel the globe, experience everything it has to offer. If I had children it wouldn't be possible." He sighed. "Besides, the world we are living in gets more terrifying every single day. It would almost be selfish to bring a child into it, knowing all the dangers and adversity they would inevitably have to face. Being a psychiatrist, I get to see firsthand the direction humanity is taking, and believe me, it's not a pretty picture."

Elizabeth sat back in her chair, completely taken back by his words. She had never given any thought to what happened after a baby was born. She had been too preoccupied with the fact that she could never get pregnant again. As much as she would love to become a mother and experience all the joy that came with it, maybe Dr. Patel had a point. Maybe it was selfish to only be thinking about how happy the child would make her, and not about the dangers and hardships she would be exposing him or her to, beginning the instant it was born.

He gave her an apologetic smile, and it immediately tore her away from her weighty thoughts. "Wow, that conversation took a turn, didn't it? Sorry to be such a damp squid."

She raised her eyebrows. "A what?"

Dr. Patel laughed. "It's an expression that basically means a disappointment. As a kid, my dad always used it in reference to me." He rolled his eyes. "He didn't realize the term is actually squib, not squid. It became a running joke between myself and my siblings."

"You're not a disappointment!" Elizabeth gave him a warm smile. "I'm having a wonderful time, Dr. Patel." Without thinking, she reached out to place her hand on top of his and felt her cheeks blaze as she watched his eyes light up. Removing it quickly, she added, "But I can definitely relate to that. I've always felt like I was a major disappointment to my mother."

"How so?"

She shrugged. "I don't know, I guess because I've been in Jane's shadow my entire life, and in my mother's eyes she can do no wrong. And now she's getting married to a doctor, and my greatest accomplishment up to this point has been not dying." She felt tears well up and commanded herself not to cry in front of him.

"Well, I think you're amazing, Lizzie," he said, and gazed at her so admiringly she couldn't help but smile.

"Thank you." She continued to smile as she dropped her gaze bashfully to her lap. "You're not too bad yourself, Dr. Patel."

He leaned forward to take her hands in his and held them firmly as he gave her a supplicating grin. "*Please*," he implored her, "call me Char."

As he walked her to her door when the night was over, Elizabeth was bombarded with panicked thoughts.

Is he going to try to kiss me? Should I let him? I don't really want to kiss him, but I also don't want to hurt his feelings by avoiding him. Oh, no, we're at the door. What should I do?

Before she could decide, he leaned in close and kissed her cheek. Then he smiled. "Thank you for tonight, Lizzie. I hope we can do it again sometime soon." He gave her a hopeful look. "Maybe catch that film I mentioned earlier?"

She grinned. "Sure. I had a great time, Dr.—Char—thank you so much."

He turned to walk away, then called over his shoulder, "I'm dying to see a film that just came out, actually. How do you feel about James Bond?"

Elizabeth's eyes widened. She frowned, unable to answer him.

"I completely agree," he jested, noting her expression. "If you ask me, Miss Moneypenny is far more appealing." With a wink, he walked away.

Chapter Twenty-Six

The following Saturday was the final dress fitting. Jane, Elizabeth, Millie, Kassy, and Andie all sat in the main room of the bridal shop, flutes of champagne in hand (in Elizabeth's case, sparkling cider) as they waited for their dresses to be brought out. Andie asked Jane if she and Will had any plans for Valentine's Day, which was in the middle of the following week.

"I think we are just staying home," she answered her. "I have to work the next day anyway, and we have spent so much money on the wedding it's probably for the best we don't go to a fancy dinner. We can just watch a movie or something."

"Netflix and chill," Millie offered candidly. "I hear that."

The others turned to give her looks of incredulity, while Elizabeth snorted into her sparkling cider.

"So, Lizzie, what about you?" Andie asked, and Elizabeth felt her smile instantly wiped from her mouth. "Have a hot date for Valentine's?"

She gave her a smugly arrogant smile, and Elizabeth had a sudden impulse to shove the glass in her hand down her throat. "No."

"Not even Char?" Andie pressed her spitefully. She turned to look at Kassy and Jane. "Did you know Elizabeth went on a date last week with Dr. Patel?"

"You did?" Jane asked quietly. She looked at her sister in disbelief. "Why didn't you tell me?"

Elizabeth cast a nasty look at Andie before looking reluctantly at Jane. "It wasn't a big deal. We went out to dinner and talked, that's all. We're just friends."

"If you're just friends, then why did he tell me you are going with him to see a film tonight?" Andie's face was full of superiority as she stared shamelessly at Elizabeth. "That sounds like a date to me."

"It's not."

"Well," Andie muttered as she leaned back in her seat and crossed her legs, "maybe tonight isn't a date—but I know for a fact Lizzie asked Char to be her date for the wedding, because he told me himself. He said he was planning on asking her all along, but then she beat him to it."

Elizabeth's face turned red as she saw the look in Jane's eyes. Just at that moment, the seamstress appeared with several dress bags slung over her shoulder. She gestured for them to follow her to the fitting rooms, where Andie offered to assist Jane before Elizabeth could even open her mouth. She watched them enter a fitting room together. Millie came up behind her and asked if she would help her with the zipper that ran down the side of her dress, so Elizabeth followed her into another room and closed the door.

Halfway through her task, Elizabeth heard Millie say, "I can be your date for Valentine's, Lizzie. My boyfriend is out of town, so I have no plans either. We can build the Lego Millennium Falcon I got from Will for Christmas." She shrugged at the less than enthusiastic look Elizabeth gave her. "Or, we can sit in the garden and smoke the Cubans I got from my friend Joe at work."

Elizabeth let out a short barking laugh. "What?! Millie, have you ever even smoked a cigar before?"

"No," Millie admitted. "Have you?"

Elizabeth smiled. "No. But I have a feeling it won't be as fun as you think. We should probably just go for the Falcon."

"Good, that's what I wanted to do anyway."

She spent the rest of the fitting, as well as brunch afterward, subdued into silence while the others talked and laughed around her. It was becoming almost unbearable to be in the same room as Andie now, with her constant derisive attacks on her character, as well as her subtle yet blatant alluding to her relationship with Charlie without actually mentioning his name. She thought there were moments where Kassy seemed bothered by Andie's behavior, as she gave Elizabeth what she could almost describe as commiserative looks now and then, but she seemed too controlled by Andie's dominating personality to say anything in front of her. Jane, much to Elizabeth's inability to comprehend, seemed to not even notice; though she supposed she could easily chalk it up to the fact that her sister had far too much on her mind at the moment to read between the lines of Andie's comments. Millie, however, showed Andie no mercy; she lobbed openly aggressive insults right back at her opponent with the ease of someone who had absolutely nothing to lose. When Elizabeth met her gaze she repeatedly gestured to her phone, as if suggesting it could all be over if she would just give in and allow Millie to blackmail Andie, but Elizabeth knew it was futile for two reasons; one, she could never stoop to Andie's level of maliciousness, and two, Andie would probably use her frustratingly effectual wit and charm to explain away the picture of her kissing the man at the bar anyway.

The day before Valentine's Elizabeth heard her phone ring, and when she picked it up she saw a number she didn't recognize. Hesitantly, she answered, and heard a familiar voice croon, "I heard you didn't have a date for Valentine's, darling."

Elizabeth frowned. "Tom?"

"Hey, Lizzie," Tom answered. "Sorry to bother you, but someone told me you were going to be alone on Valentine's, and I felt it my duty as a gentleman to rectify it immediately. Would you honor me with a lunch date tomorrow?"

She smiled into the phone. "Sure."

"Brilliant! Want to meet me at the Grand Café, inside the Royal Exchange building at noon?"

Elizabeth had never heard of it. "Sounds perfect. I'll see you tomorrow, Tom."

She hung up, her mind reeling. She hadn't seen Tom in a very long time. Why would he be calling her now, and why was he asking her out to lunch? He did mention that someone told him she was alone. It would only make sense that it was Kassy, and that the two of them simply felt sorry for her. Was she that pitiful? She would have to try and act happier around other people, so she didn't come across as miserable on the outside as she was on the inside. It was going to be difficult around Tom though; he looked so much like his brother it would be hard not to imagine he was.

She was a few minutes late meeting him the following day, as seemingly every man in London was on the tube, out buying last minute gifts for their significant others on their lunch breaks. When she entered the Royal Exchange building, a beautiful Victorian façade with towering pillars, she gasped. The lobby was absolutely stunning with its archways and windows, and in the center of the expansive room was a small but elegant café. She quickly located Tom sitting at one of the tables, and her heart skipped a beat even though she had mentally prepared herself.

"Tom!" she called brightly, determined to appear carefree.

His eyes lit up in recognition as he saw her approaching. He stood and held his arms out to give her a hug, and she nearly let out a sob when she breathed in the exact same cologne that Charlie wore on his collar. When he released her, she quickly erased the angst from her eyes and forced a smile. He grinned, then reached down to pick something up from beside his chair; a bouquet of daisies and a box of Cadbury Milk Tray chocolates.

Elizabeth's heart performed a flip-flop. How did he know that daisies were her favorite flower? Did Charlie tell him? Was it just a lucky guess? "Thank you! You really didn't have to do that, you know," she admonished him, though her cheeks were pink with delight.

"Oh, but I did," he answered, and bent down to kiss her cheek. As they both took their seats, he added, "How have you been, Lizzie? It has been entirely too long since I last had the pleasure of your company."

Elizabeth tried to smile, but it was more than obvious by the look in his eyes that Tom knew everything that had happened since the last time she had seen him, at his parents' house.

That's how he knows about the daisies—Charlie gave me a bouquet the night we met Tom and his parents. He must have remembered that tiny little detail.

She couldn't talk about Charlie with him, even if it was most likely his real reason for asking her to lunch. She had to change the subject before it even came up.

"I'm fine," she muttered. She gave him a sly smile. "How about you, Tom? Want to tell me who it was that informed you I would be alone today?"

His look of concern instantly unraveled into a knowing smile. "I believe you already know who it was, don't you?"

"She may have spilled the beans after a few drinks." Elizabeth grinned shamelessly. "I'm glad she did. It was the best thing that happened that night." She made a face.

"I heard all about it, actually," he laughed. "Sounds like you girls really embraced your status as bachelorettes."

"Speaking of which," Elizabeth smirked, "I seem to recall you saying you were a confirmed bachelor for life, Tom. What made you change your mind? When did you and Kassy start dating, anyway?"

"I met her once before, many years ago now, and I thought she was cute. But then I moved to Scotland for work, and that was that." He gave her a small smile. "Until, of course, I saw her again at Will's the night we, the night we were all there—and, well, that was that."

Elizabeth paused for a moment, lost in thought. Then she smiled. "I'm so happy for you, Tom. Kassy is really sweet. She's been so nice to me since we met." She raised an eyebrow. "So, do you think you might be reconsidering your stance on marriage too, then?"

He gave her a long, contemplative look. "Anything's possible," he replied softly. He watched her smile fade. They sat in silence for a few moments, each of them deciding whether or not to say what was on their minds. Finally, it was Tom who spoke first. "Lizzie, I'm going to tell you something about me," he began. He met her gaze. "Something I have never told anyone—not even Charlie."

Elizabeth leaned forward, intrigued, and waited for him to continue.

"In my last year at Eton, when I was nineteen years old, I met a gorgeous girl at a social. We started dating, seeing each other on and off again for almost a year. I was young and naïve, and so I fell head over heels in love with her. I had just completed my A-level exams, and had been offered a full scholarship to the University of Cambridge, when she told me she was pregnant. She didn't want to tell me, she confessed, because she wasn't certain it was mine, and she couldn't tell her parents, because they would kick her out of the house. She begged me in desperation to help her. Though I was heartbroken she had been with someone else when I believed her to be in love with me, I couldn't turn my back on her. I decided I would give up my scholarship, get a full-time job, and ask her to marry me so I could help her raise the child. I used the money my parents gave me for getting top grades to buy a ring, and was about to propose, when I found out she changed her mind and told her parents after all." He paused, tears in his icy-blue eyes. "She had apparently decided the advantages they would offer her if she agreed to have an abortion and never see me again were worth it."

Elizabeth felt a tear roll freely down her cheek, and hastily wiped it away. "What did you do then?"

"Luckily, it wasn't too late for me to accept the scholarship. I went on to complete my degree at Cambridge, and never told anyone what happened. But I never forgot. It weighed on my mind and heart for years afterward, and I closed myself off to the possibility of ever loving anyone again, not to mention the idea of marriage." He managed a small smile. "Obviously, that has recently changed." He reached across the table to take her hands in his. "I wanted to tell you about my past, Lizzie, because I want you to know that even though terrible things happen in life, things that make us think we need to close off our hearts to others in order to protect them, time has a way of helping us realize that the harm we cause ourselves by not letting others in is far worse than what could, but might never, happen if we do."

The tears were coming too fast now to wipe away, even if her hands were free to do so. Elizabeth let out a shaky breath. "Thank you for telling me your story, Tom," she mumbled. "It means so much to me that you would trust me enough to share it with me, especially since you never even told Charlie about what happened."

Tom sighed. "I should have told him a long time ago, when he was dealing with the aftermath of breaking off his first engagement. I know it would have helped him to know his own brother had his heart ripped out of his chest, if not in exactly the same way. But you should know, Lizzie, she was nothing compared to you. I saw the way he looked at you when you were together, and I can tell you with confidence he never looked at her that way—not when I was around, anyway. She was charming, and definitely knew exactly how to manipulate him into believing he loved her—but I had a terrible feeling right from the start she would end up breaking his heart, and it guts me that I didn't tell him before it was too late."

Elizabeth pressed her lips together. "And now it's too late for me," she whispered.

"No," he argued. "It's not too late for you, Lizzie. He loves you." He squeezed her hands tightly. "It's never too late."

As she walked down the busy street half an hour later, she could hear Tom's words in her head, repeating over and over.

She was charming, and knew exactly how to manipulate him.

She frowned, stepping over a puddle of muddy slush.

I had a terrible feeling she would end up breaking his heart.

Suddenly, she froze where she stood as she was hit by a shocking realization. The couple walking behind her had to divide at the last minute to avoid crashing into her, but she didn't even notice them cursing at her. She tore into the pocket of her coat for her phone, and looked for Tom's number in the call history. Once she found it, she frantically typed out a text message.

Tom, who was Charlie's fiancée? What was her name?

She waited on tenterhooks for his reply, still standing stock-still in the middle of the sidewalk. Finally, her phone vibrated.

I thought you already knew her name was Miranda.

Elizabeth let out the breath she had been holding. She had been wrong. Placing her phone back into her pocket, she began walking again. When she felt another vibration, she pulled it back out with a frown, then gasped as she read Tom's second text.

Although now that I think about it, you probably know her by her nickname—

Andie.

Chapter Twenty-Seven

*A*ndie.

Andie.

Andie.

For the next two weeks, the name echoed through Elizabeth's brain like drops of water from a leaky faucet, slowly driving her into a perpetual mental state of complete and utter despair. She couldn't remember the last time she had an appetite, and food no longer had any flavor anyway. Her restless mind wouldn't allow her to sleep, and as a result the nights were endless sinkholes of paralyzing darkness and self-loathing that began as soon as the sun dipped below the rooftops of the buildings outside her bedroom window. She couldn't even muster the energy to work, as her brain churned ceaselessly with the obsessive thoughts and regrets that were overflowing within—nearly all of them centering on Andie. Andie was the one who Charlie had been engaged to for six months. Andie was the one who broke his heart by cheating on him. And Andie was the one who managed to slither her way back into his life like the snake that she was, not unlike Satan in the Garden of Eden, and trick him into giving her another chance.

How could I have been so stupid as to not figure that out on my own? How could I have been so naïve as to believe a word Andie said to me about her relationship with Charlie when I first met her? I should have known she was lying about everything. And poor Charlie! It must have been so hard for him to see her again at Jane's engagement dinner, not to mention all the other times before we broke up. Andie obviously only pretended to be my friend so she could plant seeds of doubt in my mind in regard to Charlie's love for me. She must have been biding her time, waiting for me to screw up like the idiot that I am, so she could swoop in and steal him back. And I made it just so simple for her, didn't I? I practically pushed him right back into her cheating arms by believing all of her lies! Oh, dear God—the things I said to him on Christmas Eve! Telling him that we were never meant to be together in the first place, and that he should have been married for years by now! He must have thought I knew he was engaged to Andie, and that I was just being spiteful!

The thought made her feel sick to her stomach. No, wait—it was more than just a feeling. She raced to the bathroom, making it to the toilet just in time. Once more finding herself lying on her back on the cold tile floor, she pushed her damp with sweat hair away from her forehead and closed her eyes.

How am I going to make it until the wedding is over?

How am I going to handle seeing her with him?

How am I going to survive the rest of my life without him?

What seemed like only minutes passed, and Elizabeth awoke to the sound of running water. She opened her eyes and looked up to see Millie sitting on the edge of the tub, her hand on the tap. She dragged herself to a sitting position, her stiff muscles screaming in resistance. "Millie? What's going on?"

"I'm drawing you a hot bath." Millie dumped a container of bubble soap into the water and watched as it began to froth. "You need to snap out of this funk you've been in. And there is nothing like a good, hot bubble bath to clear your mind, so you can plot revenge on Andie." She rolled her eyes. "Or just relieve stress, I guess—whatever works for you."

"I don't want to take a bath, Millie," Elizabeth muttered as she attempted to stand. Her entire body ached from spending the night on the hard floor. "All right," she admitted, "Maybe it would help just a little."

"I'm going to run out and get ingredients to make some comfort food," she continued. "You just sit here and soak. It's going to be all right, Lizzie. Andie's a complete arsehole, and Charlie's not stupid. He's bound to run out of patience with her before too long."

Elizabeth managed a weak smile. "Thanks, Millie."

"I'll be back in half an hour. I'll make us some toasties." Millie blew her a kiss and left the room. "Don't drown yourself, all right?" she called from the living room.

Elizabeth undressed and sank into the water. The bubbles tickled her nose as she bent her head forward to tie her hair up in a messy bun. She closed her eyes and let the lavender aroma fill her nostrils with its soothing scent. The ache in her muscles was gone, but there was nothing that lavender bubbles and hot water could do for the ache in her heart. Millie's words were well meant, but they were not true. Andie's lies were one thing, they could easily be discredited; but there was no discrediting the things Elizabeth had seen and heard for herself, some of them straight from Charlie. Millie was wrong. Tom was wrong—it was too late. She hadn't even received a phone call from him since just before she left for the airport, when Jane told him she was leaving for Philly. He obviously had found a way to let her go. She had lost him, and there was absolutely nothing she could do about it now. She rubbed her eyes, forgetting about the soap on her fingers, leaving them stinging from both chemicals and repressed tears.

There was a knock at the door. Elizabeth sighed; Millie had probably locked herself out of the flat again. She reluctantly pulled herself out of the water, bubbles clinging in clumps to her flushed skin. She stepped out of the tub and wrapped a towel around her, then walked out of the bathroom and across the living room to the front door. "Millie, when are you going to stop forgetting to bring your keys with you when you leave?" She sighed as she pulled it open, then felt her heart plummet into her stomach when she saw that it was not Millie who stood in the hallway, but *Bryan*.

His eyes traveled from the towel wrapped around her diminished figure and wet skin to her messy hair with loose strands plastered against her neck and face, and then up to her hallowed cheeks and red-rimmed, bloodshot eyes. "Oh, Lizzie," he breathed, and as he stepped through the doorway with his arms extended she felt her face crumple, and stumbled into his embrace.

For several minutes he simply held her as she sobbed; his strong, familiar arms comforting her in a way only they could. Then she stepped back and looked into his eyes, which were filled with concern. "What are you doing here in London, Bryan?" she mumbled.

"I felt terrible about missing you when you were in Philly," he admitted. "I had a strange feeling you needed me, and it bothered me that I wasn't there for you. I thought about just calling, but I knew you would tell me you were fine, even if you weren't. I wanted to see how you were doing for myself, and this was the earliest I could get over here, with work being the nightmare it has been lately. I'm so sorry, Lizzie—if I had known how bad it was for you, I would have dropped everything."

"It's OK, Bryan," she croaked, "I'm just so glad you're here now."

At that moment, there was another knock at the door. Elizabeth frowned and released Bryan in order to open it. Millie stood on the threshold, holding carrier bags in her arms and her phone between her teeth. "Thorry," she muttered through a clenched jaw, "I luckd mythelf out ugin." She walked into the room and set down the bags, then raised her eyebrows as she noticed Bryan standing there, staring back at her in confusion. Millie looked at Elizabeth in her towel, then at Bryan, then back at Elizabeth questioningly.

"Millie, this is Bryan, my best friend from Philly," Elizabeth explained. She saw Millie's eyes narrow at the words 'best friend.' She turned to face Bryan. "Bryan, this is Millie, my flat mate." She noticed the hurt in Millie's eyes and added with a smile, "And my best friend in London."

Millie beamed and held out her hand for Bryan to shake. "Lovely to meet you, Bryan," she trilled happily.

"Yes, charmed to make your acquaintance as well, Millie." Bryan flashed her a signature smile, and Elizabeth watched Millie's cheeks turn pink with delight.

"Do you like toasties, Bryan?" she asked him eagerly as she unloaded her bags onto the counter.

"If I knew what a toasty was, I'm sure I would love one," he answered uncertainly.

"Lizzie's never had one either, so you are both in for a treat." She turned her back to them and began rummaging through the cabinets.

"I should probably get dressed," Elizabeth stammered. "I'll be right back out, Bryan." She left the room.

When she came back into the living room with Bingley in her arms, she found Millie and Bryan deep in whispered conversation behind the kitchen counter. As soon as they saw her enter the room they stopped talking and smiled sheepishly in her direction. Millie handed her a plate of what appeared to be a British-style grilled cheese sandwich, and the three of them filed into the living room. Elizabeth and Bryan took seats on the sofa, while Millie plopped into one of the armchairs.

When their plates were empty, and both Elizabeth and Bryan had praised Millie for her culinary masterpiece, Millie left the room to take a phone call. Bryan pulled Lizzie's bare feet into his lap and began rubbing them. "So," he began, "do you want to talk about what's on your mind?"

Elizabeth sighed. "How long do you have? It's going to take a while to fill you in on everything that's happened since I saw you last." She swallowed the lump in her throat.

Bryan gave her a commiserative look. "Lizzie," he muttered softly, "I already know everything."

Elizabeth felt a swooping sensation in her chest. "You do?"

"I do." He stopped massaging her feet and moved closer to pull her into his arms. "And I am so sorry I wasn't here, love, I, I wish…"

She could hear his voice tremble, and looked up to see tears in his eyes. She reached out to wipe one from his cheek with her thumb. "I know.

Me too." She laid her head against his chest, and he rested his chin on top of her head. After a few moments of silence, she whispered, "How do you know, Bryan? Did Jane tell you?"

"No," he answered. He removed his chin and leaned back to look her in the eye. "I have a confession to make."

Elizabeth sat up straight. "What is it?"

"I wasn't in New York for New Year's Eve." He bit his lip. "I was in Philly."

Elizabeth frowned. "You were home when I came to see you?"

"Well, no, I wasn't home when you texted me. In fact, I didn't even know you were in Philly until, well," he paused. "Charlie told me you accepted a promotion at the magazine and moved back."

Elizabeth felt her mouth drop open. "Charlie called you?"

"No. He followed you to Philly, Lizzie. Only he couldn't find you, so he came to see if I knew where you were."

"Charlie was in Philly?" she whispered.

"Yes." He sighed. "The day before New Year's Eve he showed up at my door in a panic. He had heard from someone—not Jane, I swear—that you had been offered a director position, and that you were moving back to Philly in order to accept it. He thought it wasn't going to happen until after the wedding in March, but when he tried to call you to see if it was true Jane answered and told him you were already on your way to the airport."

Jane must have mentioned the promotion in front of Kassy and Andie after I told her about it on the phone. And of course Andie would be thrilled to use it as ammunition in her mission to destroy me and Charlie.

"I was—but not permanently, at least not yet." Her chin quivered. "My dad had a heart attack. He was in the hospital."

Bryan exhaled softly. "Well, that explains why no one was home when he went to your parents' house first to look for you. I'm so sorry, Lizzie, I had no idea—why on earth didn't you call me?"

"I don't know, honestly. I should have, I know it now." She remembered Tom's words from their recent conversation. "I think I have been subconsciously not letting other people in for a long time. I'm the one who should be sorry."

He reached out to place both hands gently on the sides of her face. "You have absolutely nothing to be sorry about, love."

She smiled. "So, why would Charlie fly all the way to Philly to talk to me? He could have just called." As soon as the words were out of her mouth, she remembered seeing a voicemail from him when she got onto the plane. She never did listen to it. She also remembered with remorse all the other calls from him she missed and never returned. "What did he say to you when he got to your house?"

"He told me everything—from you finding out you were pregnant after your accident at the stables, to moving in with him and accepting his proposal, to your miscarriage and breaking off your engagement because you thought he would be unhappy if he stayed with you." Bryan gave her a pitying look. "Lizzie, I am so sorry I didn't drop everything right then and find you. I thought I would have time once he left, but by the time he did you were already back in London."

Elizabeth stared at him, in shock at the information she was receiving.

Bryan interrupted the silence with, "Honestly, Lizzie—how the hell could you actually believe he could ever be unhappy with you?"

Elizabeth hung her head in shame. "I was an idiot."

"Well, maybe you were." He smiled at the surprised look on her face. "But apparently there is no amount of stupidity on your part that can deter that man from loving you, girl. He was ready to give up everything in his life, without any certainty you would take him back, just to be near to you. He thought you were in Philly to stay, so he asked me to help him find a place to live. We spent the entire day on New Year's Eve looking at apartments in the city. That's why I wasn't home." He smirked. "And can I just be honest for a moment? I forgot what a specimen he is. Well done, darling, well done."

Elizabeth frowned again. "Wait, why would he be looking for a place to live in Philly? That doesn't make any sense."

"What do you mean?"

She sighed. "Charlie's with someone else now, Bryan."

Bryan tilted his head to one side. "What?"

"When I broke up with him, he started dating Jane's friend Andie, one of the bridesmaids in her wedding. And I'm not supposed to know this," she hesitated, "but they are engaged to be married."

"Who's engaged to be married?" Millie reentered the room with three glasses. After passing them out, she dropped down into her armchair and took a sip. Her eyes widened. "Oh, wait," she gasped. "Do you know?"

Elizabeth felt betrayed; Millie had known about Andie and Charlie's engagement and didn't tell her? "Yes, I do know," she replied angrily. "No thanks to you, apparently."

"I'm sorry, Lizzie! She told me not to tell you just yet, because she was worried it might upset you," Millie stammered.

"Since when does Andie care about upsetting me?" Elizabeth exclaimed.

Millie frowned. "Wait," she began slowly. "Who do you think is engaged?"

Elizabeth let out a slow stream of breath. "I know about Andie and Charlie getting engaged, Millie. I saw a picture of her hand with a diamond ring on it on her phone the night of the hen party."

Millie wrinkled her nose. She pulled her phone out from her back pocket and tapped the screen. "You mean this picture?" she asked, holding it out. It was the same picture Elizabeth was referring to.

"Yes." She felt more betrayed than ever. "Andie sent it to you too, then?"

"Lizzie, this isn't Andie's hand," Millie argued, pulling it back to look at it again. "It's Kassy's."

"What?"

"Kassy sent it to me ages ago," Millie explained. "She sent it to Andie and Jane as well. She wanted to send it to you, but she didn't want it to seem like she was being hurtful, considering her fiancé is Charlie's brother."

Elizabeth was stunned into silence. The picture she saw on Andie's phone, the one Andie had sent to Kassy of her hand with an engagement ring on it, was actually the other way around? It was from Kassy? She must have missed that in her rush to give the phone back to Andie. That meant Andie and Charlie were not engaged, which was what she had been thinking ever since the night of the hen party! It also meant Tom had been extremely coy on Valentine's Day when it came to whether he was changing his stance on marriage. The memory of their conversation made Elizabeth smile, knowing just how happy he must have been and still somehow managed to refrain from shouting it from the rooftops.

"Lizzie," Bryan spoke up, "I spent an entire day with Charlie, and he never once mentioned anyone named Andie. If he were engaged, wouldn't he have told me? Besides, he seemed pretty hell-bent on doing whatever it took to prove to you that you make him happier than anyone else on this earth, and that he can't live the rest of his life without you." He gave her a meaningful smile. "He would give anything, believe me."

Elizabeth looked up. She chewed her lip. "But even if Andie and Charlie aren't engaged, I know they are together, because I saw them on a date with my own eyes. Andie told me that he called her." She swallowed hard. "And when I asked him myself, he admitted that he did."

"Yeah," Millie declared. "But how do you know he was calling her to ask her out on a date? How do you know there wasn't some other reason he wanted to meet her at that bakery? I told you, Lizzie—Andie is a lying cow. She probably lied about it being a date, and then continued to lie about being his girlfriend from that point on." She made a face. "I mean, what proof do you have that she even saw him again after that one meeting, besides the fact that she told you she did?"

Elizabeth thought for a moment. It was true; she only had Andie's word to go on when it came to whether or not she was actually dating Charlie, and since when was Andie's word worth anything at all? "I don't have any," she admitted.

"I think you need to talk to Charlie," Bryan concluded, with a heart-stopping smile that made Elizabeth blush.

"And never even listen to another word that comes out of Andie's stupid mouth," Millie added, rolling her eyes. "If she even tries to stand between you and Charlie I will punch her in the throat myself."

"He loves you, Lizzie, *believe* me." Bryan took her hand in his. "He would move heaven and earth to be with you, I'm sure of it. If you want to be with him, then go find him and tell him you love him too." He saw Elizabeth open her mouth in protest and added, "Do it, Lizzie. If not for you, then for me. I need to know you will be taken care of when I leave you—because we both know you are not going to take that job in Philly."

Elizabeth wiped a tear threatening to slide down her cheek and smiled at him. For a moment, they simply gazed at each other. Then Bryan looked down at the glass in his hand.

"What is this?" he asked warily.

"Frozen butterbeer." Millie grinned. "Try it."

He took a slow sip and raised one eyebrow in astonishment. "All right," he exclaimed, "how exactly do you make this? I have to know!"

Millie beamed. Then her smile melted away into a frown. "Hold on just one bloody moment." She looked from Bryan to Elizabeth, her brow furrowed. "What's this about a job in Philly?"

Bryan stayed for rest of the day and well into the evening. It was past midnight when he kissed her forehead and hugged her for several minutes before finally releasing her. Tears rolled down her cheeks as she realized she might not see him again for a very long time, possibly even years. His eyes were also filled with tears; they brimmed over his eyelashes as he muttered with a trembling voice, "I love you, Lizzie, you know that, right? I want you to be happy. That's all I've ever wanted for you. Go find what makes you happy, even if you have to fight for it, and then never let it go."

"I won't Bryan, I promise."

"You deserve happiness, Lizzie, more than anyone I've ever met. You've been through more this past year than most people go through in a lifetime, and I can't help but feel partially to blame. You never would have moved to London if I hadn't driven you to it."

"But if you didn't unintentionally encourage me to make a fresh start with my life I would have stayed in Philly, looking for Mr. Right in all the wrong places. I would never have met Charlie," Elizabeth argued with a smile. "I have a tendency to spin my tires. Sometimes I just need a little push."

"You mean Mr. Darcy, not Mr. Right, don't you?" Bryan added with a smirk. "He was always your type."

"Not anymore." Her cheeks flushed.

"Well, I'm more than willing to be your push, love." He brushed a loose curl from her face and cupped her cheek in his palm. "Now go get that man." He opened the door and stepped into the hallway. "Oh! I completely forgot to give you these earlier," he exclaimed, and reached down to pick up something out of sight beside the door. When he straightened up again, he was holding a bouquet of twenty-four red roses. He held them out for her with a playful grin. "It is now officially Friday, after all."

She grinned as she took them from him. "I love you, Bryan."

"I love you more." He gave her a wink and turned, throwing one last smile over his shoulder at her before he walked away.

Chapter Twenty-Eight

Elizabeth felt tranquil in body and spirit as she sat beneath the willow tree. She leaned against the rough bark, closing her eyes and listening to the steady beating of her heart. She had to tell Charlie she was wrong, that she had been foolish to believe the lies Andie told her—but how? How could she admit to thinking he only wanted to marry her because she was pregnant with his child? How could she admit she thought he stopped loving her and went back to the person who cheated on him and broke his heart? It would be so humiliating to confess how badly she had misjudged him.

She continued to listen to the unwavering thump, thump, thump that seemed to grow louder and louder in her ear. Confused, Elizabeth opened her eyes. That wasn't her heart. Something else was getting louder and louder. What was it? She strained to see in the semi-darkness of twilight. The fog that had rolled in from the drop in temperature made it difficult to distinguish anything beyond fifteen feet in front of her. It was only then she realized she was dreaming, and that she knew all too well what would happen next. She rubbed the goose bumps that enveloped her arms and shivered in anticipation as she listened hard. Those were horse hooves. She was sure of it. As soon as she determined the source of the sound it disappeared. It was now eerily silent. She stood up quickly and gasped as a dark figure emerged from the fog.

Mr. Bingley?! But how—?

She studied him carefully as he began to walk toward her, from the dark blond hair peeking out from under his hat down to his white cravat and black riding boots, and back up to his face again. His lips curved upward into a playfully crooked smile, and as she gazed fixedly at his glorious dimples she was suddenly hit by a wave of sensation she couldn't seem to put her finger on. She gaped at him, jaw dropped open, temporarily struck dumb by the overwhelming feeling that perhaps this wasn't Mr. Bingley at all. Could it be—?

"Elle," he breathed when he reached her.

Her eyes widened at the sound of his nickname for her and her breath caught in her chest. "Charlie?" she whispered in a strangled voice.

He took her hands in his; they were so warm against her icy skin. "Who else would it be?" he asked, and gave her a meaningful smirk with one eyebrow raised in perfect synchronization with the side of his mouth.

She frowned. Unable to speak, she simply stared in confusion at his face. Was it possible it was Mr. Bingley, responding to the name she mistakenly called him by when she fell from the tree a second time? If that were true, why wouldn't he call her Lizzie, like everyone else? There was only one person in the world who called her Elle. "I thought you died in battle," she replied slowly, watching his reaction carefully for clues.

"You can't die if you were never alive to begin with," he answered softly. "And I promise you, my darling, I am very much alive."

Elizabeth felt light-headed. "What?"

He sighed. "I know you've been racked with guilt for being in love with two different people, Elle, but there was no need for it." He shook his head firmly. "Mr. Bingley and I were always the same person." He noted her expression filled with misgiving and continued. "Mr. Bingley is a fictional character in a book, Elle—your favorite book, in fact. He was never, and could never be, a real person. He was, however, your brain's interpretation of a real person—me. Before we met, all you knew of me was the face you saw from your hospital bed, which you then assigned to the fictional character in your dream. In your mind, I actually became Mr. Bingley. I may have talked differently and went by a different name, it was still *me*. After you woke up and we met in person at the pub, it was impossible for you to dream of Mr. Bingley and not associate him with me. It was a gradual transformation, and you may not have picked up on the subtle alterations and similarities, but eventually Mr. Bingley and I became one and the same in your mind, though you still continued to think of us as separate people."

Elizabeth thought hard, her brow furrowed. She gasped. *The day at the lake! He had a scar above his eyebrow—the scar that Charlie got from the car accident! It wasn't there the first time, but it was definitely there the second time around!* She looked for it now; sure enough, there was a thin line above his right eyebrow.

All those dreams she felt awful about having—the kisses she felt guilty about giving, the proposal she felt uneasy about accepting—it had been Charlie the entire time! Now that she thought about it clearly, of course it had been Charlie the entire time. How could it not have been? Was she ever going to stop feeling like a total idiot, even in her dreams? *Sheesh!* She watched helplessly as he flashed her a devastating smile.

Even with half of his face obscured by darkness, Elizabeth couldn't help but think, *Aaannnddd, boom. Another angel gets its wings.*

"When you made the decision to let Mr. Bingley go, and then finally made the realization that no matter how hard you tried, you just couldn't let me go," he continued softly, biting his bottom lip and staring covetously at her mouth. "Mr. Bingley went back to being a fictional character in your favorite book—" Charlie placed his arm around her, his hand firmly gripping her waist. He leaned in and whispered softly, "—and I became the only man of your dreams." He lifted her chin gently with the crook of his finger and kissed her slowly and thoroughly, taking his time. When he finally drew his head back to look into her eyes, he smiled at her dazed expression. "I missed you."

Oh, bloody hell. Yep, it's definitely Charlie.

Elizabeth swallowed hard. "You have no idea how much I missed you," she breathed. He flashed his dimples, and her knees felt weak. "I have just one question to ask you," she said quietly. "It's more of a favor, actually."

"Your wish is my command, my darling," he replied.

She took a deep breath and leaned in close to whisper in his ear.

He smiled. "Did you read my letter?" he asked, pointing to her waist.

She frowned and looked down. Tucked carefully into her sash was an envelope. She pulled it out and unfolded it to see her name scrawled across the front; it was the letter Caroline had given her at Netherfield.

She looked back up at him in confusion. "But—" she began.

He interrupted her with his lips, then took a step backward and gazed determinedly into her eyes. "Read the letter," he whispered softly, and smiled.

Elizabeth's eyes sprang open. Her heart was beating wildly in her chest as she realized she was lying in bed. Once her breathing returned to normal, her eyes drifted to the stack of boxes that lined one wall of her bedroom. Quickly, she tore the blankets off her legs and stumbled across the shadowy room, her fingers tracing the words written on the sides of each box until she located the one she was looking for. She struggled to pick it up and set it on the floor, then tore off the tape and scoured the contents, tossing everything haphazardly to one side. At long last she found it—her worn copy of *Pride and Prejudice*. Flipping through the pages, she gasped when she saw the crisp white envelope with her name scrawled across the front.

She crawled to the spot near the window where the moonlight was filtering in and softly illuminating the floor, then ripped open the envelope to get to the handwritten letter inside. She devoured every word as if they were oxygen and she was gasping for breath. When she finally reached the end, she fondly followed the loops and curves of Charlie's flowing signature. Then she clasped the letter to her chest and let the tears that had welled up fall freely to her lap.

Chapter Twenty-Nine

*I*t was the day before the wedding. Elizabeth and Jane picked up their parents at the airport, then drove them to Aunt Bridget and Aunt Tessa's, where they stayed for lunch with Will, Millie, and their parents. In the afternoon, the three girls met Andie and Kassy at a salon for mani/pedi's.

Though Andie's behavior toward Elizabeth remained unchanged since the last time they were together, Elizabeth now found it much less challenging to be around her. The secret knowledge she now possessed about Charlie following Bryan's visit made Andie's now transparent attempts to intimidate her, by alluding to a relationship that clearly never was, highly amusing, and she took great pleasure in replying to her loaded questions with only saccharine smiles and secretive smirks. For Andie, Elizabeth's mysterious newfound ability not to rise to her taunts was simultaneously infuriating and extremely unnerving.

Once their nails were finished, and their dresses were retrieved from the bridal shop and hung carefully in Elizabeth's nearly empty closet for the following morning, they dispersed to get ready for the rehearsal being held in a private room at a nearby restaurant. It was during dinner afterward, when she was sitting at a table with the rest of the bridesmaids and ushers (with the bride and groom and their parents thankfully out of hearing range at another table), that one of Andie's well-aimed shots finally dented Elizabeth's bulletproof exterior.

"So, Lizzie," she began, with a wink at Dr. Patel. "Are you excited to have Char as your date tomorrow?"

Elizabeth felt her stomach turn over. She had completely forgotten she had asked him to be her date for the wedding. She glanced over to see him beaming with delight, and found herself unable to form a reply with everyone staring at her expectantly.

Suddenly, she heard Millie speak up. "What about you, Andie? Who's your date for the wedding—is it your imaginary boyfriend?"

Elizabeth's eyes bulged. She, along with the rest of the table, turned to look at Andie, who gave a derisive laugh. "Ha! Oh, please Millie." She dug through her purse and pulled out a compact mirror, holding it out in front of her. "You want to say that again?"

Millie remained cool as a cucumber as she smiled back at her. "My boyfriend, unlike yours, actually exists. He is coming to the reception tomorrow."

Elizabeth was momentarily distracted from her unease. "He is?" She gaped at Millie. "Are you serious?"

"Yep," Millie grinned. "He called me yesterday to tell me he was in London. I can't wait for you to meet him."

"Wow," Elizabeth replied, and wrinkled her nose. "The feeling is absolutely mutual."

I'll have to work on my shocked face.

They dove into a discussion on what Elizabeth should bring with her to have him autograph, leaving the others to talk amongst themselves.

When the evening was over, everyone said their goodbyes and left for a good night's sleep before the festivities the next day. Elizabeth was alone in the coat room when she heard someone behind her say softly, "Sorry about Andie tonight, Lizzie." She turned quickly to see Dr. Patel standing behind her.

"Oh! It's all right," she replied, blushing. This was her chance; she had to tell him she couldn't be his date for the wedding, or any other night for that matter. She racked her brain for the best way to do it, but he began taking steps toward her and she lost her train of thought. "I, um, I mean," she stammered. They were so alone—wasn't there anyone left that needed their coat?

"Well, I don't know about you," he began as he took another step closer, "but I am *very* excited about tomorrow. I can't think of any date more romantic than a wedding, can you?"

Help.

She felt her heart beat against her rib cage as she looked around for a quick exit, but he had blocked her only means of escape. She took a step backward and felt the sleeves from the remaining coats brush her shoulders. His face was so close now. "Dr. Patel," she mumbled weakly.

"Please," he sighed, a determined smile on his lips. He placed one hand on her waist and drew her to him. "Call me Char." Before she could protest, he leaned in and kissed her. She was so surprised that she didn't kiss him back; but she didn't push him away from her either, so when he drew his head back he was smiling as though he had just given her an amazing gift. "See you tomorrow, love," he crooned. He walked away, leaving her standing frozen in the coat closet, speechless with astonishment.

Snow was softly falling outside the window of Elizabeth's bedroom as she looked out at the street below the morning of the wedding. Jane, Kassy, and Andie would be arriving in one hour for makeup and mimosas, and Millie's snores could still be heard through the wall, so she had a few moments to reflect on the events from the previous day as she watched the flakes pirouette through the overcast sky.

"Lizzie, I'm here!"

Elizabeth tore her head away from both her bad memories and the window to look through the doorway at her sister, who had just entered through the front door. She grinned and rushed through the living room to greet her. "It's your wedding day!" she squealed, throwing her arms around her. "I can't believe it's finally here!"

Jane beamed. "Me either! I'm going to be a married woman in less than three hours!" She sucked in her breath and bit her lip. "We need to start getting ready!"

"Where are Kassy and Andie?"

"They should be here any minute," Jane answered, checking the time on her phone. "They stopped to get some breakfast for us. There's no way I would be able to wait until after the ceremony."

"Good call," Elizabeth reassured her, thinking of Bryan's wedding.

Jane glanced at the window. "Did you know it's snowing?" she cried. "It's March, for crying out loud! Do you think it will be a problem?"

Elizabeth smiled. "Not at all. If anything, it's going to look like a winter wonderland. Not even a blizzard could stop people from coming today, trust me." Her eyes watered. "I am just so happy for you, Jane. And

I'm going to do everything I can to make this day perfect for you and Will." She gave her another hug. "I love you both so much."

Jane wiped her eyes with her fingers. "I love you too, Lizzie," she sobbed. Then she laughed. "You are so lucky I don't have my makeup on yet."

When Kassy and Andie arrived, Elizabeth left to wake up Millie, who was sleeping so heavily she had to jump up and down on the bed several times before she finally opened her eyes. "What realm is it?"

Elizabeth rolled her eyes. "Midgard." She gave her a stern look. "It's Jane's wedding day, Millie, so get your butt out of bed. We have to be at the church in two hours." She saw Millie's eyes close and gave one last enthusiastic jump near her head.

"I'm awake!" Millie shouted, before rolling off onto the floor with a thud.

Elizabeth leapt off the bed and gave her a satisfied smile. "By the way, there are pastries out there." She watched as Millie's head popped up eagerly over the edge of the bed, and she stood and walked briskly to where Elizabeth was standing. "Oh, and also Andie," she grimaced, then grabbed Millie's arm as she spun around and tried to crawl back into bed.

When they were completely dressed, with their hair and makeup done Elizabeth, Kassy, Millie, and Andie all stood back to admire Jane in all her glory. She was absolutely stunning in her classic yet modern ivory crepe sheath silhouette gown with its sweetheart neckline and beaded crepe belt. The plunging back stopped at her waist, where a row of buttons trailed all the way to the end of the chapel train. Her long blonde hair was swept up in a chignon with a beaded comb, and matching beaded earrings dangled from her ears.

"Jane." Elizabeth sighed. "Wait till Will sees you." She looked around at the others, who were equally breathless with admiration. Their own dresses were glorious concoctions of glittering rose gold that shimmered and gleamed in the light. The front was simple, with a high neckline, cap sleeves, and sheath skirt that clung to their hips and flowed down to the floor in a sweeping train like liquid copper. The open back dipped dramatically with a swath of loose fabric from one shoulder to the other. Their hair was gathered loosely at the base of their necks in a knotted updo, and their beaded earrings were a smaller version of Jane's.

"The car is here!" Millie called, looking out the window. "Oh, hell yes—it's a bloody Rolls Royce, baby."

They all gathered around her to see for themselves; sure enough, a white Rolls Royce town car was waiting for them at the curb. They all let out squeals of delight and grabbed their purses, as well as Jane's train, before making their way carefully down to the snowy sidewalk in their heels. When the car pulled up to their destination, they got out and stared drop-jawed at the towering exterior.

"I still cannot believe you are getting married at the Westminster Cathedral," Andie muttered in awe. "I am so going to have my wedding here."

Millie rolled her eyes and whispered in Elizabeth's ear, "That no one will attend, because it's never going to happen. Her funeral might be more realistic—they're going to need an adequate space to hold the crowd of people with cause to celebrate."

Elizabeth snorted. "Millie, stop it," she reprimanded her, though her eyes were twinkling.

They entered through a side door, into a small room where they would wait until the ceremony started. They could hear the buzz of conversation from the sanctuary as people made their way to their seats.

"I'm so nervous I feel sick," Jane mumbled as she paced back and forth with her bouquet in one hand and clutching her stomach with the other.

Elizabeth smiled. "It's going to be fine, Jane. Before you know it, you will be snogging Will in the back of that Rolls Royce, on your way to breakfast." She closed her eyes and sighed, thinking of the food that awaited them.

Jane shot her an amused smile. "Did you just say snogging?"

"Did I? Hmm, I guess I'm officially British now, huh?" Elizabeth smirked.

Jane's smile faded. "Just in time to move back to Philly."

Elizabeth frowned. "Jane, I—" Before she could finish, her father entered the room to tell them it was time to begin the ceremony.

They lined up at the door, and as the music began, left one by one to walk down the long aisle in the center of the magnificent sanctuary. When it was Elizabeth's turn, she pulled her sister and father into a quick group hug, kissing each of their cheeks and pausing to wipe off her lipstick. Then she began to walk down the aisle, her heart pounding in her ears as all of the people in the rows of chairs smiled appreciatively as she passed. She quickly located her mother near the front, beaming with pride. Then her eyes found

Will's as he stood grinning back at her from the altar. She gave him a wink and took her place next to Andie.

Suddenly, the music changed. Jane and her father began their slow and steady pace to the altar, both of them smiling through their tears. Elizabeth watched happily as he kissed her on both cheeks, then gave Will a hug and joined their hands before taking his seat. Jane smiled nervously at Will. He grinned back, unable to take his eyes off of her.

The minister gave his opening remarks. As Elizabeth listened to his words, her eyes wandered to the man standing at the front of the line of ushers on the opposite side—whose dark brown eyes were currently focused on hers. He gave her a wink and a knowing smile, which she only returned halfheartedly. She couldn't help but think of Bryan's wedding, when it was Charlie that stood gazing at her so intently it was as if everyone else in the room were suddenly dissolving into nonexistence. Her heart began to ache; when would she get the chance to see him again?

An explosion of applause broke her from her thoughts and she glanced around dazedly. Did she really daydream about Charlie the entire ceremony? She couldn't clap with both bouquets in her hands, so she grinned as Will dipped Jane and kissed her, then handed her back her bouquet and bent down to straighten her train before they hurried down the aisle amidst the cheers and wolf-whistles. She felt someone beside her and looked over to see Dr. Patel holding out his arm for her to take, flashing her his most charming smile. She placed her hand reluctantly on his bicep and forced a smile as they followed Jane and Will outside.

As the bride and groom were to take the Rolls Royce to the wedding breakfast alone, the rest of the bridal party were left to decide how they would get there. Sanders, who Elizabeth hadn't seen since Jane's engagement party, eagerly offered to take all of the girls in his car. Elizabeth was about to accept when Andie spoke up. "I'm sure Lizzie would rather go in Char's car, isn't that right, Lizzie?" She raised her eyebrows expectantly.

"Would you like to join us, Andie?" Dr. Patel asked.

Andie gave him a knowing smile. "Oh, no, that's all right. I'm sure the two of you would much rather be alone. I'll go with Sanders."

Elizabeth watched wistfully as they all left. She turned to see Dr. Patel offering her his arm once more. "Shall we?" he asked hopefully, and with a sigh she allowed him to escort her to his car.

When breakfast concluded, the bridal party had their pictures taken in various locations all around the city. Then it was finally time to make their way to the venue for the reception. Jane and Will, who loved the London skyline and would have held their reception in the London Eye if their entire guest list could fit inside one of the glass capsules, had chosen Altitude 360. It was a cavernous set of connecting rooms at the very top of the tallest building in Westminster, surrounded by windows that boasted breathtaking views of the city.

Elizabeth sat at a table with Dr. Patel and Millie while they waited for the others to join them. She looked up to see Kassy and Tom approaching, her heart performing its usual somersault each time she saw his familiar blue eyes and long, slender frame. She dodged Dr. Patel's arm which was aiming for her waist and stood quickly to greet them.

"Hi, Tom," she trilled nervously, giving him a brief hug.

"Hey, darling, how have you been?" He flashed her a broad smile, his dimples on full display.

She swallowed hard as she stared at them. "Good, and you?" She smirked as she turned to face Kassy, giving her a hug as well. "Do I finally get to officially congratulate the two of you on your engagement?"

Kassy glanced nervously at Tom, whose eyes widened. "You know?" she squeaked.

Elizabeth laughed. "Oh, I know," she assured her with a grin. "And I literally could not be happier for you." She reached down for Kassy's hand, which was grievously bare. "Girl, you better get that ring on your finger and start showing it off right now!"

Kassy's face turned red. She pulled a thin chain from her neckline, which held a gorgeous diamond solitaire ring that was easily four carats. She turned for Tom to undo the clasp and slide it off. Then, while Elizabeth watched in excitement, her hands covering her mouth, he gently placed it on her finger.

"That's much better." She smiled as Tom gave Kassy a quick kiss and they took their seats at the table. As soon as she returned to her seat, Dr. Patel leaned over to engage her in conversation. She did her best to appear interested until Millie took the seat beside her.

"I hope they bring dinner out soon," she muttered. "I haven't eaten since breakfast, and I just pounded a glass of chardonnay at the bar. I'm going to start a conga line soon if I don't get something in my stomach." She smiled at Elizabeth. "It looks like Sanders might be up for it, don't you think?"

They both looked over to the table next to them, where he was grinning playfully in their direction. When they saw him he gave a little wave and a roguish smirk.

When the plates were cleared away, and the best man had given his speech, which was greatly comprised of subtle but bawdy jokes and suggestively charming anecdotes that centered around his and Will's romantic encounters before he met Jane, Elizabeth took her turn with the microphone. She gave a heartfelt and eloquent speech, overflowing with love and praise for her sister that left everyone wiping away tears of appreciation.

The live band began playing, and Jane and Will took the floor for their first dance. Elizabeth watched contentedly for a few moments, then noticed other couples began to join them, including the members of the bridal party. She cringed as she realized it meant she would have to dance with Dr. Patel. Sure enough, he took her hand from where it lay on the table and helped her to her feet, then led her out onto the dance floor. She kept her body stiff as they swayed back and forth with the music, his hand resting a little too comfortably around her waist. He gradually drew her toward him until he was so close she could feel his breath on her face as he crooned in a seductively low voice, "I don't want this night to end, do you?"

I know I can't wait for this song to end.

"My feet are killing me, Dr. Patel. Maybe we should go sit back down for a while."

He smiled suggestively. "You know, I have a hot tub at my place. If you want, I can take you there so you can, you know, soak your feet. I'm sure Jane and Will won't miss us one bit." He brought his face right up to her ear and whispered, "And for God's sake, Lizzie, call me Char."

Elizabeth pulled her hand from his and took a step back. "That is so not going to happen." She wavered at the look on his face. "I'm sorry, this is my fault, really—I should have been honest with you from the start— but I'm not interested in beginning a serious relationship with you."

He gave a short laugh. Looking around quickly, he took her hand back in his and placed his other on her waist once more. "Don't worry, Lizzie," he began assertively, "I'm not interested in a serious relationship either."

"You're not?" Elizabeth frowned in confusion. "Then why did you ask me out on three dates?"

He snorted. "Three dates don't equal a serious relationship, Lizzie. They do typically equal something else, however—" he moved his hand to the small of her back "—and since *you* were the one, not me, who practically begged for the third, I can only assume you were begging for something else as well." His hand slid down to grope her backside. "It's all right—I know you want it as badly as I do."

Like the flip of a switch, Elizabeth completely lost her ability to reason. She drove her high heel down hard onto his foot, and he groaned in pain, releasing her. She turned to leave, then had a flash of inspiration and spun around again. "You might want to go home and soak that foot in your hot tub, *Char*," she snapped. "Oh, and please, *don't* call me Lizzie. In fact, don't call me at all—I don't ever want to talk to you again."

She left him alone on the dance floor and returned to her seat at the now empty table. She watched as Andie made her way over to where Dr. Patel was still standing and they exchanged a few words, then began dancing

348

with each other. She felt her eyes well up with angry tears, but before they spilled over Millie sat down beside her.

"Are you all right?" she asked warily. Elizabeth told her what he had said, and Millie jerked her head toward the dance floor. She cracked her knuckles and turned back to face Elizabeth with fury in her blue eyes. "I've always thought that guy was skeevy. Want me to end him right now?" she growled.

Elizabeth couldn't help but smile. "No, it's all right. I should have known, considering he asked me out in the middle of a therapy session at the hospital." She sighed. "And now that I think about it, I remember mentioning to him that I got a kitten the same day we were all at Jane and Will's. He probably knew it was my cat when Will told him you found one wandering around, and offered to take him so he could later guilt me into going out with him." She shrugged at the outrage on Millie's face. "Would you feel less angry if I told you I think I just pierced his foot with my heel?"

"Yes." Millie answered. "Although I still think he deserves to be punched in the face." She gave Elizabeth a smile. Her eyes drifted to the right and bulged slightly as her mouth fell open in surprise. "My boyfriend is here!" she breathed. She stood quickly, knocking over her chair. "I'll be right back!" she called, and hurried away from the table.

Elizabeth turned to follow with her eyes the trail Millie had blazed through the crowded dance floor. She smiled as she saw her throw her arms around someone who had just entered the room; someone with a slight build, chestnut hair, and thick chestnut eyebrows. They began walking over to her, and she braced herself to act sufficiently convinced of his authenticity. Just before they reached her, she gasped.

"Lizzie, I want you to meet my boyfriend Daniel," Millie gushed, and moved aside so he could step forward.

"Pleasure to meet you," he said, smiling and holding out his hand.

She reached out and shook it for an awkwardly prolonged length of time as, completely dumbfounded, she gazed into his striking midnight-blue eyes. Her brain commanded her to say something, anything, but her lips refused to comply. Instead she just continued to stare in shock as Millie gave her a self-assured smile. "We'll be back, Lizzie," she sighed, and led him away from the table to the dance floor.

The sun was beginning to set over London's majestic skyline beyond the enormous windows surrounding each table, painting the sky with pinks and oranges. The lights of the city twinkled like fireflies, sending their shimmering reflections dancing across the River Thames. Giant snowflakes swirled softly to the ground. The view reminded Elizabeth of a snow globe as she gazed admiringly from her lonely spot at the deserted table. She raised her fork and stabbed forlornly at the piece of cake before her with no intention of eating it.

The band's take on "Sweet Caroline" came to an end, and there was a light pause before the music began again. It took a few moments, but eventually Elizabeth recognized it as the Jason Mraz song, "I Won't Give Up," that had been playing the night of Bryan's wedding, when she danced with Charlie as he sang along in perfect harmony. She recalled, with a twinge of heartache, how he had waited for the interlude to tell her for the first time that he was in love with her, and that he felt as though he had loved her forever. She recalled how he told her there was something he had been wanting to ask her, and how her dad told her he asked for permission to marry her long before that night.

She listened to the words of the song, with its message of long-suffering and everlasting love in the midst of trials and heartbreak. She was reminded of a passage from the bible her father used to quote to her when she was little. She could almost hear him repeating it to her now, just as he had used it in his speech for the bride and groom only an hour earlier.

"Love is patient, love is kind.

Love bears all things, believes all things, hopes all things, and endures all things.

Love never ends.

Faith, hope, and love abide, these three; but the greatest of these is love."

With tears in her eyes, she looked out at the dance floor. She froze instantly. Standing directly in the center, his icy-blue eyes focused on hers, and hers alone, and whose intense gaze made her feel like everyone else in the room were suddenly dissolving into nonexistence, was Charlie.

Chapter Thirty

*F*or a few seconds she simply stared at him in his crisp black suit. The background noise dwindled into a dull humming sound in her ears. Then the sound of the music came rushing back and she quickly got to her feet. Like a moth to a flame, Elizabeth walked slowly out to where Charlie stood on the dance floor, without a thought in her head as to what she would say when she reached him.

Luckily for her, no words were necessary. She stopped and stood before him, her eyes locked onto his. There was a passion in his fiery gaze that made her suddenly weak, and she felt her knees buckle slightly. Without a word he reached for her hands, and, pausing to gently kiss one of her palms, placed them around his neck. Then he took her waist and pulled her close to his body. She could feel the beating of his heart against her chest as they swayed with the music, his eyes never leaving hers. Their faces gradually drew nearer until she was dizzy with anticipation from his breath warm and soft on her lips. Though he closed his eyes, he didn't kiss her; he seemed to be patiently waiting for it to be her choice.

Patience proved to not be one of Elizabeth's virtues, however, as the last lines of the song came to an end and she dove right in, blissfully unaware of the commotion around them as the next song, "Love Shack," began and the couples around them went wild. When they finally parted, she looked up at him. His blue eyes were twinkling with euphoria as he gave her a slow, crooked smile. "Do you want to go somewhere so we can talk?"

She couldn't speak, so she nodded eagerly instead. He took her hand and led her from the dance floor. On their way to the next room they passed Will and Jane talking with Tom and Kassy, and when her eyes met her sister's, she gave Elizabeth a knowing smile. Elizabeth raised her eyebrows at her questioningly, and Jane replied with a nod and a wink. Elizabeth grinned, then looked ahead once more.

Just before they turned the corner they heard a voice shout out, "Hey! Where do you think you're going with my date?"

Turning around, they saw Dr. Patel standing there, his expression full of indignation.

"I beg your pardon. Did you say something to me?" Charlie asked him calmly.

"Yes," Dr. Patel began, taking a step closer. "I did. I said get your hands off of my date."

Elizabeth spoke up. "I'm not your date, Dr. Patel." She saw Andie approaching over his shoulder, her face alight with pleasure.

"Really?" he sneered, taking yet another step toward her. "I was under the impression I was, considering you asked me to be your wedding date the night we were, you know, *together*."

"What?!" Elizabeth's heart skipped a beat. She briefly noticed Millie and Daniel join Jane's side. When she looked at her, Millie cracked her knuckles menacingly and raised her eyebrows in Dr. Patel's direction.

Charlie walked up to stand directly in front of Dr. Patel, his face perfectly composed as he looked down on him from his substantial advantage in height. "You need to leave, Patel," he threatened, his voice low and dangerous. "Now."

"What's the matter, Bennet?" Dr. Patel goaded him. "Worried I'm going to steal another fiancée from you?"

Everyone within hearing range froze in place and held their breath, their eyes wide with shock. Elizabeth's mouth fell open as her stunned eyes traveled from Dr. Patel's face to Charlie's. She had never seen him angrier than at that moment, with rage churning in his glowing blue eyes like tempestuous clouds in a stormy sky. His chest heaved with long, deep breaths, and his fists were clenching and unclenching at his sides. He looked so uncharacteristically menacing (and yet somehow insanely attractive) that Elizabeth wondered how Dr. Patel didn't shrink away from the lightning bolts that seemed ready to strike him dead at any second.

She glanced back at his face, and sure enough fear registered in Dr. Patel's eyes as he continued in a voice that lacked conviction. "At least one of them was a good shag."

Tom's voice could just be heard as he muttered out loud, "Oh, you just completely cocked up, mate."

Without hesitation, Charlie stepped back and swung his arm around, sinking his fist deep into Dr. Patel's unsuspecting face and sending him careening to the floor. He gave one last look of fury at his crumpled form before holding his hand out to Elizabeth. She took it eagerly and they turned to leave the room.

After taking only a few steps Elizabeth suddenly felt a hand on her arm yank her violently backward. She heard a sound like a crack of thunder, and both she and Charlie turned around to see Dr. Patel lying at their feet, bleeding and apparently out cold. Will, who was standing over him, flexing his biceps and shaking out his fists, barked, "Don't ever lay a finger on my sister-in-law again, you piece of shit."

Jane walked dazedly up to Will, her eyes hungry with desire. "Oh, my God, that was so hot." She grabbed his face in her hands and pulled his mouth roughly onto hers. He wrapped his arms around her and they continued to vigorously canoodle each other as their audience watched in amusement.

Andie, who up until that point had remained speechless, threw herself onto Dr. Patel's unconscious form and began wiping blood away from his face with his pocket square, mascara running down her cheeks as she ugly cried tears of anguish.

Suddenly, a voice spoke up amidst the chaos. "This is, by far, the best wedding I have ever been to." Elizabeth, Charlie, Tom, and Kassy looked over at Daniel, who was beaming, thoroughly entertained by the melodramatic scene he had just witnessed.

Elizabeth felt yet another hand on her arm; and this time she could sense an urgency in its gentle touch. She turned around. Seeing the desperate look in Charlie's eyes, she followed him wordlessly from the room. When they reached the hallway they kept walking until Charlie stopped at a door labeled, *Roof.* With a mischievous smile he opened it and gestured for Elizabeth to go through first. She smiled back at him, then stepped through the doorway and out into the cold night air. She rubbed her arms as they were both immediately covered in goose bumps. Charlie removed his suit jacket and draped it around her shoulders, and she turned to face him with a grateful smile.

They took a moment to gaze out at the splendor of the city. From where they stood they could see nearly the entire skyline lit up like a fairyland. The snowflakes were still falling, and as she watched them gather in his hair she was reminded of Christmas Eve, when he had come to her flat to try and explain why she had seen him with Andie at the bakery. *Andie! Dr. Patel!*

Dr. Patel was the person Andie had cheated on Charlie with!

Her heart suddenly lurched. "Charlie," she blurted out, "Dr. Patel, I, I had no idea about him and Andie," she stammered.

"Neither did I." He gave her a rueful smile. "I don't know why, really. It makes complete sense now that I look back on it." He groaned and examined his bruised hand. "I hope I at least broke his nose."

"Charlie, I was never with Dr. Patel," she assured him. "I only went to dinner with him once, because I felt obligated to thank him for bringing Bingley home when he was lost. But I never had any feelings for him. And it certainly never, you know, went beyond dinner." She gave him a remorseful look. "I should never have even agreed to that."

"It's all right, Elle," he soothed.

"And I had no idea Andie was engaged to you, Charlie, I swear. She told me when I met her that you only dated for a few months. She said she broke up with you because you didn't want to get married after your fiancée broke your heart." She dropped her gaze to her feet. "She basically lied to me for months about the two of you being together again. And I believed her."

"And I am so sorry for not telling you about the engagement in the first place. The night you met her was also the first time I saw her since I broke it off. She asked me not to even mention it to you. She said she was ashamed of who she was back then and didn't want you to think badly of her. I guess I thought maybe she had actually matured and decided to give her the benefit of the doubt. So you see, I am no better than you when it came to believing her lies—I'm worse, in fact—since I was fool enough to believe them the second time around." He exhaled disdainfully through his nose and shook his head. Then he lifted her chin with the crook of his finger to look her in the eye. "She did tell the truth about one thing," he began, "I never did want to get married after everything I went through with her." He smiled at the look on her face. "But that was before I met you."

She bit her lip. "My dad told me you asked his permission to marry me back in June."

"That I did," he admitted. "If I had the chance to ask him the moment we met, I would have."

"And Bryan told me you followed me to Philly."

"I had to," he insisted. "You left me no choice when you wouldn't answer my calls. Kassy told Tom you were accepting a job in Philly after the wedding, so I knew I would have to find a place to live over there, nice enough for both of us once I convinced you to marry me. I thought I had a bit more time, but when Jane told me you were on your way to the airport, I panicked, thinking you were already leaving. I chased after you, you know," he admitted, one eyebrow raised. "It was exactly like one of those cheesy romantic comedy films, where they run through the airport to stop the love of their life from boarding a plane. I had already gone through security, so I was barefoot and everything."

Elizabeth tried to keep a straight face at the mental image. "I am so sorry. I should have answered your calls, but I was too afraid to hear you tell me for yourself you were in love with Andie. I went to Philly because my dad had a heart attack."

He nodded. "I know. I spoke to both your dad and your mum before I came back to London, actually."

Elizabeth smiled. "You did?"

"I did. After I searched for flats with Bryan—who, coincidentally, I had a surprisingly brilliant time getting to know, by the way—I drove back to your parents' house with the hope you would be there. They told me you had left that morning for London, and invited me to stay with them for the night before my flight the next day. Your dad told me about a conversation the two of you had before you left." He gave her a wearying smile. "It seems he and I have a lot in common when it comes to the obstinate, headstrong women we have chosen to love."

She frowned. "Charlie, the things I said at the hospital—" she carefully wiped away the tears in her eyes so as not to smear her mascara "—when I gave you back the ring. I didn't mean them. I was just so afraid you wouldn't be happy if you married me, with everything that happ—with all of my health problems." She unknit her eyebrows. "Although, I went back to the doctor recently and he told me my kidney was perfectly healthy for the time being, so that's something, right?"

"Elle," he whispered, and smiled. "There is absolutely nothing on God's green earth that could keep me from wanting to marry you, even if it means I have to take videos of every significant moment for the rest of our lives, in case you forget them."

Elizabeth thought hard. "Actually, I don't think I've forgotten anything for a while now! At least, I don't remember forgetting anything."

She laughed. "You know what I mean. I guess maybe you were right, that the memory loss was only a side effect of the concussion."

"Well, that's a relief." He sighed happily as he dropped to one knee. "Because I would really love to do this just one more time." He reached into his pocket and pulled out the ring. Then he looked up at her and smiled, his dimples making her heart beat faster in her chest. "Elizabeth Poppy Baker," he began, and she wrinkled her nose at the mention of her middle name. "I have wasted entirely too many years of my life apart from you already—I cannot imagine living another one without you as my wife. If you'll let me, I'll try my hardest to make you happy for every minute of every day, for the rest of your life. Because, darling, you are all I could ever need to make me happy for the rest of mine." She grinned at him as he took her hand and slid the ring onto her finger. "Will you marry me?"

"Yes," she answered, clearly and without any hesitation whatsoever. He stood quickly and wrapped his arms around her, then lifted her off the ground and spun her around once before setting her back down again. Pulling her closer to him, he reached up to hold her face gently with both hands as he kissed her, his lips warm and soft against hers.

She pulled her head back abruptly and squinted up at him. "What do you think my chances are of convincing you not to use my middle name again?"

He leaned his forehead against hers and smiled with his eyes still closed. "Not good at all," he whispered, and pulled her closer. She wrapped her arms around his neck and nuzzled her nose against his, then smiled up at him. He flashed his adorable crooked grin and kissed her again as the softly falling snow dusted his eyelashes and covered her auburn hair in a lacy veil of white.

When they reentered the building, most of the wedding guests were already gone. Dr. Patel and Andie were nowhere to be seen, presumably having left together to nurse each other's physical and mental wounds. Tom, Kassy, Millie, Daniel, Jane, and Will were all still out on the dance floor, so Elizabeth and Charlie joined them for one last dance. When they got close enough to the bride and groom, Elizabeth showed Jane the ring on her finger and staggered as she was nearly knocked over backward by her delighted embrace. Will clasped Charlie's hand firmly, each of them grimacing in pain from their injuries, then leaned in for a quick hug. The others rushed over to congratulate them as well, and then they all said their goodbyes.

Charlie took Elizabeth back to his flat, where they stayed up all night long talking, at least when their lips weren't otherwise occupied.

The next morning, Jane called Elizabeth and asked her to meet her for a late breakfast. She was leaving for her honeymoon that afternoon, but she wanted to say goodbye to her sister first. When they arrived at their favorite café, they sat in their usual spot by the window and sipped their coffee while they waited for their food to arrive.

"Do you remember the first time we came here?" Jane asked with a smile. "It was the night I told you I was setting you up on a blind date."

Elizabeth wrinkled her nose. "I vaguely recall it, yes." She smirked. "You told me he wasn't your type, but that *I* might like him."

"Right. Not my best moment, I'll admit." Jane gave her a sheepish look. "I wonder how good ole Simon is doing these days. Did I tell you he quit teaching?"

"No, but I didn't tell you that I received an invitation to his wedding a while back." Elizabeth smiled, shaking her head in disbelief. "He and Emma are getting married, can you believe it? In Pennsylvania! They are going to live there, I guess. I can't imagine how hard it must be for him to leave the first love of his life."

Jane's lip curled. "You?"

"No." Elizabeth rolled her eyes. "His mother."

They both laughed. "So Simon is moving to Pennsylvania, huh? That should be interesting," Jane teased.

Elizabeth caught her meaning. "Yeah," she began with a knowing smile. "Good thing I'm not."

Jane's eyes widened. "You're not accepting the job in Philly?" she asked hopefully.

Elizabeth grinned. "No, I'm not. It's an amazing opportunity, but it's not for me." She sighed happily. "There are far too many reasons why I could never leave London," she admitted, as she glanced down at the ring on her left hand.

She looked back up at Jane, who she was surprised to see had tears in her eyes and was suddenly looking extremely coy. "I think I might have one more to add to your list," she offered, and bit her lip. "I just found out yesterday that I'm pregnant."

Elizabeth's mouth fell open. "Are you serious?" she gasped. "I'm going to be an auntie?" She watched the apprehension leave Jane's face as she nodded. Elizabeth jumped to her feet and threw her arms around her sister. "I'm so happy for you and Will!" she cried. "And I'm so excited!"

"Really?" Jane muttered, relief flooding her features. "Because I was a little worried to tell you, to be honest. I didn't know how you would take the news."

"I could never be anything but thrilled that my best friend in the entire world is going to be a mom!" She beamed. "Besides, Charlie was right—we can always adopt. There are so many children out there that need loving families, you know?" She let out an excited squeal. "I can't even wait to hold my niece in my arms!"

Jane laughed. "Niece? It could be a boy, you know."

Elizabeth shook her head adamantly. "No, it's a girl. I'm sure of it."

Jane grinned. "So, you and Charlie had time last night to talk about your future together?" she asked slyly.

"Oh, maybe just a smidgen." Elizabeth blushed. "By the way, did you tell him to come to the wedding?"

"I might have called him," Jane answered shamelessly. She gave her sister an exasperated look. "I had to, after finding out you asked Dr. Patel to be your date for the wedding. I was a little worried you might do something you would later regret. I knew seeing Charlie in person would knock some sense back into you." She smirked. "I did not anticipate him knocking some sense into anyone else though, I'll admit."

Elizabeth cringed. "Jane, I am so sorry about the whole thing! I had no idea that Dr. Patel was the man Andie cheated on Charlie with. He told me later that he never knew either, which is probably why he lost his temper and punched him right then and there." She chewed on her lip. "I have never seen him like that before."

Jane raised one eyebrow suggestively. "It was pretty hot though, right?"

Elizabeth shuddered, closing her eyes. "It really was." She frowned. "But still, I know if he were thinking clearly he would never want to do anything to ruin your night."

Jane let out a short laugh. "Are you kidding me? Ruin my night?" she exclaimed. "Watching Will lay out Patel with one punch was the sexiest thing I have ever seen in my entire life!" Her eyes unfocused at the memory and she gave Elizabeth a suggestive smile. "If I wasn't already pregnant, I would be now."

Elizabeth laughed. Then her smile faded. "I can't believe I didn't realize what a sleaze bag Dr. Patel was. He seemed so nice at first. I even went to see him at the hospital, and he was so attentive and compassionate as he listened to me talk about my anxiety issues." She rolled her eyes.

"Don't beat yourself up, Lizzie," Jane reassured her. "No one knew until last night, when he showed his true colors. Will told me this morning he wishes he had never asked him to be his best man. He spent a lot of time getting reacquainted with Tom since he started dating Kassy, and I think they might be besties now." She laughed. "By the way, did you know they were at Eton together with Prince Harry? I almost lost it when I found out."

"Wow, really?" Elizabeth snorted. "Didn't Andie say she wanted to marry him? Guess she missed out on that love connection, huh?"

"Speaking of Andie, and wishing I had never asked someone to be in the wedding," Jane muttered. "I am so glad to be rid of her. She was driving me off the rails, and had been since the moment I asked her to be a bridesmaid. The only reason I didn't kick her out was because I thought maybe it would upset Will, since they worked together. But as it turns out, Will never could stand her either." She gave Elizabeth a look of disgust. "And if I had known how badly she was going to treat my baby sister, and how she did her best to come between you and Charlie after breaking his heart in the first place, I would have sent her to the seventh level of hell, where she belongs."

Elizabeth grinned. "I love you, Jane."

"I love you too, Lizzie," Jane replied with a smile.

Chapter Thirty- One

*I*t was New Year's Eve. Softly falling snow slowly transformed the cars on the quiet street below into giant marshmallows. Sporadic partygoers trudged through the drifts in their evening wear, scrambling to deliver their champagne bottles before the midnight toast. Muffled laughter and music reverberated down the hallway of the building; the vibration from the speakers producing a steady humming that traveled through the narrow walls.

Beyond the door labeled 207 in faded brass markers there was even more evidence of it being an extraordinary evening. Bouquets of wildflowers were gathered on the kitchen counter, the cheerful daisies and vibrant bluebells gathered with silky blue ribbon. Powder-blue bridesmaid dresses with sweetheart necklines were carefully hung in a row beside an ivory crepe sheath strapless gown with an off the shoulder panel of sheer lace that tapered just below the belted waist. The lace sleeves ended in a row of buttons near the wrist, and the trail of buttons on the low back pointed to the flowing chapel train.

Elizabeth, Jane, Millie, and Kassy had just finished putting on their makeup. Elizabeth, whose hair was loosely braided across the back of her head with the rest hanging down her back in thick curls, smiled around at the rest of the girls as they admired her nearly finished look.

"All that's left is the dress!" Jane exclaimed, and turned to retrieve it from its place in her closet.

Once they were completely ready they donned their light brown faux mink stoles and stood before the mirror to fully appreciate their effect.

"All I need now is the iron throne," Millie muttered under her breath, staring at her reflection with a fervid gleam in her narrowed eye.

They made their way outside to Jane's car. As soon as they reached the sidewalk, however, Millie spoke up. "I have a little surprise, girls." She pointed to the street, where a gleaming, fully restored 1964 silver Aston Martin DB5 stood out among the snow-covered mounds surrounding it.

"Millie, where did this come from?" Elizabeth asked breathlessly.

"I borrowed it from my boyfriend," Millie answered proudly. She grinned. "I promised not to drive too fast."

"In this snow?" Jane cried. "You better not, Millie! I have a baby now, remember?"

They piled in and drove (slowly, much to Millie's chagrin) to the stables. When they arrived they saw a beautiful white open carriage and two majestic matching horses waiting for them, and after climbing in, snuggled together under the white fur blankets as the carriage made its way over to the barn. As it stopped in front of the open doors, they all gasped in unison. The inside of the barn was almost unrecognizable, with strands of fairy lights and paper lanterns suspended from the rafters. Rows of white chairs lined either side of the barn wood center aisle, their occupants wearing coats and white fur blankets across their laps. At the end of the aisle stood a rustic altar made of birch logs with garlands of wildflowers draped from one side to the other, and standing in front of it, wearing a crisp black suit and a devastating smile, was Charlie.

Elizabeth grinned at him as one by one they climbed carefully down the steps of the carriage. The live quartet in the back corner began playing an instrumental version of "Marry Me," by Train. Kassy began her walk down the aisle, followed by Millie. Jane gave her sister a kiss on the cheek, then took her turn.

Elizabeth's dad joined her side and smiled at her through the tears that were glistening in his eyes. "Ready?" he mouthed, and she nodded back at him excitedly.

As they made their way down the aisle, Elizabeth couldn't take her eyes away from Charlie's. When they finally reached where he stood, her dad placed his hands on her arms and kissed her cheek. "I love you, my darling girl," he whispered in her ear, then left to take his place beside her sobbing mother and wrapped his arm around her.

For years to come, Elizabeth had to admit to herself she may have experienced one last incident of memory loss, as she could never seem to recall the minister's words in the short but sweet ceremony; though in that one circumstance it had absolutely nothing to do with a head injury. Instead, she blamed it entirely on the man who stood before her, holding her hands in his and gazing at her as if no one and nothing else existed in the world.

She did, however, remember the kiss he gave her after they exchanged their vows, as it was more unforgettable than all of the kisses they had shared up to that point; it was their first kiss as husband and wife.

They walked back down the aisle, hand in hand, amidst the raucous cheers from their family and friends. He helped her climb back into the carriage, then jumped in himself and sat beside her on the bench, tucking the blanket in around their laps. Just before the horses took off, Millie ran up and called out for them to wait. When she reached the side of the carriage, she held up a set of keys. "I'm catching a ride with Will, to watch the baby while he and Jane get drinks with Tom and Kassy. I don't suppose you could drive the Aston Martin home, and bring it to breakfast tomorrow, could you?" she asked Charlie, then gave Elizabeth a playful wink.

Charlie looked in astonishment from Millie to Elizabeth. "Pardon me, darling—but did you just say Aston Martin?"

As he was too shocked to move, Elizabeth reached out to take the keys. "Why yes, Millie, we would be delighted." She grinned, mouthing her thanks to Millie over Charlie's head.

The carriage pulled away, the guests waving until they could no longer be seen. Then Charlie leaned in to kiss his bride, placing his arm around her and pulling her close as she leaned her head against his shoulder.

Once they were both seated inside the car, Charlie started the engine. He then stared, unblinking, at the steering wheel for several seconds with his mouth gaped open in appreciation.

Elizabeth smirked. "Are you going to be able to drive, Mr. Bond?"

"Just give me a moment," he whispered. "I'm having a bit of a cathartic experience, I think."

"Take your time," she laughed. "There's no need to rush."

After a few seconds, he turned and made a face. "So, promise you won't laugh if I make a confession?"

"I promise."

He reached into his jacket and pulled out a pair of black rimmed glasses. "I need these to read and drive now, apparently." He put them on, and Elizabeth bit her lip.

"I look ridiculous, don't I?" he mumbled. "Not very Bond-like."

Elizabeth felt her cheeks grow warm. "Maybe not, but he hasn't had the same appeal for me since Daniel Craig took over for Pierce Brosnan anyway." She smirked. "You do remind me of another celebrity, though—who not only plays an even cooler secret service agent, but also happens to be Mr. Darcy."

They had nowhere they needed to be, as the wedding breakfast was the next morning and everyone was dispersing to celebrate New Year's Eve on their own. Therefore, it only made sense to Elizabeth to make a stop at the place where it all began. The place she stumbled into, weary after an unfulfilling blind date, and met the actual man of her dreams sitting at the end of the bar. Where they had talked till closing time, feeling as if they had known each other their entire lives.

They walked hand in hand up to the building, gazing at the familiar ivy-covered brick walls, window boxes twinkling with fairy lights, and gingerbread style roof. Before they entered Elizabeth smiled up at the sign that hung over the second story window, on which a bird perched on a branch could be seen underneath the words, *The Nightingale.*

As it was ten o'clock on New Year's Eve, the pub was nearly full. Every table in the room was occupied with people laughing and talking, drinks in hand. Elizabeth and Charlie made their way to the surprisingly empty bar, catching some appreciative looks in their wedding attire, and sat down together on two stools at the far end. Long since having sworn off alcohol, Elizabeth ordered a mint soda after Charlie asked for a beer. Once they received their drinks, they toasted each other and reminisced on the first time they sat at the bar together.

"I remember thinking I had absolutely no clue as to what I was going to say if you showed up," Charlie admitted. "I guess I was just hoping you wouldn't slug me in the face."

Elizabeth laughed. "I remember not thinking at all. The instant I saw your flowers, I ran out into the street barefoot to look for you. I didn't even have time to change into regular clothes before meeting you here. I was worried you would think I was a weirdo for being so overdressed."

"When I saw you sitting there, so unbelievably gorgeous in that white dress with your hair exactly the same way it looks right now," he began with a bashful smile, "please don't think me a mental case—but I just knew right then and there that one day you would become my wife."

Elizabeth blushed. "And here we are again, sitting on the same exact stools as the night we first met."

"You know, I think you're right!" He chuckled. "Let's see, I believe the first thing I did was introduce myself." Smiling, he held out his hand. "I'm Charles Bennet," he said. "But you can call me Charlie."

She grinned. "I'm Elizabeth Baker," she replied, taking his hand. "But you can call me Lizzie."

"No love, you got that part wrong," he reprimanded her, his eyes twinkling. "Your name is Elizabeth *Bennet*." He flashed his dimples and leaned in to kiss her.

When the clock switched over to 11:59, the crowd in the pub began a thunderous countdown to midnight. Elizabeth and Charlie joined in, "3...2...1..." and felt the entire room rumble with the tumultuous cry of *HAPPY NEW YEAR!*

Elizabeth stared into Charlie's eyes and thought happily of all of the kisses that were being given around her, and everywhere at that moment. "Happy New Year, Charlie," she sighed.

"Happy New Year, my darling," he agreed, and pulled her into his arms.

The following morning was the wedding breakfast. Elizabeth wore a simple but classic white cocktail dress, and Charlie put his black suit back on. Though they had kept the guest list as intimate as possible, between their family and friends they still required almost as many tables as an a full-blown reception. Will and Jane joined Elizabeth and Charlie at the head table, along with their two-month-old daughter, Elle, as well as Tom and Kassy, whose recently acquired wedding bands glinted in the sunlight. Millie, who was without a date but was making plans to move to New York City to be closer to her boyfriend, held her niece in her arms, laughing as she followed with bright eyes Millie's owl earrings as they swayed back and forth.

Bryan and James, who had come from Philly for the wedding so that Bryan could be Charlie's second best man, gave Elizabeth advice on how to decorate her flat after Millie left, as she and Charlie would soon be moving in with Bingley. Elizabeth begged Millie to let her keep the living room just the way it was and Millie wholeheartedly agreed, with the exception, of course, of her Hogwarts tapestry and wand collection.

Elizabeth's parents Marianne and Henry sat at the next table with Aunt Tessa and Aunt Bridget, discussing their upcoming move from Philly into their aunts' flat after they married each of their individual boyfriends; who were too occupied reprimanding their tiresome daughters to join in the conversation. Another table held Charlie's parents and Will's parents, who had become fast friends with their dads' mutual admiration of British tea, and their mothers' mutual admiration of bragging about their children's accomplishments.

Simon, who was expecting twins with Elizabeth's oldest friend Emma, described to Sanders with overzealous gusto the shelves he had just finished putting in the closet of the nursery all by himself, without the help of his mother. Sanders appeared to be listening attentively, but was actually lost in lustful thought as he gazed dazedly at his new girlfriend, a redhead with freckles across her nose named Wendy. Juliet watched Simon babble awkwardly for a few moments, then turned to greet Graham McKenzie and his fiancée, who had insisted on attending when Elizabeth called to tell him she was getting married. He brought with him author signed copies of the entire *Twilight* series, which Elizabeth received with a sheepishly delighted smile.

When breakfast was over, everyone milled around talking and dancing. Elizabeth found Jane alone at their table, looking through her purse for a stick of gum, and sat down beside her. "Jane, I have something for you," she said quietly. She handed her a rectangular package wrapped in delicate paper and tied with a ribbon.

Jane took the gift from her sister and gave her a dubious look. "This isn't another Colin Firth film, is it?" she asked warily. "I had to hide the last one you gave me in my nightstand, because I felt so guilty for how bad it made me want him when I watched it with Will."

Elizabeth laughed. "No, it's not. I promise."

Jane tore off the paper. Underneath was Elizabeth's well-loved copy of *Pride and Prejudice*. Jane glanced at her sister uncertainly, then opened the cover and read the inscription, *to my beloved daughter, may you find your own perfect happiness.* Her eyes welled with tears as she looked back up at Elizabeth questioningly.

"I want you to give it to Elle when she's ready for it," Elizabeth explained, her own eyes glistening. "It's time for a new generation to appreciate just how amazing a story it really is." She gave her sister a meaningful look, then wrapped her in a tight hug.

When she left Jane, Elizabeth wandered the room looking for Charlie. She finally saw him from a distance, sitting at an empty table and cradling her niece in his arms, and smiled. As she made her way over to him, she heard him singing softly to the baby, and her heart skipped a beat when she recognized the song.

"If your dilly dilly heart feels a dilly dilly way,

And if you answer yes,

In a pretty little church, on a dilly dilly day,

You'll be wed in a dilly dilly dress of,

Lavender blue, dilly dilly,

Lavender green,

Then I'll be king, dilly dilly,

And you'll be my queen."

He looked up to see Elizabeth gaping at him through her tears as she stood watching in disbelief. "Hello, my love," he sighed happily.

"How do you know that song?" she asked him quietly, taking a seat beside him.

He smiled. "My mother sang it to me every night when I was little. It was my favorite time of the day, listening to her beautiful voice until I fell asleep."

They both looked down to see the baby sleeping peacefully in his arms, then back at each other and smiled.

"Elle," Charlie began slowly, then grinned as her namesake fluttered her eyelashes and sighed in reply. "I never told you why I called Andie and met her at that bakery."

Elizabeth bit her lip. "I guess I forgot all about that." She raised an eyebrow. "So, why did you call Andie and meet her at that bakery?"

He gave her a guilty look. "I asked her for a copy of your medical chart. She said she would give it to me, but only if I took her out for lunch. I didn't want to, obviously, but it was the only way I could know for myself exactly what was happening to you."

"Why would you need to know what was happening to me?" Elizabeth asked, her eyes narrowed in suspicion. "And how did Andie not get in trouble for stealing my chart?"

"Oh, she did," he confessed. "She was sacked for violating privacy policies. Apparently she is jobless and living with Patel now, driving him mental and using him as a human cash machine." He wrinkled his nose. "I would feel a smidgen sorry if they hadn't both gotten exactly what they deserve." He gave her a devilish smirk when he saw the look on her face. "I told you, some moments are worth breaking the rules for, my darling."

"Wow," Elizabeth whispered. "That's just terrible, really." She smiled. "But you didn't tell me why you needed my chart."

Charlie grimaced. "Please don't be angry with me—but when I was in Philly, I took it to an endocrine specialist."

"Why would you do that?" Elizabeth asked.

"Because I wanted to know if it would be possible for you to have a baby of your own if you had two healthy kidneys."

Elizabeth frowned. "But I don't have two healthy kidneys, Charlie."

Charlie smiled. "You would if I gave you one of mine."

Elizabeth's mouth fell open. She blinked a few times. "You would do that for me?" she whispered.

"When I asked you to marry me I said I would try my hardest to make you happy every minute of every day, for the rest of your life." He paused. "I know how badly you want a baby of your own, and I would do anything in my power to make it possible."

Elizabeth suddenly remembered something Bryan had said when he came to visit her. *He seemed pretty hell-bent on doing whatever it took to prove to you that you make him happier than anyone else on this earth, and that he can't live the rest of his life without you.* "How do you even know you could give me one of your kidneys?"

"Because I also had testing done while I was there to find out," he confessed. "And they called me a few months ago to tell me I'm a perfect match." He smiled. "So if you want, we can start the process whenever you decide you're ready."

She grinned. Then she leaned over and kissed his cheek. "I cannot believe you would do something like that for me," she sighed. She waited a moment. "But I don't think it will be necessary."

He looked at her, confused. "It won't?"

She gave him a secretive smile. "I also went to see a specialist a while back, right after Jane's wedding. I had a strange feeling the doctor at the hospital's opinion might not have been entirely accurate, so I wanted to find out if another doctor thought I might be able to have a baby with just one kidney. He did a ton of tests, and when the results came back he said there should be no problem whatsoever with trying again. I would still be considered a high-risk pregnancy, but as long as I have frequent checkups and get enough rest, I should be able to deliver a perfectly healthy baby!"

"That's amazing news, Elle!" Charlie exclaimed, and cringed as the baby in his arms startled. When her tiny body relaxed once more, he added in a whisper as he gestured to her, "So when do you want to try for our own little girl?"

"Oh, no," Elizabeth contradicted him. "I would want it to be a boy. One that looks just like his daddy, with blue eyes and dimples."

Charlie laughed. "All right, a boy then." He gave her an inquisitive look. "What would his name be, you think?"

Elizabeth smiled meaningfully. "How do you feel about the name Henry?"

"I love it," he agreed. "When would you like to try for little Henry?"

Elizabeth smiled and chewed on her lip. "Well, actually," she admitted. "There's something I've been meaning to tell you."

Epilogue

"So, Mr. Bennet," a low voice growled, "You thought you could get classified information about one of my patients from someone on the inside." He laughed—a deep throated cackle reserved only for the most diabolical of villains. "Well, you were wrong, weren't you? If you had any brains at all in that debonair head of yours, you would have had the foresight to know she was working for me the entire time." He kept his gun pointed directly at his prisoner's chest as he turned to look across the room.

The agent followed his gaze to the shadowy corner, where the outline of a voluptuous woman with glossy black hair wearing a shimmering arctic-blue evening gown could be easily traced. As she took a few steps into the light, the entire room dropped in temperature from her biting glare. Bennet felt a shiver go down his spine as he struggled against the bindings on his wrists tied above his head.

"Miss Frost," the villain summoned her. "Please show our guest what happens when he crosses Dr. Fatale." He sneered menacingly as he watched her approach the exam table. Bennet's heart beat faster in his chest to fight the chill that coursed through his extremities as she advanced on his supine form. She reached out and placed an icy hand on his arm.

Instantly, blue streaks appeared where her fingers made contact with his skin, sending intense pain screaming through his entire body; yet as his panic rose, so did his curiosity. He lifted his head off the table, the only part of his body not tied down. "Pardon me," he asked politely, "but what did you say your name was?"

The villain's evil grin faded away. "What?"

"Your name." Bennet raised an eyebrow. "Did you say it was Fatale?"

The villain frowned. "Yes—why?"

Bennet glanced at Miss Frost questioningly. "Like femme-fatale?" he inquired, his lips twitching.

"What?" Dr. Fatale bellowed. "No!" In his consternation he let his gun fall to his side. "Like fatal—you know, causing death!" He raised the gun again and pointed it at the agent's head. "Which is exactly what I'm going to do to you, Mr. Bennet!"

Bennet let his head fall back onto the table. "Hmm."

"What is it?" Dr. Fatale seethed, unable to stop himself.

"Pardon?" Bennet raised his head once more to look at him. "Oh! It's nothing, really. It just sounds like you are referring to yourself as a femme-fatale—you know, an attractive and seductive woman, who will ultimately bring disaster to any man who becomes involved with her, that's all."

Dr. Fatale groaned. "It's French!" he bellowed. "It means fatal in French!" He groaned again, then stomped across the room to stand over him. "You think you are so suave, don't you, Bennet?" he crowed. "But *I'm* the one who stole not one, but *two* women away from you."

"How's that, now?" Bennet asked conversationally.

"Well, you see," Dr. Fatale snarled in a stereotypically nefarious manner, bending down so close to him that his foul breath was hot against his face. "First, I seduced Miss Frost here and convinced her to betray her loyalties—one of them being you—so I could infiltrate your secret intelligence service." He jabbed the end of his revolver into Bennet's cheek, forcing his head to one side, and continued. "Then I commissioned her to befriend the love of your life, all the while pouring lies into her trusting ears, so I could seduce and steal her away from you as well. And it was all so effortless, because she never really loved you in the first place."

"Ah, but that's where you're wrong, Fatale," Bennet muttered insolently, pushing his face against the gun in resistance. "You've got it backward."

"What are you talking about?" he snapped.

"The night she met me at that pub, I believe she was coming straight from a date, wasn't she? A first date that was never followed by a second?" He smirked. "And if I'm remembering correctly—and I think I am—wasn't that date with *you*?"

"So," Dr. Fatale barked. "What's your point?"

"My point is," Bennet whispered, so softly that Fatale had to remove his gun from his cheek and lean in close to hear him. Once the villain's ear was hovering over the agent's lips, he concluded with, "*I* was the one who seduced and stole her away from *you*, mate."

He drove his forehead upward into Dr. Fatale's eye. The villain cried out in pain as he shrank away from the table, knocking Miss Frost aside in the process. She stuck her arm out to break her fall, accidentally grabbing onto the ropes that bound Bennet's ankles together and freezing them solid.

They were now brittle enough for him to kick apart, freeing his legs. "Thanks for the assistance, love," he crooned, and flashed her a heart-stopping smile.

He somersaulted backward off the end of the table and slid the ropes from his wrists, but before he could reach for his gun he felt the barrel of Dr. Fatale's revolver against the back of his head and froze in place.

"You're going to pay for that, Bennet!" Dr. Fatale whimpered.

Suddenly, the rumble of an approaching motorcycle could be distinguished outside the building. It grew louder and louder, until the sound dissipated and was replaced by an ominous silence. Dr. Fatale, Mr. Bennet, and Miss Frost all stood stock-still, fervidly staring at the closed door in anticipation.

Like a crack of thunder the door was blasted off its hinges. It flew across the room to land with a deafening crash onto the floor. When the inexplicable smoke cleared, a young woman with blazing auburn curls tumbling over her shoulders stood smoldering with her feet spread apart and her hands on her hips. She was displaying an inordinate amount of bare flesh in her red leather bustier, superfluous skirt, and thigh-high boots. Hanging from her waist was a rolled up lasso. A metal shield was slung on her back, and each forearm was encased in a bronze gauntlet.

"Ah, Miss Baker," Dr. Fatale jeered. "So we meet again."

"Dr. Fatale," she countered. "I believe you have something that belongs to me."

"Please, call me Char," he replied tersely. "And if you are referring to my heart, you're absolutely correct."

Elizabeth grimaced. "Ew." She removed her lasso and unraveled it slowly. "Let Mr. Bennet go," she threatened, "and things won't have to get—" she glanced around the room at the medical supplies "—*physical*."

"As much as I love our witty repartee, Lizzie," Dr. Fatale began. He paused and jerked his head sideways to give Mr. Bennet a condescending glare. "That's *French*, by the way," he muttered exasperatedly, then turned back to face Elizabeth. "It's such a bloody damn tease. Watching you and Miss Frost 'get physical' would be far more satisfying."

He nodded to Miss Frost, who slithered toward her like a cobra. "It doesn't have to be this way, Lizzie." Her voice was cold and unfeeling. "I still consider you a friend, you know. We could use skills like yours on our side—and you know deep down in your heart he loved me more than you, anyway. Let's kill him together and become allies." She held her hand out for Elizabeth to shake.

Noticing the deceitful gleam in her frosty glare, Elizabeth removed the shield from her back just in time to deflect the stream of ice that shot out of the end of Miss Frost's hand. It rebounded off the metallic exterior and hit Miss Frost directly in the chest, freezing her instantly and transforming her into a crystal-clear ice sculpture. "Consider this the end of our friendship, you frigid bitch," Elizabeth retorted. She clobbered the human block of ice with an aerial kick and watched in satisfaction as it careened to the ground and smashed into smithereens. "Oh, come on now, Andie, there's no need to be so broken up about it."

She spun around. Dr. Fatale still had one arm hooked around Mr. Bennet's throat and was pointing the gun at his temple with the other.

"It's not too late, Lizzie," he insisted. "You can still choose to be with me."

Elizabeth considered him. "If I do, will you let Mr. Bennet go and promise to never harm him again?"

"Sure, sure, whatever, I promise," Dr. Fatale blurted impatiently.

"All right. Let him go," she conceded.

He removed his arm from Bennet's neck and shoved him aside. As soon as he recovered his balance, Bennet reached for his own gun lying on the table and fired it, but wasn't fast enough as Fatale's bullet struck him in the shoulder. He pitched backward into the wall clutching his arm, his face contorted in pain.

"You just made a huge mistake, Dr. Fatale," Elizabeth seethed, her voice low and dangerous and her eyes fiery with rage.

"For the love of God, woman!" Dr. Fatale screeched. "How many times do I have to ask you to call me Char?" He fired two consecutive shots at Elizabeth. She threw her arms out in front of her, and with an excessively exaggerated clanging sound the bullets ricocheted off her gauntlets and buried themselves in the opposite wall. She whipped her lasso around in one rapid rotation and threw it at Dr. Fatale. It snaked itself around his hand, forcing him to drop his weapon.

"Elle!" Bennet cried, and tossed his wedding band to her. In one fluid motion she caught the ring, yanked the lasso and Fatale toward her, and grabbed onto his arm. The ring sent an electric shock coursing through Dr. Fatale's body. He writhed and shook with violent tremors before she released him and he fell to the floor, dead.

Elizabeth kicked his smoking corpse with her toe, grimacing as she watched it sizzle. "I suppose it would be rude not to call him Char at this point, don't you think?" she asked Mr. Bennet, who joined her side. She gave him a smirk. "Although Char-*broiled* would be more fitting."

He laughed, then winced as he cradled his injured arm.

"Are you all right?"

He gave her a playfully crooked smile. "I'm fine. Just a little shaken." He paused for dramatic effect, turning his head to give a nonexistent camera his most convincing smolder as he removed his black rimmed glasses from the breast pocket of his jacket and put them on. "But not stirred."

Elizabeth grinned. He took her in his good arm and kissed her so intensely that she herself was not just shaken, but most *definitely* stirred. "Let's get out of here," she declared.

They climbed into Mr. Bennet's silver Aston Martin. Elizabeth took the wheel, as Mr. Bennet was unable to drive with his wounded shoulder. She revved the powerful engine and sighed appreciatively. Mr. Bennet let out a soft groan as his eyes traveled from her flaming curls down to her waist, and then from her thighs to her boots.

Elizabeth frowned, incorrectly interpreting his discomfort. "Don't worry, I'm going to get you to a hospital as soon as possible."

"I've got time," he insisted, opening his suit jacket and checking his wound. He flashed his dimples in her direction, then looked past her through the window to the crowd that had gathered on the sidewalk. "I just wish we had a little more privacy."

She raised an eyebrow. "It's funny you should mention privacy," she began, "because I had a new feature installed in your car." She winked, then pressed a button near the steering wheel. The car, as well as the two of them, seemingly vanished into thin air.

"An invisible car!" Bennet exclaimed. "Now there's a gadget that will definitely come in handy!"

Elizabeth giggled. "Speaking of handy, I know you're an expert at unlacing corset stays…" She gave him a provocative smile. "But how are you with reinforced steel?"

Charlie sat straight up in bed, his heart drumming a rhythm in his ears. "Whoa." He waited for his eyes to adjust to the darkness, then turned his head sideways to see his wife sleeping peacefully next to him. The dream had felt so real he almost expected to see a gauntlet on the arm stretched across his leg. He lifted it carefully, leaning over to plant a kiss on her fingers before placing it gently at her side. Then he got out of bed to make a bottle for the tiny baby stirring in his bassinet.

Juliet Evans and Graham McKenzie will return in

And There You Were

Acknowledgments

As always, I would like to thank my insanely beautiful and talented editors, Courtney Whitman and Marlene Engel. Without your superhuman abilities there would be no book at all, or at least not one I can be proud of. A huge thank you also to my insanely beautiful and talented cover artist, Stacey Leonard. I am thoroughly convinced she has magic in her fingertips. Thank you to my husband Mitchell for putting up with me every time I disappeared into my mind palace to think of ideas. Thank you to my children for entertaining themselves so I could crank out the final chapters on their summer break. Another big thank you to my fabulous mom Claudia for being my biggest fan and cheerleader. I hope I always make you proud of me. Thank you to my friend Kassy Andrade, who let me borrow her name as long as the character's happy ending included a hot guy.

I got you, bestie.

And thank you once again to the immortal Jane Austen.

It might sound silly, but thank you to my characters Elizabeth and Charlie. They really do feel like old friends at this point, and I will miss writing about their love story. But then again, who knows? They might just pop in and give us an update at some point down the road.

(Winky-face emoji)

About the Author

Samantha Whitman is the author of *Ditching Mr. Darcy* and the sequel, *Becoming Mr. Bingley*. She is currently working on her third novel. Samantha loves spending time with her own Mr. Bingley, their five children, and their fur babies. The most recent addition to the family is a black and white kitten named Tom, who was found abandoned by his mother in their attic. He is not only the most spoiled cat on the planet, having been bottle-fed and pampered like the human he thinks he is—he is also the inspiration for Elizabeth's cat Bingley in *Becoming Mr. Bingley*.

Praise for Ditching Mr. Darcy

"This book deals with demystifying some of those unrealistic romantic expectations we have in life, in a fun romcom format. You'll be pleasantly surprised, especially if you are obsessed with all things *Pride and Prejudice*. Definitely give it a go!"

—Sense and Spontaneity

"This story is an entertaining and enchanting read for readers who dream of waking up in Elizabeth Bennet's shoes and experiencing *Pride and Prejudice* firsthand. I'm so excited to see what sort of adventures are in store for these characters in Ms. Whitman's sequel – *Becoming Mr. Bingley*!"

—Austenesque Reviews

"I loved the fresh take on the *P&P* we all know and love. Elizabeth was so funny, quirky, and loveable. The whole novel was so easy to get into. It started right off as that perfect narration for me. I'm sure there is some technical term, but it's that way you start a book and just 'hear' the main character? Yes, that."

— State of Inelegance Blog

"Samantha Whitman puts a modern, fun twist on the Austen classic, *Pride and Prejudice*. With a cast of characters you won't soon forget and a story that will have you hoping for a sequel, Samantha is sure to be an author everyone will be talking about for a long time to come."

—Book Mama Blog

Made in the USA
Columbia, SC
10 December 2018